The Pearls and the Crown

Book Two

The Crown

Deborah Chester

ACE BOOKS, NEW YORK

THE BERKLEY PUBLISHING GROUP
Published by the Penguin Group
Penguin Group (USA) Inc.
375 Hudson Street, New York, New York 10014, USA
Penguin Group (Canada), 90 Eglinton Avenue East, Suite 700, Toronto, Ontario M4P 2Y3, Canada
(a division of Pearson Penguin Canada Inc.)
Penguin Books Ltd., 80 Strand, London WC2R 0RL, England
Penguin Group Ireland, 25 St. Stephen's Green, Dublin 2, Ireland (a division of Penguin Books Ltd.)
Penguin Group (Australia), 250 Camberwell Road, Camberwell, Victoria 3124, Australia
(a division of Pearson Australia Group Pty. Ltd.)
Penguin Books India Pvt. Ltd., 11 Community Centre, Panchsheel Park, New Delhi—110 017, India
Penguin Group (NZ), 67 Apollo Drive, Rosedale, North Shore 0632, New Zealand
(a division of Pearson New Zealand Ltd.)
Penguin Books (South Africa) (Pty.) Ltd., 24 Sturdee Avenue, Rosebank, Johannesburg 2196,
South Africa

Penguin Books Ltd., Registered Offices: 80 Strand, London WC2R 0RL, England

This is a work of fiction. Names, characters, places, and incidents either are the product of the author's imagination or are used fictitiously, and any resemblance to actual persons, living or dead, business establishments, events, or locales is entirely coincidental. The publisher does not have any control over and does not assume any responsibility for author or third-party websites or their content.

THE CROWN

An Ace Book / published by arrangement with the author

PRINTING HISTORY
Ace mass-market edition / December 2008

Copyright © 2008 by Deborah Chester.
Cover art by Matt Stawicki.
Cover design by Judith Lagerman.
Interior text design by Laura K. Corless.

All rights reserved.
No part of this book may be reproduced, scanned, or distributed in any printed or electronic form without permission. Please do not participate in or encourage piracy of copyrighted materials in violation of the author's rights. Purchase only authorized editions.
For information, address: The Berkley Publishing Group,
a division of Penguin Group (USA) Inc.,
375 Hudson Street, New York, New York 10014.

ISBN: 978-0-441-01657-0

ACE
Ace Books are published by The Berkley Publishing Group,
a division of Penguin Group (USA) Inc.,
375 Hudson Street, New York, New York 10014.
ACE and the "A" design are trademarks belonging to Penguin Group (USA) Inc.

PRINTED IN THE UNITED STATES OF AMERICA

10 9 8 7 6 5 4 3 2 1

If you purchased this book without a cover, you should be aware that this book is stolen property. It was reported as "unsold and destroyed" to the publisher, and neither the author nor the publisher has received any payment for this "stripped book."

Ace Books by Deborah Chester

The Ruby Throne Trilogy

REIGN OF SHADOWS
SHADOW WAR
REALM OF LIGHT

Lucasfilm's Alien Chronicles™

THE GOLDEN ONE
THE CRIMSON CLAW
THE CRYSTAL EYE

THE SWORD
THE RING
THE CHALICE

THE QUEEN'S GAMBIT
THE KING BETRAYED
THE QUEEN'S KNIGHT
THE KING IMPERILED

THE PEARLS
THE CROWN

Praise for

The Pearls

"The characters are compelling, the plot is action packed—with complicated twists that fantasy fans crave . . . This is truly an all-around satisfying book. The sequel can't come soon enough!"
—*Romantic Times*

"An enchanting fantasy filled with magical and mundane intrigue, enhanced by a hint of romance."
—*Midwest Book Review*

Praise for other novels by Deborah Chester

The King Imperiled

"Chester is a world-class fantasist."
—*The Best Reviews*

The King Betrayed

"Epic fantasy at its romantic best."
—*Midwest Book Review*

The Queen's Gambit

"A powerful, romantic sword-and-sorcery tale that readers will gain tremendous pleasure from perusing . . . delightful . . . a fantastic fantasy."
—*Midwest Book Review*

The Sword, the Ring, and the Chalice trilogy

The Sword

"A compelling fantasy that shimmers with magic . . . mesmerizing."
—*Romantic Times*

The Ring

"A lyrical fantasy that is as much about character as it is about magic."
—*Romantic Times*

The Chalice

"A riveting tale of destiny, treachery, and courage."
—*Romantic Times*

Chapter 1

At dawn on the last day, Lea E'non—sister to the emperor and princess of the people—awoke to a tickling of her nose and the unwelcome stench of unwashed male.

When her eyes flew open, she found herself face-to-face with piggish eyes above a set of puckered lips. His hot breath stank of parsum, jerky, and cheap wine.

"How's 'bout a kiss, pretty?" he asked.

Her fingers tightened around the smooth river stone she'd slept with, and she slammed it into his forehead.

With a grunt, he toppled backward. Laughter rang out around her, and a shout went up. *"Drakshera!"*

Lea sprang from her bedroll in a flurry of long, tangled skirts and unbound hair. Glaring at the laughing mercenaries who were slapping their knees and shoving each other, she dodged a playful grab at her haunch and flung the stone at another man who was coming at her with his arms held exaggeratedly wide, smacking his lips grotesquely for a kiss. Her aim was good, but he skipped aside. The rock thudded harmlessly to the ground.

Whistling at her through a gap in his rotted teeth, he

grinned while his friends swiftly riffled the pockets of the man she'd knocked unconscious.

"*Drakshera*, eh, Crad?" one thief said, laughing. "Let's cut off his eyelids and see if he can sleep without 'em."

Crad was still grinning at Lea, still puckering his lips suggestively.

Repulsed, Lea glanced around the ramshackle camp for the commander, who did not permit these games involving her.

"Ain't here, is he?" Crad said, spitting through the gap in his teeth. While he spoke, the other men gathered behind her, blocking her retreat.

Lea's heart was thumping, and she found herself breathing fast. It took effort not to look away, not to cry out for help, but she had learned a lot in the difficult weeks since her capture. This morning, the men were in an amiable mood, but they could turn ugly fast. She knew she must not show fear, she must not beg, and she must not call out for help.

It was dawn. Overhead, the sky looked pearlescent above the cedha trees surrounding the camp. The air stung with the sharp cold of approaching winter, and after the warmth of her bedroll, she could not help but shiver.

Crad took another step toward her and stopped.

She frowned, aware that he was playing with her, teasing her. The men at her back jostled and snickered in anticipation. The dangerous games they called *drakshera* had been adapted to include which man could fondle her or kiss her before she fought back or the commander punished them. The men delighted in unnecessary risk. Lea had stopped trying to understand why. She only knew how to play to survive.

Now, with the commander absent, she used her special gift to silently summon the earth spirits to her aid.

"Come on, pretty," Crad said softly, the amusement in his ugly face darkening to lust. "Let's have a kiss, then. A good long one before old Ironguts comes back."

"No."

He pounced. Lea dodged, but he was quicker than she and grappled her swiftly into an embrace. His mouth, coarse and hot, covered hers, and she nearly gagged on his sour breath. Twisting her face away, she pushed at his chest, bruising her fists on his armor.

There came a slight tremor in the ground beneath her feet, signifying the approach of an earth spirit.

"Dust!" she cried.

Dirt shot up into the air between Lea and Crad, parting them with a force that knocked him sprawling. Stumbling off balance, Lea was caught by one of the men behind her. He pinched and groped, while she elbowed her way free.

Dirt shot up again into the air, and the ground rumbled and shook enough to scatter the men away from her. Swearing oaths and clutching their amulets, they scuttled for cover as though under attack, leaving Lea standing alone on the rippling, unstable ground. She sent her thanks to the earth spirit, but it seemed fretful and unappeased, rumbling again and shaking the ground until little pebbles bounced on top of the hard soil.

Then, without warning, it vanished.

The air crackled and grew heavy as though a thunderstorm was imminent. But there were no clouds in the dawn's sky, only a glow of sun radiance. The commander stepped into view and paused among the trees to survey the camp. A rim of sunlight shone behind him, casting his face in shadow and making his black armor look even darker than usual.

Shadrael tu Natalloh, ex-commander of an Imperial legion, praetinor of the empire, and discredited hero, wore his shadow-sworn magic like an inky cloak of dark misdeed. From the spikes at his shoulders to the polished silver bars of rank embedded in his breastplate to the heavy war gauntlets held in one hand, everything about him, including his posture, short-cut hair, and clean-shaven jaws, was in sharp contrast to the slovenly men in mismatched armor who served him.

An eagle among crows, he gazed at the camp of scattered

bedrolls, a small cooking fire burning unattended, the unconscious man lying in the dirt, the rest of the men crouched and wary, and Lea standing straight and angry in her ragged, travel-stained gown, her hair spilling in an unbound tangle down her back, her blue eyes hot with indignation.

She did not have to say anything. He obviously knew what had happened.

Ducking his head beneath a low-hanging branch, the commander strode forward with all the dangerous assurance of a general about to order inspection. As he drew nearer to Lea, however, she saw the pallor of his face and the almost feverish darkness of his eyes. He looked haggard from lack of sleep and whatever else preyed on his conscience. Although he gave her only one glance, she saw no mercy for herself in his eyes, no softening.

And it was the last day. A ragged sense of disappointment welled inside her, but she capped it swiftly, refusing to think about that now.

"Commander," she said, "have I permission to go to the stream? Alone?"

His gaze was on his men. He gestured to them, and they emerged from cover, looking guilty and sheepish as they silently formed up.

Lea drew an impatient breath. "Commander?"

He nodded curtly without looking at her.

Swiftly Lea folded her bedroll into a neat bundle and gathered up her fur-lined cloak. Without looking back, she walked swiftly away into the trees, knowing the commander would not grant her much time for privacy.

She could hear his voice berating the men, laced with magic and pitched to hurt. It pained her to listen; she could not bear him like this, so harsh and hostile to everyone, so cruel and wrapped in shadow.

As soon as she gained the cover of the cedhas and squatty pines, she ran.

The woods were sparse, with almost no undergrowth besides occasional patches of short, brittle scrub. Not much

could grow on this parched, stony ground. Her red boots—
once so pretty but now worn and scuffed—crunched over
shale and hard soil until she fetched up at the edge of the
stream. It was tempting to cross and just keep running, but
there was nowhere she could go that the commander would
not find her.

The men could track her easily. The commander kept a
finger of awareness on her at all times. She had no hope
of running and hiding herself, unless she slipped *between*.
Yet without the power of her special necklace, which he'd
stolen from her, she could not slip from this world un-
aided.

Sighing, she rubbed her chilled, reddened hands dry on
her skirts before raking her long blond hair forward over
her shoulder, combing through the worst of its snarls and
tangles with her fingers and plaiting it loosely.

A soft splash startled her. Upstream, a large blue-
plumaged bird on long stiltlike legs fished for its breakfast.
It did not seem afraid of her as it plunged for a fish and
swallowed it in one great gulp.

How I wish you were Thirbe, riding to my rescue, she
thought. But remembering her gruff, tireless protector,
who had died in his attempt to rescue her, only made her
sad. She pushed his memory away.

It was time to return to camp before someone came to
fetch her.

When she shifted her gaze from the bird, however, she
saw a face staring at her from the bushes across the stream.

Her hands clenched involuntarily on her gown, and her
breath froze in her lungs.

It was a Choven face, as young as her own, with delicate
masculine features and a pair of large, fawn-brown eyes.
The barest touch of something warm and gentle brushed
against her senses, something kind, without menace.

A rush of gladness and relief overwhelmed her. Trembling, she barely stopped herself from jumping to her feet
and screaming for help. She must not, she told herself

breathlessly, squander this chance. *Be sensible,* she warned herself. *Be careful.*

She lifted her hand in the Choven manner of greeting. "May the three harmonies find you well, my friend," she said in the tongue of the People.

The large eyes blinked at her, then vanished. But the youth emerged cautiously from the thicket and ventured as far as the water's edge. He was as alert and wary as a deer, tilting his head to listen to the occasional shouts and murmurs coming from the camp.

His garb, woven intricately of many colors and hues, was not that of any clan she recognized, nor fashioned in the styles worn by Choven who mingled readily in the towns and settlements of the empire. For a moment she feared he would retreat as abruptly as he'd come, without answering her greeting.

But then the youth slowly lifted his hand in response and his mouth quirked in a fleeting smile before he made the gesture of farewell and turned away.

Lea shot to her feet. "Wait," she called softly, afraid some of the mercenaries would hear and come running. "Please don't go."

The youth hesitated, turning back to face her with visible reluctance.

An earth spirit bumped the ground beneath her feet, momentarily distracting her. *"Do not change the future,"* it warned her silently. *"Do not. Do not."*

Lea frowned, and the earth spirit moved away.

But the youth had vanished.

Disappointed, she looked both upstream and down, wondering if she dared cross the stream and go after him. For the first time in her life, she knew annoyance with an earth spirit for interfering.

The large water bird spread its wings and lifted ponderously into the air, gliding upward into the sunlight, its feathers radiant in colors of blue and gold.

One long tail feather drifted down in its wake, swirling

momentarily over the surface of the water before landing
on the bank near Lea. She picked it up, twirling it in her
fingers so that its rich colors shimmered, but her attention
wasn't really on it.

"Please," she whispered, and extended her inner *quai*.

The youth emerged from cover once more, his gaze fastened on the feather she held. In the tiny clearing, all became quiet and peaceful, the *jaiethqual* as calm as the
surface of a lake on a clear day. The youth warily touched
his *quai* to hers, flinching away from that initial contact,
then touching again.

His *quai* was as gentle and warm as a child's sleeping
breath, as pure and untainted as the sky. In contrast, she felt
the scars in her own, scars that the commander—and her
recent experiences—had created.

Even so, it felt good, this *sevaisin*. Smiling, Lea closed
her eyes and let balance flow between them. The tranquil
peace of the youth's spirit refreshed hers, and although she
urgently desired to ask for his help, for a moment it was
enough just to share.

He withdrew first. Opening her eyes, Lea pulled back as
well, although she was reluctant to break the joining. They
exchanged shy smiles, their *quaieth* still touching very
slightly, as was polite.

"You are blessed," he said, his voice low and melodic.
"The feather of the pa-crane holds both powers of water
and sun within it, perfect balance, good blessing."

Lea twirled the feather in her fingers once again. "Are
you in migration?" she asked, knowing she could not plunge
straight to the point. "Do your people travel to the glaciers of
Trau or farther away?"

"We are Gosha bi Choven," he replied. "Of the Tol
tribe, of the north lands. Weavers of cloth and leather."

"My greetings to your tribe, your elders, your family,
and to you."

He nodded. "All the Gosha will be honored to learn I
have conversed with Lea of E'nonhold."

Frowning slightly, she did not correct him. The hold where she'd been born and lived the first eight years of her life stood no longer, thanks to the Thyrazene raiders who had burned it. The Choven were like birds, migrating according to old instinctual patterns of wind and land. Walls and towns might rise or tumble, but the land, forest, and rivers remained for them to follow.

"There is trouble in your heart." The youth tilted his head to one side, listening to a sound she did not hear. "Your *quai* carries sorrow."

"I have been stolen," she said, seizing the opening he'd finally given her. "I know much sorrow and trouble. Will you take me from here and hide me among your people?"

Looking startled, the youth actually stepped back. "Why would you join us? Our clan is small, our harmony careful. Why do you seek this?"

"Because I have been stolen. I must get away from my captors and return to my home. Please, can you help me?"

Confusion and alarm filled his face. Lea started to resume *sevaisin* with him, but he blocked the joining so swiftly her *quai* bounced back to her.

"You ask many disharmonious things," he said. "I must consult my elders before I could give you an answer."

"I understand," she said, forcing her impatience under control. She knew she had handled this wrong. He was frightened now and unlikely to listen to any request. "Forgive me for breaking harmony. Will you carry a message instead? Talk of me to others in the migrations, so that word of me is carried to Light Bringer, my brother."

The youth's expression grew solemn indeed. His slim shoulders hunched as he drew up his clenched fists and crossed them over his chest in a gesture of worry. "Light Bringer?" he whispered.

"Yes. I am his sister."

"Light Bringer is our father. We honor him although he does not claim kinship with the People."

"He is not enlightened," Lea replied. She and Caelan

had argued that point many times, for she did not approve of his decision to conceal his Choven heritage. "But he is a good emperor and fights shadow."

"Can he not find you?"

"No. I am guarded by shadow magic."

Hissing, the youth backed away.

"Please!" she called to him, forcing her voice to stay low. "I ask this of the People as one who was born of them."

"You are not full blood."

"My mother was of the People," Lea insisted. "You know this." She extended her *quai*, and he touched it lightly but still blocked full *sevaisin* between them. "In kinship," she said, "I ask for help."

"We are Gosha," he replied, his eyes darting nervously. "We cannot fight shadow magic. We are not of the tribe of Otha, makers of protections and warding keys."

"This, I know," she agreed although it cost her much not to argue. "Will the People of Gosha carry my message, the news of my plight from one family to another, from one clan and tribe to another?"

He said nothing.

"I do not ask you to change your migration," she said. "When your tribe joins another in its journey, could news of me be shared?"

He remained silent.

"Do you know the tribe of Mu?"

"Makers of jewels," he said reluctantly.

"Yes. They go often to the emperor. To Light Bringer."

"Never have I seen families of Mu." His frown deepened, and with his fists still clutched to his chest he rocked slightly from side to side. "Our tribe comes to this desert to meet the *nameid* weavers called Druth of Jawnuth. Know you them, Lea of E'nonhold, sister to Light Bringer?"

"I do not."

"They are born of this land. They are not of the People, but we count them friends."

Lea could no longer hear the mercenaries talking in the

distance. *I'm out of time,* she thought frantically, aware that if she didn't head back to camp now someone would come looking for her.

Still, she dared not allow her urgency to show in her voice as she said, "There is the tribe of Kero."

"Builders."

"Yes."

He nodded. "Kero families sometimes walk with ours."

"They build for the emperor, for Light Bringer. They could carry my message to him. Would you tell the People of Kero of my troubles?"

The youth spread out his hands in a gesture of apology. "Winter comes. Our migration goes far away from these mountains. How can this help your sorrows?"

It was all she could do to stop herself from running across the stream to him and pleading for more than he could give. "Just let the message be carried," she asked. "It is no more than the rain cloud shadowing the sun, its trouble to the People light and fleeting, barely disruptive to harmony."

"Sorrow is sorrow. I grieve for you." He paused, thinking things over. "If I went to my elders—"

"Would your elders not praise you for granting aid to one in trouble?" she interjected quickly.

"I do not know."

"Are your elders close by? If I could speak with them, ask them to take me *between* and hide me there—"

The youth looked shocked. He crossed his wrists, looking sharply here and there into the woods as though anxious to go. "You would bring shadow to us? Is this the way of friendship?"

His rebuke, however mild, shamed her. Lea looked down swiftly, biting her lip in an effort to compose her mixed emotions. She'd known it was wrong to ask such a thing. And now he knew her to be a coward.

She lifted her gaze slowly to his, fighting back the tears that burned her eyes, for she did not want to use such wiles to persuade him.

"Oh," he whispered, staring at her. His *quai* stopped resisting hers and resumed *sevaisin* briefly, just enough to share his compassion with her. "It is disharmonious to be afraid. I am sorry. I am sorry."

She shook her head. "I am the one who should ask pardon of you."

Slowly he lowered his arms to his sides. "My elders will know what is best. Their wisdom will decide whether we carry the burden of such a message as yours to the far north and back again or whether we should tarry in this land and speak to the weavers in Kanidalon. They cross paths with many. They know the shouting ones."

"Soldiers?"

He nodded.

Gratitude filled Lea. She smiled at the youth. "I give you my thanks."

"It pleases my *quai* to tarry near Kanidalon," he said shyly. After slight hesitation, he drew a slender ribbon of deepest blue from the folds of his garment. "This is my token. I am intended for a *nameid* maiden. We are in courtship."

Lea's smile faltered slightly, but she forced herself to be courteous. "I share in your happiness and wish you a long life together," she said as custom required. "May your courtship prosper."

He held the ribbon aloft, watching it flutter in the breeze. "Your blessing honors me," he replied. "Now I must go."

Lea looked down at the long, beautiful feather. "May I bestow this gift on you?" she asked.

He made a gesture of refusal. "That is your blessing. You have need of it."

"It would honor me to share it with you and your intended."

He hesitated, but she held out the feather with a look of appeal. Smiling, he ducked his head shyly and stepped into the stream toward her.

There came a swift whistling through the air, and a metal
star thudded into the Choven's chest. His large brown eyes
flared wide, and he seemed suspended in midstep, his arms
outflung in shock. Blood welled around the star, bright and
bubbling as it stained his clothing. Bewilderment spread
across his face before it puckered with intense agony. He
fell facedown in the stream, his blood staining the clear water. The blue ribbon of courting flowed away, and the pa-
crane feather—dropped by Lea—swept downstream after it.

Chapter 2

$\mathcal{T}$he shock of *na-quai* hit Lea. She felt the youth's death as though the throwing star had pierced her heart. The whole world seemed to break as the tranquil *jaiethqual* of this clearing shattered. Agony poured through Lea. Crying out, she staggered back on legs that suddenly could not support her and collapsed on the ground.

An earth spirit rippled the ground next to her, bumping her in gentle agitation. Desperately she dug her hands into the soil until she touched it.

Rough, gritty energy flowed around her, absorbing her agony until she was released from the lingering connection with the boy. Spent and gasping, Lea lay limply on the ground. Her mouth tasted of soil, and she felt cold as though the hand of death touched her still.

Her fault, she thought. Her fault that the young Choven had died. She should have let him go the moment he first flinched from her *quai*. Curling up, she began to cry.

Footsteps crunched across the hard ground to her. A scuffed boot toe nudged her shoulder.

"No," Lea whispered.

He nudged her again.

Lea stared up at the commander silhouetted against the sky. His face was in shadow although his eyes glowed like fire. He wore death like a cloak, and carried violence as his shield. Loathing him, she choked back her tears, and could not bring herself to speak.

Perhaps he read her feelings in her face, for abruptly he turned and splashed across the stream to the floating corpse now snagged on rocks. He gripped the back of the youth's colorful tunic and half-dragged, half-flung him onto the bank. Rolling him onto his back, the commander bent over him, only to abruptly straighten.

"Choven!" he said.

Whether he was surprised or disgusted, Lea could not tell. She kept her fingers in the soil, feeling the rough comfort of two more earth spirits who had joined the first. With their comfort, she regained her strength.

"I am a coward," she thought to them. *"I have caused an innocent's death and broken harmony."*

One of them bumped her repeatedly until she finally sat up. It bumped her once more, hard, and when she righted herself her fingers brushed against a tiny stone lying in the loosened soil.

The moment she touched it, she felt the special hum of *gli*-energy. Her fingers closed quickly on the stone. It was an emerald, a mere sliver compared to the magnificent jewels in the necklace the commander had stolen from her. But however small, the little jewel gave her fresh hope. The earth spirits did not judge; they simply gave her what they could. Now, despite what had happened, she no longer felt helpless.

The commander—having retrieved and cleaned his weapon—came back, splashing through the water with long strides. His face looked as grim as granite. Swiftly Lea concealed the *gli*-emerald in her pocket, praying he would not sense it and take it away from her.

"On your feet," the commander said harshly.

She scrambled up, jerking away when he reached for

her. "There was no need to kill him. How could you do that to a harmless Choven?"

Nothing—not the slightest vestige of shame—flickered in the commander's gaze. "We're breaking camp. Come on."

Lea stood her ground. "He is to be buried, not left here to pollute the stream. He must have the four sayings of—"

"Gods! Am I to waste half the day digging a hole that won't hold out scavengers?"

"You murdered him!"

"What of it?"

"By law, by all custom and decency, they are *never* to be harmed."

"Then he should have kept away from you. What were you about to give him? A message for your brother?"

A tide of heat rose through her face.

He nodded. "I thought so. Blame yourself, not me."

"I take the blame I deserve. You didn't have to kill him."

"Then he should have stayed on his side of the stream."

The heat in her face became fire. "Is *that* why you killed him? Because he was crossing to me?"

"You were handing him a message."

"No, a feather!"

The commander blinked. "What feather? I saw no such thing."

She held her hands apart. "This long. A tail feather from a pa-crane."

"A what?"

"A pa-crane. That's what he—" Choking, she gestured at the dead youth. "That's what he called it."

"No such bird exists. Pa-cranes are a myth."

"It was there," she said, pointing. "I saw it fishing."

"You saw a dream the Choven put into your mind."

She sighed, well aware of the difference between visions and reality. If the commander hadn't seen the bird or the feather from its exquisite plumage, it was because shadow blinded him to such beauty. "And you," she said sadly, "killed a Choven boy for no reason."

"Oh, I had a reason."

She flushed. "At least honor his death."

"Why should I?"

She gasped. "Because he has died in violence. His *quai* is not—"

"Mael's plague on his damned *quai*. I've no time for Choven superstitions. Come along."

"I owe him a proper final rite."

"You owe him nothing." The commander's gaze narrowed. "Do you think delaying me will save you? It won't."

"You enjoyed killing him, didn't you?" she said in a low, angry voice. "It gave you pleasure."

"Yes."

"You think that if you make me hate you, giving me to the Vindicants won't hurt so much."

In answer, he gripped her sleeve, pulling her along without directly touching her. "Think what you like," he said gruffly. "It doesn't matter."

"But it does matter! You aren't one of them—"

"I don't want to hear that. You had your chance before, and you didn't take it. Don't start puling to me now."

"But—"

"Be silent! Or I'll muzzle you."

She choked back her protests, aware that he was perfectly capable of silencing her with magic.

His glare held hers for a moment longer before he shifted his gaze away. Glancing up at the rising sun, he winced as though the light hurt him, and hurried her back to camp.

The men were waiting, ready to go. Lea felt the force of their eyes upon her. Someone murmured low. Another nudged his neighbor with a sharp elbow. They all smirked as though they thought the commander had been enjoying a dalliance with her in the woods.

"Attention!" rasped out a hoarse, strangled voice.

The men snapped to stiff silence.

Fomo—second in command—led the commander's saddled horse forward. Rugged and vicious, the former centruin

was a battle-scarred veteran who carried a whip to enforce
his orders. He never looked at Lea except with flat resentment, sometimes even hatred. She would as soon have
handled a poisonous snake as spent a moment alone in his
company.

The commander took the reins Fomo handed him. "Did
the scout return?"

"Aye. The road looks clear toward the pass. Said a patrol
goes through twice a day." Fomo coughed and spat. "It'll
be tight, getting through without stirring 'em up."

"If we make the pass, they'll never catch us in the Broken Spine country," the commander replied. "It's worth the
risk."

"Sir—"

"Hold my stirrup."

Glowering, Fomo obeyed, and the commander mounted
swiftly. His horse champed and shifted, lather dripping
from its bit. Its ears were flat to its neck, and its eyes rolled
back until the whites showed. He controlled it with the
same uncompromising authority as he controlled his men.

Lea's gentle heart felt sorry for it, for she well understood its fear of such a rider. A man with no soul, who did
not even cast a shadow in the morning sunlight. A man who
seemed to have no heart as well.

The commander glanced down at her as though he could
sense what she was thinking. His dark eyes were too bright,
too angry in the pallor of his face.

Shadow magic is destroying him, Lea thought. Cruelty
did not come naturally to him; he'd learned it, just as he'd
learned how to handle a sword and command men. She believed he could have been a fine, valiant man. Instead, he
persisted in clinging to the sour bitterness of disappointed
hopes. By his own choice and lack of courage, he refused
to change. His stubbornness was going to cost them both
dearly, she thought, and for what purpose, except to cause
more suffering?

"Hand her up, Fomo. Gently."

With a grunt, the centruin lifted her, and the commander caught her by the back of her gown, hoisting her in front of his saddle. His arm went around her to hold her securely, and she shivered from his touch.

"You should wear your cloak."

She frowned, thinking, *He doesn't like me. He doesn't care about me. It isn't kindness, only seeing that I'm alive and well when he delivers me for payment.* If he cared, why did he not stop before it was too late?

Turning her head, she sent him a beseeching look of appeal. His dark eyes were as dark and impenetrable, however, as the obsidian basilisks in the Imperial Palace.

"We'll cross Ismah Pass today," he told her. "By nightfall you'll be delivered to the Vindicants." His gaze swung away and he raised his arm. "Eh, men? Vindicant gold in your pockets tonight!"

Their cheers rang in the air. And only Lea was silent.

Chapter 3

In the race to reach Ismah Pass before nightfall, darkness won.

During the day, the commander pushed his men hard, leading them at a steady trot along dusty mountain trails.

Lea could sense nothing from him save angry prickles of temper, like a hedge of thorns keeping her out. His proximity was a torment to her, his taint of shadow magic nearly unbearable to her senses.

Lea stayed silent and asked no questions. Despite her cloak's protection and the bright sunlight, she felt cold and dispirited. The death of the Choven youth still distressed her. Her anger with the commander weighed heavily on her heart, for it was not her nature to lose her temper or hold grudges. Yet how to forgive what he'd done? How to accept it? She did not think she could.

It was past midday when trouble crossed their path.

As the road climbing Ismah Mountain twisted steeply, the men were put under orders to keep quiet. Sound could carry a long way through the canyons of this desolate land, and the commander was clearly on the alert for patrols despite his scout's report. The road inclined so steeply that the horses struggled, and the men trudged at a slow pace, breathing heavily, their heads down.

Partway up, the road leveled for a short distance.

From ahead came the clattering sound of shod hooves, and two riders in Imperial armor rode into sight around the bend and halted, blocking the narrow road. They looked as startled as the mercenaries.

"Mael's bloody breath," the commander breathed above Lea's head. "Cover your hair. Quickly."

She obeyed him, drawing up her cloak hood and tucking her long braid out of sight. Her movements of course called attention to her, and one of the soldiers, a decivate, gazed at her hard.

She stared back, her heart thudding fast with hope. This had to be the patrol that guarded Ismah Pass, the patrol the commander had worried about avoiding. The emblem of the Ninth Legion shone on their breastplates, and their rank insignias glittered in the sun.

Certain that Captain Hervan would have reported her abduction to New Imperia, Lea believed the entire army must have been alerted by now that she was missing. Although she might be far from the province of Chanvez, where she'd been captured, all Imperial forces had surely received orders to watch for a woman of her description.

She went on staring hard at the soldiers, knowing her pale skin and blue eyes could not fail to be noticed in this sunbaked province of swarthy people, but when a little prickling sensation drifted over her she realized with dismay that the commander had draped her in a thin veil of shadow magic. Gault alone must know how she appeared to the soldiers.

The decivate who'd been staring at her blinked and shifted his gaze to the commander. Lea's heart sank.

Her throat swelled with the urge to cry out for help, but as though he could read her mind the commander pricked her in the side with his sleeve knife. Stiffening, she sat dry

mouthed and miserable, her mind racing to think of some
way to save herself.

Riding sleek bay horses and wearing polished armor,
the young officer and his aide looked strong, experienced,
and capable. Unlike the mercenaries, they bore no blasphemous tattoos; their faces shone with health and were not
raddled with dissipation.

In contrast, the mercenaries were clad in mismatched armor and rags, their faces dirt-streaked and unshaven. Even
the commander's black armor was dulled with dust, ill
cared for of late. But the mercenaries greatly outnumbered
this pair of young soldiers. Lea saw the decivate glance at
the ground where Commander Shadrael's shadow should
have been but wasn't.

"You there!" the decivate called out. "State your name
and purpose on this road."

"Orders?" Fomo whispered from the corner of his
mouth without glancing the commander's way. "We can
take 'em—"

"Shut up," the commander breathed.

Lea noticed how Fomo's cold, cruel eyes narrowed. He
sat his horse alertly, keeping his face slightly averted from
the soldiers to conceal the blasphemous army tattoo on his
left cheek, a tattoo not crossed through to show him unsworn
to Beloth. Although he rested his hand casually on his thigh,
from her vantage point on the commander's taller mount,
Lea could see a dagger sheathed inside Fomo's boot top,
within easy reach.

When Commander Shadrael remained silent, the decivate frowned. "You in the black armor—"

"You will address me as Commander. I'll take no im-
pertinence from a decivate on his first posting."

The two soldiers exchanged swift glances, and the decivate reddened a little. "All right . . . *Commander*," he said,
putting a slight emphasis on the word. "I—"

"Identify yourselves," the commander broke in, his voice
stern with authority. "By whose orders do you question me?"

"Decivate Lukare and aide," the young officer replied
with equal crispness. "Ninth Legion, posted to keep order in
this province by Imperial decree. No one can travel north-
ward by this route without a pass. Produce that at once, and
state your name and purpose for traveling."

"I'm Commander Buthrel, of the Legate special forces.
My orders come from the Imperial Council and are sealed.
Yield the road."

His tone and air of confidence as he lied had both the
soldiers straightening, but neither saluted. Nor did they
obey him.

"I'm not interested in your orders, Commander," the decivate said firmly. "Only in mine. Show me your pass, or
you must turn back."

The commander snorted. "So the Ninth is still bandit
chasing for the warlord of this sorry province. Wouldn't you
rather be slaughtering Madruns on the border and gaining
glory for yourself?"

Lukare's eyes narrowed, and whatever expression
crossed his face was too fleeting for Lea to recognize. She
suspected, however, that the commander had somehow insulted him.

"I may be chasing bandits, sir," Lukare said stiffly, "but
you and your men look like them. Once again, sir. Your pass."

Lea held her breath, expecting the commander to order
an attack, but instead he produced a grubby fold of vellum,
which he handed to Fomo. The centruin kicked his horse
forward and gave it to the aide, who in turn handed it to the
decivate.

Lukare took it with an expression of distaste, his gaze
lingering suspiciously on Fomo before he unfolded it. He
read only part of its contents before glancing up in surprise.

"This is a praetinor's pass," he said.

"What of it?"

"But you—I'm sorry, sir. This is a praetinor's pass."

"And an old one," the aide said, staring at it over Lukare's
shoulder.

"There are no restrictions on praetinors," the commander said harshly. "Or expirations." He gestured, still holding his small knife concealed at Lea's side, and Fomo leaned over to pluck the pass from the decivate's fingers and return it to the commander. "Yield the road."

Lukare's frown deepened. "But you're—that is, where is the praetinor himself?"

"Sealed orders. Yield the road."

"Sorry, but I must know your purpose."

"And I'm not permitted to give it."

They glared at each other. Lea could feel the commander coiling his shadow magic like a viper preparing to strike. The disguise spell he was holding over her shivered as though his control was slipping. When she drew an involuntary breath, his knife poked her sharply, and she froze. The gathering force of imminent violence pressed along her back. Not wanting these young soldiers to die, she surreptitiously slid her hand deep into her pocket and curled her fingers around the tiny *gli*-emerald. Its power thrummed gently within her touch, and she prayed the commander would not notice.

"I think," Lukare said, "that we had better escort you and your . . . men"—his nostrils flared in disdain—"to my cohort leader for further—"

"Your refusal to yield to a praetinor's pass is tantamount to disobeying a direct order," the commander broke in. His voice held enough anger and threat that both soldiers reached for their weapons.

The mercenaries drew theirs first, and the pair of officers froze although they still seemed unafraid.

"That pass is stolen," Decivate Lukare said firmly. "Just as your armor and horse are stolen. Legion armor, a horse under cavalry saddle, a praetinor's pass written under the former regime, a band of thugs at your back, and a—a woman who—"

The spell of disguise covering Lea vanished as the commander dropped it in order to fling shadow magic at

the decivate. Lukare gasped, reeling as though he would
topple from his saddle. Beside him, the aide grabbed a
horn and blew it loudly.

At the same time, Lukare straightened and spurred his
horse forward recklessly, brandishing his sword. Commander Shadrael lifted his gloved fist and *severed*, reaching for
his threads of life.

The sudden explosive action caught Lea by surprise despite her anticipation. Her fingers pressed the small *gli*-
emerald deep into her palm, and she closed her eyes,
drawing swiftly on its power.

Light flowed through her, buoyant and strong. She tried to
cast it over the decivate as a shield but was too late. The
commander snapped one of Lukare's threads of life. The decivate screamed, doubling up, and Commander Shadrael
turned on Lea, gripping her shoulder hard.

When she struck his hand away, light and shadow col-
lided with a terrific bang so loud it nearly deafened her. A
buffeting force of magic swept Lea away from the commander and threw her *between*.

Breathless and shaken, Lea picked herself up and
stood looking about in a place she did not recognize. The
sunlight and mountains were gone. Instead, she found herself on flat ground with featureless walls rising on all sides.
They curved slightly overhead. It was as though she stood
in the bottom of a bowl. The little *gli*-emerald was alive in
her fist, pulsing hard and fast.

Well aware that there were many layers of *between*,
ranging from the deepest and darkest in what the followers
of Beloth called the Hidden Ways, all the way to the joy-
ous, rainbow-hued refuge where the *chi'miquai* spirits had
sheltered her when she was a child, Lea supposed this must
be neutral ground at neither one extreme nor the other.

The little *gli*-emerald went on pulsing in her fist, casting
a nimbus of light around her.

Knowing how easy it was to become lost in such places, Lea dared take no step forward. A sound from behind her, however, made her turn.

She saw Shadrael standing a short distance away. His threads of life stretched out from him in a dark knotted cluster, and most of his body was concealed by shadow. In contrast, Lea looked down and saw her own form glowing golden white as though illuminated from within.

"Shadrael!" she called.

He did not seem to see or hear her.

She started toward him, but the air around her suddenly rippled and shimmered, and a warm fragrant breeze blew against her face.

The sinuous grace of an air spirit flowed around her to hold her back. *"Come away,"* it murmured to her mind. *"I will guide you to safety."*

Shadrael cried out.

Lea saw a dark, indistinct figure looming above him, clutching his threads of life in its talons. It tugged him this way and that like a puppet.

Thorny vines grew around the commander's legs and torso, tearing open his armor and rending his flesh. His eyes were glowing red like burning coals. He writhed about, trying to break free.

Compassion filled Lea's tender heart. "No!" she breathed. "What can we do?"

"Come away," the air spirit urged her. *"Do not watch."*

"I cannot leave him," Lea said. "I must help him."

Shadrael looked at her, shouting something she did not understand. Flames came from his mouth, and flaming words and symbols flew at her. They struck the light shielding her, and exploded into ash.

Startled, Lea felt neither strike her. But Shadrael recoiled as though the flaming words had smote him instead. With his face contorting in agony, he dropped to his knees.

The thorny vines grew over his shoulders, trying to pull him down. Yet whatever held his threads of life yanked him upright with such cruelty Lea feared they would snap and destroy him.

Pushing through the air spirit, Lea hurried to Shadrael. He was still struggling against the vines that nearly covered him. At her approach, some of the writhing brambles turned to lash at her, but the light glowing around her charred and crumbled them.

"Shadrael!" Lea said as loudly as she could. "Come forth!"

As she spoke, she reached through the thorns and gripped his hand. He was trembling violently, but she held hard to his fingers and pressed the glowing little *gli*-emerald against his flesh.

His scream tore her heart open, and an unseen force knocked her away from *between*. She felt herself flying through the air in a confusion of light, sound, and blazing colors she could not comprehend. And all the while, the air spirit was murmuring in her mind, *"It begins. It begins. It begins."*

Chapter 4

She landed back in the hard world of reality with a jolting thud. All went black and still for perhaps as long as one heartbeat; then she felt herself scooped up and dragged across the ground.

There was a great deal of noise close by, whoops and talking and laughter. Over the commotion, someone was repeating her name insistently, but she did not care. This darkness seemed safe, just as when she was very small and her father's stern voice would rise briefly in another room, forceful and harsh, its tone cold with censure.

If I keep my eyes shut and do not move, Lea thought, *I will be safe.*

Water splashed into her face, shocking her awake.

Sputtering and sitting up, she blinked, and saw Fomo's scarred face glaring into hers.

"That's right, witch," he snarled. "You open those big blue eyes and get busy."

"I don't under—"

"Him!" Fomo pointed at the commander, lying unconscious in the scant shade cast by the hillside above them. "Get him up and moving."

"But I—"

Fomo gripped her shoulder hard, his fingers digging in. Before she could even gasp, his dagger was at her throat. "One more protest from you, and *zzsst!*" he said, sliding the flat of his blade across her throat.

She flinched, and he smiled without mirth, leaning so close she could smell his sour breath.

"You done this to him. You undo it now. Get him moving. Hurry!"

Lea turned her gaze toward the commander. Blood was running from his nostrils, and he looked ashen. Slowly she slid her hand into her pocket.

Fomo shoved her hard. "Be careful, witch!"

Lea righted herself, wondering how she was supposed to help the commander when Fomo was too frightened to let her move. "It's the shadow magic that's killing him," she said carefully. "Each time he uses it, he grows weaker. You know that."

"I know you hit him with a spell. Now get busy."

Lea dared not argue with his illogic. She pulled herself unsteadily to her feet and saw the pair of Imperial soldiers lying dead and coated with dust, sprawled like the abandoned rag dolls of a careless child.

Only this was no child's game, Lea thought, feeling sick. The sun shone bright against her aching eyes. The smell of blood and male perspiration filled her nostrils. Surrounded by violence and *na-quai*, she could not achieve inner harmony. Miserably closing her eyes, she sought a prayer mantra for the soldiers she'd failed to save.

"Keep quiet," Fomo ordered the men, lashing one across the shoulders so that he yelped. "Get your gear and—"

"Wait, Centruin," one of the men protested. "It's our right to strip 'em. You'll get your share."

"Aye!" another man spoke up. "I need new boots and—"

"You can skin 'em and make their hides into a hat for

yourself," Fomo answered, "but keep quiet. Fools! That patrol will be coming soon."

The men rolled their eyes at each other, smirking without concern. As soon as Fomo turned away, they pounced on the bodies of the decivate and his aide, tugging and snarling over the loot like dogs. One man tried on the decivate's boots, and another hacked off the stiff, coarse bristles of the young soldier's helmet before trying it on for size.

"You!" Fomo said hoarsely, returning to her. "I told you to get busy."

He shoved her over to the commander so hard she stumbled to her knees, banging one of them upon a stone. Pain filled her eyes with tears, but she checked her outcry. The commander had not moved. He looked ghastly. She feared she'd already done too much and dared not touch him.

"Hurry," Fomo breathed behind her. "Hurry."

"Centruin!" someone called out. "The commander dead yet? If you're taking his armor, I want some of it."

Fomo whirled around, driving them back with the whip, his dagger ready in his other hand. "He ain't dead, you hear? He ain't dead!"

The men looked sullen, nudging each other and muttering, but before they could challenge Fomo, a horn sounded in the distance. Lea's head snapped around, and the mercenaries froze in alarm.

"Mael's eye," one of them swore. "That's a legion horn."

The mercenaries grabbed their packs and scattered like qualli into the brush, abandoning Lea, Fomo, and the unconscious commander.

Swearing, the centruin crouched by Commander Shadrael. "By the eye of Mael, you ain't leaving me stiffed like this," he muttered in determination. "Got something coming to me after all these years standing at your back. M'lord, to arms! We're under attack!"

But the commander did not rouse. Lea heard the faint thunder of galloping hooves echoing through the mountains and canyons. She could not tell how close the patrol was,

but it was coming fast. As the horn blew again, she hurried
to the center of the trail, her heart beating fast in anticipation.

"Help!" she shouted with all her might.

"Damn you!"

Fomo grabbed her long braid and yanked her around,
slamming her into the cliff wall. Half-stunned, she gasped
in pain as Fomo marched her back to the commander's side.

"Ain't telling you again. Fix him now, witch, or die here
and now."

Wary of the wild alarm in Fomo's eyes and the dagger
jerking nervously in his hand, Lea said, "You won't kill me.
He needs me for payment."

"Your pretty scalp will do for that," Fomo replied in his
rasping voice. "I got nothing to lose. Take your spell off
him now, or in Beloth's name I'll gut you."

Swallowing hard, Lea turned back to the commander,
although her hands were shaking and her breath came shal-
low and fast.

The commander lay as still as death. The pallor of his
handsome face stood in stark contrast to the blood dripping
from his nostrils. Despite what Lea had seen while they
were *between*, here his armor and clothing were untorn.
His flesh showed no wounds from the thorny vines of her
vision, yet now she knew how cruelly they tore at the inner
man. She did not know how he had borne such torment for
so long without going mad. He had a depth of strength and
courage beyond anything she'd ever known.

Lea took his hand between hers. His flesh felt cold and
strange, not quite like death but very wrong. Despite all
that he was and had done, she felt fresh compassion over-
taking her. *I do this to him,* she thought sadly. *I want to
help him, but I make him suffer more.*

"Oh, Shadrael," she whispered.

Fomo prodded her, making her flinch. "Hurry. Hurry!"

Lea slid her fingers across the commander's palm.
There, stuck partway into his flesh like a splinter, was her

tiny *gli*-emerald. She pried it free with her fingertips and slipped it into her pocket.

"What was that?" Fomo asked suspiciously. "What have you there? What are you doing?"

Lea's heart shot into her throat, but she forced herself not to hesitate or even look over her shoulder. "Helping him," she replied with a calmness she was far from feeling. "As you asked me to."

While she spoke she reached into the commander's cloak pocket to draw out her necklace of large *gli*-emeralds. The commander uttered a sighing moan.

At once, Fomo knelt beside her, his shoulder bumping hers as he bent over the commander. "M'lord, you must rouse. Sir!"

But the commander did not stir again.

"Give him time," Lea whispered, and backed away.

Sunlight glittered on the jewels in her hand. She turned the necklace over, delighting in having it once again. Although the emeralds were large, they could not be considered beautiful in the usual sense of the word. Bumpy nodules marred the shape of some of the jewels. The center stone of the nine was cracked almost in half, yet as she held them she could feel a response to her touch as though the necklace was coming alive. A warm, uplifting sense of security flowed into her arms. Suddenly she felt complete, whole. Her *quai* gathered around her, and she was centered once more.

Smiling, she fastened the necklace around her throat.

"Here now!" Fomo rasped out. "Give me that!"

With renewed confidence, she lifted her chin, meeting Fomo's gaze without fear. "I shall walk down the road to meet the patrol," she said. "You and the commander will have time to hide, get away. That much I'll do for him."

Fomo swore something horrific under his breath. "You ain't escaping that easy," he growled, avidly staring at the jewels. "If the commander's lost, he's lost. I ain't walking out of this with nothing."

"You—"

He sprang at her, but Lea skipped aside. His dagger whistled harmlessly past her. Fomo staggered to catch his balance, and whirled to strike again.

"Earth spirits!" she called.

They came promptly, shaking the ground beneath Fomo's feet and toppling him. Part of the ground cracked open beneath him, but he twisted like a cat and saved himself from falling in. His dagger skittered over the edge and was lost as he rolled to his feet, spitting oaths. "You damned—"

"Go!" Lea commanded him, pointing toward the pass. "This is finished."

"Not quite," the commander said from behind her.

Startled, Lea spun around to see Shadrael on his hands and knees, struggling to rise. Impatiently he swiped the blood from his nose with the back of his hand.

"Commander!" Fomo said urgently. "To your feet, sir! We're under attack."

"You," the commander said in a rage to Lea. "What did you—"

"Commander, no time!" Fomo broke in. The centruin ran to help him up. "Patrol's coming. We've got to go."

Lea pointed at the rocky slope rising above their heads. "Help him up there into cover," she said. "I'll tell the patrol that all of you ran away. They will not bother to search for you when I—"

"Ran away?" the commander said with a ghastly attempt at a laugh. "Shadrael tu Natalloh *ran away*?"

She could have stamped her foot in frustration. Why would he not take the chance she offered? "Does it matter what I tell them? Go while you can."

"Quickly, Commander," Fomo said, looking past her down the road. "I'll help you."

"Mael blight your help!" the commander said, shaking him off. He drew his sword, swayed, and held himself upright with a visible effort. "It does not end here, Lady Lea. Your offer I refuse."

He took a step toward her, but Lea lifted both hands to her necklace and backed swiftly away.

"You've lost," she said. "I am no longer yours to order. Good-bye, Shadrael tu Natalloh. I—I thought things could be different, but now—"

"Save the pretty speech of farewell," he said harshly. Lifting his hand, he spoke a word of magic that thundered in her ears.

Caught by surprise, Lea tried to use her necklace's protective force as a shield, but his stronger magic broke through her defenses, and her hands dropped to her sides. She found herself frozen, unable to move or speak, unable to run.

Astonished, Lea berated herself for not running away while she could. She'd assumed he was too weak to attack her with magic.

Staggering over to her, the commander gripped her arm and paused for breath. His face was contorted with effort, his skin gray and drawn tight. His dark eyes were those of a stranger's, blazing fierce and . . . quite mad.

"No, Lady Lea," he said, his voice strained and raw. "Not over. You've broken me, but so will I see you destroyed in turn."

The cruelty of his threat made her flinch. She wanted to speak his name and could not.

"They're nearly on us, sir," Fomo said. He ran to grab the bridles of their nervous horses, leading them back to where the commander and Lea stood. "Hear 'em? Be coming around that bend any—"

The commander pushed himself away from Lea. For a moment she felt the spell holding her falter. She lifted her hand, but the commander crushed his magic around her again with such force she would have cried out had she still a voice.

The patrol of Imperial soldiers swept into sight. Lea heard the startled neighs of their horses and the shouts of

the men. She saw the vivid banner of the Ninth Legion flying in the breeze. Sunlight gleamed on burnished armor
and upraised swords. The officer leading them shouted in
surprise and reined up his horse abruptly.

Time seemed to freeze for a moment. The officer's eyes
met Lea's, and his mouth dropped open in recognition.
Gowned in rags, her golden hair half falling out of its braid,
the emeralds gleaming at her throat, Lea could do nothing
but stare at him in mute appeal, while inside she screamed
and struggled with all her might to draw on her necklace's
power and break free of the commander's spell. The effort
made her temples throb, yet she could not prevail. Her vision blurred, and she could not fully breathe. She had to
abandon her struggles in order to remain conscious.

Attack, she thought. *Attack now while he is still weak.*

But the patrol was not coming forward. Bunched together awkwardly on the narrow road, they stared, a few
even pointing with their swords.

The commander spoke a word of magic, opening the
Hidden Ways. Behind her, a ghastly breath of rot and evil
exhaled from the bowels of the shadow world. Astonished
that he could do this, as weak and injured as he was, Lea
knew she'd hurt him. He was damaged, so how in Gault's
name was he holding on to his magic like this?

Not through Gault's name, she thought in despair. Beloth's.

She realized then that because she had removed her
emeralds from his pocket, they were no longer hampering
his abilities. But now . . .

I've helped him reach fully back into shadow, she
thought, and could have wept.

"Men, advance!" the patrol leader shouted, and spurred
his horse forward.

In a surging thunder of horses, the soldiers came at
them. Sunlight glinted off swords and armor. The men
were shouting, their voices ringing off the cliffs in a deaf-
ening din. Lea saw their eyes, furious and determined. She

saw their strength and valor. She felt the heat of their battle lust, like a wind of violence.

This time, she thought, the soldiers would reach her in time.

She was wrong.

The officer swung his horse beside her, so close she could have touched the animal's heaving flank had she been able to move. He reached down to her, his hand so near she could see the freckles in his skin beneath a mat of gingery hair. She struggled against the spell, striving to grasp his fingers. Almost she broke the commander's spell; almost she managed to move her hand.

But almost meant nothing.

A dark, icy cold mist engulfed her from behind, drawing her beyond the officer's reach. His horse reared in fright, blundering into another shying mount. Suddenly all the soldiers were shouting and fighting to control their bucking, terrified horses while already it was too late for Lea. The Hidden Ways closed around her, and a veil of shadow separated her from the chaos on the mountain trail. Their voices grew fainter until she heard them no more, saw them no more. Around her, there was only the cold silence of murk and rot and defeat.

No! she wanted to scream. *No! No! No!*

But shadow won, and all was darkness.

Chapter 5

 $\mathcal{T}$ heɣ emerged from the Hidden Ways with a jolt so painful Shadrael could not suppress his groan. Gasping for breath, icy sweat running down his face, he leaned against a boulder, pressing his cheek to the gritty stone, and focused on getting his breath.

It was dark here. Night had fallen while he'd concealed Lea from rescue. Now the wind blew cold, making him shiver. And he had not reached the Vindicant camp.

The horrible idea that he'd lost the markers and come out at some opposite end of the empire possessed him. He lifted his head, struggling to stand fully upright. Had to find his bearings, had to *know* . . .

"Commander?"

Fomo's rasping voice, sounding strangled and uncertain, made Shadrael gather himself as best he could. He could not *sever* the pain grinding through his chest. It had to be borne the hard way, through sheer willpower. And although he wanted to sink to his knees and pass out, he held himself up, bracing one gloved hand against a boulder.

"Centruin?" he responded wearily.

When Fomo hesitated, Shadrael looked through the gloom at the man's shadowy figure. If he wanted reassurance or perhaps just orders, Shadrael had neither to give.

As for Lea, she sat heaped at his feet, huddled beneath her tattered cloak. Her silence was a blessing. Shadrael did not think he could cope with her at the moment. She had damaged him, draining his powers to the dregs. He had so little left, having squandered nearly all his carefully hoarded reserves of magic to bring her here, and now . . . and now . . . if he'd failed this time to reach his destination, it meant the end of everything.

"M'lord?"

"Yes, Fomo."

He forced himself away from the boulder's support and set about taking his bearings. They stood near a mountain summit, well above the tree line, just as before. Above him in the inky sky, the star Kelili glowed steady and bright with her sisters. He turned his face eastward. Before him stretched a breathtaking vista. Dahara Peak, its snowcapped top shining in the moonlight, stood tall and majestic in the distance. Foothills gathered along its hem like the ruching of a lady's finest gown. Shadows, dark and soft in the twilight, filled the folds of canyons and softened the angular edges of cliffs. Ahead lay the unmistakable Valley of Fires, a land creased and folded into strange shapes of stone that long ago had flowed hot and molten. Gigantic boulders lay tumbled about as though once they had been pieces in a game of spillikins for the gods. Across the valley, cliffs rose to a plateau that he recognized as the Anvil of Hadra. He stared, imagining he could see the black mouths of caves riddling the cliffs. A cloud of bats flew overhead, momentarily dark against the spangled stars, then was gone.

It was very cold. Shadrael could smell snow in the air, in the bank of clouds lying on the north horizon beyond Dahara Peak. And behind him rose Ismah, the mountain he'd been climbing at midday. Ismah Pass, and the patrol checkpoint, lay to his rear.

He had made it through the Imperial line. He was safely in Broken Spine country, where no Imperial patrol could track him. He was . . . home, where he could die as a Ulinian should.

A tremor of sheer relief passed through his body. Shadrael tipped his head back and closed his eyes.

"Steady, sir." Fomo's hand went under his arm, supporting him.

Realizing he was swaying, Shadrael stiffened his body and pulled free, turning about to face Fomo.

"It's all right, Centruin," he managed to say. "We're close enough to the meeting place. They'll arrive soon."

"Have some water," Fomo whispered.

Shadrael pushed away the proffered waterskin. His mouth was parched, but he feared if he tried to swallow liquid he would spew his guts. A clammy sensation spread through him, and then he felt hot and dizzy. He dropped to one knee, swallowing hard.

Fomo crouched beside him. "Easy, sir. Take the water and rest. How long before they come?"

Shadrael could not answer. A chorus of whispering, dreadful voices clamored in his mind. He felt the sucking glee of madness drawing him down, and it seemed too hard to shake it off.

Yet he knew he must try. He had to hang on for just a short time more. He was Shadrael tu Natalloh, and he'd never been defeated in battle. He would not die now a failure.

"Call them," he murmured.

"Sir?"

"Call them. Damn you, must I say everything twice?"

Fomo sat back on his heels. "How?"

Shadrael grunted. "Help me up."

"Sir—"

"Do it!"

With the centruin's help, he struggled to his feet. Fomo would have supported his weight, but Shadrael pushed away and managed to shoot one feeble burst of magic sparks into the sky. Then he walked unsteadily over to the girl.

She sat motionless and silent, her hands folded together. He realized belatedly that he was still holding her under a spell. He released it, feeling a fresh razor slash of pain as he did so.

Lea drew an audible breath and brought her hands up to her face.

Sorry for how he'd treated her, Shadrael wanted to apologize, wanted to offer her comfort, but he had none to give. Angrily he closed the momentary tenderness in his heart. They could not go back, any of them, he thought. Nothing could be undone now. He had to go forward, had to gain the soul the Vindicants had promised him. He saw his end approaching, and was afraid. He could not die without a soul.

"Get up," he said to her.

She lifted her face slowly to his. The moonlight gleamed upon her pale face, and there was a soft radiance to her hair and skin and eyes that even her fatigue and fear could not diminish. The *gli*-emeralds at her throat glowed brightly, casting a nimbus around her.

Shadrael frowned. His dizziness was fading, and he could breathe more easily now, with less pain. Which meant that perhaps death was stepping back from his shoulder for the time being. Even so, he knew it was vital to make no more mistakes. He could not risk leaving the *gli*-emeralds in her possession.

He did not want the cursed jewels near him, but he had no choice. They were too valuable to waste on priests.

"Get up," he said again.

When the girl did not obey his order, he gestured at Fomo, who yanked her upright and gave her a good shaking.

"When he speaks, witch, you jump," the centruin snarled at her.

Still courageous, still defiant, Lea ignored the centruin and met Shadrael's gaze, lifting her small chin high.

"You are too ill to command me now," she said, touching her necklace. "I shall call the earth sp—"

Shadrael snapped his fingers, but Fomo was already moving, pinning her bodily against a large boulder. He jerked her hands away from the necklace, twisting them behind her back so that she cried out.

The agony in her voice made Shadrael frown, but he did not stop Fomo. Lea had cost him too much, more than he could forgive.

Then Fomo did something that made her gasp and stop struggling. The centruin was laughing.

"Would you rather have a kiss or a broken arm?" he rasped, licking her cheek.

Lea shuddered, straining to avert her face.

Fomo laughed again, a low, evil sound. "Right. Then—"

Lea screamed, sinking halfway to her knees before Shadrael said, "Enough."

Fomo's head whipped around. "Have a heart, m'lord. It's time to sport a bit with this fancy piece of—"

"You've had enough," Shadrael said, barely keeping his temper. "Keep her still."

"Yes, sir."

He forced himself to ignore the faint whimpers she was making beneath her breath. Her face remained averted, but in the gloom he could see how violently she was trembling. Compassion sparked briefly to life in him before he stamped it out.

The last thing in the world he wanted was to touch that damned necklace of hers, but he steeled himself and jerked it from her throat.

The touch of it burned through his glove and made him shout hoarsely. The necklace went flying through the air, falling in a heap on the dusty ground.

Lea's courage seemed to go with it. She shrank a little in Fomo's merciless grasp. Tears were glistening on her face. "Please," she whispered. "Please!"

When Shadrael picked up the shining necklace, the light

in it lanced through him. He somehow shoveled it into his cloak pocket, his hand throbbing. Already he could feel what scant strength he possessed draining away, exhausted by the necklace's proximity. He struggled to endure it.

All his hatred of light, all his resentment of her brother, all his bitterness since his disgrace came boiling up inside him. He drew on the night itself, shielding himself from the power of *gli*. This was simple magic, hill magic, the kind a mere child could do, but it served to mute the necklace, diminishing its effect to a bearable level.

"Let her go, Fomo."

The centruin released Lea, giving her a rough little push that staggered her. She rubbed her wrists as though they hurt, and dabbed tears away from her face with the backs of her hands.

Whatever she might have said to him was silenced by the sudden appearance of the gray Vindicant raven. It flew from the night sky, swooping down at Shadrael's head so close he felt its talons skim his hair.

"About time!" he yelled at it. "Bring your master and hurry!"

The bird wheeled above him and flew past Lea, making her flinch before it vanished into the darkness.

"You cannot really mean to do this," she said now, her eyes huge pools in the tear-streaked pallor of her face. "How can you give me to them? Why not to your brother, for ransom?"

"Be quiet."

"No, you must listen to me—"

"Why should I?" Shadrael broke in angrily. "I've heard everything you have to say."

"Can't I appeal to any mercy in your heart? And don't say you haven't any because I know better. You aren't wicked, not truly. You couldn't really—"

Fomo started snickering, slapping his leg in mirth. Lea sent him an uncertain look before turning back to Shadrael.

"Please," she continued. "You don't have to—"

"Stop begging," Shadrael broke in. "Show some courage, at least."

"Why? Will it alleviate your conscience if I do not cry or plead? If I show you a brave face and meekly accept this fate you've dealt me, will you then pretend I am not terrified, or that no harm will come to me?"

Her words were like needles. He forced himself not to listen. She was his death, his misery. If he listened to her now, he would go mad for certain.

"Shadrael—"

"No!" he snarled. "Cry if you must, but shut up. Shut up!"

"Why should I be silent to please you? Don't you realize what the Vindicants will do to me?"

He tightened his mouth and didn't speak.

"They're lying to you," Lea said, her pretty voice spinning its poisoned web of doubt and fears in his head. "No matter what they claim, they cannot give you a—"

"Be silent!" he said.

"I would rather you killed me than submit me to their cruel torture," she replied. "Fomo has said they'll pay you even if I'm dead."

Shadrael glared at his centruin. "Fomo lied."

"Slaughter me, if you care so little!" she cried. "Let my end come at your hands, and not theirs."

"They will not kill you," he muttered.

She sighed. "You've lied to yourself, and now you lie to me. Is this a praetinor's honor?"

Never before had she spoken to him with contempt. It hurt. Shadrael felt some thin vestige of pride stir in defense. Angry resentment started to smolder in his heart. It was *donare* anger, dangerous and cruel, while temptation dug in its thorns.

Kill her, whispered the harsh voice of madness. *Kill her and drink her sweet blood. Crush her dainty skull against these stones and offer her to Mael. You want to. Consider what she's done to you. You want to.* Grimly he compressed his mouth, refusing to be manipulated.

"I can understand your brother's motives," she said. "But what good can come of selling me to such evil?"

"I do not serve good."

"You aren't evil, Shadrael. You aren't! You have only to accept the light, to believe in yourself again."

He turned on her, gripping her by the throat and drawing his dagger. But Lea's blue eyes met his, and he could not strike.

Frustration and *donare* rage flailed inside him. He needed to kill, had to kill, and yet he did not want to harm her. Desperately he tried to *sever* the madness, but failed. The agony exploding in his chest made him certain his heart had burst. Dropping his dagger, he released Lea and staggered away, sweating and wracked in torment.

All his world was crashing down; his honor, his prowess—the last few desperately cherished pieces of his life—were gone. He choked on his agony and shame, and faced a terrible truth: He was *donare* no longer, a warrior no longer. His magic was gone, expired. He had squandered it all for this blue-eyed wench, and now . . . and now . . .

He wanted to weep, to scream. Instead, he found himself laughing, the sound hollow and wrecked.

"Shadrael," Lea whispered gently.

Fomo stepped between them. "M'lord," he said, his voice cold but careful. "They're coming. Pull yourself together."

From a distance came soft chanting. Shadrael recognized that prayer, knew what it was for. A small shiver ran up the back of his neck. Fomo was right, he thought dully. He could not face Urmaeor unmanned like this. Bowing his head, he unclenched his hands and slowly straightened. The pain in his chest was easing slightly.

His dagger lay shining on the ground where he'd dropped it, moonlight gleaming on its blade. He felt too unwell to pick it up, and pointed for Fomo to fetch it for him. The centruin watched him in silence, making no move to obey.

Regret and wariness mingled inside Shadrael. For years Fomo had served him ably, but only because he was strong. Now he knew from the centruin's stance that there was trouble to come. "Fomo . . ."

His voice came out as a thready croak. He cut off the rest of what he was about to say. Legion commanders did not plead, did not ask for help. Not even destroyed ones.

The chanting abruptly stopped, leaving silence except for the sighing wind. Listening, Shadrael turned his head. He caught not even the whisper of a footstep, yet the Vindicants were coming.

Lea, he saw, had retreated up the trail as though she meant to run. There was, of course, nowhere for her to go, unless she threw herself off the precipice.

"Here, m'lord." Fomo picked up his dagger and came close, holding it out.

Thinking he meant to stab it deep, Shadrael stiffened, but the centruin merely caught him close and slid the dagger into its sheath on his belt. When he stepped back, Fomo held the emerald necklace in his hand. A triumphant little smirk twisted his mouth, and he tucked the jewels swiftly from sight.

Furious, Shadrael grabbed for them, but Fomo gave him a rough shove. "Got to look out for myself, don't I?" Fomo asked. "You ain't going to now."

Before Shadrael could answer, Fomo gave his commander a mocking salute and vanished into the darkness, climbing the hillside swiftly and angling away from the trail.

Chapter 6

A light pelting of sleet began to fall on the mountain, just as the moon vanished behind a cloud. Frightened, Lea backed against a boulder and sought some last means of escape. But the commander blocked the trail in one direction, and the Vindicants in the other. And somewhere on the dark hillside lurked Fomo. There was nowhere for her to go.

Garbed in long, flowing robes, the Vindicants blended with the shadows so well she could not count how many had gathered. Silent, seemingly unaffected by the sting of wind-driven sleet making her shiver, they stared at Lea with palpable intensity.

One of the Vindicants approached her. He was almost as tall as her brother and gaunt beneath his robes. Although he wore no cowl or hood, she could not clearly see his face. She did not think she wanted to. His *quai* was all spikes and barbs, poisoned and black with rot. He stank of blood and ashes. Although she could not see his eyes, she could feel them boring through her.

She stared back as a mouse might at a cobra. It was suddenly difficult to breathe. Her heart raced beneath her breast.

"Light Bringer's sister," he said, speaking Lingua with a patrici accent. His voice was a deep, oily baritone.

The smug satisfaction in it, the ringing note of triumph, made Lea swallow hard and glance involuntarily in the commander's direction. She believed that he could still save her if he wished. These ex-priests and their charlatan tricks were no match for a *donare*. He could *sever* their threads of life, yes, even the knotty cords of such evil men as these. Although he was ill, he had but to sweep out his hand and do it, and she would be free.

I will plead with Caelan on his behalf, she thought to herself. *I will gain a pardon for him, and we . . .*

The sleet stopped falling with a faint rattle of ice upon the rocks. Overhead, the clouds parted, and moonlight shone down again just as the pale raven flew to sit on the commander's shoulder. It pecked the spikes of his armor and flicked its tail up and down as its talons scrabbled for purchase on the metal.

With a blink, Lea realized what she was thinking, what she was wishing for. Appalled by the violence of her desires, she buried her face in her hands and burst into tears of shame.

I have not changed him, she thought bitterly. *He is changing me.*

"**L**ady Lea," the ex-priest said, "come to me."

Panic swelled her throat. Fighting it, Lea choked back her sobs. There were pearls in her palm, gleaming white and soft in the moonlight, pearls formed by her tears. Curling her cold fingers around them, she lowered her hands to her sides and did not obey the order she'd been given.

"Commander," the Vindicant said, "bring her to me."

When the commander did not immediately respond, hope sprang to life inside Lea. She found herself certain that this time Shadrael would save her . . . and himself.

But after a pause, he hitched himself forward, moving

slowly and awkwardly without his usual grace. When he drew near enough, she saw how deeply his eyes had sunk into his skull; saw, too, the grim slash of his mouth and the furrow of his dark brows.

Their eyes met in the darkness, hers yearning and afraid, his holding tiny flickers of red flame that came and went, like a sputtering fire. After a moment, she dropped her gaze. There was something very wrong with him, something damaged and strange. He'd tried to kill her, and now he was looking at her as though he'd never seen her before.

"Commander," the Vindicant said impatiently. "I have waited long enough."

The commander gripped Lea's sore wrist, the one Fomo had twisted earlier. She flinched, drawing a sharp breath. The commander shifted his grip to her elbow, but when he tugged at her, she held back.

"Please, no," she whispered. "For your sake, for mine, stop this now."

Although he said nothing, he stopped pulling her. His face was a mask of light and shadow, without expression.

"I believe in you," she whispered urgently, desperate to reach him. "They never will. Shadrael, please listen to me. I love—"

The Vindicant's voice uttered a word of potent magic. A small blazing ball of fire formed in the air, striking the commander so hard he staggered and dropped his hold on Lea. She was close enough to feel the backlash of the blow he'd taken. Hot prickles of shadow swept across her. Shocked, she flung her pearls at the Vindicant before she had time to think.

Several of them hit his robes and burst into flames, driving him back a step. Yet before she could feel even fleeting satisfaction, the flames died, leaving the air stinking of sulfur and ash.

The ex-priest straightened, dusting off his robes. "Your pathetic element magic has no real power," he said contemptuously. "You will not play such tricks again."

As he spoke, he raised his hand. A glowing nimbus of green and yellow magic swirled around it, then shot toward Lea.

Too late for her to form an inner triangle of resistance, too late to even dodge. His magic struck her hard, as hard as his previous blow to the commander. Like ice, it stabbed through her vitals, robbing her of breath and nearly her reason. Cold tendrils of it knotted around her heart and lungs, squeezing . . . squeezing . . .

Unable to speak, much less fight it, she feared he would kill her, but she could not draw enough breath to scream surrender.

"Urmaeor, enough," the commander said.

But the Vindicant only squeezed harder, making the moonlight spin around her while shadows danced across her eyes. She felt her *quai* crumbling. Her hands clawed the air as she struggled to breathe, yet somehow she retained enough sense to resist using the tiny *gli*-emerald in defense. *Not yet,* she thought, praying that Urmaeor would not kill her on the spot. *This is only the beginning. It will get much worse.*

A ghostly echo of laughter entered her mind as though he'd read her thoughts, and then the Vindicant lowered his hand.

Released, Lea collapsed in a heap, struggling to breathe. She felt chilled to the marrow, defiled, and sickened. Her *quai* lay in pieces, its harmony broken. Even so, she summoned enough defiance to raise her head and glare at him.

He was smiling smugly. "Is your first lesson to be one of many, or do you learn fast, Lady Lea?"

Drawing a sharp breath, Lea swiftly emptied her mind of all thought of *gli*-emeralds.

The Vindicant tilted his head a moment, pursing his lips, before shifting his gaze to the commander. "Jewels?" he asked. "Emeralds?"

"Given to my men," the commander replied.

"I wonder."

The commander said nothing. He stood motionless, his dark armor as one with the mountain shadows.

Urmaeor approached Lea, who remained kneeling on the ground. She hardly dared breathe, in an effort to keep her mind a blank. When he bent to caress her hair, she flinched. He chuckled, the oily sound of his amusement making her gentle mouth tighten.

Touching the cold ground, she called inwardly for an earth spirit.

The Vindicant stamped on her hand. Pain throbbed through it, making her cry out. For an anguished moment she thought he'd broken it.

He yanked the back of her hair hard enough to raise tears in her eyes. And all the while her hand was throbbing and swelling as she cradled it.

"A slow learner," Urmaeor crooned to her. "There are many lessons for you to learn, and the first is obedience."

"I follow the teachings of harmony," Lea replied, her voice shaking. "I shall not obey you."

"Really? In that case, we have much to do. It will be a pleasure to corrupt you, Lady Lea."

She opened her mouth, but he was too fast for her. His spell hit her hard, harsher and crueler than any of the commander's, and she never felt herself fall.

When Lea slumped to the ground, Shadrael took an unsteady step forward, but Urmaeor was quicker, moving between him and the unconscious girl.

"No, Commander," the priest said softly. "Do not interfere."

"I did not bring her here to be tormented."

"You brought her to me because I hired you," Urmaeor said coldly. The power crackling through his voice drove Shadrael back. "Your involvement with her is finished. Leave her to us."

"It's her brother you want to harm. She's no—"

"Must I waste breath debating stupidity?" Urmaeor turned away from Shadrael and gestured at his minions.

Several of the Vindicants surrounded Lea. One of them picked her up, and Shadrael saw how small and delicate she looked in the man's arms. Suppressed as she was within Urmaeor's spell, the pale radiance of her hair and skin had faded. Not even the cold touch of moonlight rekindled it.

An anxious pang pierced Shadrael. "Take care!" he said sharply. "She's more fragile than she appears."

"Why, Commander," Urmaeor said in a silky voice, "do you dare instruct us?"

The warning was all too clear. Fighting back his tangle of feelings, Shadrael swallowed. "If she dies before you maneuver the usurper into your trap, our effort is for nothing."

Urmaeor stared at him coldly, but instead of answering directly he produced a small knife and cut off a strand of her pale hair. He held it aloft so that its silky length fluttered in the cold wind.

"Here!" he cried. "A fresh prize for your victory banner."

The insulting mockery cut deep. Shadrael fought to hold his temper.

"Take it," Urmaeor insisted. "You have earned the right."

"Am I some barbarian, some Madrun piece of filth hanging scalps from my tent pole?" Shadrael asked. "Enjoy the prize I've brought you, but do not mock me again."

"Don't be a fool! Take the girl's hair to the usurper. Tell him our terms."

"I'm not your lackey," Shadrael replied harshly. "I've done my part. Pay me, and let's be done."

"What? Coin for your jackals? But no, you've paid off your men, or so you said."

Resentment washed through Shadrael in a tide of heat. He could feel the forces of shadow around him, the very darkness that should have strengthened him. Now, thanks to Lea, its comfort was denied him. *No magic, no future,* he thought bleakly.

"I want the soul you promised me," he said.

"Of course." Once again the Vindicant held out Lea's hair. "Here is a piece of her beauty to keep close by. Call it a trophy, and let it sustain your memories on the cold winter days of regret."

Shadrael reached for his sword, although he lacked the strength to draw it. Urmaeor's laughter rang out, echoing off the rocks before he abruptly cut it off.

"Whatever spell she's cast on you, shake it off. There is work to be done, and more service for you."

"I'm done, and I want payment."

"Lord Barthel intends you to do more."

"No."

Urmaeor drew his pale robes more closely about his tall person. "I told you before we have need of the strongest *donares*, need of able-bodied commanders. This is but the first phase of our . . ."

Shadrael's concentration wavered. Drawing a ragged breath, he felt the knot of pain in his chest throbbing so insistently now he wanted to groan. Thinking he might swoon, he gritted his teeth in an effort to hang on.

"Commander, are you listening to me? I said—"

"I want the soul promised to me," Shadrael whispered, pressing one fist to his breastplate. "I must have it. *Now*, priest. Now!"

Without warning, fire shot from Urmaeor's hand and knocked Shadrael off his feet. He went tumbling, crashing hard to the ground, and lay, winded and helpless, the priest's magic burning along his limbs like sweet fire. His craving for shadow consumed him, and for a moment he sank deep into the chattering, screaming voices that were babbling madly inside his head.

"Make no demands of me!" the priest shouted.

Shadrael shuddered, fighting his way back from the precipice one more time. Even so, he did not think he could hold on much longer. Certainly not if Urmaeor continued to play his stupid games.

"On your feet," Urmaeor said. "Face me and receive your orders."

Rot with Beloth, Shadrael thought, and closed his eyes.

The next thing he knew, Urmaeor was kneeling beside him. "What's happened to you?" the priest asked quietly. "Shadrael? Do you hear me?"

There was almost kindness in his voice, but Shadrael knew better than to trust it. Turning his face away, he could not bring himself to answer.

"Shadrael . . ." The priest's hands touched his limbs, his clammy face. Suddenly his long fingers tightened on Shadrael's head, tightened as though they meant to crush his skull. "What have you done?" His voice was hoarse with surprise. "What ails you? What have you *done*?"

Shadrael tore his hand from his face. "My soul," he gasped out. "I must have it now, before I die."

Urmaeor backed away. "Did she do this to you? Did she?"

"What does it matter?"

"You are not of shadow now." Urmaeor's voice held revulsion. "You are something . . . something . . . How much power has she? Quickly! What else does she command besides element magic?"

"In Beloth's name, Urmaeor, carry me to the place where I may receive a soul."

The priest turned away, staring at Lea, who was still lying unconscious in his minion's arms. "We must rethink our plans for her. Lord Barthel will be most interested in this. We must not underestimate her again."

"We made a bargain, damn you!"

Without answering, Urmaeor strode away.

Fury clawed through Shadrael. He forced himself to his feet, although the effort left him shaking and dizzy. This, he recalled, was how he had felt after that fateful day of *shul-drakshera* when he'd lost his soul. Lying on his cot, wracked in horror, he'd first known the touch of madness before Urmaeor saved him. The priest had the power to help him again, and by the gods, he must do it.

"Urmaeor!" Shadrael called out weakly, panting in an effort to speak. "Damn you. I brought you the usurper's sister, as agreed. I brought her!"

The priest spun around to face him. "At what cost, Commander? You have no magic left."

"I have enough."

"For what?" Urmaeor almost spat the question at him. "What good to us are you, if you are no longer *donare*, no longer strong? She has crippled you, destroyed you. You were a fool to let her!"

"You'll pay my price, damn you. If I have to spit at you from Faure's hell and haunt your dreams, I'll see payment rendered to me."

"Why should I bother? You cannot force me," Urmaeor said. "You cannot even withstand the smallest flick of my power. At our last meeting you withstood me but now I could make you kneel, even eat soil, if I chose."

"And is that reason to break our agreement?" Shadrael asked. "To refuse to honor our—"

"Honor?" Urmaeor laughed without amusement. "She has corrupted you, rendered you useless. Why should I honor *you*?"

"Because I'm not as useless as you believe," Shadrael said, twitching his wrist so that his sleeve knife slid down into his palm. "What I've given you, I can take back."

Urmaeor gestured impatiently, and the knife in Shadrael's hand blazed white hot as though made of Choven-forged steel. Feeling his flesh blister and sting, he dropped it.

"Have done with your threats and false bravado," Urmaeor said scornfully. "Would you rather I crushed you like an insect beneath my heel? Begone!"

It was exactly the reaction Shadrael had maneuvered him to make. With the priest focused on taking the knife from him, Urmaeor's attention dropped from suspending the spell that held Lea unconscious. Shadrael gathered himself, but Urmaeor threw up his hand.

"Don't," he commanded. "Haven't you realized that without a *donare*'s quickness your intentions are easy to read? It's pathetic, like watching a blind man swing a sword."

Humiliation burned through Shadrael. He clenched his fists, ready to physically knock Urmaeor down, but he feared the attempt would collapse him flat on his face. His helplessness, his *failure*, left him raw with frustration.

"Hear me. Your task is not finished."

When Urmaeor pressed the length of Lea's silky hair into Shadrael's hand, he almost flinched, yet found his fingers closing on it while he shivered.

"Take this to Warlord Vordachai as proof that we have her."

"What?" Shadrael stared in astonishment. "After—"

"You will persuade him to give us his army, to stand ready to attack the usurper when he comes."

"Vordachai won't join sides with you."

"It's now your job to see that he does. We need his army. You will get it for us."

"Be d-damned!" Shadrael said.

"You serve me now as surely as though I put my mark on you," Urmaeor said coolly. "Now you will atone for your blunders."

"I—"

"You let her beguile you, suborn you. Where do your loyalties truly lie, Commander? When I gaze into your mind, I see confusion and . . . compassion. To pity her is to defy us. No, Commander, if anyone's broken faith here, broken our agreement, surely it is you."

"You hired me to abduct one Imperial princess," Shadrael said, barely controlling his temper. "I brought her to you. That's all I will do."

Urmaeor moved quickly, suddenly gripping Shadrael's head as he had before. His fingers burned icy cold against Shadrael's skin, yet before Shadrael could pull free, the priest was inside his mind, digging deep.

This time, there could be no *severance*, no resistance. Shadrael felt the mad whispers stop raging in the back of his mind, felt the fire in his veins flicker and cool down, felt the knot of throbbing pain in his chest loosen and fade. A sense of well-being flooded him, a healing of the wound that had gaped deep inside him for years, a restoration of all that had been missing for so long. It was as though he were sixteen again, newly commissioned into the army, young, strong and vital, and filled with ambition to be the best soldier among the emperor's legions.

And it felt . . . it felt *good*, so good he could not imagine it, almost could not endure it. Had he been able to remember what tears were, he would have wept for the blissful pleasure of what he was experiencing. He felt reborn. What did Lea know? What need had he for light, when shadow brought him such delight as this?

Something inside him, something gnarled and bleak and hard, softened and unfurled. Hope filled his heart.

"Yes," he whispered.

Urmaeor dropped his hands from Shadrael's face and stepped back. Abruptly the feelings of joy and completion vanished. Bleak emptiness of heart, the corruption of spirit, the barren waste of shattered dreams and hopes . . . all came back, colder and harsher than ever before. His pain returned, clawing his chest. If he could have drawn sufficient breath, he would have cried out for the loss.

Urmaeor watched him. "What you are. What you can have," he murmured, his words slurring slightly together as though the effort to walk Shadrael's mind had tired him. "You want your youth back. You want to be strong and vital."

Craving burned inside Shadrael. "Yes."

Flames suddenly blazed in Urmaeor's eyes. "Liar! You want a soul to gain her affection. You have foresworn shadow and your oaths to Beloth, all for *her*. You are a coward, unworthy of shadow and its notable gifts to you. And now you crawl and cringe, fearing death, mewling for mercy."

"I—"

"Lord Barthel wants to be vital and whole again, Shadrael," Urmaeor said harshly. "We all want it. Why should we reward *you* with a soul first, while the rest of *us* continue to suffer?"

"Then we are through!" Shadrael shouted. "Carry your messages? Never! I'll warn—"

"Enough! You will serve my master, as I serve. You will do his bidding as once you swore to obey Beloth."

"Barthel is *not* Bel—"

"You are shadow sworn, Commander. You will remain so, no matter how your loins yearn for that witch of light. And no one will be healed before our master. No one!"

Shadrael's feet were rooted to the ground, keeping him from simply striding away. He could not believe he had been such a fool as to forget the ways of shadow, especially the wiles, tricks, and stratagems of the Vindicants. *Never trust; never believe; never hope,* he thought bleakly, repeating the old motto of his training.

His gaze strayed involuntarily to Lea, still unconscious, her face bathed in moonlight. He knew he had been a far bigger fool than even Urmaeor claimed. He never should have brought her here. Never should have accepted the Vindicant offer.

As though you had so many other options, he thought harshly. Regrets were a waste of time. He threw them away.

Urmaeor watched him in silence, no doubt reading his mind and fully aware of all that was flooding Shadrael's thoughts.

I can reach him, Shadrael told himself. *One plunge of my sword, and he is dead.*

But what would it gain? What would it gain?

"Nothing," Urmaeor said aloud, staring fearlessly at him. "I am legion, and my master's reach is long. Do you think you'll warn the usurper against us? You won't. Do you think you'll persuade your brother not to side with our cause? He'll never listen to you, not after your betrayal. Crawl into the wastelands," Urmaeor said, pointing toward Broken Spine country, "and die there alone, as you deserve. The demons will feast on your bones gladly. And when you are dust, who will praise your name or speak your laurels? A disgraced officer, broken from service. A blight to your family's name. A traitor to your god. A betrayer of your word. A coward to the very last . . ."

As he spoke, he flung a slender bolt of magic at Shadrael, and knocked his medal away. It landed on the ground, gleaming in the moonlight. *Praetinor ad duxa . . .* the highest distinction an emperor could bestow on a legion officer. It had been his talisman for years, his one remaining piece of honor. Praetinor for life. No one could take that away from him.

Urmaeor laughed, and spoke a word that made the air crackle. Tiny flames erupted across the surface of the medal, making the edges blacken and curl.

Shadrael could no longer restrain his temper. With a shout, he drew his sword and lunged at Urmaeor.

He was slow; he was weak, but his rage carried him forward despite a roaring in his ears and the taste of blood in his throat. He heard Urmaeor shout a defensive word of magic, one that should have knocked him back, but Shadrael used his anger as a shield. He fed it with old resentments, hatreds, and bitterness, focused into one last, glorious thrust, one final plunge of his sword through Urmaeor's vitals. The priest would die, and so would Shadrael, equally damned together.

Urmaeor shouted again, and the tip of Shadrael's sword wavered. Sweating, Shadrael held the weapon with a grip like death, feeling Urmaeor's magic vibrate up the blade into his hand and wrist. With teeth gritted and bared, ignoring the thundering agony in his chest, Shadrael drove himself forward.

A stone thudded into his skull, glancing off his temple and making the night explode with stars and vivid color. As though from far away, Shadrael heard himself grunt. Another stone hit his armored shoulder with a clang. He staggered, half-conscious from the sucking blackness in his head, feeling a chill flow from the top of his pate into his

limbs. His sword suddenly weighed twice what it had before, and he seemed to be moving in deep mud.

Another rock hit him, and another, more striking his
face, head, and legs. His knees buckled, and he went down.
The Vindicants closed in, surrounding him. Grim faced and
merciless, they stoned him like a peasant caught stealing.
No sword thrust of honor. No beheading after trial. Nothing worthy of an officer. Just this beating of flesh and spirit
as he lay on the ground with his hands shielding his head,
tasting blood and dirt in his mouth, his mind and body on
fire with agonized humiliation.

A beggar's execution, he thought, knotted with hate.
Damn them. Damn them. Damn them . . .

Chapter 7

The market town of Kanidalon might be a famous crossroads of important trade routes; it might be a notorious black market center; it might even be a bed of iniquity, vice, corruption, and depravity. To Thirbe, riding in on a cold afternoon, wind knifing his back and dust stinging his eyes, it was the first sign of real civilization he'd encountered in weeks and a welcome sight for sore eyes.

The moment he slid, bone weary, off his horse, someone tried to pick his pocket.

He turned, spitting an oath, and slugged the thief. The man went down in a heap, a bundle of filthy rags, and Thirbe whirled back to grip the accomplice's wrist before the second thief could slice his purse strings.

Howling, the man writhed in an effort to break free. Thirbe held him long enough to make sure he hadn't stolen anything else, then released him with a kick to the backside to speed him on his way.

Across the crowded street, couple of soldiers lounging about on their spears laughed at the show. Thirbe dusted himself off, hitched up his sword belt, and sent them a sour look.

"Thanks for the help, you lazy swinegullets," he muttered.

After he'd stabled his horse and taken a room at an inn costly enough not to steal his possessions while he was out, he headed for the legion camp and approached the gate sentry on duty.

He flashed his pass. It was a thin rectangle of bronze engraved with his name, rank, present duty assignment, and service stamp. "Requesting admission to speak to your legion commander on Imperial business."

The sentry wasn't interested. "You and a hundred others every day. Try tomorrow."

Thirbe bristled. Maintaining camp security was one thing, but denying entry to an Imperial Protector was another. "You want to rethink that answer?" he barked. "I'm here on official—"

"Heard it before," the sentry said indifferently. "Every tramp at the gate has an Imperial pass, is here on Imperial business."

Thirbe held up his pass again, and the sentry shrugged. "See a dozen or more of 'em every day, forged over on Kettle Street, behind the plaza. Try tomorrow."

Tired, saddle galled, filthy, and aching, Thirbe had not crawled his way across Ulinia to be thwarted now by a slow-witted sentry swelled up with his own sense of importance.

"So you can't tell the difference between a forged pass and an authentic one," he said, putting more bite in his voice than before. "You can't recognize service armor from civilian—"

"Bought and sold, all the time."

"Can't tell real insignia—"

"Copied."

Thirbe saw a decivate and his ten approaching from behind the sentry, and raised his voice: "When the Imperial

Eagle comes in, you salute it! You don't question it, you step aside! Who in Faure's hell trained you to think for yourself, soldier?"

"Go buy yourself an ale, old man, and stop blocking the gate."

Waving him aside, the sentry motioned for a pair of dusty messengers to ride through. They did so, the horse of one jostling Thirbe almost off his feet. The decivate veered over to speak to the messengers, without glancing at Thirbe once.

Having enough, he bared his wrist and stuck it under the sentry's nose. "How many forged tattoos like that do you see every day?"

The man blinked. "You're Twelfth? Old Twelfth?"

"That's right. Pre-Reform, cheating, lying, dirty-minded Twelfth," Thirbe said.

Planting the butt end of his pike in Thirbe's chest, the sentry shoved him back. "We get old cankers like you crawling around the gates, wanting to reenlist, begging for free brew and a hot meal. Move along, old sot!"

Thirbe knocked the pike aside, and was reaching for his sword when the eager gleam in the sentry's eyes brought him back to good sense. Struggling to master his temper, he knew that if he attacked a sentry he'd end up in the guard-house with execution scheduled for dawn, and no questions asked. Even so, his frustration was so great he could barely force his hand off his weapon.

Grinning, the sentry gave him another poke. "Lost your nerve? An old veteran like you?"

"You cloth-headed, itty-witted dunce, if it's a bribe you want, you can stand there until your case of pox burns you blind. I have an Imperial pass, and I'm here on the emperor's business. And if you continue to block me, the blood of Her Imperial Highness will be as much on your hands as—"

"Problem, Sentry?" asked a voice. It was the decivate, his attention captured at last.

"No, sir! Just an old reprobate trying to cause trouble."

Thirbe, however, had his identification ready and held it so the decivate could see the sunlight flash across the mark of the Imperial Stamp. He shoved open his cloak, flinging it back over his shoulders to fully reveal his protector's insignia, already ignored by the sentry.

The decivate drew in an audible breath, suddenly snapping alert. "Your name, sir?"

"Thirbe, protector to Her Imperial Highness—"

"Lady Lea?" the decivate asked. "Light Bringer's sister?"

"Yes."

"By Gault you've been quick. This way, sir. At once!"

Snapping a salute, the decivate gestured for Thirbe to step through the gate before turning on the sentry. "Dolt! You were told to be on the watch for any news of Her Highness. Obviously you slept through the briefing."

"Decivate, I—"

"I'll deal with you later." With a glare at the crestfallen sentry, the decivate turned to Thirbe. "And your men, sir? Quarters for how many?"

"I'm alone," Thirbe said.

The decivate's frown told him how that sounded. For a moment Thirbe thought the young officer might push him back through the gate.

Instead, he said, "Come, sir. I'll escort you to the commander's office."

Legion Commander Pendek Drelliz was a tall, slab-shouldered man, with a long, broad face and the slightly tilted eyes of a Chanvezi. His skin was tanned by the harsh Ulinian sun, as brown as his hair. Only his eyes, small, and a startling green, gave his face any color or distinction. Although on duty, with orderly little stacks of vellum arranged in precise rows across his desk, he wore no armor. He had the spatulate ink-stained fingers of a clerk.

The decivate saluted smartly. "My lord, this is Lady Lea's protector."

Commander Pendek rose to his feet, blinking. "Merciful gods, but you've been quick. You must have intercepted my courier on the road."

Thirbe felt his heart stop. "She's found?"

"A sighting only. My men could not reach her in time."

"Where was this?"

"Near Ismah Pass, a mountain road running—"

"How long ago?"

"The afternoon before last. I sent my courier yesterday."

In silence Thirbe strode over to a map pinned to the wall and squinted at it. The decivate joined him and silently traced the mountain and road with a fingertip for him. It was all Thirbe could do not to pull out the magical opal in his pocket and compare his map to this one, but he restrained himself. He didn't want to land in the guardhouse on charges of using shadow magic.

"Then there's time," he said. "Which way was she being taken?"

Pendek didn't answer. Thirbe swung around, and found the commander staring at him in apparent confusion.

"I don't understand," Pendek said.

"Simple enough question. Which way?"

"But if you've read the report—"

"Haven't," Thirbe broke in. "I've tracked her into Ulinia, but I need a good map of this province. Never saw so many damned mountains and switchback trails that dead-end into canyons. I'm assuming you've already started systematic search parties through the area, but I'd appreciate two or three decims of men if you can spare them and will be joining the search myself as soon as I can get fresh provisions. Any assistance you can provide, information on the local government, its factions, and so on, will be welcome. By now, I suppose you've sent notice to every outpost in your jurisdiction to be on the watch for her."

Pendek blinked at him for a long moment. "You say you've tracked her here," he repeated slowly. "But you haven't read my report."

Thirbe expelled his breath, trying hard to be patient. But Gault above, he was tired, tired to his very bones, and in no mood to deal with a commander like this. He should have waited until he'd eaten and rested before coming here, he told himself, fully aware that he could not have borne to do either with Lea still in danger.

From outside came the sounds and activity of a legion camp: the stern shouts of centruins, the tramp of boots on packed parade ground in the distance. This small mud hut was furnished like any other legion commander's office in any permanent posting. The legion's standards were propped in one corner like so much fishing clobber. There were a utilitarian desk, a small assortment of wooden stools, and a duff chest to hold gear. Even the smells of camp were as Thirbe remembered from years ago when he'd been an ordinary foot soldier in the Twelfth. Oil for armor and leather, camphor ointment for sore muscles, and the reek of latrine lime when the wind shifted just right.

The decivate cleared his throat, breaking the silence. "It seems you are at cross-purposes, sirs."

"Are you alone?" Pendek asked. "Where are your men, the rest of the lady's armed escort?"

"Killed, along with their officers." Thirbe hesitated a moment before adding the lie, "Ambushed by the mercenaries that took her. I've been on her trail since."

"Dispatches apprising us that she was missing reached here only four days ago," Pendek said. "And then my patrol came in with this report—"

"Good," Thirbe said. "Then I'm close. We'll get—"

"Do you expect to keep searching here?" Pendek asked in astonishment. "But she's far away by now."

"She's in Ulinia," Thirbe said.

"Impossible. They took her through the Hidden Ways."

"So?"

Pendek sighed. "If you aren't familiar with that particular method of travel available to shadow users, then—"

"I am."

"Then I needn't explain how quickly someone can cross great distances. I daresay she's at the Madrun border by now, being handed over to those wretched savages."

Thirbe stared at him. "You haven't initiated searches?"

"No need."

"There's every need! I tell you I've tracked her as far as these mountains." Thirbe stabbed the map with his finger.

"Broken Spine country," the decivate informed his commander.

"Bad area," Pendek said. "I don't allow my patrols to venture into that region. Too risky for losing men."

"Too risky," Thirbe snapped. "Poor reason for refusing to rescue the emperor's sister."

"Nonsense!" Pendek's voice was equally sharp. "How dare you put words in my mouth? A refusal would be treason."

"Yes, it would be, right enough."

The decivate reached for his sword, but Thirbe drew his quicker. "Don't try it, son," he said quietly, his voice cold and hard. "I have more years than you, but I ain't slow yet."

"Put away your weapons, both of you!" Pendek said angrily. "I will not have this, do you hear? Decivate, you know better than to challenge a protector. Come to order at once!"

Looking surly, the decivate took his hand off his weapon. Thirbe did not.

Pendek turned on him. "Now you see here," he went on, his color high. "The patrol did its best to rescue her, but could not follow her abductor into the Hidden Ways. I have sent my report to the palace. I have done my duty, exactly as I should. Insulting me and casting doubt on my loyalty as an officer may relieve your spleen, Protector, but I will not stand for being told I am derelict in my duty."

Thirbe sucked in a couple of deep breaths and got his

temper under control. "Right," he said in milder voice. "I tender my apology, Commander."

"Accepted." Pendek exhaled. "Now, you can ask the quartermaster for accommodations tonight. Glad to provide you with all you need. Will you be heading to New Imperia in the morning?"

"No!" Thirbe said in astonishment. "I'm not quitting."

"Very commendable, but the Hidden Ways—"

"Mean nothing," Thirbe told him. "He's been trying to move her through them for weeks, but without much success. I figure he hid from your patrol until it moved on, and then he came out again."

Pendek stared at him blankly.

"Shadow magic don't work right these days for most of 'em," Thirbe said with more patience than he felt. "I figure Lady Lea's interfering as much as she can. He never uses magic long, and he doesn't go far. Like I said, he just hides and comes out again. The quicker we get some search parties sweeping that area, the better."

"You're welcome to your interpretation of the events," Pendek said, still looking baffled. "But there's no reason for her abductors to linger in Ulinia."

"Plenty of reason. The knave we're after is Shadrael tu Natalloh."

"The praetinor? Commander of the Eighth?" Pendek said in astonishment.

"Ex-commander."

Pendek cleared his throat. "Yes, of course. I meant to say ex-commander. Discharged in the Reforms. A sad day for the army, losing someone of his valor and skill. Had to be done, of course," Pendek added hastily as Thirbe's eyes narrowed. "No question of it. Had to be done. Pity he could not forswear shadow."

"While you're lamenting the army's loss of an officer, consider that he's Ulinian by birth," Thirbe said.

"Is he?" Pendek suddenly scowled. "And here, seeking to stir up trouble. I know exactly how to deal with that."

He picked up a piece of vellum and began writing across it. "Decivate, this order is to be conveyed to Lord Vordachai immediately, requesting that he conduct a search across this region at once." Pendek smiled at Thirbe, flourishing his signature and handing over the order to the decivate, who saluted. "Nothing better than using the locals when possible. The warlord's men are expert trackers."

Thirbe blinked. "Are you mad? This is an Imperial matter, not a provincial one!"

A tide of crimson surged into Pendek's face. "Remember whom you are addressing, Protector. I can make allowances for your state of mind only once. Control yourself in future, and address me with respect."

"Do you think the emperor will *respect* your decision to hand his sister's safety over to the local warlord, a man known to be conspiring to commit treason?"

Pendek's face grew even redder. "I have no solid proof that Lord Vordachai is involved in these recent acts against Imperial authority. He has promised full cooperation with my efforts to establish order here. I am to keep Ulinia quiet and loyal."

"Don't care. Lady Lea's safety—"

"My orders are to maintain peace in this province and keep the trade routes clear of outlaws. This week, one of my road patrols was attacked. I've had officers killed."

"Hazard goes with the job," Thirbe muttered.

"Not like this. Not robbed and left mutilated." Pendek clenched his fist atop a stack of papers. "The constant insurgency of bandits and outlaws is threatening to escalate quite out of control. My men must quell this trouble before any caravans are threatened."

"By all means, leave the princess in jeopardy while you protect rugs and hammered pots."

"That's quite enough! For these ruffians to dare ambush Imperial officers is outrageous. Now there have been shadow users nearby, and a sacred festival is coming up. I have more than enough on my hands at the moment, but I can assure you that this year there *will* be order, even if I have to set a curfew before sundown."

Thirbe opened his mouth, only to close it again in silence. Obviously Pendek was no field officer. How he'd ever achieved the rank of legion commander must be something of a miracle—or else his family had bribed him through the promotions necessary. He'd probably been posted to this backwater province because of some career-blighting blunder. He showed all the marks of having burrowed deep into this dreg posting like a dung beetle, determined to clerk his way through reports and regulations until his hitch ended and he could retire with his pension. He was worse than Hervan Hothead, Thirbe thought in disgust. A pen-pushing, minimum-effort bureaucrat too stupid to see that helping rescue the emperor's sister would restore his fallen fortunes faster than sunshine could dry a puddle.

"Let me explain the situation to you more clearly," Thirbe said at last. "Shadrael tu Natalloh, the man who's probably kidnapped Lady Lea, is Lord Vordachai's younger brother."

"Is he?"

"The local warlord's a troublemaker, known to be agitating to pull Ulinia from the empire. I'd wager a month's pay that he's behind these so-called bandit attacks up and down the caravan roads. And probably behind the attack on your officers."

Pendek frowned.

"Now Vordachai's brother—who just happens to be a wicked brute, a shadow user driven from the army because he was too evil to accept reform, a *donare* with a heart as black as his armor—has stolen Lady Lea, probably on Vordachai's orders. She's being held at one of Vordachai's strongholds. I'd stake my life on it. And I say that we forget asking for his help in looking for her and start searching his—"

"No!" Pendek said explosively, rising to his feet. "You

must be mad if you think I'm going to accuse Lord Vordachai of complicity in treason, without solid proof."

"I—"

"Ulinia is a hotbed of political unrest. The least thing,
the slightest insult, could set it ablaze. I manage a careful
balance here to keep order, and by Gault, I won't have
someone like you stirring things up."

"The lady's life depends on me doing exactly that."

Pendek's green eyes met Thirbe's glare for glare. "Protector, the lady's life depended on your having kept her
safe in the first place."

"You want to see the hole in my back that I took de-
fending her?"

"No, I want to see proof backing up these wild accusa-
tions."

Thirbe clenched his jaw. *Damn you, Hervan,* he
thought. *If you'd done things properly I wouldn't be in this
mess now, with no authority behind me.* "Lord Shadrael's
Ulinian. He's Vordachai's younger brother, and he has
brought her here. The pieces fit too neatly to be ignored."

"Loose evidence. I need facts, Protector. Not your sup-
positions."

"Tracked 'em as far as the badlands, where I lost the
trail and was forced to come here for help." Thirbe drew a
deep breath and spread his hands wide in appeal. "I'm asking you, Commander Pendek, for that help."

Pendek gestured curtly at the order in the decivate's
hand. "I've supplied it."

"Gods, man! If Vordachai is part of this, he'll laugh
himself sick. It's plain enough that Shadrael is heading
straight for his fortress."

"You said the badlands," the decivate said. "Lord Vordachai is based in the Jawnuth Mountains. The ones overlooking this city."

"There!" Pendek said triumphantly. "Not the same location at all."

Thirbe scowled. No legion commander could be this

stupid, he thought. Which meant Pendek was on the take, or . . . "What's the size of the reward offered by the emperor for her return?"

Pendek's jaw dropped open. "Are you implying—"

"Sir," the decivate said, stepping forward, "withdraw your implication or accept my challenge."

"Shut up, you damned little banty cock," Thirbe growled. "We've been through that already."

"That was before you accused my commanding officer of accepting bribery."

"That will do," Pendek said, glaring at both of them. His green eyes blazed at Thirbe. "Now you listen to me. However you may have botched your duties, Protector, it doesn't mean I'm going to botch mine. I'm too old to be busted down in rank, and too smart to take the word of some rough-shaven ruffian with a protector's pass and a hot temper, trying to force me to commit the biggest blunder of my career."

"And you don't think Vordachai might have hired his brother to abduct her? That he might intend to use her as leverage?"

"The warlord is not that big a fool."

"Then why was the girl brought here?"

"That's for an agent to find out," Pendek said. "My report is on its way—through correct channels—to the palace. I do not need you telling me how to run an investigation, or whom to trust."

"There's more to an investigation than insisting on proper chain of command."

"It matters, sir! It matters! Without order, there is only chaos, chaos that undermines the empire. I am holding this province together despite every imaginable difficulty and hardship. You Itierians will never understand. You—"

"I don't understand you bleating about roads and keeping order," Thirbe said furiously, "when my sweet lady's life is at stake. You have no idea how special she is, how precious to the empire, to the emperor's heart. These brutes have dragged her about, subjecting her to Gault knows what kind of brutality, and you intend to sit here and do nothing."

"I've heard the lady is beautiful, even that she performs miracles and is an oracle of wisdom," Pendek said flatly. "But I have done my duty and I will continue to follow my orders from correct channels, not go jumping to rash conclusions based on guesses instead of proof."

"Can't you use your common sense?" Thirbe cried.

Pendek frowned. "Bring me real proof, and I'll sweep the warlord aside, lay siege to his fortress, and claim his lands for the empire, but I won't judge him guilty on your word alone."

"What must I do, lay her corpse on your desk?"

"That's enough," Pendek said. "You have followed regulations and correct procedure in reporting to me on your arrival in Kanidalon. I will make a note of it, and this information will be routed through the proper channels back to New Imperia. Until then, I will wait for direct orders."

"Listen, you—"

"That is all."

"You damned scab-brained—"

"That is *all*. Dismissed!"

Thirbe seethed, gathering himself for another try. The decivate, however, stepped toward him.

"Sir," he said in a steely voice, "you will accompany me outside or I'll be forced to summon sentries to escort you to the guardhouse."

Thirbe went on glaring at the top of Pendek's bent head. The commander had resumed his writing, his pen scratching firmly as he worked. After a moment Pendek looked up.

"The decivate will escort you to the warlord's citadel tomorrow," Pendek said. "Talk to Lord Vordachai about the missing girl. Ask for his help. Don't demand it. And don't accuse him to his face of treason. Decivate?"

"Sir!"

"I'm relying on you to keep the protector from starting an incident that could inflame this province."

As he spoke, Pendek glared firmly at both Thirbe and the young officer, then returned to his writing.

The decivate saluted Pendek before turning to Thirbe. "Report to the north camp gate at the bells of *naoin*," he said in a surly voice.

It would be, Thirbe knew, a complete waste of time. Mastering himself with an effort, he spun on his heel and stormed out.

Chapter 8

Snow was falling upon the valley of Falenthis, shrouding the bleak ruins and turning the tiny stream bordering the old Imperial road to slush.

"It was here, Excellency," the agent said, pointing.

Caelan drew rein, his horse snorting and pawing the crumbling pavement of the old Imperial roadbed. Orders rang out down the line, and his armed escort halted.

He had three companies of legion soldiers marching with him, one full squadron of auxiliary cavalry in bright blue capes and tall fur headdresses, tassels swinging from the hilts of their curved swords, and fifty members of the Imperial Guard—over four hundred men in all, bristling with weapons and unease, their breath misting white about their faces in the cold.

Since he'd turned onto this road and entered the deserted valley, Caelan's mood had grown grimmer by steady degrees. Now he swept an expert gaze across the site where the ambush had happened, noting how the road bordered the wooded hillside where there would have been plenty of cover to hide the waiting force. The stream ran between low

banks in places, but here the near bank lay flat and wide
while the opposite bank rose sharply. He imagined the attack and its confusion. He imagined his sister trying to gallop away, while her horse slipped and scrambled up that
muddy slope.

"According to Barsin's report," the agent in charge of
the investigation was saying, "the attack hit the head of the
column approximately *there*." He pointed.

Caelan saw a veritable thicket of brambles and vines
now outlined in snow.

"In short, Excellency," the agent said, "a perfect ambush site. Scant room for cavalry to maneuver because of
the stream and that bank. They lost half their force in the
opening strike."

Caelan abruptly reined his horse aside and crossed the
stream to ride into the ruins of the village. By the look of
the place, it had once been a large, thriving town. The
buildings had fallen in, and dead vines had grown over the
rest of the rubble. He could barely find evidence of streets
among the crumbling foundations or occasional wall jutting up. The silence was eerie, with not a creature in evidence. Caelan saw no birds on the wing, spotted no tracks
of snow hares, field mice, or their predators. Over the creak
of saddle leather, his heart was drumming in his ears. His
horse snorted and minced along, ready to shy.

Riding at Caelan's stirrup, his protector was breathing
audibly, his gaze shifting back and forth. Two lieutenants,
three centruins, his aides, and a decim of Imperial Guards
rode bunched together, their hands close to their weapons.
No one said a word.

It was indeed, Caelan thought, a terrible place. Its bleak
emptiness as oppressive as the worst sites of shadow
magic, the very ground cursed. He could sense something
foul here, as though hands were reaching from their graves
for him. Whatever had gone wrong for the inhabitants of
Falenthis, it was too terrible for even time to repair. Some-

thing wretched lingered here, its ancient misery overlaid
by the recent events of Lea's abduction and the slaughter
of most of her entourage. A terrible sense of rage boiled up
inside him. That Lea—his gentle, sweet sister—should
have been brought to such a foul place, exposed to its
heartbreak and violence . . .

"Hervan was a fool," he said curtly.

The agent glanced at him without expression. "Yes, sir.
That fire in Brondi was set by arson."

"You think he was bribed to turn onto this road?"

"I found no definite evidence of that, Sire. He *was* in
debt, but then most officers in the Crimsons are."

Caelan frowned. The Household Regiment was notorious for its high expenses. "What else have you to show
me?"

The agent cleared his throat and set his horse picking a
careful path through the rubble lying half-concealed under
the snow.

Caelan was well aware of what they were all thinking.
For the emperor to have left his palace and ridden all the
way to the remote, and unimportant, province of Chanvez
to inspect the capture site in person was extraordinary, especially given the press of the emperor's other obliga-
tions and responsibilities. It did not bode well for the
regiment's future that His Excellency was unwilling to
simply accept the official report, or the findings of his in-
vestigative agents.

This agent, selected to conduct him out here, looked
nervous enough, as though he feared his own work might
next be held to close scrutiny.

Let them all be afraid, Caelan thought angrily.

"Magic has been done here," Caelan said, pointing at
the broken walls of a fallen hut. "Is this where they called
the dead?"

Looking startled, the agent shot Caelan an uneasy
glance. He hesitated long enough to make the other officers

stare at him, before he said hoarsely, "Yes, Sire. According to the testimony of the captain's servant who followed him that night. You can see here, and here, my stakes marking the spot."

Caelan glowered at the wooden stakes that had been driven into the ground. Brightly hued scraps of cloth fluttered from the tops of the stakes. *Evil on top of evil,* he thought. *A curse that goes on and on, regenerating itself with new victims.* He knew he would never discover what had first befallen this valley so many years or perhaps centuries ago. It hardly mattered. Sometimes evil went so deep, remained so pervasive it could not be stamped out.

Abruptly he wheeled his horse around and guided it out of the ruined village and back across the stream to the road. He reined up there, his men watching him anxiously, and squinted against the driving snow toward a dimly seen smudge of hills to the north. Some instinct told him the mercenaries had ridden that way with Lea. And yet . . . his gaze swung northwest. The evidence left behind, the scattered weapons of Thyrazene make, had not convinced him. He knew that trick as well. It was as old and shabby as the pre-Reform army.

A feeling of despair surged through him, making him bow his head. He had indeed been foolishly impulsive to come here. He'd discovered nothing except confirmation of the reports. Leaving his palace exposed, leaving Elandra and their child without his protection, and for what? To punish himself? To feel that he was doing something worthwhile to recover Lea?

She was not in Chanvez. He had known that before he came.

The agent's report in person had not deviated from the one he'd written and sent by courier to New Imperia. Meeting this investigator had confirmed for Caelan only one thing that he'd already suspected.

There was deceit wrapped around the matter, layers and layers of deceit. They were all—from Lea and her call for help to this agent to the commander of the Crimsons—all, for whatever reason, lying to him.

"A false report!" the agent sputtered that night, standing white faced and rigid. "Sire, I beg you not to believe such a thing. Every effort—"

"False," Caelan insisted.

They were in the commander's quarters at the outpost at Brondi, a wretched little provincial market town on the banks of an unremarkable river. The log-fenced fortress had the same weathered, weary look of similar remote outposts across the empire, too insignificant to be well supplied, too often overlooked in cases of merit, a mediocre posting for mediocre officers.

Outside, a cold winter wind was howling around the corners of the cabin, worrying at the log chinking and rattling the shutters. Caelan heard the shrieking wail of wind spirits out there, sensed their furious hunt for some unwary soul foolish enough to venture unprotected into the night.

Indoors, Choven warding keys shone above every shuttered window and bolted door. The firelight glowed brightly, casting uneven warmth and flickering shadows about the room. The agent and his assistant investigators stood before him as though too shocked to move. Caelan's protector and guards were present, but no officers. This meeting was private.

"Excellency, how have we erred?" the agent pleaded. His eyes shone wet and liquid in the firelight. "I realize the report is inconclusive, but—but until Captain Hervan is found and questioned, there can be no establishing whether he still searches for Lady Lea or has deserted."

Caelan drew a sharp breath, but he could almost hear Elandra's calm voice, sensibly warning him to keep his temper.

"You have also talked to an officer of the Crimsons, haven't you?" Caelan said now, and watched the man squint

involuntarily, then force his expression to one smooth and
impossible to read. "Who came here?"

"Excellency—"

"Damn you, do you dare lie to your emperor?"

Again the agent's eyes shifted. He stared at the floor
even as he said, "Please, Excellency, there is no lie—"

"Name the officer!"

"The Crimsons would not suborn an Imperial agent."

"Then who was the man? Speak up! Or do you want to
be held on charges of complicity?"

"Sire, it's not like you think." As though realizing what
he'd just blurted out, the agent grimaced and fell silent. Behind him, his men exchanged worried glances.

For a long moment the only sound in the room was the
hissing crackle of the fire. Caelan stepped closer to the
agent, looming head and shoulders over him, letting the firelight glint off his silver-hued eyes, using his physical size to
intimidate in the way he'd learned during his years as a gladiator.

With Lea's survival at stake, Caelan burned to take action, whether right or wrong, burned to be doing something,
anything to help her. Gods, if only he had an enemy standing
before him, one he could fight, then he would know what to
do. But this slippery intrigue, this constant sifting for grains
of truth within the sand of lies . . . he hated it.

"You had better explain," he said coldly, and watched
the agent flinch. "And the truth this time! Do you think you
can deceive Light Bringer?"

The man turned ashen and sank to his knees. "Please,
Sire. I—I didn't change anything in my report that would
jeopardize the lady. I swear it!"

Caelan's sigh came from the depths of his soul. "Talk."

Chapter 9

The emperor's return to New Imperia was as unexpected and sudden as his departure had been. On his first afternoon back in the palace, His Imperial Majesty had closeted himself with his privy council most of the day, messengers and couriers going in and out of the palace at a rapid clip.

When Lord Tinel Hervan was seen entering the palace, bets were laid on whether the House of Hervan had fallen at last. When Colonel Dreseid of the Household Regiment entered the palace, grim faced and striding fast, rumors flew that the regiment was being disbanded.

Spies skulked everywhere. Money changed hands in the galleries and behind columns and in corners. Whispers and lies, speculations and rumors, snippets of fact and complete supposition were all woven together in the palace gossip.

The throne room, constructed in the shape of a nautili-cone, its walls and floors lined with porphyry, marble, and alabaster, was closed. His Imperial Majesty did not sit to-day on his emerald throne, an enormous jewel the size of a

boulder, cut into innumerable facets by master Choven
craftsmen and resting on a gold base stamped with symbols of wisdom and protection. According to clerks dourly
revising their lists and schedules, no audience would be
given.

Palace officials stood about with grim faces. The pair of
heavy doors leading to the privy chamber remained firmly
shut. No one, not even the chamberlains, could listen at the
keyhole. The doors were flanked by members of the Guard,
standing rigidly at attention with drawn swords held across
their chests to indicate that the emperor was still inside.

Without warning, the heavy bronze doors crashed into
the walls as though propelled open by an invisible force.
Jinjas came pattering out, hissing and spinning about as
though glad to be released, only to scatter as the emperor
emerged.

Wearing his Choven-made crown—an intricate web of
finely spun gold, diamonds, and emeralds—Caelan strode
out past his hastily saluting Guards while pages ran before
him, shouting, "Make way for the emperor! Make way!"

Although he always moved in a rush, his usual custom
upon leaving the privy council was to pause in his progress
to acknowledge those courtiers in favor or exchange a few
words with minor officials.

This time, however, his long legs carried him rapidly
through the parting crowd. He spoke to no one. His brow
was like thunder and the steely anger in his eyes forbade
anyone to approach him.

"Excellency!" It was Chancellor Brellit who called after
him from the doorway of the private chamber. "Please,
Sire! Excellency, I beg you to wait!"

Fuming with every step, Caelan strode down the gallery
as though he did not hear and went out through a set of tall
doors into the shelter of a long loggia. The downpour had
stopped, but the garden beyond was glistening with water,
its plants drenched and the pathways full of puddles. Water

being channeled through gutters and drains gurgled into the palace cisterns.

Too furious to continue, Caelan halted. He had no intention of going into the session gallery, or seeking out the women's pavilion where Elandra was supposed to be resting after her part in a morning ceremony. He had found it a hard journey home from Brondi, through snow, sleet, rain, and mud. He was tired and frustrated, and although today's meeting had been necessary for the sake of procedure it had accomplished nothing.

He wanted to strike out, to destroy something, even if it was only to childishly trample these flowers. He did not want to be soothed, or listen to reason. Above all, he wanted no more lies or empty assurances.

A pair of gardeners, busy tying up leggy flowers now sodden with rain, stared at him in awe. A curt gesture from Caelan's protector was enough for them to grab their tools and flee. The Guards secured the area to ensure the emperor's privacy.

Scowling, his thoughts confused and angry, Caelan paced out into the garden toward a bubbling fountain, turned abruptly to his right, and followed a flower-bordered path to a sundial. By the time he'd circled the tiny garden, Colonel Dreseid and Chancellor Brellit had managed to follow him. They stood beside the fountain. Brellit wore an expression of long-suffering patience, Dreseid a scowl of outrage.

Dreseid, sunburned and tall with a fringe of white hair around his bald head at variance with his unlined face and athletic build, carried off the vivid uniform of the Crimsons with an air. From his short red cape trimmed in tawn-cat fur to his spotless white gauntlets held correctly in his left hand to his shining, immaculate boots, he epitomized the ideal of the most famous cavalry regiment in Caelan's armed forces. Medals swung at his throat and glittered on his right breast. He carried his helmet, with its long horsetail plume, tightly clamped under his left elbow. However handsomely attired, at the moment he looked less than confident. His brow was furrowed in a ferocious scowl, and his jaw muscle kept twitching.

"Excellency," he said, his voice brusque, "I protest this decision to throw out Adjutant Barsin's testimony as invalid and to discharge him dishonorably from the Crimsons. He did his duty. He is not at fault for what occurred."

"Protest all you like," Caelan said, equally curtly. "Your primary witness is useless."

"Excellency, the boy has been seriously shocked. He—"

"Adjutant Barsin has been coached so carefully he might as well stand mute."

"Sire—"

"The Crimsons," Caelan broke in, not taking his gaze from the colonel, "are covering up a botched mess at the expense of my sister's safety. It's obvious Barsin has been got at."

Whatever his feelings, Dreseid had not become a senior commanding officer by losing his temper when provoked. He swallowed hard, his mouth tight-lipped. "There can be no question of this officer's loyalty."

"No? Is it loyalty to me, or loyalty to preserving the honor of the Crimsons at any cost?"

"Great Gault, Excellency! The poor judgment of Captain Hervan should not be blamed on—"

"Do you think I am a fool!" Caelan shouted. "I do not blame the adjutant for Hervan's misdeeds. I blame him— and you—for lying to me."

The colonel closed his mouth without a word. His face might have been carved from stone except for the anger blazing in his eyes.

"Now, then," Brellit said, stepping slightly in front of him. Portly, short of stature, afflicted with a nose far too large for his face, Brellit had proven himself to be a level-headed diplomat and a useful chancellor. "Now, then, let us keep our tempers. Let us think this through carefully."

"There's been too much thinking," Caelan said curtly. "Too much lying."

"Excellency—"

"No!" Cutting off the chancellor, Caelan glared at Dreseid. "The time for worrying about your regiment's reputation is over. I want real answers, and I want them now. Is Barsin lying on your orders?"

"No, Sire!"

"Then on whose?"

"Barsin was not part of any plot," Dreseid said. "I know the young man and his family. Barsin is an excellent young officer. I won't have him broken in rank, blamed for what happened, simply because you can't get at Captain Hervan or Lieutenant Rozer."

Caelan drew a sharp breath while Brellit watched them both with alarm. "You think I'm making a scapegoat of the adjutant?"

"I fear it might happen, Sire."

Caelan snapped his fingers at an aide. "Bring Lord Tinel to me."

Looking startled, the colonel and Chancellor Brellit exchanged glances. Caelan resumed his pacing. Dreseid stood stiff and motionless while Brellit tapped his fingertips together.

"Dear me," he muttered as though to himself. "Dear me. Dear me. This is a most serious charge. Most serious."

If his comment was meant as a warning, Caelan ignored it.

"Excellency, I am at your disposal," said a breathless voice.

Caelan turned to see a man stopping to bow beneath the loggia. Lord Tinel Hervan looked flustered. He was a handsome man, middle-aged, his girth starting to thicken. Attired in the richest materials, he wore a heavy chain of plaited gold, and a jeweled pomander hung at his belt. His accent was soft and unquestionably patrici. He ruled one of the oldest, wealthiest, most prestigious houses in Itieria, yet as he ventured out into the dripping garden a light sheen of sweat could be seen on his upper lip and temples.

Nervous? Caelan wondered. Or hurried too much by the Guard to answer his emperor's summons?

"Thank you, Sire, for receiving me." The baron bent in a courtly bow. His tone was laced with gracious charm. By all accounts he'd been at court for weeks, attempting to gain an audience. "May I express the tremendous concern I and my family feel regarding Lady Lea? I have the utmost confidence that my son is doing everything he can to rescue her from whatever has befallen—"

"No doubt," Caelan broke in, ending his speech. "I have some questions for you."

Lord Tinel was an adroit courtier. Straightening, he gazed at his emperor with a look of utter compliance. "Whatever might please you, Excellency?"

"How long did Adjutant Barsin serve with your son?"

"Barsin?" Lord Tinel looked blank. "Oh yes, young Barsin! A delightful boy, Excellency."

"I'm waiting for your answer," Caelan said harshly.

"Hard to say—"

"Over a year, Sire," Dreseid broke in crisply. "According to records."

Caelan did not bother to shoot the colonel a glance of exasperation. "Long enough," he asked, "for a bond to form between the two young men?"

The baron frowned. "Really, Excellency, I don't know."

"But he was a guest at your home. You entertained him?"

"My son always brings home friends on leave," Lord Tinel said. "I believe young Barsin comes from a fine, though not prominent family. He's a second, no, third son and must make his way in the world."

"Not a wealthy young man, then?"

"To my knowledge, no."

"A loyal young man, reputedly excellent at his work, lacking enough funds but serving in a regiment notorious for high expenses. Ripe for bribery."

"Excellency," the baron said in a bewildered voice, "I do not understand."

Caelan thought of the vision he'd seen, that wavery image of the wooded stream with Lea kneeling beside a slain officer wearing captain's bars while her captor stood over them both. "I must tell you that Captain Hervan has been killed."

All three men started, but it was Lord Tinel who turned white to the lips and staggered back.

"Gently, man," the chancellor said. "Hold yourself together."

"But . . . but . . ." Wildly, Tinel glanced from Caelan to Dreseid's impassive face. "Colonel, how come you by this news? Have they been found?"

"That is for the emperor to say," Dreseid replied.

"Your son is dead, and my sister remains missing," Caelan said harshly. "There is no more need to try to salvage your son's career, no more need to cover up what actually happened. Whatever you've said to Barsin, whatever you've paid him to keep quiet, I order you to rescind your instructions. We need the truth from him, not your meddling."

The baron looked stunned. He kept blinking, his usual air of assurance gone. "Oli dead," he whispered. Grief filmed his eyes. "I cannot believe it. He would go after her, Sire. He would never quit until he saw her safely rescued."

"Then you insist he was a good officer?" Caelan asked. "When your attempt to conceal his mistakes from me says otherwise?"

"I—I—" Lord Tinel's gaze darted to the colonel and back to Caelan. "Yes, he is an excellent officer. The very best. Commendations, praise from his superior officers . . . Colonel, please assure His Excellency that my son is a shining example of the finest—"

"Captain Hervan was heavily in debt," Caelan said.

"A few gaming notes, nothing serious." Lord Tinel shrugged and wiped his brow with a shaking hand.

"How often did he ask you for money?"

"Frequently! All my sons do."

Caelan nodded. That answer at least held the ring of truth. "And if he were desperate enough for money would he have accepted a bribe to take my sister to Falenthis?"

Lord Tinel stiffened. "I protest this maligning of my son most strongly!"

"Careful, Baron," Brellit warned him. "Remember whom you're addressing."

Tinel seemed not to hear. "Excellency, this is an outrage! He would never—"

"But he suddenly abandoned his official route," Caelan said. "His duty was to keep her safe! He failed. You may coat that with every excuse at your disposal if you choose, but the fact remains that my sister has vanished without a trace, and other than the wounded men left behind in Adjutant Barsin's charge, the Crimsons responsible for her safety have disappeared, too. Whether they have deserted, or perished like your son, I do not know, but let us have no more prevarication. You tampered with the Imperial agent assigned to investigate the matter. Have you also tampered with Barsin's testimony to protect your son's reputation and career?"

"Sire, I assure you that I would never—"

"Don't compound your treachery by continuing to lie," Caelan said, drilling his gaze through the man. "Or destroy the House of Hervan for the sake of one misguided son."

The baron turned white. Gasping, he dropped to his knees before Caelan and clasped his jeweled hands together. "Sire, please! Let me explain. Please, hear me!"

Caelan sighed.

"I feared this misconstruing of events," Lord Tinel said desperately. "That everyone would think the worst, would believe Olivel had gone mad and committed some terrible act. He didn't. Hasn't. I know my son. Whatever turned him toward that accursed valley was a mistake, a simple error in judgment. He is loyal to Your Excellency. As am I. On my House, on my very honor, I swear it."

Caelan stared at him unmoved. "Did you talk to Barsin before he came to the palace?"

"Yes."

"Did you bribe him to keep him quiet?"

"I—I assured him I would pay a healer's expenses for the wounded men, and I would see him into another regiment if he loses his commission in the Crimsons. His father cannot afford to help him." Lord Tinel sent Caelan an imploring look. "Why should I not do what lies within my means?"

Behind him, Brellit sighed, closing his eyes for a moment. And Dreseid began to frown.

Caelan compressed his mouth. "You would not have to ask him to lie, would you, Baron? A boy already known to admire your son, a boy with over a year's service under your son's influence, and you, stepping in with such assurances. What else could he do but shield the captain?"

"But—but, Sire, please!" Lord Tinel pleaded. "You're assuming that Olivel is guilty of—of misdeeds. Can you really believe he would be involved in some plot against Lady Lea? He's in love with her! He hopes to marry her. There, I realize I speak rashly, but a young man's love *is* rash. How can he possibly withstand her beauty?"

Again Brellit stirred as though longing to warn Tinel to be quiet. Caelan felt his temper blazing through his body and throbbing in his temples. He wheeled away, striding furiously back and forth in an effort not to seize his protector's sword and eviscerate this presumptuous fool.

"Excellency," Brellit dared say behind him. "You cannot believe young Hervan would shirk his duty, or—Gault forbid—bring Lady Lea to harm in some plot."

"Indeed not!" Tinel added eagerly. "My son likes his pleasures. He is young and headstrong and too sure of his charm with the ladies. But those are the failings of many young men of his class and station. Hardly grounds for assuming him guilty of—"

"Enough," Caelan cut him off. "Let us stop trying to be-

lieve this officer so doggedly followed her trail that he
never bothered to send a messenger, report her abduction,
request armed assistance, or generally follow regulations at
all." His gaze swung to Dreseid. "We've had this conversation before, Colonel, and I'm weary of it. Is there any explanation for this lapse of procedure?"

"Not so far, Excellency."

"No, indeed. And Barsin, who should be clearing up the
mystery, has nothing to say except some mad chatter about
ghosts."

Dreseid drew a breath. "Sire," he said reluctantly, "it's
possible, as you've said, that Hervan and his men have deserted."

Lord Tinel averted his face, his throat working. For an
instant Caelan felt compassion for his distress, but then he
thought of Lea—gentle, sweet, and lovely—who'd come to
jeopardy because of Captain Hervan's blunders. There were
too many unanswered questions remaining, too much rushing to escape blame instead of finding explanations. As for
Lea's part in this . . . her own complicity . . . Caelan could
not consider it without feeling pain. *I must not judge her actions until I understand everything about this business,* he
told himself. *Perhaps I should not judge anyone as yet.*

He lifted his gaze to the colonel's, and saw there a look
of intense shame, as though desertion was worse than
death. In the colonel's world, no doubt it was.

Red faced, grim, Dreseid continued. "The . . . reputation of the Crimsons was earned by our loyalty, courage,
and accomplishments, Sire. We do not rely on trickery or
deceit. But if evil has been done, if there has been complicity in this matter . . . I swear to you that the truth will be
uncovered. I personally will question Barsin again."

"Sire," Lord Tinel whispered in an anguished voice. "I
know my son. He has his faults, but he's a good officer and
a loyal one. Please let him defend himself. He—"

"He is dead," Caelan said in a quieter voice. "I know
this absolutely."

"But—"

"Accept it. Go and pray for his soul."

"Excellency, please," Tinel said, almost moaning the words. "We are loyal. I swear to you that we are loyal. We have changed servants, removed certain possessions, unsworn old oaths. I even had the family chapel's symbols of Beloth chiseled off the walls. My son never served in the old army. He enlisted under Your Excellency's reign. He has been loyal to you from the beginning. There is—was no corruption in him, no real vice. I assure you, Excellency, that he feels the honor you dealt him with this mission most profoundly. We all do. We—"

"Lord Tinel, I will consider your situation at another time. You have my permission to withdraw."

The baron hunched his shoulders as though in pain. Bowing, he left without another word.

In the little silence that followed, Brellit cleared his voice and said, "A harsh way to learn about the death of one's most promising son."

Dreseid was frowning, holding himself erect in his bright uniform, saying nothing of what he thought.

Caelan ignored the chancellor's remark and went on staring steadily into the colonel's eyes. "Calling the dead. Are you familiar with that practice?"

The colonel's sunburned visage changed color. He hesitated long enough to make even Brellit stare at him, and then he said hoarsely, "Yes, Sire. An old ritual in honor of fallen comrades, now banned."

"Did you know," Caelan asked, "that I have a report that lists the membership of the Talon Cadre?"

Colonel Dreseid blinked. "Former membership, surely. It and all the other secret societies for officers and enlisted have been officially disbanded."

"You belonged to the Talon Cadre, didn't you, Colonel?"

"Yes, Sire."

"It's my understanding that the Talon Cadre still exists."

"Probably, Sire."

There it was, a flash of defiance. Caelan's suspicions hardened. "Young Hervan was most certainly a member."

The colonel's frown deepened. "At the risk of contradicting Your Excellency, like myself, he withdrew membership upon your orders."

"Are you certain?"

"I discussed it with him at the time. He said . . . his father insisted that he withdraw."

"What else does the Household Regiment have to hide?"

"Nothing, Sire."

Their eyes met, clashed, held.

Caelan said softly, "Send out an order to all the provinces for the arrest of Hervan's men."

"And if they haven't deserted? Can Your Excellency not wait?"

"For what? My sister's plight to become a bigger tragedy?"

"Imperial reprisals against these men will not help her if she's been taken for ransom. Until their side is heard, until there is a trial, I protest with all due respect the public disgrace of good men."

The colonel's remark was dangerously close to insubordination. Caelan flushed. "Your protest can be officially lodged. My order will be sent."

Dreseid, his face very red, saluted crisply.

"As for Barsin's dishonorable discharge," Caelan said, "delay that. See that Lord Tinel speaks to him. Then question him again."

"Yes, Sire."

"Ask him in particular why the dead were called."

"I've told you, Sire. That's an old custom of honoring fallen comrades."

"I'm not interested in your assumptions," Caelan said impatiently. "Ask him! Or my predlicates will."

"Excellency—"

"That is all."

Dreseid's mouth clamped to a rigid line. He saluted and

marched away, his back ramrod stiff, the back of his neck as fiery red as his cloak.

$\mathfrak{I}t$ was starting to drizzle, but Caelan, hot faced and seething, took off his crown and tucked it beneath his arm, shaking back his shoulder-length hair. He made no move to retreat indoors. "None of this," he said wearily, "helps Lea. Not one interrogation brings us closer to finding her."

Chancellor Brellit sighed and let his fingers dabble in the bubbling fountain for a moment. "In which case, is it wise, Excellency, to make enemies of the Crimsons?"

"You had better ask Colonel Dreseid if it's wise to make an enemy of *me*," Caelan replied. "I'm not Kostimon, willing to ignore corruption when it suits me."

"Once you start condemning members of the patrici and confiscating their personal fortunes, where does it stop?"

"Are you saying I'm becoming a tyrant?" Caelan asked angrily.

"Not at all. But why make enemies of your allies? Tinel's no traitor. An opportunist, certainly, but his loyalty has gone unquestioned until now."

"He had no business tampering with that boy's testimony. Or an Imperial agent's!"

"Certainly not. But consider a father's grief, a father's natural desire to protect his son. And his House. Imperial reprisals have been harsh since the Terrors. Many decent men walk in fear, and is it really your desire, Light Bringer, that they do so?"

Caelan fumed a moment, trying hard to control his resentment of this gentle admonishment. "Perhaps we should consider a brother's worry. If she falls into the hands of my enemies . . ."

"There is no *if* about it. You know she has, Excellency," Brellit said quietly. "The only question is which among many. And you'll know that once the ransom demand comes in."

Caelan scowled at his chancellor. "Thyrazenes, Madruns, Vindicants, or Ulinians? I would prefer to strike now, rather than wait."

"And strike at which of them?"

Baffled, Caelan shook his head. "All of them, if I could."

"That's exactly what this plot seeks to accomplish. Luring you from the palace to attack, probably the wrong enemy. Result? Chaos, a disordered empire, and a chance for someone else to seize the throne." Brellit spread out his pudgy hands. "The oldest maneuver in politics."

"Yes, yes, I know. So you have said before. Elandra agrees with you." Caelan swept back his damp hair. "But I am a man of action, and Lea is far too precious to risk."

"They know that, Sire. They're counting on you to think exactly like that. You must be an emperor now, before you are a brother. You must guard your center of power, and you must outthink them. Make them take the first move and betray themselves."

"In capturing Lea, they've already done that."

"No, no. You must be patient and strong."

A chill fell through Caelan. He realized his clothes were becoming soaked. "And while I am patient and strong, being clever and waiting and guarding my throne, what becomes of her, Chancellor? Will you next advise me not to pay her ransom? Because once I crumble to one demand, no one I love will be safe?"

Sympathy filled the old man's eyes as he lifted them to Caelan's. But he did not answer those anguished questions.

He did not have to.

Chapter 10

The Golden Cup rang with noise. Travelers and locals jostled shoulder to shoulder in the taproom, calling out for ale and hot zivin—a regional drink made from fermented goat's milk and unmentionable ingredients. It was Mrishadal, the sacred winter festival for all Ulinians, and revelers sang and danced in the dark streets of Kanidalon, now and then bursting into the jammed tavern on blasts of wintry air, shouting for drink and food.

In the darkest corner of the taproom, Shadrael sat with his back propped against the wall, nursing a cup of tepid zivin while he fingered the flask of blood in his left hand. The blood—some nasty potion mixed with herbs bought in a grim little dark alley—was supposed to help combat the buzz of imminent madness in his brain. No doubt, Shadrael thought sourly, it was just a quack's remedy made of spittle, weeds, and dyed water. He swallowed a deep mouthful of zivin instead. The potent drink had weakened his legs and numbed the ache of his bruises, but best of all, it seemed to be holding off the shakes and snakes. No tremors, no agonizing bursts of pain, no hallucinations. Just a happy, warm glow of intoxication.

What more could a man ask for?

Perhaps an uncaring stupor, he thought, and took another swallow.

Shucked of his armor and weapons—now pawned to pay for this drinking spree—and unshaven and sour breathed, he lifted his cup in a silent toast to the Vindicants, who hadn't stoned him to death after all.

Apparently it had been enough for them to cheat and humiliate him. Protected from serious internal harm by his armor, he'd lain in the dirt for a long time after they left, but he hadn't died, not even from losing his magic. There had been only the cold darkness of the night, the mountain wind gradually cooling the feverish fire in his limbs, and Fomo crawling cautiously up to him. Fomo, emerging from the shadows, to stealthily loot the corpse.

Surprise, guilt, or perhaps a vestige of military discipline had stopped the centruin from cutting Shadrael's throat and taking what he pleased. Instead, Fomo had helped him up, groaning and barely able to walk, and urged him along. It had been Fomo who brought him here, Fomo who pawned his armor and weapons, and Fomo who'd kept most of the money.

Shadrael hadn't seen the man today. He didn't know if Fomo would return or not. It hardly mattered. When Shadrael had not died that night, he knew he was destined to go mad before he perished. That was the fate of those who lost their souls . . . slow torture, the worst kind, and no more than he deserved.

All he wanted now was to forget everything that had happened, especially the memory of Lea's beseeching eyes and that little tremor in her sweet voice as she'd begged him for mercy.

He raised his cup in another silent toast. To gentle, lovely Lea E'non, who had struck him down with light and torn his magic from him. The cruelest enemy of all.

Fomo slid through the crowd, jerked a tipsy youth off his stool, and shoved him sprawling before scooting the stool close to Shadrael and sitting down with a grunt. "Time we was going," he said hoarsely.

Shadrael didn't glance at him. "Later."

"You said that yesterday. Ain't you drunk enough of that foul brew yet?"

"No."

"Your luck's running out. Someone's bound to tell the warlord you're here," Fomo said, his narrowed eyes watching the crowd. He'd untied his hair, letting the stringy hanks fall over his face to conceal his army tattoo. "Best we pull out soon."

"When I'm ready."

"When's that to be?"

Shadrael scowled into his cup. "When I'm drunk."

The wailing music of guinars and tambours struck up a lively tune, and people in the crowded taproom jostled toward the walls in an excited surge. Men's voices called out eagerly, and through the crowd came a trio of dancing girls swathed in robes and wearing dowry headdresses made of innumerable coins linked together. In the center of the room where space had been cleared for them, they grouped themselves in a circle, back to back, and faced the leering men.

Fomo grinned, licking his lips and leaning forward.

To Shadrael, their faces were blurs; their dark eyes—heavily lined with kohl—no comparison for blue.

The music struck a flourish, and the girls flung off their robes to reveal lithe bodies clad in little more than flowing scraps of silk and long strings of clashing coins. As a loud shout roared up, they began to dance, swaying and undulating to a primitive beat. The watching crowd swayed, too, mesmerized or singing lustily while busy waiters threaded through the throng, refilling cups and taking payment.

Without taking his gaze from the dance, Shadrael drained his cup to its bitter dregs. Shuddering, he wiped his mouth with the back of his hand and slumped lower against the wall. The room was warm, and the dance whirling before him was making him drowsy. His eyes grew heavy.

Something bumped into his table, startling him back to alertness. Fomo was gone. Someone else stood there.

"Looking for an ex-legion commander named Shadrael," a gruff voice said beneath the crowd's hubbub. "You know the man?"

Shadrael let his gaze drop. "No."

"Thought you had the look of old army. That other fellow, too, before he took off."

"Never served."

"Sorry. Maybe it's the short hair or the boots, or that sword callus on your thumb."

Shadrael's gaze flickered up, taking the trouble to focus this time. He saw a gray-haired, stocky man with a barrel chest and a mean eye. Gaunt as though he'd recently come through hard times, he wore armor in disregard of Mrishadal's edict of peace. The folds of his cloak hung over any insignia his armor might bear, but he carried a sword that was short enough to be legion issue, its hilt fashioned in the predlicate style. He held himself alert, balancing on the balls of his feet, his stony eyes shifting warily about to watch his surroundings.

A fleeting sense of caution passed through Shadrael before he knocked it away as he might a crawling ant. Whoever this old man was, and for whatever reason he was seeking Shadrael, he wasn't official or he would have come in with soldiers at his back.

Silence stretched between them, unfriendly and suspicious on both sides. Shadrael went back to watching the dancing girls, his thoughts blurred by the music and hard drink.

"Mind if I sit here?" the stranger finally asked. "Come a long ways, and I'm fair parched."

Shadrael slid the useless blood potion into his pocket

and kept his other hand firmly on his empty drink cup. "Suit yourself."

The stranger waved for a waiter, who came sliding expertly through the crush, nodded impassively at the order for hot mead, bit into the coin paid him, and a short time later brought a flagon of cheap homemade ale. Shadrael watched with an appreciative eye while the stranger blew gingerly across the drink's surface, frowned, and sipped cautiously.

His face screwed into a sour pucker before he spat out his mouthful. "What kind of damned horse's piss is this?"

"Home brew," Shadrael told him.

"Gah! I'd sooner drink slops than this cold . . ." Letting his voice trail off, he shot Shadrael a look of speculation. "Cheated me, didn't he?"

"Yes."

"Dirty little Ulinian pox mark. How much is ale?"

"Half the price of mead, which has to be imported and taxed at customs."

"Knew what he'd do, didn't you?"

Shadrael shrugged.

Scowling, the stranger took another, unwilling sip, only to shudder and slam his cup down hard enough to slosh its contents. "Damn this stinking town! The food this bad?"

"Might be."

"For a stranger, you mean."

"Maybe."

"I'm getting all the hospitality Ulinia has to offer, ain't I?" As he spoke, the stranger watched a steaming dish of food being carried past him. "That smells good."

"Is good," Shadrael said, remembering to slur his Lingua slightly without military inflection. He gestured for a waiter and tossed his empty cup aside. "Call it *kuvslaka* when you order."

"What is it?"

"Stew. Goat meat and . . ." Shadrael gestured vaguely.

"If I order it, this *kuvslaka*, will I get it?"

"Ulinian word gets Ulinian service. You pick up our language quickly."

The stranger's gaze bored into Shadrael, sizing him up so openly that again Shadrael felt that flicker of caution. "Didn't say I couldn't speak Ulinian, now, did I?"

Shadrael didn't answer. Across the room, he glimpsed Fomo in the crowd, scowling at him and making a gesture of warning. Best to go, Shadrael thought, before this man asked him real questions.

At that moment, however, his waiter came, bringing a cup of fresh zivin. The man set it on the table and fetched a hot poker from the enormous hearth. Plunging it into the cup with a mighty hiss of steam, he let the contents boil and froth, then removed the poker, accepted a coin with a quick grin, and hurried away before the stranger could snag his attention.

"Served you pretty fast," the stranger observed.

"I," Shadrael said with a grand gesture, gulping down several swallows of hot liquid that burned to the pit of his stomach, "am *aziarahd mahal*. Of course I am served well."

"You're drunk, boy."

"Am I?" Shadrael asked in wonder, taking another sip. "I think I might be drunk, but I am no longer a boy."

The stranger suddenly grinned, although his smile never reached his eyes. He held out his hand in a friendly way. "M'name's Thirbe. Yours?"

"Nothing." Sobering abruptly, Shadrael glared down into his cup, inhaling its potent fumes. "My name is nothing. Strangers do not share names here. I warn you of this because I like you."

Thirbe withdrew his hand in a disgruntled way and went on staring at Shadrael. "You must get around this province, if you work the roads, eh?"

"I did not say I am a bandit." Shadrael frowned. "You carry a predlicate sword. You ask questions like a predlicate. Maybe you *are* a predlicate." He waved his cup about, nearly dropped it, and drained the rest of it so fast his ears rang and he felt dizzy. "It's Mrishadal," he said, slamming his cup to the floor. "Time to celebrate."

"I need to hire a guide, a skilled tracker to get me around these parts. You familiar with Broken Spine country? I'll pay you for the job."

"Got money," Shadrael informed him with dignity. "Pawned my . . . pawned . . . Got money."

Thirbe almost grinned as he leaned forward. "You ever work for a man named Shadrael? Come on. You know who he is. I can tell by your eyes every time I mention his name."

The music struck a flourishing crescendo and the dancers spun to a halt. A loud shout roared up. Shadrael shouted with them, only to catch his breath sharply and bend over, pressing his fist to his chest.

Thirbe gripped the back of his tunic and pulled him upright. "You sick?"

Shadrael gasped for air, feeling clammy until the weakness passed. When he could breathe again, he leaned back against the wall, letting the tremors pass down his legs.

"Better slow down on that stuff you're drinking," Thirbe advised him. "You're looking like a raw recruit on his first bender."

Shadrael hardly heard him. Thirbe, he was thinking. The name Lea had sometimes whimpered in her sleep. The name of her . . . protector.

Alarm pinned Shadrael, and for a moment he felt breathless and cold. *He knows me,* he thought. *He has tracked me here—how?—and he toys with me now like a cat with its prey.*

But the momentary panic faded along with the ache in his chest. He even grinned a little, thinking this was the best game of *shul-drakshera* of all, the Dance with the Enemy.

"Hey, you!" Thirbe finally caught a waiter. "Bring me some *kuvslaka* and make sure it's hot."

Scowling, the waiter told him the price.

"Payment when I'm served," Thirbe said, showing him money but tucking it away.

With a shrug, the waiter picked up the cup Shadrael had dropped, filled it with more steaming zivin, heated it with a hot poker, and pressed it into Shadrael's hand. When Shadrael fumbled to pull out a coin, however, he found his purse empty.

"You must pay," the waiter said in Ulinian, reaching for the cup.

Shadrael gripped it tightly. "Lord's privilege," he snarled in the same language. "I pay with lord's privilege."

The waiter stared at him round eyed, and suddenly backed away with a bow, glancing over his shoulder as he hurried into the crowd.

"What's that mean, lord's privilege?" Thirbe asked.

Shadrael shot him a narrow look, remembering belatedly that Thirbe had said he understood Ulinian. *Get away from him,* warned a sensible corner of Shadrael's mind. But the rest of his thoughts urged, *Stay and torment him, tease him . . . later, kill him.* In the back of his mind he could hear laughter, shrill and wild. Without answering Thirbe's question, he drank deep and fast until his wits were spinning and the laughter died down.

"Something to do with being *aziarahd mahal,* ain't it?" Thirbe went on. "Kind of the local aristocracy."

Before Shadrael could speak, Thirbe's food was brought, a mounded plate of steaming food. The protector counted three coins into the waiter's hand. "Very tasty," he said, wolfing down several mouthfuls before he wiped his chin and shot Shadrael a look of appraisal. "Come down in the world, ain't you, Lord Shadrael, if you're hanging around a place like this?"

A shiver of alarm passed through Shadrael, but not very strongly. He wondered if a legion patrol was waiting outside right now to arrest him. "I am not the man you seek," he replied.

"Pity. Would save me a lot of time if I could find him fast."

Shadrael shrugged. He was starting to feel warm and muzzy again although he had the feeling there was something he needed to do. *No,* he reminded himself, *you are finished. All your tasks are done.*

Thirbe went on eating, chewing with rapid appreciation as though he hadn't enjoyed a good meal in days. "You know, there can't be that many noblemen in Ulinia. Bound to know each other, don't you? So it seems kind of strange that you wouldn't have anything to tell me about this man Shadrael."

"If you know his name, you know enough about him," Shadrael replied, staring into his cup.

"He used to be a legion commander, but fell on hard times," Thirbe said, wiping his plate with a morsel of flat bread. "Been doing some road work here and there, I hear. Picking up coin."

Ignoring the slang words for outlawry, Shadrael swirled the zivin around in his cup.

"Just makes sense that you'd know something about him. Sure, you Ulinians are tight-mouthed with strangers, but what's it going to hurt you to sell me a little information?"

Shadrael turned his dark gaze on Thirbe, who'd stopped eating and was staring at him hard. Defiantly Shadrael stared back. "Maybe the warlord's sword through my spine."

"Fair enough. Tell me nothing, but guide me to his hideout." Thirbe turned over his hand and uncurled his fingers to show three shining ducats on his palm. "Worth your while, friend?"

It was a *lot* of money. Shadrael stared at the coins, mesmerized by the wealth they represented. He felt tempted to carry the game further, to take the payment and lead this fool out into the Valley of Fires. No one would ever find the old man in a back canyon, not even his bones picked clean by scavengers.

Abruptly Shadrael lost interest. It was too much trouble.

All he wanted was to remain in this dark corner, staying drunk and being left alone.

"Well?" Thirbe coaxed him. "All you have to do is show me where to find him."

"Can't."

The protector clamped his hand on Shadrael's wrist. "Can't? Or won't?"

Shadrael tried to pull free, but Thirbe had a grip like iron.

"We can keep this friendly," he said softly. "I'll pay you like I said. Or we can do this the hard way, where I drag you out back and beat the information out of you."

Shadrael grinned at him, feeling the fumes of his drink wreathe around his brain. "Hard way."

"All right," Thirbe snarled, standing up and giving Shadrael a jerk. "On your feet, you drunken lout!"

Smiling muzzily, Shadrael lifted his arms. "Going to buy me," he crooned.

Thirbe swore a blistering oath; then a hand clamped on Shadrael's shoulder. He pressed a bruise hard, and Shadrael winced, trying to shrug free.

"Easy!" he said. "No need to be so—"

"On your feet," said a gruff voice unfamiliar to him, a voice that spoke Ulinian. "And no trouble."

Turning his head, Shadrael looked up into a hawkish face with fierce dark eyes. "'Nother stranger," Shadrael announced. "Never seen so many strangers. Fomo should start counting all of you."

The man gripped his tunic front and hauled him to his feet. The room tilted wildly, making Shadrael laugh. Nearby he glimpsed Thirbe arguing hotly. Then Thirbe was shoved aside, and Shadrael found himself flanked on either side by grim warriors in head wraps and long cloaks.

"Come on. Come on!" they urged him.

Shadrael swayed, opening his mouth to protest, and felt the sharp prick of a dagger point in his ribs. He looked down at the hairy hand holding the weapon. "You could hurt me with that," he said.

"You're right," the man agreed. The dagger point jabbed him impatiently. "Move!"

Gripping his arms, they shoved him forward past a scowling Thirbe. Shadrael could not lift his arm to wave farewell, so he let his head loll back. "Good hunting, Thirbeeeeee!" he called.

The room kept dipping and swaying with as much abandon as the dancing girls. By the time Shadrael managed to refocus his eyes he found himself being shoved out of the Golden Cup.

The cold night air was like a brisk slap to his wits. Swaying, he blinked against the blaze of torchlight and now saw that his escort wore Choven protections and the insignia of the warlord on their cloaks. Vordachai's men.

Frowning, Shadrael dug in his heels. "I do not want to go with you."

"Never mind what *you* want," one of them growled.

Another motioned. "Hurry before he gathers his wits and fights us."

Shadrael opened his mouth to knock them senseless with a spell, but he couldn't think of one. By then they were trussing his wrists behind him. *Sever,* he thought hazily, supposing he should resist. It seemed that his brother had found him earlier than he'd expected.

"There are," he announced solemnly as the knots were yanked tight, "no free drinks."

"Why doesn't he fight us?" someone asked.

"Shut up! Hurry and get him on that horse."

It seemed suddenly very funny to Shadrael that he should go to his execution this way. The warlord's men gathered around him and grimly hoisted him belly down across a horse like a sack of fodder. Dangling upside down made his head spin worse, and that was funny, too.

"Caught," he said, slurring his words. "But with dig-dignity and honor." That had been his father's favorite motto. "Dignity and honor! I give you leave to carry on. Hoo!"

And as they mounted their horses and bore him away like a stoat to slaughter, he let his face bounce against the saddle leather while his laughter echoed down the narrow street.

Chapter 11

At dawn, however, Shadrael was not laughing. He was, in fact, sitting on a hard cot in a bare, dusty cell, holding his head between his hands and longing to die. He'd puked up his guts already in the musty floor straw, and now he sat there with his head five times its usual size and throbbing in time with the cadenced marching and orderly shouts of the changing of the ramparts sentries.

He felt as though he'd been turned inside out and flailed, and as the effects of his drinking bout faded, the beating he'd taken from the Vindicants made his muscles cramp and shiver. He ran both hot and cold. The shakes and snakes were definitely coming over him. A *mesderah* horn—low and carrying—had already sounded the time of day, splitting his head in twain. He thought an axe cleaving his skull would have been more merciful.

The sound of footsteps approaching from outside gave him warning just before a key clattered in the lock. The door to his cell slammed open with a boom that echoed down the passageway and burst open Shadrael's head.

He flinched, shutting his eyes as fresh sweat broke out across his brow. He lacked even the strength to swear.

"Shadrael, you filthy, lying leper!" Lord Vordachai roared.

He stormed in, halting just across the threshold, his bulky body blocking most of the light streaming in behind him. Clad in brown finery that made him look like a wine barrel balanced atop thin legs, he glittered from a gold chain hung with jewels and a seal ring banding his thick finger. A large teardrop ruby swung from one ear, the fine stone as scarlet as the temper in his bearded face. His dark eyes snapped ferociously.

"Where is she?" he shouted. "What have you done with her?"

Squinting against the sunlight that spilled through the doorway behind Vordachai, Shadrael tried to pull himself together. "Go away," he mumbled.

"Where is she?"

His bellow was loud enough to bring down the mountain. Shadrael winced, holding his head, and didn't answer.

"What have you done with her? Speak up! And don't lie to me about taking her to Muhadim. I know she isn't there."

"Never found her—"

Growling deep in his throat, Vordachai yanked Shadrael upright, shaking him as a dog might a rat. "I'd sooner spit you on the end of my *minzeral*'s pike and leave your skull hanging outside my window for the crows to peck. And when they eat their fill of you, they can line their nests with plugs of your hair and raise their young in it. At least in *that* respect you will have done someone a worthy service. Better than you have served me."

Shadrael swallowed back another heave of nausea and sent his brother a mocking little smile.

With an exclamation of disgust, Vordachai shoved him sprawling across the cot. "Gods," he said with loathing, "how you stink. I see what you've done these past weeks, you pus-filled demon! Lounged about the alehouses and drunk all the gold I gave you."

"Why not?" Shadrael muttered.

Vordachai gave him a hefty kick that nearly drove his head into the wall. "Lying dog! I know you captured her. You had her in your hands." He shook his meaty fists. "And you've done what? Lost her? Sold her? Answer me!"

Shadrael closed his eyes, clutching the blanket that was bunched beneath him. He longed for Vordachai to go away. "Never found her. My men deserted. Never saw—"

A golden strand of hair, the one Urmaeor had cut and given to him, landed on the cot beside Shadrael. He stared at it, feeling a surge of unwanted emotions go through him, and forced himself to sit up.

"And what is this souvenir you keep in your pocket?" Vordachai asked. "A bit of your horse's mane? Now, the truth this time. Where is she?"

"Vindicants."

Vordachai drew an audible breath, but the shout Shadrael expected never came. Shadrael managed to lift his aching head enough to see his brother empurpled. With eyes bulging, his hands clenching and unclenching, he looked as though he wanted to throttle Shadrael, or else he was on the verge of apoplexy. "And this is how you've repaid my trust," he said at last. He sounded hurt, even bewildered. "I relied on you."

"Shouldn't have."

Vordachai struck him, knocking Shadrael off the cot into the dirty straw. Tasting the coppery warmth of blood, Shadrael didn't bother to struggle up. He didn't have to. Vordachai picked him up, only to strike him again. This time the blow rang through Shadrael's skull, and tiny black dots danced in his vision.

Vordachai was breathing hard and fast. "You've given her to—to . . . *gods!* I cannot look at you, cannot bear the sight of you, or the stink of you." Abruptly he shoved Shadrael sprawling. "Clean up and stand in my hall to

explain yourself, or damn your eyes, I'll see you thrown off
the cliff alive, and fed to the vultures."

With a slam of the door, he was gone.

$\mathcal{B}y$ the midday horn, Shadrael thought he might—
perhaps—live long enough to see his execution. His head
still ached, but it had shrunk to its normal size. He could
eat nothing of what was brought to him, but his nausea was
gone, thanks to a brewed drink supplied to him by Ban, the
warlord's valet.

Shaved, washed, and wearing clean attire, Shadrael
emerged blinking from his cell into the glare of day and
could not quite mask his flinch of pain as the sunlight hit
him. Many of his brother's warriors were lounging about;
undoubtedly they'd been waiting to see the notorious Lord
Shadrael who'd made such a name for himself . . . and
come home in chains.

Tight-lipped, Shadrael limped grimly along. The sunlight
seemed to be burning him raw. He endured the discomfort,
determined not to squint or moan. His knees were weak and
shaky beneath him, and he focused his attention on not
stumbling. Before he'd walked a dozen steps, he was panting
for air. His aching head tended to swim whenever he glanced
over the parapet wall at the dizzying plunge below. *I've become as much a flatlander as an Itierian,* he thought in self-
scorn.

The citadel of Bezhalmbra was both fortress and palace,
built at precarious angles up the vertical slope of Jawnuth
Peak, its stone walls shrouded in clouds and mist.

They descended infinite steps in silence, with warriors
and workers staring everywhere. In his wake, Shadrael
heard them mumble over their amulets when they saw for
themselves that he indeed cast no shadow. Once he would
have delighted in scaring them; today he felt ashamed.
Many of these people he'd known since birth. He hadn't

been back since the day at sixteen he'd left for the army, but this was no homecoming.

Just when he feared they were going to walk halfway down the mountain to the palace, its tiled roof a sun-faded red amidst the brilliant color of the gardens, the guards wheeled smartly and escorted him instead into the armory.

The shade of its interior gave him such respite that he gasped aloud and would have tripped on the threshold had not one of the guards steadied him. An officer reprimanded the man curtly, and Shadrael nodded to himself. Had he been well, he would have seized the guard's weapon and fought his way out.

But he was too dizzy and weak to cause trouble. The exertion of walking down so many steps had made his chest hurt again, the way it had before he'd drunk enough zivin to dull the pain.

"Come on!" Vordachai's impatient voice yelled, echoing through the vaulted central hall. "I've waited long enough, damn you."

Pride and sheer grit stiffened Shadrael's spine. He reminded himself that he was still a praetinor, even if his medal was now a dishonored scrap of charred metal, still a man who'd once won battles for the glory of the empire, still a man who'd been given a triumph by the emperor, still . . . a man, however disgraced. Drawing a breath, he swaggered down that long expanse to the scuffed wood dais where generations of Ulinian fighters had been rallied to war.

The hall was empty save for the guards, Vordachai, the warlord's protector, and a gray-bearded *talhadar*, a holy man. Along the walls hung racks of weapons and draped hides of wild animals. The room was old, impossible to heat, and full of memories that Shadrael shut firmly away.

He understood what Vordachai was doing in bringing him here. His brother was not a sophisticated man and undoubtedly thought that he would soften Shadrael with a

flood of memories and the kindness of old servants, but
this was not home. The army, Shadrael reminded himself
stiffly, had been that. Now there was nothing.

Liar, he thought with a burst of anger. *Lie to him. Lie to
all of them, but not yourself.*

Perhaps halfway along the hall, he lurched to a sudden
halt. A wave of clammy trembling, impossible to control,
washed through him. Little glimmers of half-seen people
and faces danced along the edges of his vision. Sweating,
he blinked them away, struggling to concentrate. He did not
want to collapse here, not in front of his brother. He did not
want Vordachai to see him reduced to a pathetic madman.

Please. Please, he prayed desperately. He had to face
Vordachai and take whatever his brother chose to mete out,
like a soldier, like an Imperial officer. Not collapsed in a
heap, gibbering at things that weren't there.

Vordachai stopped fidgeting about and was watching
him. Shadrael heard the guards approaching from behind
him as though to shove him the rest of the way. His head
came up. He struggled to force the glimmering shapes
from his vision.

"Shadrael?" Vordachai said.

Grimacing, Shadrael walked the rest of the way to the
dais and halted, panting for breath. He looked up into his
brother's frowning face, blinking as it wavered before him.
Another clammy tremor swept down through his body, but
he'd locked his knees to keep them from failing beneath
him.

"Gods, but you're still a sorry sight," Vordachai said.
"Didn't Ban give you the remedy? I don't want you puking
in here."

"I won't."

Vordachai drew in a breath, expanding himself. His
dark brows knotted above eyes still hot. "Did you intend
this betrayal from the beginning? Don't stand there like a
stone. Start talking!"

"What would you have me say? It's done."

"I would know your reasons."

Shadrael felt a sense of unreality, as though he were floating. "Reasons are a waste of time. It's done. Finished."

"Not finished!" Vordachai roared, clenching his fists. "Is this all you will say to me? Is this how you repay my trust? I relied on you!"

"Which makes you a fool."

The guards' hands went to their weapons, but Vordachai did not rise to that bait. He stood there, red faced and making a sort of growling sound in his throat.

"Do you realize what you've done?" he asked. "I was this close. *This close!* I was ready, my warriors mustered, my barons summoned, my armory filled." He gestured with a thick arm. "And what do I have? *Nothing!* Nothing but Imperial suspicion aimed at me."

"You—"

"Did I not instruct you to throw the blame on Thyraze? Did I not tell you to take the girl swiftly to Muhadim? You should have been there weeks ago! Instead, you've dawdled along, laying a trail a blind idiot could follow straight to my door. Explain that!"

"I don't give excuses."

Vordachai snorted. "Army discipline, I suppose, eh? Did you know I've had a decivate up here? A prancing little decivate still wet behind the ears daring to question *me*. By the gods, that legion may have put my largest city under martial law, ordering my people about and thinking it rules this province instead of me, but some things I won't stand for! And the girl's protector right here with him, accusing me of being involved in her abduction."

"You were."

"But thanks to you, I don't have her! Why should I be blamed for what I do not have?"

Shadrael looked away. At the best of times his brother's faulty logic was difficult to follow. Right now, it was too much bother to sort out.

"Had I hired the laziest, verminous, most pox-riddled

blackguard in a mire of filthy pigs, I would have been better served than by you."

"Naturally—"

"Don't mock me!" Vordachai broke in, his voice savage. "I'll not stand for that."

"If you're going to execute me, why don't you get to it?" Shadrael said wearily.

"I'll throw you to the vultures when I'm ready and not before! I can see what you're doing! Trying to make me lose my temper so I won't think. I see your game. Yes, I see it clearly."

"Stop looking for conspiracies that aren't there," Shadrael said. "If you want your gold back, it's spent. You made a poor bargain, my lord. The girl went to a higher bidder. That's all."

"It's not that simple," Vordachai said suspiciously. "Nothing with you is ever simple. As for those filthy Vindicants—"

"Will they not accomplish your objective?" Shadrael broke in. "If it's war you want, there'll be one. And already I've served you better than you deserve, for the decivate found no captive here. You've been spared arrest, and nothing can be proved against you. Let the priests take the blame."

"I don't want war like this," Vordachai said, stamping his feet. "I'll be called up by that pompous legion commander to supply auxiliaries."

"What of it?"

"Blast your eyes, I haven't had my chance to pluck the Imperial purse strings!"

"Spoken like a true bandit."

Vordachai drew a sharp breath, and even his protector took an involuntary step forward at that remark.

Eyes ablaze, Vordachai held up his hand to stay the man and said softly, "Under the old law, it's death to insult the warlord. You know that. You *know* that!"

Shadrael raked him with a look of contempt. "Old law or Imperial, you haven't the spine to obey either. You yell and bluster, but you're soft inside, afraid that your thick wits will lead you into a corner you can't escape. As for the Vindicants stealing your plan . . . Beloth's black heart, man, can't you see that they likely put it into your skull from the beginning?"

"It came to me in a dream," Vordachai insisted. "I told you that."

"And they have dream walkers."

Looking baffled, Vordachai sputtered a moment and then scowled. "You're lying to me, trying to confuse and trick me. But I won't let you. The priests are outlawed and toothless. Their magic is gone."

"Not quite. They want your allegiance."

"My *what*?"

"They want your army behind them."

"What talk is this?" Vordachai asked, raising his hands. "Are you now their envoy? Would you have me join those devils?"

Shadrael said nothing. Every breath he drew hurt his chest. He felt immensely tired. The fact that he was still obeying Urmaeor, like some puppet hireling, shamed him to his core.

"Drink has rotted your wits," Vordachai said. "Beloth is broken. Shadow is broken. The priests are the weakest of the factions opposed to the usurper, and you ask me to join them? You've gone mad."

Laughter rose in Shadrael, a wild, reckless howl he could not control. "Oh, well said, my lord. Well said! And what is done with mad dogs in Bezhalmbra? Let's see, the cliffs await me. What else? A piking, a beheading, and the crows to peck my eyes. Not enough to destroy a *donare*, you know. I think you had better draw and quarter me, chop my bones into pieces, and boil me in hot pitch. Then you can throw me off the cliffs, but watch out . . . watch out because I might—come—*back*!"

The consternation in Vordachai's face made Shadrael throw back his head and laugh harder, only to abruptly

choke and sink to his knees. The pain was terrifying, robbing him of breath and wit. He doubled up, groaning.

"Shadrael? Shadrael, what ails you?"

"M'lord," a man was saying urgently. "Stay back from
him. He is surely possessed."

"Be quiet, fool! Shadrael, can you hear me?"

Gasping, Shadrael could not answer. He thrust out his
trembling hand toward his brother, but touched nothing.
Fear flashed through his heart. *I am a ghost,* he thought
wildly. *I have passed into damnation, and I am lost.*

Chapter 12

He came to slowly, adrift on the eddies of semiwakeful-ness, and found himself in a bedchamber hung in pale draperies. His bed was an oasis of comfort, the blankets soft and warm. The carved cabinetry of the bed was as fa-miliar to him as the lines in his palm.

Lazily he reached out and let his fingers trace the old carvings of his childhood. Those legendary kings and he-roes of Ulinia before it was conquered and made a part of the empire . . . their representative figures were cut into the aged wood panels: Nontepi standing with his flock of goats while the sun rays of Adruu, most ancient of gods, shone over him and called him to greatness; Jendralha holding a mighty sword over the kneeling enemies he had van-quished; Seltet the Lawgiver with a scroll in one hand and a spear in the other, standing on a hillside as he rallied his warriors to battle.

Shadrael let his smile fade. His fingers slid away from the carvings. A boy's dreams . . . a boy's ambition to grow up into a mighty warrior as legendary as these heroes of his lin-eage . . . was that all that had driven him these many years?

He blinked, staring upward at the ceiling of his bed cabinet, feeling strangely lazy. It surprised him to find he was still alive, and for the moment comfortable and without pain. The usual buzz of voices and torment in the back of his skull was absent.

The relief of it was so immense he felt tears prick his eyes. O Gault, he thought, to stay here in this warm cocoon, this haven of rest.

"You're awake," a voice said.

Hastily Shadrael blinked his tears away. He turned his head to see a stranger lifting back some of the hangings to peer in at him.

It was a kindly face, with gentle eyes and smiling mouth, a face of wisdom and compassion, seamed by years and burned by the sun. Shadrael did not have to see the man's white robes or their patterned band of blue at the throat to recognize a healer.

He understood now why he felt so lazy and content, why nothing hurt. "You have *severed* me." His voice came out thick and slow.

"Yes, my lord. A deep healing *severance*, as deep as I've dared. I'm surprised to find you awake, in the circumstances. Your injuries are—"

"Thirsty," Shadrael broke in, not wanting to discuss his problems. "Very thirsty."

"So I imagine." Liquid gurgled into a cup. The healer lifted Shadrael's head to help him drink.

But Shadrael smelled the potion and turned away. "Want water."

"Later perhaps. You need nutrients now."

"No—"

"This will help you. Do not fear it."

Shadrael frowned, but something in the healer's voice reassured him. He drank, and although the liquid was unpleasantly thick it held no foul taste. When he had swallowed it all, he found his lassitude sinking deeper, drawing him down.

And as he crossed the threshold between wakefulness and slumber he heard another individual come in and stand beside the healer. Survival instincts forced Shadrael to open his eyes, but they were too heavy, his vision too blurred for him to see.

"Is he at all better?" rumbled Vordachai's voice, trying to be quiet. "Is there any hope?"

The healer's answer was only a babble of sound, like the running water of a stream. Shadrael slept.

$\mathcal{T}$he next time he awakened, his head was clear, his body rested. He sat up, thrusting the soft hangings aside, and with a soldier's honed instincts listened and observed.

He had not dreamed about being back in his old room. This was his bedchamber, the furnishings unchanged since he left to join the army. Only the clutter of his possessions was absent, his old collection of weapons and hunting gear, the ragged pile of cloth his favorite dog had used for a bed, his boots and game boards and hawking jesses and maps were all cleared away. Nothing remained except the large bed, a chair, a clothing chest, and a fine old, sun-faded carpet.

Shadrael frowned, refusing to let memories engulf him. Perhaps Vordachai had meant to be kind in lodging him here like a favored houseguest, like a member of the . . . family. The past, however, meant nothing to Shadrael now except a prickle of thorns he wished to avoid. He found clothing in the chest and put it on, feeling lost without his weapons.

His bruises from the stoning had faded. The wound he'd taken from that last fight with the Crimsons had healed to a small scar and was no longer sore. Estimating that he'd lain here for several days at least, he knew he should be hungry, but his lean, concave belly felt no pangs of emptiness. The lingering effect of *severance*, he thought. It had not entirely worn off.

He felt baffled and lost, like a ghost no longer part of this world, no longer belonging anywhere. Not dead yet, but not wholly living either.

Experimentally he rubbed his chest, wondering if the damage inside was mending or permanent. Where his reserves of magic had been, there now remained only a hollow emptiness . . . except for a tiny amount. Like the last drop of liquid in a bowl that eludes a spoon. Not even enough to reassure him.

The magic might, he told himself, serve briefly as a puny kind of weapon. He certainly had nothing else for protection, not even a sleeve knife.

A click of the door latch was his only warning when the healer entered his room. They stared at each other in surprise, Shadrael stiff and defensive, the healer astonished.

"A good way to eat a dagger," Shadrael said gruffly.

The healer's brows shot up. "What need of violence, my lord, when you are sheltered within these safe walls? I did not mean to startle you."

Shadrael gestured dismissal, but the healer approached him instead.

"You should not be up, my lord. Are you in pain?"

"No."

The man blinked, his frown deepening. "Still *severed*? And you are able to stand and converse? I—" He broke off, muttering to himself, then sent Shadrael a wary look. "*Donare!* Of course. I should have realized."

"Now you have," Shadrael said curtly. "You may go."

Instead, the healer held up a flask. "I have brought you more nutrition. There is no need to go seeking food within the kitchens today, if that's your aim."

Shadrael scowled. "I want none of your vile brew."

"Not vile, my lord. Its taste is pleasant and soothing. Surely you've swallowed far worse concoctions while participating in the rites of Alcua."

"What know you of those?"

The healer shrugged, appearing unconcerned by Shadrael's hostility. "You are not interested in my past," he said. "Will you not return to bed now, and partake of this?"

"I've slept long enough."

"Whatever you feel at the moment, you are far from well, my lord."

"Well enough to do what's necessary."

"Which is what?"

Thin lipped, Shadrael glared at him. "I don't answer to you!"

"My lord misunderstands. I do not ask from idle curiosity. Please," the healer said, making a conciliatory gesture at the chair. "At least sit down for a short time. You should not be this active so soon."

Shadrael headed for the door, only to find his path blocked by the healer. Angered, he stopped, his nostrils flaring. "How dare you hinder me? Step aside!"

"No occasion requires you to hurry, my lord. Must I remind you that you are still in a healing *severance*, and not yourself?"

"I've been in the care of a healer before. I know what it's about."

"Then you know that you should not exert yourself. Please sit down and drink some of this—"

"No," Shadrael said curtly, thrusting aside the proffered flask. "I want to talk to my brother."

"Tomorrow will do for that. In the meantime, why not rest?"

"To what purpose?" Shadrael glared at him. "What's happening to me cannot be cured."

Regret settled over the healer's weathered face. His eyes held sympathy, but he did not contradict what Shadrael had said.

"Better, in fact," Shadrael continued bitterly, "if you had used a pillow to smother me while I slept. Then it would be over."

"My purpose is to restore health, not take life," the healer replied, and smiled briefly. "Besides, despite your present discomfort, is it not better to endure withdrawal? Are you so tied to the shadow god that you cannot accept freedom?"

"What if I am?" Shadrael snapped, thinking the man a fool. "What does it matter?"

"Of course it matters! You must not give up hope, my lord. There is a period of severe shock and suffering, naturally, but with time and expert care—"

"Don't lie to me. My ability to *sever*, is it permanently damaged?"

"I cannot answer that question unless I know what caused the injury."

"Element magic struck me, just as I was about to snap someone's threads of life."

Looking shocked, the healer blinked, and had nothing to say.

Dour amusement spread through Shadrael. So much for provincial sophistication, he thought. This healer was evidently accustomed to splinting broken bones and smearing salve on kitchen burns, not coping with confessions of attempted murder gone awry.

"Normally element magic is too mild to harm me," Shadrael went on casually, as though it meant nothing to use the dark forces. "I've suffered minor injuries before, but nothing like this."

"When you attempt to *sever*, where does the pain occur?" The healer gently touched his chest. "Here?"

Shadrael flinched, and the healer drew back swiftly.

"Ah yes, I noticed that. I have mitigated the pain there all I can. Time must do the rest."

"Time," Shadrael said grimly, "is my enemy, not my friend."

"Time," the healer replied, meeting his gaze steadily, "is all someone in your condition can hope for. Even a *donare* such as yourself will end up diminished, as undoubtedly you know. I have found much scarring from your heavy reliance on shadow. Like this." As he spoke, he laced his fingers together. "All built upon a web of very old damage from a severe injury that was never tended properly. Frankly, my lord, I'm surprised you lived through it, given the botched mess done to you."

Shadrael scowled. He was not going to discuss what he'd gone through to survive losing his soul.

"You see," the healer continued, "no matter what you've been told, the potions of Alcua cannot go on mitigating a progressive course of repeated damage and injury forever. Every deferment means less true healing, until it becomes too much for your body to handle. How long have you been *severing* to endure withdrawal shock?"

Shadrael's opinion of this man began to change. He found himself answering honestly. "Since the Terrors."

"Three years . . . nearly four," the healer said thoughtfully. "Very few could last that long. Your, um, strength has been your undoing."

"You mean—"

"The effects of transition can only be worse than usual."

Shadrael barked a short laugh. "Honesty over reassurance. Is that your dogma?"

"Lies will not help you, my lord."

"Then answer what I've asked you. Will I be able to *sever* again?"

"If you rest and allow yourself a chance to heal properly, perhaps. You will never regain the full ability you had before."

"How soon?"

"You must learn to govern yourself, as you are perhaps not used to. That means getting sufficient rest and not forcing yourself to unnatural extremes of exhaustion." The healer paused. "The way you are doing now."

"When can I *sever*?"

"Weeks, perhaps not even then." The healer gave him a very serious look. "If you ignore my advice and *sever* too soon, the damage could be permanent, or even fatal."

Shadrael shrugged. "I'm dying anyway—"

"Everyone thinks so in the first and second stages of shadow withdrawal. It's a common reaction, but not always a correct one."

"I've seen men die by the hundreds. I've seen *donares* go rogue," Shadrael said angrily.

"Cared for by Vindicants?" The healer sniffed, his expression eloquent. "Had you sought a properly trained healer from the beginning, you could have avoided much of this suffering now."

"Are *you* a properly trained healer?"

The man said with quiet dignity, "I trained in Trau, and I am descended from *nameids* on my mother's side. I may have not been to the Imperial Court, my lord, but yes, I know what I'm doing."

Oh yes, Shadrael thought resentfully, he knew what he was doing. A true member of his profession, the healer obviously believed he possessed all the answers. A patient was expected to shut up, swallow what was given, and be blindly obedient so that everything would come right. Typical of all healers, Shadrael thought, to examine a new patient, criticize what had been done by a predecessor, and offer a new, far more wondrous line of treatment. Vindicant or otherwise, urban or provincial, they were all the same.

Shadrael had no intention of being gullible enough to swallow any reassurance this healer offered. Without a soul, he knew there was nothing that could be done for him, absolutely nothing. To his mind, this conversation was a meaningless waste of time. Except that now he knew he possessed the means to *sever* his own threads of life.

Thanks to the healer's efforts, he was strong enough to at least do that. He knew, from the kind of care he'd been given and from being installed in his old bedchamber inside the palace, that already Vordachai had decided not to execute him as threatened. But then, his brother could never be relied on.

"The more rest you get now, the longer the healing *severance* I've given you will last," the healer said, breaking the silence. "I don't need to tell you why that's to your advantage."

"You mean," Shadrael said harshly, wanting to be rid of him, "as long as I lie here trapped in this room and drinking your potions, I can pretend I'm not going mad."

"That is not quite how I would put it, my lord. The effects of shadow dependency vary and are difficult to gauge, much less treat. However, I heal hurts of the body, not the spirit. Madness and afflictions of the mind are not my specialty."

"So unless I begin to rave and drool spittle, you won't know whether I'm crazed or not?"

The healer permitted himself a slight smile. "You joke, my lord, but lunacy is to be pitied, not ridiculed."

Anger flowed hot through Shadrael, momentarily thawing the effect of *severance.* At once he felt the strength leaking from his body. Instead of striking the healer, his hand shot out desperately to brace himself against the wall. His breath came unsteady and fast.

The healer took his arm. "Let me help you back to bed, where you belong."

Shadrael shook him off, although the effort nearly made him dizzy. "Get away from me! Do you think I want your kind of healing, where I am left a cripple, locked in my brother's turret to spend my days beating my skull against the walls? Get out!"

Although shorter and older than Shadrael, the healer was sturdy enough to hold him fast in an expert grip. "Were you truly out of your mind, my lord, raving and hurling about wild, destructive spells of magic, you would now be restrained in the strongest possible bonds of *kwaibe*, with Reformant priests and holy men standing watch over you.

Instead, you are a free agent, are you not? However ill advised it might be, you are at liberty to go where you please."

Shadrael stared at him in consternation, his temper collapsing. The healer touched his forehead, and *severance* flowed back into place, steadying him. Even so, he felt very tired now.

"It's you who have cut off the voices, the hallucinations," Shadrael said, his voice dull. "Thank you, but they will come back."

"Then I am sorry for you, but if necessary that can be treated. Humanely. And kindly. You will be made comfortable. There is nothing, my lord, noble about suffering."

A cold chill sank through Shadrael. "You mean, take my mind away. Take away memory. Take away everything."

"If necessary. But I think we should focus on a more hopeful outcome."

From outside came the low wail of a *mesderah* horn, followed by glad shouts of merriment and laughter and the jingling of Mrishadal bells.

"Happy sounds, aren't they?" the healer said. "People are going to the feast. Tomorrow is the last day of celebration."

Still horrified by what he'd said, Shadrael refused to be distracted by thoughts of revelry. He took a step back, pulling free of the healer's touch. "You are an evil man," he said softly. "An evil, cold man to offer me *that*. Can you believe it will comfort me? I would rather go out of here to my death than sit about, drinking your filthy potions and believing your lies, until my reason is taken from me."

"You insist on dwelling on the worst possible outcomes," the healer replied calmly. "That, too, is an effect of withdrawal. You need to rest, and let your family come in here to visit you. Surround yourself with what is positive and good, rather than morbid thoughts of madness and death."

"I *am* death," Shadrael replied harshly. "I have brought it to others many times. I am darkness. I wear it as my mantle, and I will not don another."

The healer flinched, as Shadrael had meant for him to, but he did not back down. "I have not lied to you," the man said. "Can you not deal truthfully with me in return? Do you think I do not understand the hopelessness in your questions? You intend to gather yourself for one last try at *severing* your own threads of life."

Shadrael started to speak, but the healer held up his hand. "Don't deny it. You babbled enough in your feverish moments for me to understand your fears."

"That's not—"

"Your circumstances are terrible," the healer went on, his mild voice containing no sympathy now. "But what of it? We all bear our burdens. You have been a coward long enough."

Shadrael curled his fists. "I'm no coward!"

"Aren't you? Pitying yourself. Clinging to shadow customs and charlatan cures, harming yourself repeatedly by misuse of *severance* instead of finding a decent healer to help you through transition. When you hide behind such lies and shams, then you are a coward."

"If you were not protected by your calling, I would see you dead," Shadrael said hoarsely.

"If you wish to destroy yourself from some sense of guilt, admit it as such, but do not claim despair as your excuse."

They glared at each other, but it was Shadrael who was the first to look away.

"This conflict is not good for you," the healer said. "Truth can be hard to swallow, even painful to receive. But I have given you my professional opinion. I hope you will think hard and long about what I've said."

"Be damned."

"No, my lord," the man said firmly. "If you do not change soon, if you do not make the effort to save yourself, however difficult, then it is you who are damned."

"Why should that matter to you?"

"Because I have served the lords of Natalloh all my life.

Strive to make your peace with Gault, my lord. Accept harmony. Otherwise . . ."

Shadrael's mouth tightened. He did not want to discuss his damnation with this man, with anyone. He turned in silence, pushing the healer aside, and strode out.

Chapter 13

In her tiny cell, Lea sat hunched and shivering against the stone wall, gazing upward at the narrow ribbon of sky that was her only view. She had been lowered into this hole at dawn, and thus far she had no inkling of what was to befall her. Whether it was a dry well or a shaft that had once led into a now-collapsed mine, she could not tell. All she knew was that her only way out was if someone lowered a rope to her.

It was bitterly cold, and her tattered cloak was not enough protection. She was thirsty and hungry, but no food—not even a cup of water—had been given to her. At some point she'd dared call the earth spirits, hoping to escape into *between* with their guidance, but none had obeyed her summons.

She did not blame them. The place crawled with a filthy type of magic, something foul and raw, too primitive to call shadow. It was oppressive, wearing on her nerves, taking advantage of her fatigue and hunger to gnaw at her emotional defenses.

Without warning something fell on her, bounced, and hit

the ground with a soft thud. She picked up a piece of fruit, now squished on one side, and sniffed it cautiously. Something else dropped on her, pieces of flat bread, stale and dry. She gripped the food gratefully, peering up in hopes of getting water.

"Please," she called. "I am so very thirsty."

A face looked down at her from the top of the shaft, blurred and gone before she could tell much about it. Moments later, a water skin was lowered to her by a thin piece of rope. She untied it, and at once the rope was jerked out.

"Thank you!" Lea called.

No answer came, but she hardly cared. Crouching on the ground, she brushed dirt off the bread and fruit and ate rapidly, drinking deep of the tepid water until it occurred to her that she might not be given more through the day.

She was right. No one came back. No one spoke to her. No one brought more food and drink. It grew dark and colder than ever. She sipped her dwindling ration of water, reminding herself that she'd gone hungry before and survived. Huddling beneath her cloak, unable to stretch out flat, she curled herself in a shivering ball and tried to sleep.

In the morning, she was sitting quietly, fighting the distraction of ravenous hunger and tracing triangles on the ground to keep up her hopes, when a stout rope came snaking down and fell across her shoulder.

Startled, she scrambled to her feet and looked up. Three faces were staring down at her, silhouetted against sunlight. "Hurry," one said to her.

Lea wasted no time in making a clumsy knot in the thick rope and clung to it, her heart thumping hard as she was hauled out.

Bruised and breathless, she got to her feet and looked around. She was standing in a small clearing of sorts surrounded on all sides by towering stones and heaped boulders of a porous black rock unfamiliar to her. On all sides there were what seemed to be caves or overhangs of rock. Men—how many she could not count—concealed themselves well away from the thin sunlight shining through a scrim of cloud. Silent, motionless, like quiescent toads lying flat and concealed among the grass in a garden, they watched her with palpable hostility.

In all her life, she had never encountered such overwhelming, intense hatred. She steeled herself, aware that *sevaisin* with Shadrael had made her stronger and more knowledgeable of evil. She feared it no less, but it no longer possessed the power to completely disconcert her.

She heard no sound, save for the sighing whisper of wind through the rocks. The men said nothing to her. Their stares, coming at her from all directions, were no worse than the leers of the mercenaries.

Slowly Lea turned about. When no one came forward or spoke to her, she gathered her dirt-streaked skirts and headed for a pathway that seemed to lead out of this circle of stone.

Hissing came at her from all sides, but she did not falter or glance back. She climbed atop a stone, teetered there in her scuffed red boots, and stepped onto the pathway.

A man in the saffron-hued robes of a Vindicant appeared as though from thin air, blocking her way. He was tall, and seemed thin despite the bulk of his robes. A hood shaded his face too much for her to see it clearly.

"Lady Lea," he said, and she recognized his deep, smug voice from the night Shadrael had abandoned her. Shadrael had called him Urmaeor. "Welcome to our temple."

As he spoke, he gestured with patrici grace at the barren place of stone and dust. A glimpse of his hand showed her pale flesh mottled an angry red, as though he'd been burned, but he shook his wide sleeve over it and partially turned on the path.

"You will follow me."

Lea thought about protesting and being difficult, but it seemed better to bide her time and wait for a true opportunity of escape. Antagonizing these former priests without a plan seemed as sensible as poking a nest of hornets for amusement.

"Sensible," he said in approval.

Startled, she blinked at him and thought she saw him smile beneath his hood. She could not stop herself from drawing a sharp breath. *Be careful. Be careful,* she warned herself.

"Do as you're told and you have nothing to fear," Urmaeor said. "Come."

He led her through strange formations of rock to a widemouthed cave partway up the hillside. She hesitated there, not wanting to enter such dank darkness.

"Come," he said impatiently.

"Where are you taking me?"

"To meet my master."

For a frightened instant she thought he was referring to Beloth, but then a measure of sense returned to her and she knew that could not be true.

"I thought you ruled here," she said. "Who is your master?"

"Flattery, like your questions, is futile. I see I must teach you another lesson."

"No—"

Magic flicked out from his fingertips, raking her with pain that stung and left her feeling numb. Doubling over, she gasped for breath and found herself trembling. Not so bad, she reassured herself although her heart was racing and skipping much too fast. Afraid that he would do much worse, however, she hurried into the cave, only to stop again, shivering.

"Better," he said, "but not quite good enough."

"Please!" she said involuntarily, gazing up at him with beseeching eyes.

He chuckled, the sound like a spider skittering across the back of her hand. "Lord Barthel has not been well of late, but I think you will amuse him, sister to Light Bringer."

Lea raised her chin. "What ransom do you intend to ask for me? My brother will not—"

"Don't negotiate!" Urmaeor said, his voice cracking

like a whip. "You have nothing to bargain with, Lady Lea. Nothing!"

The force of his voice made the unlit torches along the walls burst into flame. Lea knew the priests were full of theatrical tricks, but she could not stop herself from jumping.

Even so, this time Urmaeor was not amused. He leaned toward her. "Too vital," he murmured, pushing back his hood so that his dark, cold eyes glimmered in the gloom. "Too vivid. Too alive. Too much for Lord Barthel in his condition. Let me diminish you a little."

Fearing he would mesmerize her, Lea looked away from his eyes. *I am of the light,* she thought. *I am joined to harmony and I walk in unity with it.*

"Not anymore," Urmaeor said, reaching out toward her. She flinched, but his spell was already descending upon her, as though a dark veil smothered her hair and face. "You belong to shadow now, Lady Lea. You are ours, and ours you will stay."

The hanging gardens of Bezhalmbra, even at the start of winter, held a beauty Shadrael had never seen equaled in all his travels. Shivering outdoors with no cloak to shield him from the biting wind, he stood gazing at paradise through the ornate metal gate. Magic had created the gardens long ago, carving terraces for them in the stony side of the mountain, and magic preserved them still. He did not believe the spell would permit him entry, but longing to see his mother's beloved refuge one last time, he dared set his hand on the gate.

It swung open at his touch, inviting him in.

He hesitated, wary and unsure, then drew a deep breath and walked inside.

The barrier of magic raked across him, but it was no more painful than being snagged by a rose's thorns. Past the gate, the air blew warm and fragrant against his cheeks, for he had left autumn behind at the gate. It was a relief that allowed him to straighten his hunched shoulders. He stood sheltered and untouched as a frosty gust of air swirled dead leaves along the paving stones on the other side of the gate. Then he turned and surveyed the loveliness before him.

Spring forever blessed these gardens. Year-round, storms never flattened them; lightning never split the trees or struck the fountain; frosts never killed the flowers. The beauty was a marvel to all who saw it, legendary in this desert province.

As a boy, Shadrael had pelted the sentries with ice balls and thrown himself into deep snowdrifts beside the stables until he was shaking with cold. Then he would run into the gardens to thaw out, shedding his cloak and fur-lined gloves as he went. Sometimes—when no servant was watching to disapprove—he would paddle and float in the warm waters of the fountain, laughing at the snowflakes that swirled in the air above the garden without ever falling on it.

High on Jawnuth, shaded by the summit from the harsh afternoon suns and wind, sheltered by stone walls, and watered by the gentle, misting rains that never reached the lower desert elevations, the garden paths meandered between lush plantings of slender sentinel cypress and red-blooming oletha bushes that should not have been able to grow this far above the tree line. The magnificent vines, their shaggy trunks as thick as his waist, sprawled over the terraces to hang, vibrant with cerise, white, and lavender racemes, over both garden and palace walls, even growing down the cliffs. Roses, fragrant with heavy blooms, brushed Shadrael's shoulders with perfumed pink petals that showered the path in his wake. His boots crunched faintly on the raked gravel, now and then crushing creeping herbs that sent up a delightful spicy aroma to his nostrils.

The fabled gardens of Bezhalmbra, rumored to have been formed by Ancient Ones breathing magic over this mountain to create an oasis like no other. Gardens traditionally tended by *nameids* whispering magic into the plants to make them thrive. In this high place of stone and sky where even

weeds clinging to cliff and precipice beyond the walls had
to struggle against a scourging wind, the juxtaposition of
such astonishing beauty below ramparts bristling with defenses was beyond imagining.

Shadrael halted amidst intoxicating splendor and let
himself drink it in. For years he would not let himself even
think of Bezhalmbra, for it was not his, would never be his.
He could not have borne the early days of army life and
training, its brutality and the cruel shocks, if he'd allowed
himself to be homesick. He could not have made the army
his home, his family, if he had not renounced Bezhalmbra
and its very memory.

But, gods, here he stood, where he'd never thought to
return. And no matter what he suffered for all eternity, at
least the final moments of his life would be spent in this
small paradise.

It gave him no comfort.

Lea, he thought involuntarily, would have loved it here.
It might have been created for her. He indulged himself a
moment, imagining her skipping with delight along these
paths, running from flower to flower to inhale the perfumes.
A smile touched his lips briefly before it faded. For Lea,
thanks to his betrayal, would never see any garden again.

Veiled in shadow, feeling sick to her stomach, Lea was
led through dark passageways deep into the ground.
Torches hanging in iron sconces burned along the tunnels,
casting ruddy, uneven light difficult to see by under the best
conditions. Whenever she stumbled or faltered, Urmaeor
spoke a word that hurt her.

Eventually the passageway opened into an underground
chamber fitted with assorted chairs with high backs, fine
cushions now as soiled and tattered as her gown, a table of
fine inlaid-wood marquetry that was scratched and dented,
and a stack of battered traveling chests spilling pieces of
tapestry and silk hangings as though no one had packed

them properly. Torchlight flickered and smoked, making the air hot and unpleasant. Symbols of Beloth had been painted on one wall. It hurt Lea's eyes to even look at them. She could smell blood, old and rotted, and saw a dark stain upon a crudely fashioned altar stone. The altar held dented bronze bowls and a chalice purloined of its jewels. The empty settings looked like wounds in the scratched and dented metal. Even so, dark steam curled from inside it, as though fire burned and smoked within the cup.

Fearing they meant to pour some perversion down her throat by force, Lea found her mouth too dry to swallow. Swiftly she averted her gaze, trying not to think, trying not to let fear overwhelm her.

Sounds whispered through some of the passageways, echoing so that it was impossible to tell their direction. She heard voices and snatches of chanting as soft and furtive as sin.

Urmaeor pointed. "Wait there. Do not speak or move, by my command."

Coerced by the spell he'd laid on her, she could do little save obey him. Through the dark scrim of his magic, she found her vision blurred, the torchlight dim, and her hearing muffled. *Do not fight it,* she told herself. *Perhaps it is a mercy.*

But in her heart she did not believe that Urmaeor understood the concept of mercy.

A pair of men in brown robes emerged through a low doorway cut into one wall of the chamber. They stared at Lea suspiciously, muttering questions to Urmaeor too softly for her to hear. He replied, his voice deep and assured.

Glowering, they reluctantly stood aside, and Urmaeor turned to her.

"Lord Barthel will receive you, Lady Lea." His voice abruptly hardened. "Go inside."

Her ears roared and she could hardly catch her breath, yet she was moving obediently, compelled to do what he said. The interior of the next chamber was dim and murky.

It contained a cushioned platform. Reclining on it was a
grotesquely fat figure draped in the ornate stole of a chief
priest. Lea had never seen a man so obese. His body over-
flowed the platform, huge rolls of flesh quivering beneath
capacious robes of fine silk. In the quiet, she could hear
him wheezing for breath. His eyes, small and almost lost in
folds of skin, glittered at her. They were as yellow as the
eyes of a snake, rheumy and rimmed with red, with puffy
flesh sagging beneath them.

He studied her with those inhuman, yellow eyes, his
breath wheezing and laboring. One of his hands, almost as
small and dainty as hers, waved in excitement. "Closer!"
he commanded. "Closer!"

"Be careful, Master," Urmaeor cautioned. "She has not
yet been fully conditioned."

"Closer!" Lord Barthel hissed.

Urmaeor pointed. "Go to him."

Lea tried to resist, but the spell pushed her forward. She
stopped within touching distance and despite her impaired
vision she could see that the silk robes were grimy. A peculiar stench—doughy and repugnantly sweet—wafted out
from Lord Barthel's person. Lea tried not to inhale it.

A heavy weight pressed down on her shoulders. Determined not to bow, Lea struggled until she felt perspiration
bead along her hairline. Yet despite her efforts she was
pushed to her knees. She felt raw humiliation at having to
honor this vile creature.

"Stop!" Lord Barthel commanded.

The pressure crushing her abruptly vanished. Lea
gulped in a breath of relief, her muscles trembling with exhaustion.

"You are governing her too much," Lord Barthel said,
his voice reedy and high-pitched. It was an ill-tempered
voice, cross and impatient. "And why do you keep her en-
spelled? I cannot see her properly. Is she pretty? I was told
she was pretty."

"Lady Lea is dangerous," Urmaeor replied, coming up beside her. "I have muted her for your protection."

"Bah! I am ill, but far from a weakling. Do you think I am afraid of a maiden like this?"

Urmaeor bowed again in silence.

"Girl! Look at me!" Lord Barthel commanded.

Lea turned her gaze in his direction, and felt another wave of revulsion shudder through her.

"Unveil her," Lord Barthel said. "Quickly. Quickly!"

"Master—"

The chief priest snarled something, and little sparks of fire blazed around Urmaeor before fading with a stink of decay and ashes. Urmaeor gestured at Lea, and the dark gauzy feeling of being half-smothered fell away from her.

The room remained poorly lit, but it was not as murky as she'd first thought. Her hearing came back in full. She smelled damp and sickness and the filth of rats. The *jai-ethqual* here was nothing but depravity and fear permeating the very stones.

Lea turned her gaze on the chief priest. "Why do you not seek treatment for your shadow sickness? Aren't you aware that chewing est-weed induces dreamy lassitude only for a short while before its effects cease to work? You would do better sending for a healer who understands the proper nature of medicinal herbs."

A terrible, spasmatic wheezing alarmed her before she realized that Lord Barthel was laughing. His delicate, fine-boned fingers wriggled in delight. "And are you a trained healer, Lady Lea?" he asked.

"My father was," she replied, forcing herself to meet those yellow eyes. One had started watering copiously, seeping pus at the corner. She tried to ignore it. "Of course, perhaps you are burning est-weed more than you chew it, but the effect—"

"Silence!" Lord Barthel commanded.

Lea cut off her sentence.

Lord Barthel stared at her avidly, his mouth hanging open a little while he struggled to breathe. His fingers wriggled and fluttered. For a moment it seemed he would reach out and actually take her hand in his. Instinctively she shrank back.

"Don't rise, Lady Lea," Urmaeor said. He held no spell over her now, but the authority in his voice kept her still: "Give him your hand."

Lea could not do it. Wheezing, Lord Barthel shifted his massive body enough to lean forward, reaching out. His skin was flaking from a half-healed rash. A shudder rippled through Lea. *If he touches me,* she thought, *I shall . . . I shall . . .*

His fingers nearly brushed the back of her hand, but at the last moment he flinched, abruptly drawing back.

Lea saw that he was shaking, his fat rippling under the tawdry silk robes. His face drained of color to an even more pronounced pallor.

Relief flashed through her. *He dares not touch me,* she thought gratefully.

"Too vital. Too vivid," he murmured, much as Urmaeor had done earlier. His gaze flashed up, caught her staring at his trembling hands, and narrowed. "An excellent candidate, Urmaeor," he said in a stronger voice. "I must have this. I must!"

"Then shall I begin the task of conditioning her, Master?" Urmaeor asked.

"Yes, yes, yes!" Lord Barthel licked his dry, crusty lips. "Make her ready. Hurry!"

Urmaeor uttered a sharp word, and pain lanced through her. Lea cried out, dropping to her knees. He spoke again, and it was as though a thousand red-hot needles pierced her flesh. She writhed on the ground, struggling to breathe, her heart nearly bursting.

Then the agony was gone, leaving her limp and spent on the cold ground. She drew in shaky breaths, grateful the attack was over, and dared not think what might be coming next.

Urmaeor crouched beside her, his robes rustling faintly like a serpent's scales sliding over dead leaves. Fearing that he meant to punish her further, Lea tried to shift away, but he pinned her with his hand and bent down, his face next to hers. Swiftly he inhaled one of her breaths, holding it in his mouth before blowing it into what looked like a chunk of crystal that clouded swiftly. Then he bent, and stole another of her breaths, blowing it into a second piece of crystal that clouded as rapidly as the first.

Only then did he release her and back away.

Uneasily, Lea pulled herself to a sitting position. She felt light-headed and tired, as though he'd taken more from her than her breath.

"Get up," Urmaeor said. His voice was as hard as stone.

While she struggled up, swaying on her feet, he handed the crystals to Lord Barthel's attendant. The chief priest was whimpering eagerly, stretching out his hands to clutch the crystals.

Lea was glad to leave. As she followed Urmaeor from the oppressive room, she said, "I cannot help that man. And if you have convinced him otherwise, you do him no service."

Urmaeor's thin face smiled in satisfaction. "Are you so without mercy, Lady Lea, that you cannot spare your breath to an ill man?"

"That's not what you're doing. You're feeding him part of me."

"Better your breath than your blood," Urmaeor said calmly, and pointed at the passageway. "Go."

She realized that the moans coming from Lord Barthel's chamber had stopped. "That's what he wants, isn't it? My life? My essence? To keep himself alive, like some kind of—of—"

"You have more than enough vitality to spare," Urmaeor

replied. "Now, do you want another lesson? Or will you leave my master in peace?"

Too horrified to stay there longer and face the sick truth, Lea fled.

Chapter 14

$\mathcal{T}$he *mesderah* horn blew from one of the fortress towers higher up the mountain, its low wail signaling the end of prayers. Still wandering the garden paths, Shadrael heard a sudden babble of voices and laughter as people spilled from the chapel just over the south garden wall.

He concealed himself in the shrubbery just in time to avoid a pair of women hurrying along the path. Dressed in finery, one was his sister Nachel, holding the hand of a skipping child. She swept the little fellow along so fast his small feet barely touched the ground. But when the child dropped his toy, so bright and new it had to be a Mrishadal gift, he wrenched free with a wail and came running back for it. He saw Shadrael standing silent and motionless in the bushes, and froze, his young eyes wide and unsure.

Shadrael lifted his finger to his lips and smiled. The boy smiled back, then ducked his head shyly and ran to catch up with the women who were now calling to him.

Probably he would tell them he'd seen a stranger, Shadrael thought. But perhaps Nachel and her companion would be too preoccupied to listen.

Impatiently he waited in hiding until he heard music strike up in the larger courtyard. Lutes, he thought, accompanied by the sprightly tootling of panpipperies that heralded the coming of Oued'Fiet and his sack of treasure. Family, guests, and servants alike would be gathering to greet the legendary figure of *nameid* folklore. Oued'Fiet would enter through the massive gates, leading a tame sacred deer with tiny burning candles tied to its antlers. He would carry his leather sack from child to child, pronouncing a blessing on each one before pulling out a gift, typically a piece of colored sugar to suck on or perhaps a tiny deer carved of wood. All sentimental nonsense, Shadrael thought.

Emerging from the shrubbery, he brushed small leaves from his shoulders and strode on past the splashing fountain. He'd dawdled long enough. His body was tiring, and his heart was sore. It was time to end this.

Even so, his mind filled with the old stories often told about his mother, of how—proud and unwilling—she had been brought to Bezhalmbra to marry his warlord father in an arranged match. She would speak to no one at first, would not eat, would not drink, would not even look at his father who'd tried daily to woo her.

But when she saw the gardens, it was said that her fierce heart softened. She had smiled for the first time since setting foot in Bezhalmbra, and allowed her new husband to lead her along the fragrant paths, showing her its many wonders. From that day forward, the marriage prospered. And she had borne her husband three children, two sons and a daughter. She had taken Ulinia into her heart, and she had made it her home.

For years she sewed Shadrael's undertunics of fine linen, and sent them to him by courier. She died the year Shadrael was given his triumph in Imperia by Emperor Kostimon. He did not think his mother had ever known that he lost his soul playing *shul-drakshera* as a young, foolish new officer. Her letters to him had held pride in his accomplishments, victories, and promotions.

And this is the price I now must pay for that glory,
Shadrael thought bleakly. *The reckoning comes to us all.*

Ahead, he saw the end of the path, where a bench stood
nestled against the stone wall. He climbed atop the bench
and stood with his hands pressed to the gritty, sun-warmed
stone. Short of breath, weary from his exertions, he gazed
over the wall at the sheer, plunging infinity of the abyss below him.

There was, he thought grimly, no need to cut his own
threads of life when all he had to do was drop.

The healer's accusation roared in his mind, but Shadrael
forced it away. With a soul, with a chance, Shadrael might
have listened to him. As it was, he had nothing. The Vindicants had stoned his last hope.

Mesmerized, he stared down into the endless chasm. He
could hear nothing but the singing of wind across the
mountain slopes and the thunder of his heartbeat.

Then there came the harsh cry of an eagle.

Involuntarily he lifted his gaze and saw the majestic
birds circling on the wind currents. As a child he'd tagged
along behind Vordachai, climbing to the cliffs where the
large birds nested. They'd crouched behind rocks, watching
until the adults flew away before venturing to peer inside
the nests at fierce young chicks hissing and flapping their
useless, stubby wings. Twice he and his brother had caught
chicks and brought them home, attempting to train them for
hunting, but unlike hawks these mountain eagles would not
be tamed. Refusing to eat, they had pined and died, and after that Shadrael would not go back to the nests with his
brother to capture more.

Now he stared out toward the horizon with tears stinging his eyes and a sense of longing for something he could
not name.

Before him rose the mysterious, cloud-wreathed Dahara
Peak, and to his right the less formidable slopes of Ismah
Mountain gilded by fading sunlight. Somewhere between
them, among the canyons and ridges and secret caves, lay

the Valley of Fires, and somewhere hidden in that strange valley of frozen black rock was Lea.

Since the night he turned her over to the Vindicants, Shadrael had refused to let himself feel the crawling shame of what he'd done. He felt it now. He missed her so acutely it was like losing his soul all over again. An essential part of him had been cut away. Strange that he had been foolish enough, arrogant enough to believe she would not affect him. Without him realizing it, those weeks of daily proximity had worn down his defenses and won his heart. Even now he had only to close his eyes to see her gentle face, the trusting blue of her eyes. He could hear her voice, musical and sweet, asking him intelligent questions or speaking some courtesy to one of the brutes under his command. How gracefully she moved, even when performing the most mundane task. And her spirit, irrepressible despite everything he'd done and said to her, was as fine and perfect as a cut diamond. All the mud and filth smeared upon it could never cloud it or mar its value. Although Beloth knew he'd tried.

Lea had become a part of him, when he'd believed no one could ever matter. She'd maddened him with her goodness and infuriated him with her attempts to reform him.

Now, when he stood at the edge of what a man could endure, there was no need to close out thoughts of her, no need to avoid admitting what he'd done. His feelings opened a floodgate. He was bitterly ashamed of what he'd done to her.

Perhaps the healer was right and it was time to face the truth. At Ismah Pass, when she'd pleaded with him for mercy, he'd thought only of saving himself, of reaching out to the lie promised him by the Vindicants. He'd betrayed her out of cowardice and selfishness. There was nothing noble, nothing excusable about what he'd done.

In remorse, he drew the lock of her hair from his pocket and dropped it into the chasm below, watching the golden threads spinning out of sight.

Lea! he called silently with all his might, knowing it was too late. Hooking his elbows over the wall, he pulled himself on top of it. *Lea,* he called again, *forgive me!*

Awakening abruptly from a disturbing dream, Lea pulled her blankets tighter and lay shivering on her thin mattress. She coughed, frowning as she tried to catch her breath, and struggled to sit up so she could get more air. It was afternoon. The sun's rays almost touched the bars of her window where she now lived among the ruins of some building half-fallen in. The Vindicants had made her a shelter apart from their caves, well away from them, although she was never left unguarded.

Her dream had been of Shadrael. He'd been calling to her, trying to tell her something, but she did not know what it was.

Sighing, Lea rubbed tears from her cheeks. She seldom cried these days, for there were creatures here that fed on sorrow and misery. She had learned to bury her emotions where they could not be stolen, to feel as little as possible in order to bear her broken heart.

Most of the time she simply felt numb, as though the things said and done to her happened to someone else. She tried hard to daily recite the mantras she'd been taught by the Choven, to keep her *quai* strong. The priests had not been kind to her, but neither had they mistreated her in any serious way. They seemed a little afraid of her. The burns on Urmaeor's hands, she'd learned, had come from his touching her. Now no one wanted to approach her too closely. They guided her with harsh words and magic, pointing and glaring whenever she had to leave her quarters.

A sound of bars being lifted from across her door alerted her. She straightened her shabby clothing swiftly and pushed back her hair before sitting straight and outwardly composed with her pale hands folded in her lap. Inside, her heart was racing. A sick, wild feeling of despair threatened to choke her.

Not again, she thought.

The door swung open, and Urmaeor stood there, his eyes alight with anticipation, a faint smile stretching his lips. She could not suppress a swift shiver at the sight of him. How he enjoyed stealing her breaths. The very act excited him and obviously gave him a sort of sick pleasure. No doubt, had contact with her skin not burned his, he would have been forcing her to actually kiss him. The idea of it nauseated her.

"Lady Lea," he said in greeting, sounding almost cheerful. "I am pleased to inform you that my master's health has improved, thanks to you."

Lea looked away. A scathing comment rose to her lips, but she no longer spoke without permission.

"I know," Urmaeor said, his deep voice as smooth as oil, "that you share our delight."

"Yes," she said tonelessly.

"Then you will be eager to take the next step."

Alarmed, she glanced at him and caught him staring at her the way a cat might a mouse, intent . . . predatory. Her mouth went dry.

Although she tried to suppress her emotions, Urmaeor's smile widened. "Ah, there it is," he whispered. "That tiny trickle of fear escaping your attempts to conceal it." He closed his eyes and inhaled sharply. "Delicious!"

Lea felt her emotions churning beneath her attempts to control them. She'd never been very adept at concealment and guile. Instead, she began to mentally go through a mantra of harmony.

"On your feet!" Urmaeor said sharply, distracting her. "Come at once. My master wants you."

Her alarm intensified. Gathering her cloak about her thin shoulders, Lea obediently left her cell. She had lost weight. Her clothes were becoming too large for her. As she walked in the direction Urmaeor pointed, she shivered despite her cloak's protection. Every passing day seemed to grow colder. She sniffed the air surreptitiously, finding it dry with no scent of snow. *If the weather holds fair, Caelan will come,* she assured herself.

The Vindicant settlement bustled with an air of new purpose today. The priests, well wrapped to shield their skin and eyes from daylight, much like lepers, seemed busy with myriad tasks. Instead of chanting, she heard conversations and the sound of hammering in the distance. A soldier, clad in mismatched armor and wearing his hair tied back to expose his blasphemous tattoos, swaggered into sight, leading a horse laden with supplies. Another soldier joined him. Lea heard them laugh, and one punched the other's shoulder as they talked.

"The first of our army," Urmaeor said, walking beside her. "Are you impressed?"

Lea shot him a swift glance. "A few mercenaries will cause my brother little trouble. He is served by the best."

"The *best* have been discharged. The Imperial Army is left with nothing but weaklings and light worshippers," Urmaeor said coldly. "No one fights as fiercely as a man who's been wronged."

Meeting his gaze, Lea could not help but think of Shadrael and his bitterness. Injustice had been done to him, and it had festered within him until he was raw with hate and anger, unable to change or move forward into a new life. She pitied him, for he had elected to believe lies instead of truth, but she refused to let herself wonder where he was now. He'd made his choice, and she must live with it.

And then she was inside the warren of caves and torch-lit passages that led to Lord Barthel's chamber. After the sharp, clean air outdoors, she found the room fetid with stale, lifeless air and the stink of sickness. The chief priest reclined on his platform, a helpless, disgusting mountain of flesh barely able to move without assistance. To Lea's eye, he looked more pallid than ever. Small wonder, she thought, lying down here in the darkness day after day.

Three priests in the brown robes of service were with Lord Barthel. One was swabbing his face with a cloth and smoothing his robes while the others busily cleaned the chamber. One of them was complaining about some matter in a voice that rose and fell in short, staccato bursts of unhappiness. "The ceremonial strella is going bad almost before I take it off the fire," he was saying. "The bitter herbs rot as soon as they are stirred into the blood potions. It's all because of *her*—"

Urmaeor cleared his throat, and the complaints broke off abruptly. The trio came scuttling out. The two carrying buckets would not look at Lea, but the one who had been attending Lord Barthel's person glared at her, his face dark with dissatisfaction. He muttered something as he brushed past her and vanished into a dark passageway.

"Have you brought her?" Lord Barthel's shrill voice called out. Lea heard him wheezing and wallowing about on his cushions. "I cannot see her. Where is she? Urmaeor, have you made her ready? Completely ready?"

Afraid, Lea tried to turn back, but Urmaeor stopped her with a gesture. His cold eyes bored into hers. "Be quiet and do exactly as you are told," he said in a low voice. "I'll see you get more food tonight if you cooperate."

Lea's heart was thudding wildly. She fought the need to cough. "Am I to be bought so cheaply?"

He frowned, his expression suddenly ugly. "You—"

"Urmaeor!" Lord Barthel called querulously. "You promised she was ready."

"And so she is," Urmaeor replied, glaring at Lea. He leaned down to her ear and murmured, "You will not resist him. He is barely well enough for this, and you must help him."

"I—"

"Hear me!" Urmaeor's fingers dug into her arm. "Do

what you're told, and do it willingly. Any tricks from you—any difficulties—and I promise to leave you blind and dumb for the rest of your pitiable life." He paused, his face set and cold. "And that is only the beginning."

"Shadrael!" exclaimed a voice behind him. "Is there no blasphemy you will not commit?"

Startled from his thoughts, Shadrael spun around and found himself facing his brother.

Lord Vordachai, thickset and square in a scarlet tunic slashed with blue, his gold chain straining across his massive chest, stood in the doorway of the council hall, his bearded face as red as his garb.

"So this," he said, stepping over the threshold as the guards closed the thick door behind him, "is how you repay my kindness. This is how you find yet another way to insult me." Vordachai spread wide his thick hands, his face puckering with perplexity. "Attempting suicide—blasphemy!—during Mrishadal, staining my household with dishonor."

"I—"

"I gave you shelter. I invited you beneath my roof, offered you my hospitality, and you do this to me."

Shadrael shrugged. "I'm not exactly a guest here, am I?"

"Damn your black heart!" Vordachai said hoarsely.

"Vordachai—"

"No!" The warlord turned away from Shadrael, hunching his big shoulders. "I don't want your mockery. I'm offended by this. I thought you could at least honor Mrishadal, but, no, you must defile everything."

Shadrael swallowed a sigh. "It's nothing to do with you or the festival. I was—"

"Stop!" Vordachai broke in. "I shan't hear your lies. Don't you care who you hurt? If you want to waste your life, go out into the desert and do it far from my door, but *this*—do you know how much money I wasted paying that

healer to tend you when I could have left you in the citadel
to rot?"

"What? Purse-pinched again?"

Glowering, Vordachai stomped over and struck him.
Shadrael went down hard, the blow making his head ring,
and crashed into the sturdy leg of the table. He clung to it,
gasping and tasting blood.

Vordachai loomed over him. "Get up!"

Severance held back any pain, but Shadrael did not
want another beating. He hauled himself back on his feet,
assisted by Vordachai, who gripped the back of his tunic
and hoisted him with more vigor than compassion. Warily,
still probing his cut lip with his tongue, Shadrael faced his
brother's ire.

Vordachai was not yelling, not slamming things about
or breaking chairs. Steaming, his dark eyes narrowed to
beady, intense slits, he stood clenching and unclenching
his powerful fists, his jaws grinding together.

"I'm sorry the child saw me," Shadrael said now. "But
he doesn't understand—"

"And that makes it all right, eh?" Vordachai said,
sweeping this apology aside. "Our nephew sees you about
to throw yourself into the chasm, and he won't understand
it? Even a young child knows what suicide means, you
thickheaded dunce. And what of our sister? I have just left
her crying fit to break her heart."

"Nachel barely knows me. I was facing execution anyway."

"*I* decide who dies here!" Vordachai roared, losing control. "Not you! *I* choose when, and how, and why. Not you!"

"Then, damn you, get it over with!" Shadrael shouted
back. "Stop messing about with the festival and take care of
your responsibilities. Bringing me into the palace, slapping
me back together with potions and remedies . . . letting me
see Nachel and the boy. That isn't kindness. It's cruelty, the
worst torture of all. I just want it done!"

Vordachai plucked a dagger from his belt and threw it at him. Instinctively Shadrael jerked to one side. It missed, thudding into the battered council table and quivering there while Shadrael tried to catch his breath.

"Liar," Vordachai said harshly.

Humiliation clawed deep into Shadrael. He clenched his jaw, refusing to speak, while his feelings burned *severance* away. Without its support, he felt his strength draining swiftly. The truth lay between them, and he hated Vordachai for forcing him to acknowledge it.

"You've come this close to dishonoring a sacred festival," Vordachai said. "All for a lie. If you wanted to die you would have let me kill you." He pointed at the dagger still projecting from the table. "And now what's it to be? A grand execution? One more chance to wear your armor and medals, to walk through the sunlight casting no shadow and frightening dogs and small children before you put your neck on the block? Wrong, brother! I'm not giving you that satisfaction."

Surprised, Shadrael frowned at him.

"No," Vordachai said, staring him down. "You don't deserve a hero's beheading."

"Then you're throwing me over the cliff as you promised," Shadrael said with a twist of his mouth. "I was just going to save you the trouble—"

"Shut up! You may have been a hero once, and there was a time when I even admired you, but that's gone. You are nothing to me—no hero, no legion commander, no praetinor, no valiant warrior. I see only a liar and cheat, a traitor too filthy to wash pigs. And so I'm giving you a traitor's end." His eyes met Shadrael's firmly, cold with contempt. "I'm turning you over to the legion in Kanidalon, where you'll be charged with Lady Lea's abduction."

Astonished, Shadrael stared first, then scowled. "Now, just a—"

"It's decided."

"You can't do that!" Shadrael protested angrily. "You

fool, you're behind the plot. You'll be condemning yourself with me."

"Will I?" Vordachai asked. "Who will believe you, Shadrael? You're a broken officer with a dishonorable discharge. A known bandit, wanted for crimes in several provinces. A traitor who abducted the emperor's sister and turned her over to sworn enemies of the empire for payment." He shrugged. "Name me in the plot if you dare, but my standing with Pendek is better than yours. There's no proof against me, but when the lady is ransomed she can testify against you."

The idea of being denounced as a traitor and led back to New Imperia in chains filled Shadrael's mind with memories of the Terrors, when men had been hunted down ruthlessly and tortured for their actions under the reign of shadow. A traitor's death was the worst . . . Penestrican magic burning away his entrails while he hung, still alive, from the gibbet. He would swing there day after day, wracked with unspeakable torment while the Reformant priests tore asunder the last bit of spell holding his soulless form together. They would send him to an unspeakable hell and leave him in a place worse than the nine curses of Mael.

"No," Shadrael said, dry mouthed. "You will not do this."

Vordachai didn't bother to argue with him. Sighing, he called for his guards. They poured in, surrounding Shadrael with drawn weapons while his wrists were bound. A Choven ward was hung around his neck, its magic tormenting him already.

"Vordachai!" he shouted.

But the warlord turned his face away and would not watch as they pushed Shadrael from the room.

Chapter 15

Too stunned to weep, Lea was hastened back to her cell by an escort of frightened Vindicants led by Urmaeor, who kept stinging her with quick, angry bursts of magic. Her jailer, pallid and round eyed, flung open the door and she was pushed inside.

"I warned you," Urmaeor said furiously from the doorway. "I warned you not to resist him!"

Wearily Lea turned to face him. Twilight was closing in, yet she hardly noticed or cared. Her lungs were aching as though she'd inhaled ground glass, and she felt almost too weak and dizzy to stand, yet she forced herself to meet the priest's angry gaze. She knew it was pointless to explain; there was nothing she could say or do that he would heed. Urmaeor was tight-lipped and rigid, his emotions pouring off him with such intensity she feared he would blind her as he'd threatened. But she refused to show fear. What was done was done. It was not her fault.

He raised his hand, his fingers curling like clutched talons, and Lea braced herself for the strike. Instead, Urmaeor abruptly stepped back and gestured at the jailer. "Lock her up," he ordered, and strode away.

The door slammed shut and the bars were dropped into place across it. Surprised, Lea plopped down on the edge of her narrow cot. She could not believe he had spared her, not after what had happened. The echo of Lord Barthel's screams was still ringing in her ears.

She realized her heart was thudding almost as hard as when she first walked into the chief priest's chamber. She caught herself rubbing her mouth with the back of her hand, rubbing and rubbing until her lips felt swollen and sore. Shuddering, she forced herself to stop.

It was very cold in her cell. In her absence someone had left an extra blanket folded on her cot. Drawing it about her as night gathered close, she felt no comforting warmth. The coldness lay inside her, a terrible draining of her very life force. With all her heart she longed to lie down and take refuge in the blessed oblivion of slumber. Yet she dared not. She knew she had to stay strong if she was to survive here. If she collapsed, the priests might decide her breath was no longer enough to sustain Lord Barthel. Once he started feeding upon her blood instead, she would be finished.

Accordingly, she forced herself to sit composed and silent until she heard the approaching footsteps of her jailer.

He set a tray on the ground, grunting as he bent down, and slid it through a narrow opening in the bottom of her cell door. Normally he backed away, but tonight he lingered at her door. "There's poison in your food tonight," he growled in warning. "Eat it, and you'll be the one rotting away, not him."

Listening to his footsteps trudging away, Lea marveled that he had chosen to warn her against the food. Especially since she'd burned his master.

The smell of hot food brought back unwanted memories of Lord Barthel's fetid breath. Lea had been commanded to

kneel before him, her face level with his obese one. He'd
stunk of decay and putrescence and est-weed combined. At
first she hadn't known what to expect until he strained to
put his peeling, fleshy lips close to hers. Wheezing and eager, he'd poised himself to catch every quick breath she exhaled. He'd fed and fed, moaning and whimpering to
himself, pausing only to slurp and gasp for a few moments
before resuming. He'd been coated with spells to guard
him, slimy protections of shadow magic that made her sick
to her stomach. But then he ceased to merely catch her exhaled breath and began to draw it from her, greedily,
avidly. She had felt an icy coldness descending through
her, and knew he was draining some vital part of her. She
was smothering, fading . . . needing to break away, desperate to survive.

When she drew back, his delicate hands had been unex-
pectedly strong and quick. They clamped her head to hold
her tight, and before she could struggle, his mouth trans-
formed into an orifice with tiny, waving tentacles that
gripped her face painfully, drawing the very life from her.

Not until she was actually fainting had he let her go, his
mouth sliding away across her cheek like a slug leaving a
wet trail. And he'd whispered to her in that shrill, reedy
voice, "Delicious. Delicious! Come back to me tomorrow."

It was then that white flames had erupted on his hands.
He lifted them, blazing like torches, his eyes wide with horror. The tiny tentacles in his mouth fluttered frantically and
then blazed white, too. He fell back, screaming, the smell of
burning flesh filling that dank chamber. That's when Urmaeor and the others had rushed in, shouting as they extin-
guished the white flames with clouds of shadow magic. And
all the while, Lord Barthel's mountainous body was jerking
and quaking.

He'd moaned piteously then, and she knew he was still
alive, still in agony as the Vindicants sought to save him.

Now, sitting in her dark, cold cell, Lea broke down,
burying her face in her hands as she sobbed. She tried to

muffle the sounds, wanting no one to overhear her. Yet her
grief and terror were such that violent sobs wracked her
thin frame.

Never before had she harmed anyone. She had dedi-
cated her young life to sustaining the principles of harmony, to living as peaceably with all living creatures as she
could.

What had she become, to do something like this? Had
she been truly Choven, truly of the spirit as she'd striven
since adopting the teachings of Moab, she could not have
done this terrible thing.

She could almost hear Moab's quiet voice saying, "One
does not fight violence with violence, or terror with terror.
One transcends wrong and accepts."

But I do not accept this evil, Lea thought, drawing an
unsteady breath. *I cannot.*

And she understood something that she'd been trying to
deny since the day that Commander Shadrael had abducted
her. She was no longer a sheltered, spiritual creature deli-
cately tethered to this world. She had changed, been forced
to change, in order to survive. And however much her tender heart and empathy for others had made her believe she
must escape all that caused pain and grief, however much
she longed to live in peaceful serenity, embracing the good
in all creatures, she'd learned that evil would not keep its
place unless forced back.

A rustling sound outside her cell alerted her. Lifting her
head, she listened. Something not human scratched at her
door, whispering, "Sweet weeping. Sweet sorrow. Let me in.
Let me in."

Lea gathered the handful of pearls formed by her tears
and crouched by the door. Pushing her food tray aside, she
opened the bottom of the door and flung the pearls through
the narrow space. Something squalled and spat, scrambling
away with a howl of pain. She thrust the tray of poisoned
food out through the tiny opening, slammed it shut, and began pacing back and forth across her small quarters.

Doubtless her fate hinged on whether Lord Barthel lived or died. Poisoned food was the first retribution, but she knew there would be others.

Her hand slid deep into her pocket and fingered the tiny *gli*-emerald she'd secreted there. Until now she hadn't dared use it actively, fearing they would take it from her. But she knew now she couldn't survive by remaining a docile, model prisoner. If she could not escape, then she had to thwart the evil here as much as she could. She had to hold them back, make them distracted or even fearful of her.

The Vindicants had set so many shadow guards and protections around her cell that she was cut off from the element spirits, but with the power of the *gli*-emerald she might be able to break those protections.

Her fingertip rubbed the tiny stone, feeling its warm energy tingling into her hand and restoring much of what Lord Barthel had drained from her. It was all she had, but despite its diminutive size it carried considerable power, enough to shatter Commander Shadrael's magic, enough perhaps to destroy what gathered here. Even if she used it only once before they confiscated it, that was better than doing nothing. But she believed she would prefer to keep its use small and undetected, undermining their magic subtly . . . and for a longer length of time. The magical stone had been given to her for a purpose—what as yet she did not know. She would not risk its loss recklessly.

She thought of her brother, Caelan, who had set aside his Choven heritage in order to take up a sword. He had fought shadow for the cause of light, and he had prevailed.

Now it was her turn.

Surrounded by four Ulinian guards, Shadrael rode down a treacherous mountain switchback trail on a horse that feared him. They'd left Bezhalmbra in late afternoon, against custom, but Vordachai apparently could not bear to let him remain on Natalloh land a moment longer. With

their late start, darkness had swiftly engulfed them. Now
they picked their way down the perilous trail, hindered
by the weak light of a moon on the wane. The men were as
uneasy as the horses. They'd hung a Choven protection on
him to mute his powers, and Shadrael supposed that with
his brother's usual lack of attention to detail he'd forgotten
to inform his men that Shadrael was a shattered *donare*,
barely able to hold himself together much less attack their
threads of life.

Despite his bleak mood, he felt amused. Let them fear
him in this last journey down the Jawnuth. Let them sweat
and quake and hide their terror behind bravado. What did he
care?

The horses snorted, spooking at the least movement,
tossing their heads as the wind blew the men's cloaks and
fluttered the ends of their head wraps. Shadrael's mount
was the most nervous of all, flinging up its head and prancing on its toes as though it meant to bolt at any moment.
Periodically it balked, backing its ears and stretching its
neck as the man leading it tugged harder on the reins.
Everyone cursed it, and Shadrael expected it to pitch him
off into the chasm at any moment. That would, he supposed wryly, solve a number of problems.

As soon as they were well beyond the citadel's walls, the
guards cut Shadrael's hands free and gave him his reins,
permitting him to manage his recalcitrant horse himself. It
was more a matter of practicality than the courtesy due a
warlord's brother, and certainly no chance to break free.
Short of plunging to his death, there was nowhere Shadrael
could go until they reached the bottom of the mountain.

No one chattered. It was too cold and dark for conversation, and Shadrael was in no mood to talk. His thoughts
were busy, his heart still burning from the knowledge that
for once Vordachai had seen the truth quicker than he could
himself.

The healer had—under the close supervision of the
guards—applied new *severance* to see Shadrael through this

journey. His nourishment potion swung heavily in Shadrael's pocket. None of this was kindness, of course. Shadrael understood that Vordachai wanted him strong enough to stand trial.

Damn you, Shadrael thought.

Shivering in the icy wind and feeling naked without his armor, Shadrael knew what he must do. He marveled that it had taken him so long to see his path, yet he felt calm and settled, as though on the eve of battle when all the strategy was set and the preparations done.

The coward's way was closed to him. He scorned whatever temporary weakness had made him consider it. And he was not going tamely to the fate Vordachai had chosen for him. He would not be dragged to New Imperia in chains, and the usurper would never pronounce his death sentence; of that, he was determined.

Which left him with only one other true option: saving Lea.

Despite the effects of *severance*, Shadrael could feel exhaustion in his body, but it hardly mattered. His mind stayed focused and alert as he sought the opportunity he needed.

Between the last road checkpoint and the distant lights of the town, he found it.

The steep trail leveled out, merging with a wide trade road that was dry and dusty from much travel. The horses jogged into a trot, as though eager to reach Kanidalon and a stable. Wrapped and shivering in their cloaks, the guards stayed bunched around Shadrael and did not bother to bind his hands again.

Ahead, a caravan of merchants was camping next to the road. The wagons had been parked close together for security. The campfires were still burning, and people moved about, cleaning after their meal or talking, for it was not yet late enough for sleep. The fact that they had not pressed forward the last half league to Kanidalon announced that their wagons were empty of goods and their master was inexperienced.

The bandit in Shadrael assessed their numbers and longed to burst onto them, seizing their profits, but before he could even suggest it to his guards they turned off the road to skirt the camp. Even so, some of his guards were glancing toward the camp in curiosity, and Shadrael thought this was the best opportunity he was likely to get.

He opened his mouth to cajole his guards into stopping, but before he could speak the man in charge swore at the undergrowth, which was growing across their path in a thick, thorny barrier. When he tried to push forward, his horse shied back.

"Back to the road, Hultul?" the man on Shadrael's left asked.

"Not yet. There's bound to be a trail through this thicket."

"You'll hunt it all night, and my bones are freezing," complained the man on Shadrael's right. "What good is this duty if we arrive in Kanidalon too late to enjoy the pleasures of Last Night?"

Listening to them argue, Shadrael smiled to himself. They had relaxed enough to forget he was their enemy.

"Wait here," Hultul ordered, and turned his horse aside.

No sooner had he vanished into the night than Shadrael reached for the Choven protection around his neck and snapped the chain. It stung and burned his hand, but his state of *severance* enabled him to handle it long enough to fling it away. Leaning to his left, he plucked that guard's dagger from his belt, plunged it deep through mail and surplice, and shoved the man from the saddle.

The man on his right shouted, but Shadrael was already twisting to attack him. His bloody dagger was deflected with a clash of steel. Aware that he'd lost the element of surprise, Shadrael kicked his nervous horse hard in the flanks. Neighing, it half-reared and bolted straight into the thicket before the others could do more than shout after him.

They came galloping in pursuit, but Shadrael yanked his horse around, letting it bounce and nearly buck beneath him as he stood in the stirrups to grasp a slender tree branch overhead. He swung himself up onto the branch, which dipped alarmingly before supporting his weight. His horse—reins dangling and stirrups flapping—shied off just before the pair of men came crashing through the undergrowth beneath Shadrael's branch.

He dropped onto the closest, dragging the man from the saddle so that they crashed together into hard ground. By the time they'd rolled over from the momentum of their fall, Shadrael had cut his throat and scrambled away to rise and meet the attack of the remaining man.

Leaning from the saddle, drawn sword in hand, the guard charged him, yelling a war cry.

Cursing the man, Shadrael had no time to grab a sword from the guard he'd just killed. He threw himself into a thornbush to avoid the charge and felt a sword blade whisper death just above his head.

Still yelling, the guard swung his horse around and charged again with bared teeth gleaming in the starlight and the ends of his head wrap streaming out behind him.

Shadrael dodged right, then left, yanked the dead man's sword from its scabbard, and met his foe's attack with an expert twist of his wrists that caught his opponent's sword and sent it sailing into the brush.

"Nine thousand curses upon you!" the man swore, and threw a star.

Shadrael deflected it with his sword, sending it spinning harmlessly to the ground. Even as the man kicked his horse into another charge, Shadrael was pouncing on the throwing star. He scooped it up, cutting his hand on the sharp edge of steel, and spun about. The horse was too close; he'd been too slow. He stumbled back, pushing against the horse's sweaty shoulder to gain momentum, and flung the star without aim.

It bounced off the guard's mail shirt but flew up, cutting his jaw instead. With a howl, the man swayed in his saddle, and Shadrael sprang at the horse, causing it to shy sideways. The rider lost his balance, and Shadrael gripped his

stirrup, tipping him from the saddle, then pouncing on the
man as he tried to scramble to his feet.

Their fight was brutal, messy, and brief. Panting hard,
Shadrael staggered to his feet, shaking off the sweat streaming into his eyes. He felt spent, so out of breath he was almost dizzy. Swaying, he almost sank to one knee, then
gritted his teeth and forced himself to stand upright. Out of
habit, he cleaned his weapons, wiping blood with the edge
of his cloak. He sucked at the blade cut on his hand, feeling
nothing at the moment, and pulled a thorn from his shoulder. At the moment, with killing lust pounding through him,
he did not know whether his healing *severance* had held or
not. He did not care.

Someone from the nearby camp called out a question,
and was swiftly hushed. Shadrael could not see them but he
imagined a swift argument was taking place. The merchants would not dare venture out of camp to investigate
trouble that didn't involve them. He was more concerned
with Hultul, who would also have heard the commotion
and doubled back.

Hearing hoofbeats, he slid swiftly into cover despite
getting scratched ruthlessly by thorns. Sweating in the cold
air, clutching the stitch in his side, and wrapping one corner of his cloak around his cut hand to stop the bleeding,
Shadrael kept still while the remaining guard searched
warily in the dark.

A moan nearly startled Shadrael from hiding. He listened to Hultul's voice, shooting questions, and the groggy
answers that told him he hadn't killed the first man he
struck down. The temptation to attack burned inside him,
but Shadrael gritted his teeth and forced it under control.

"Kalfim? Sarthu?" Hultul called.

Silence.

Shadrael waited grimly, letting the lone man work it out
for himself. Three armed companions downed in short order
by an unarmed man supposedly kept under control by
Choven magic that had failed. In the end, Hultul decided he

did not want to hunt a ruthless *donare* in the dark by himself. He gathered the wounded man and retreated.

As soon as he deemed it safe, Shadrael moved swiftly, breaking cover to seek his horse. The animal had managed to catch one of its reins in the brush and was caught fast. Snorting, it shied from him, but he tied it more securely and set to work.

It was simple enough to strip one of the bodies and change clothes, although he struggled to fit inside the man's mail shirt and surplice. The head wrap was warm and itchy. Finding the belt too long, Shadrael sliced off the excess length with his dagger. Then he put his clothes on the dead guard, and struggled to lift the man across the horse he'd been riding. Trussing the corpse swiftly in place, Shadrael caught the guard's horse and climbed into the saddle.

Shadrael rode cautiously, leading the other horse carrying the dead man.

The city gates were closed for the night, and numerous wagons were parked outside the walls. The guards, however, were still admitting a few travelers through the eye gate, provided they carried the right kind of pass.

Well aware of the annoying habits of bureaucracy that required every guard to carry a duplicate pass, Shadrael dug into saddlebag and pockets until he found a writ of arrest signed by Vordachai. Clutching it, he approached the gates, nervous in the torchlight, and answered the questions put to him.

"Bringing in a prisoner on the warlord's orders," he said, using a broad *dramen* accent. He remembered to slouch in the insolent curve of the true *dramen* horseman, and did not look the centruin on duty in the eye as an officer would.

The centruin studied his writ with a narrowed eye. "What in Gault's name would my commander want with some renegade?"

Shadrael shrugged. "Does m'lord tell me such things? He says, 'Deliver a traitor!' and that is what I do."

"This isn't some weird festival joke, is it?"

"To ask that is to insult my religion."

The centruin raised his hands. "Gault knows, we don't want to do *that*. But treason's a stiff charge."

Shadrael mentally swore at the fellow and tried to look bored. "He gives me the orders. I follow the orders."

"Right. You know nothing about nothing, and I'm supposed to let you into town with a dead man charged with treason during a festival when violence is forbidden. So how'd he get dead?"

Shadrael let his gaze wander indifferently. "It is a long way down the mountain from m'lord's citadel."

The centruin grinned, giving Shadrael a friendlier look. "Is it now? And you're bringing him in all alone."

This time Shadrael did meet his gaze. "Does he look like he needs a full escort?"

"Nope. He don't, at that."

"It's cold, eh? If I get him delivered before the taverns close . . ."

"You won't," the centruin said gruffly, his sympathy dying fast. "Got to file a report first. No one on duty in camp will accept a corpse on a night like this. Might as well roll up over there"—he pointed—"and wait for morning."

Shadrael felt grudging admiration for the man's training. He was doing his job exactly as he should. "There is a reward," he said. "M'lord says I am to collect it from the commander."

"Reward for what?"

"Delivery of traitor called Shadrael—"

Stiffening, the centruin stepped back. "Pass!" he shouted loud enough for the sentries to hear. "Man and prisoner coming through."

An echoing shout replied from the other side, and the eye gate swung open. He feared the centruin would detail an escort for him, but the cold night and a hot barrel fire seemed to be working in his favor. The men on guard duty barely looked his way. He rode down the street until he was out of sight of the wall sentries. Then he dropped the reins of the horse he'd been leading, abandoning it and its burden. He tossed away his head wrap and turned his cloak inside out to change its color. Flinging it around his shoulders, he rode through narrow, twisting streets, avoiding crowds singing in groups as the festival wound down, and keeping away from crooked dark alleys where thieves lurked.

Eventually, in the guild quarter, he found what he wanted—a large tavern ablaze with lights and roaring with celebration. A dozen or more horses were tied at the rear. Shadrael secured his mount among them and hastened off on foot.

By the time he reached the pawnbroker street he was short of breath and inclined to stumble if he wasn't careful. Frowning, he pulled out the flask and sipped at the potion in an effort to regain some strength. He hoped the healer hadn't put anything in it to make him sleepy.

After a moment of enforced rest, he regained his wind and skulked along the row of darkened shops until he reached the one where he'd pawned his armor. An expert jimmy with his dagger opened one of the shutters. The shop remained silent inside, with no dog on guard to sound an alarm, and no Choven warding keys to hinder his entry. All he heard was a faint rumble of snoring from upstairs.

Shadrael hoisted himself inside the window. Slowly and cautiously, he threaded his way through the stacks of goods, making no more sound than a ghost, searching patiently until he put out his hand and touched his breastplate.

"Thanks to Mrishadal," Shadrael murmured, aware that it was forbidden to sell weapons and armor during the festival. Legal to buy, but not legal to sell. A convenient law, in the circumstances, for it meant the pawnbroker had not yet dispersed his possessions.

He shed the uncomfortable mail shirt and buckled on his breastplate with the familiarity and ease of long years of practice. His sleeve knives were gone, but he dug around in the shop until he found replacements. He located his sword, fastening the scabbard to his belt, and hooked his fang-

point axe at the small of his back where it felt at home. The
borrowed belt he wore had no hooks for throwing stars. He
frowned at that, but let it go, taking instead a boot knife and
two more daggers. His helmet took longer to find, and he
was growing impatient before he located it on a cluttered
workbench. It smelled strongly of oil as though someone
had been polishing it, and he tucked the greasy thing under
his arm with relief.

The snoring overhead stopped. Shadrael froze, his heart
thumping hard. He was tired and cold, and there was much
left to do. He didn't want to kill a harmless shopkeeper
nosing downstairs at the wrong time.

But after a moment the snoring resumed. Shadrael
eased out his breath and left. Back in the street, he clamped
his hand firmly on his sword hilt, put an assured swagger in
his step, and walked where he chose, aware that no thief
was likely to attack an armed man.

At the tavern where he'd left his horse, a sizable crowd
had gathered, yelling drunkenly and slurring Last Night
blessings to each other. One by one the patrons came stumbling outside, ejected by the landlord who was trying to
close down his establishment before curfew.

Impatient with the delay, Shadrael retreated to avoid
both crowd and torchlight. If they didn't break up soon, the
soldiers would come to disperse them. He didn't want to be
rounded up with drunks and questioned. There was always
the risk of being recognized.

"Make way! Make way!" a man called out. "Let us pass!"

Shadrael saw a portly man shaking his staff at the crowd
in an effort to get through. By his clothing and rings he was
a wealthy man. With him were a cluster of sleepy-eyed servants and a wheeled litter that doubtless held his wife or
mistress. The curtains were firmly closed, and yet something about the conveyance caught Shadrael's attention.

He found himself staring hard at the litter, his curiosity
sharpening. He sensed something familiar and unwelcome,
something he had to acknowledge. Before he could stop

himself he stepped away from a doorway's shadow into the torchlight.

Pushing his way through the revelers, who were shouting good-naturedly at the rich man without letting him through, Shadrael yanked open the litter curtains and peered inside.

A pair of startled eyes, heavily painted, stared back at him. The woman's mouth parted in surprise, but it was not her plump, coarsely attractive face that held Shadrael's attention. It was not her lush figure or the gawking maidservant with her that made him stare.

Around her neck hung Lea's *gli*-emeralds, the green stones huge and glowing as they reflected the torchlight. They dangled in their settings of intricate Choven gold, all nine stones holding enough power to bring down a mountain and burn his flesh like fire.

"How dare you?" the woman cried, although her painted eyes appraised him openly. "Get back from my litter at once! Husband, I am being accosted!"

Her cry to her husband wasn't loud, however. The man, busy arguing with the revelers, did not hear her.

Grinning, Shadrael leaned inside audaciously to press her mouth to his. She tasted of wine and scented lip wax, her perfume a heavy cloud. Her lips, frozen only for a moment in surprise, parted beneath his with a willingness that told him everything. Her fingers slid through his hair.

"Bad man," she whispered against his mouth. "Join me quickly. The maid can go."

Shadrael had no intention of obeying. Kissing her so expertly she moaned and melted, he unfastened the necklace adroitly and was gone, tucking the jewels into his cloak pocket as he went. The woman shouted in annoyance, then screamed, but Shadrael was already mixing into the crowd. He escaped into a dark alley, turned corners as more shouts went up behind him, and ran until there was only cold dark night and sleeping houses.

Stumbling to a halt, he leaned against a wall to catch his breath. He ached all over. His strength was spent. Possession of Lea's emeralds was already making him restless and uneasy. He felt that dull, heavy ache around his heart return, and his spirits dropped. The magic in the jewels had done nothing in the past but weaken him. He would be a fool now to keep them, for he could not afford to waste his scant strength resisting their effect, much less concealing them from the Vindicants.

She'll need them, he thought.

Still gasping for breath, he shook his head at his own impulsive stupidity and stumbled on through the night.

Chapter 16

Coated with dust, his hips and knees aching from too many hours in the saddle, Thirbe was standing once again in Commander Pendek's plain office. He had just been offered a cup of hot mead, but slammed it down untasted. "Got away?" he said. "You're saying you had Lord Shadrael in your fist, and he got away?"

Looking stout and authoritative in full armor, his insignia glinting on his breastplate, a crimson cloak of thick Ulinian wool hanging from his shoulders, Pendek had likewise just come in from outdoors. They had met at the door, and Pendek had invited Thirbe inside and offered him a drink to help warm him up before telling him the news.

Standing with his back to the fire, his hair windblown and his cheeks reddened, Pendek did not immediately answer Thirbe's outburst. Instead he drank his mead in what seemed to be a display of indifference, but when he lowered the cup, his green eyes were troubled.

"According to Lord Vordachai," Pendek said carefully, "he arrested Commander Shadrael and sent him here to be charged officially with treason."

"On what grounds? Abduction? Does Vordachai have Lady Lea?"

"No."

"You don't believe that, do you? Or did you even ask?"

Pendek reddened. "Of course I asked. I have made full inquiries. Lord Vordachai says he caught his brother for reasons of outlawry and theft. He also says that you informed him that his brother was under suspicion and wanted for Imperial questioning. He sent him to us."

"Except Shadrael just *happened* to escape," Thirbe said. His throat felt raw, as if he'd swallowed a roadside thistle. "How lax is your security on the guardhouse?"

"The man never reached Kanidalon," Pendek said huffily. "You needn't lay blame *here*, Protector. The Ninth does not lose its prisoners."

Thirbe was shaking his head in disgust. "Plague smite that wind-swelled liar! Sitting up there on that mountain, safe behind his walls, and laughing at us. He's spread this lie to cover his own involvement; of that, I'm sure."

"Well, I'm not. Three of his men were killed by Lord Shadrael," Pendek said. "The warlord has no reason to lie."

"He has every reason!" Thirbe burst out. "Gods, man, how can you believe such a feeble tale?"

"One of the dead men was found tied to a horse wandering Kanidalon streets," Pendek said, picking up a pen from his cluttered desk and putting it down again. "Stabbed through the—"

"What does that matter? The—"

"Of course it matters!" Pendek said, looking shocked. "Every detail in this affair could be important."

"Every detail in a lie still adds up to a lie," Thirbe told him. Unable to keep still, he stomped over to the small window overlooking the camp and back again. "You can't approach this like a clerk, organizing old ledgers, Commander. It's strategy, and he's outmaneuvered us."

"I don't—"

"Nothing holds together. Vordachai wouldn't surrender his own brother voluntarily—"

"He did," Pendek insisted. "Which means your talk with him the other day accomplished something."

"Aye, proved my point. Both of 'em involved. My visit must have spooked him, made him worry we were closing in, perhaps considering arrest. So he pretends to surrender his brother as an act of good faith, and Shadrael conveniently escapes before he reaches the guardhouse. Very tidy, damn his eyes."

Pendek gave Thirbe a flat, unblinking stare, the kind only a Chanvezi could produce. "Your interpretation is . . . creative," he said eventually. "But why not view the positive side of the situation?"

"What's positive about it?" Thirbe asked. "We've lost our one solid lead. *If* Shadrael is even still in the region. There's no proof that any of this happened, no matter how much you want to believe Vordachai."

Pendek shook his head. "Well, I do believe him. He's not clever enough to create the kind of complicated intrigues Itierians love so much. Don't you see how positive a step this is?"

"No."

"Lord Vordachai is beginning to trust me. I believe he can be—"

"Trust!" Thirbe broke in. "There's no trust, you—" Just in time he stopped himself from completing the insult. Exhaling fiercely, he tried again. "If he *trusted* you, Commander, he would have followed the proper procedure by clapping his brother in chains and sending for an escort from the Ninth to take him. There would have been no convenient escape, and we'd have our prisoner sitting tight and tidy in the guardhouse, ready for me to question."

"This is exactly why you should leave diplomacy to the experts," Pendek said. "Permitting my men to remove Lord Shadrael from his property would break every law of hospitality a Ulinian knows."

"Do you think I care about etiquette, you great—"

"I think you had better take care, Protector."

Thirbe threw up his hands. "Right. Let's throw army regs off the mountaintop and bend ourselves double to honor local customs. Meanwhile, you've left a loophole big enough for Shadrael to gallop a horse through, while the warlord folds his hands and looks innocent. Bah!"

"You can look at it that way if you choose."

"I do!"

"Well, we are all disappointed, but—"

"Disappointed!" Resisting the urge to swear, Thirbe instead circled the office again. "Sir, you can't natter about diplomacy and positive progress, not when Lady Lea's still a prisoner, still in need of rescue. Until she's found and safe, I'm not going to stand about and talk disappointment. Or worry about hurting a provincial warlord's feelings. Gods!"

"Move past this setback and consider how close we've come. We know Lord Shadrael is in the area."

"He was," Thirbe muttered darkly. "Wager you a year's pay he's in the next province by now."

"I've sent a courier to alert the Thyraze border. They can assist our search with dragon scouts."

"Useful," Thirbe admitted grudgingly. "But they won't fly into the Broken Spine. And that's where—"

"You seem obsessed by that location, Protector," Pendek said, pouring himself another cup of mead. "The evidence indicates that the commander—er—former commander has headed elsewhere. He'll be found. In fact, if you wish to co-ordinate our efforts with the Thyrazenes I'll authorize it."

Thirbe had no intention of being deflected off on that kind of wild qualli hunt. He said nothing.

"I'm also authorizing a reward to be issued for any information regarding Lord Shadrael's whereabouts," Pendek said smugly. "That should bring results."

You'll be so swarmed by fools and greedy swindlers, Thirbe thought sourly, *that you won't have time to sign your name to paper, much less search for her.* He swallowed the remark, however, and stood there fuming, frustrated by the combination of incompetence and ranking authority before him. He'd spent the past week combing through a small portion of the badlands with trackers that could not get him where he wanted to go. The opal still glowed when he held it over that location on the map, but dimly. Every day its light grew feebler, and he was worried to his bones that he would not reach Lea in time.

My lady, my good, sweet lady, please hold on, he prayed.

Now he'd come dragging back to the legion camp, weary to the bone, and nearly frozen from camping every night in the open. He and the decim of men assigned to him had run out of food and supplies and needed fresh horses. And this was the news that greeted his return. He'd met plenty of fools in his long career, but Pendek Drelliz was a thick-necked, boneheaded, lumbering idiot with the judgment of a gnat and the gullibility of a raw recruit in his first crap game.

Aware that he could shout all day and never budge the commander's decision, Thirbe sighed. "The messenger that brought you Vordachai's news—"

"Ah yes." Pendek rooted among the papers on his desk. "A fellow named Hulthul. No . . . Hultul. Rather difficult, these local names."

"I want to see him."

"Really?" Pendek frowned, his green eyes suspicious. "For what purpose? I can't have you casting blame with your usual lack of tact."

Thirbe swallowed the temptation to tell him where he could stick his tact and said in a strangled voice, "Just a few questions."

"No . . . no, I think it would be best if you refrained. I have spoken to the man. He was competent, and acted quite exasperated about losing his prisoner. Of course, it would be difficult to contain someone of former Commander Shadrael's abilities. His reputation is remarkable. For

him to turn renegade . . . a pity." Pendek sighed and shook
his head. "No, best to leave it as an unfortunate event. I've
tightened controls in the city. There are extra men posted at
every gate. Extra patrols on the streets. We're watching,
Protector. We're very close now. Despite all you say, we're
making definite progress."

Impatient with the time he'd wasted on this leather-
headed noddy, Thirbe saluted, spun on his heel, and
tramped outside into the cold wind. He snagged the first
centruin to cross his path.

"Sir?"

"Heard a Ulinian messenger came in this morning, reporting an escaped prisoner."

The centruin coughed and looked sharply about the
bustling camp before giving Thirbe a brief nod. "Sorry, sir,
but I can't stand here. I'm due for a guardhouse inspection."

Thirbe took the hint and fell into step with the taller
man. They crossed the camp, dust fogging everywhere, and
skirted the parade ground where men were being drilled by
a pair of centruins with lungs that could outshout a gladiator trainer. At the end of a row of perfectly aligned tents
stood a ramshackle commons, a building for the men to
gather in for meals or games of chance in their off-duty
time. The centruin's brisk stride paused there.

He coughed again, glancing around, and casually pulled
Thirbe's dagger from its sheath. "Got a loose rivet in the
hilt. See?" he said, handing the weapon back.

Thirbe slipped him a coin as he took the weapon and
peered at it. "So I do. Better check it with the armorer."

"You do that, sir." Saluting, the centruin strode on.

Thirbe pushed open the door to the commons and ducked
under the low lintel. Inside, the room was dim and shadowy,
lit by a roaring fire and some smoking lamps. The air stank
of sweat, leather oil, damp wool, and the dried dung patties
fueling the fire. At one table several foot soldiers were swap-
ping jokes and howling at their own wit. A trio was drinking
together in a corner, perhaps nursing festival hangovers. And

a Ulinian wearing the warlord's coat of arms sat alone on a bench with his back to the wall, dourly gnawing on a piece of stale flat bread.

"You!" Thirbe said to him. He jerked his thumb over his shoulder. "Come with me."

Hultul was short, slight, and wiry, the kind of man that could ride all day in the desert without food or drink. Wrapped tightly in his cloak, the ends of his head wrap flapping in the wind, he peered up at Thirbe with small dark eyes as helpful as stones. To every question, he shook his head.

Frustrated, Thirbe switched from Lingua to Ulinian, using the official, most common dialect. Hultul said nothing.

"Damn you, I know you understand me. You spoke to Commander Pendek."

"He is commander of Ninth," the man replied. "You are . . ." He shrugged.

Thirbe twitched aside his cloak to show his insignia. "I am protector to her Imperial Highness, Lady Lea."

Hultul shrugged again, his gaze a dark flick of indifference.

"Have you sisters?" Thirbe asked, struggling to keep exasperation from his voice. "Have you daughters?"

Hultul did not answer.

"If you do, consider what you would feel if one of them was carried off by a bandit. Frightened, mistreated, perhaps hurt. Would you not want her back?"

"Would *take* her back, like this!" As he spoke, Hultul grabbed the air in a quick gesture. "Would not stand around, asking stupid questions."

Thirbe's fist shot out and connected with the man's jaw, knocking him flat. Hultul was rolling onto his feet as soon as he hit the ground, but Thirbe caught him by the front of his cloak and twisted it around his throat before pinning the man with a thud against the flimsy wall of the commons. Hultul stretched his lips in a dangerous little smile and kicked, but Thirbe blocked that move.

Twisting the cloak harder around the man's throat, he

force-marched him around to the back of the building, out
of sight of the rest of the camp. There, he drew his dagger.

"Listen to me, you little wart," he snarled. "I've taken
all the lies and tricks I'm going to."

Hultul just smiled and said nothing. His dark eyes held
flat defiance.

Thirbe, however, had not been trained as a predlicate for
nothing. Deftly, he slid the point of his dagger beneath the
neck of the man's mail shirt and pulled out his *harnush*, his
birth amulet. Hultul's eyes widened fractionally, and all
other expression vanished from his face.

"Got your attention, don't I?" Thirbe said. He twisted the
cloth noose he'd made a little harder, so that the man
grunted.

Thirbe cut the cord holding the amulet and at the same
time kicked Hultul's feet out from under him. The Ulinian
squirmed frantically, lunging for the amulet, but Thirbe
was quicker. He stamped on Hultul's wrist and kicked the
amulet out of reach before dropping on Hultul's midsec-
tion with his knees. He heard the whoosh of air knocked
from Hultul's lungs, and noted the man's desperate gasps
with satisfaction. His left hand clamped hard on Hultul's
throat as he brought the dagger point up right between the
Ulinian's eyes.

"Now," he said in a mild, conversational tone, "I'm all
for following regs, doing things by the book. I'm all for
congenial relations between provinces and local govern-
ments. But my allegiance is to the emperor, see, not your fat
warlord with the strange name. And I'm a little tired of getting the runaround since I came to this worthless dust hole."

Hultul squirmed in an effort to throw him off, reaching
for a weapon that Thirbe took away from him. While Hultul glared at him, Thirbe began tapping his dagger point
between the man's eyes.

"Now," he went on as though he hadn't been interrupted,
"Commander Pendek likes to honor the local customs.
Thinks it keeps things peaceful. I know a few local customs

myself. One is that you devils think your soul perishes if you lose that birth amulet."

Hultul's mouth twisted in contempt. "An old legend, nothing more!"

"Then you won't mind so much when I take yours down to the Plaza and sell it for drinking money."

Hultul twisted and heaved desperately to throw him off, spitting angrily. Thirbe held him, ducking to avoid the spittle.

"You been lying to me," Thirbe said, "and I don't like it."

"I have said nothing to you, foreign dog! Nothing!"

"You been lying to Commander Pendek."

"That fat swine. He is—" Hultul barked out a rude epithet in Ulinian.

Thirbe grinned. "I agree. But he's legion, see? That puts him above you, dung beetle. You shouldn't lie to him."

"No lies! I brought a true message, as my lord bade me!"

"So Lord Shadrael's running free, is he?"

"He escaped. He killed three of my best men."

Thirbe nodded as though he believed this. "Doesn't say much for you or your best men if an outnumbered prisoner could get away from you."

"He is *donare*! He is fierce and kills without mercy."

"Snapped threads of life, did he?"

Hultul tried to shake his head, but Thirbe's hand was still clamping his throat.

"You're lying, dung beetle," Thirbe said. "Your master's lying. Lord Shadrael's his heir, ain't he?"

Hultul stopped struggling for a moment and stared up at Thirbe. "If my lord has not been blessed with children, how is that your concern, *cumith'el daed*?"

"You can leave my ancestry out of this discussion," Thirbe said. "So your oath of allegiance is just as strong to Shadrael as it is to your warlord."

"Not the same!"

"I think it is."

"You know nothing. You understand nothing. Lord Shadrael is—is not—he is not as other men. If you saw him, you would know he is *muibe oedui*. Without a soul."

Thirbe tucked that information away with the grim intention of worrying about it later. "So where can I find him?"

"He is like the shadows of night, nowhere to be found unless he wishes it."

"Now, I happen to know another local custom," Thirbe said, still tapping his dagger point between Hultul's eyes. "It's said that a blind man cannot enter Paradise—"

"No! There is nothing about that. Nothing!"

"—because it is sacrilege to enter the Sacred Gates and not be able to see the blessings beyond them. Ain't that right?"

Hultul stared at him with teeth bared, his dark eyes snapping with fear and anger.

Thirbe bent close and snarled in his face, "You know exactly where Shadrael is!"

"No!"

"You know exactly where they are keeping Lady Lea!"

"No!"

"When I pop out your eyeballs I'm going to keep them moist and juicy, take them straight over to Kettle Street, and have them cooked into a tasty dish. A man who eats the eyes of his enemy forever rules him. Isn't that your Ulinian proverb?" Thirbe smiled. "And if my knife slips and plunges too deep into your worthless, flea-ridden skull . . . well, not having a birth amulet to bless your passing isn't important. That's what you said."

Hultul's face went ashen. Although Thirbe was no longer squeezing his throat, his breath came in short gasps. His eyes flashed with hate. "May the plague rot you from within, you—"

Cutting off his air expertly, Thirbe pressed the point of his dagger right at the bottom of the man's left eye and flipped upward.

Hultul's scream was silent, for he had no air. Thirbe released his throat, and the man dragged in a shuddering breath. His eyes were clamped shut. Blood was trickling down his cheek where Thirbe had cut him. Swiftly Thirbe clamped his hand over Hultul's left eye, holding him when Hultul would have thrashed.

"That's one," he said. "I now own half of you. Do you start talking, or do I take your second eye?"

"She is not . . . My esteemed lord does not keep her prisoner. He knows nothing of this evil that Lord Shadrael does," Hultul babbled.

"Where is she? Where in the Broken Spine are they keeping her?"

"The refuge of the Vindicants."

"Vindicants," Thirbe whispered grimly.

"My beloved master has nothing to do with them. Nothing! He despises the evil ones."

"I reckon he despises them so much he's given them refuge on his land. Maybe he even sends them supper every night."

"Would you risk a Vindicant curse if the evil ones came to you for hiding? Would you deny them and suffer thereafter plague and rotted crops and tainted water and no kids born to your flocks? Would you?"

Thirbe was too busy thinking about Lea in the clutches of those shadow worshippers to answer.

"My beloved master is angry with Lord Shadrael for selling the girl to the evil ones. So angry he sent Lord Shadrael here for arrest. He said the emperor would order Lord Shadrael to be given a traitor's execution, and it would be much deserved. I swear to Gault the Most Holy that this is true!"

Thirbe abruptly released Hultul. He wiped clean his dagger point on his knee and sheathed it. No good being horrified, he told himself, pushing down his emotions. If he started thinking about what might be happening to

Lea, he'd be unmanned and of no use to her at all. And it was no good taking this information to Commander Pendek, who would find some boneheaded reason for taking no action.

"What is this?" Hultul said, lowering his hands. He blinked about him, his brow knotting in perplexity before he gingerly felt his left eye. Although the cut beneath it was still trickling blood, Thirbe had not blinded him at all. "You have not taken it. You—" He stared at Thirbe in dawning anger. "You *tricked* me—"

Thirbe held up his amulet, letting it swing from his fingers. "So?"

Hultul rushed at him, but Thirbe gave him a rough shove backward. "Got a job for you," he said. "I need a guide who can get me to where the Vindicants are hiding out."

Already Hultul was shaking his head, making a sign of warding with his fingers, and trying to back away. Thirbe grabbed him and shook him as a dog would a rat. "A guide," he said gruffly. "No tricks or leading me through dusty canyons to nowhere special. Straight to their camp."

"No, this I cannot do."

"You want this amulet back?"

Hultul glared at him. "You prepare for me another trick."

Thirbe stuffed the amulet into his pocket. "Now, you listen to me, you gutless wabbie," he said fiercely. "I've got your confession that Lord Vordachai's involved in the girl's abduction up to his fat jowls—"

"No! I said nothing like that. Nothing!"

"You think the emperor will let Ulinia stand if anything happens to his sister in this rat heap of a province?"

"Always he is against us. Always! He hates us!"

"You think the emperor won't haul your master before a board of inquiry faster than old Vordachai can spell his name? You think *you'll* escape a traitor's execution yourself? Maybe they'll make you swallow the slow fire that burns through your entrails, or maybe they'll just quarter you, but I swear that I'll eat both your eyes long before they stick your head on the palace gates to rot."

Hultul gave him a strange look. "I count your threats as nothing. Give back my *harnush*, and I will guide you as you desire."

"You'll get it when the girl is found," Thirbe replied grimly. "Move!"

"Are you mad? It will be dark soon."

"Then we ride as far as we can," Thirbe said, ignoring the temptation of a hot meal and a good night's sleep. He could not shake the feeling that Lea needed him desperately. "There's no time to waste."

Chapter 17

Shadrael walked across the dusty ground where mercenaries were straggling through a drill. The men were poorly equipped, carrying personally owned weapons, including spears, mauls, and swords. Their armor was scanty at best. Using a flat-topped boulder as his vantage point, he watched them blunder about in what should have been an infantry maneuver. His dark gaze instantly picked out the handful of men who executed it correctly.

"Halt!" he shouted.

His voice echoed off the stony ridge behind them, and the men turned around to stare at him.

In the sudden quiet, they stared at each other—recruits and new commander. He sensed someone climbing onto the rock behind him, but did not turn his gaze away from the men.

"Start over, and this time move left." He pointed. "Go!"

"You're wasting time," Urmaeor's deep voice said. "There's no need to teach them how to maneuver."

Less than pleased at being interrupted, Shadrael said, "By the last report, Light Bringer is sending four legions to

Ulinia. Together with the Ninth already in place, that will
be twenty-five thousand men against these four hundred. If
they can't maneuver, this rabble will die in the first charge."

Urmaeor chuckled. "Such a dismal perspective. Are you
so easily cowed these days, Commander?"

"Faster!" Shadrael barked at the men, before glancing at
the priest beside him.

Lines of fatigue were carved into Urmaeor's face, and
the rash mottling his skin was worse. Shadrael had seen
lepers that looked healthier. His bloodshot eyes looked
feverishly bright. He kept his hands tucked out of sight
within the wide sleeves of his robes, but Shadrael saw the
peeling blotches of skin on his throat and smelled the rot of
his body beneath a mask of herbs and other fragrances.
Lea is doing this, he told himself, then closed away all
thought of her.

"Dregs," he said now, "versus Imperial soldiers. Call
that dismal if you want."

"All these men need do is attack on command and hold
their weapons properly."

Shadrael quelled his annoyance. No emotions, he reminded himself. Since the day he'd come to the Vindicants,
he'd shut away damaged pride and resentment in order to
take command of this ragtag force, ignoring the triumphant
little smirk on Urmaeor's face. He didn't allow himself to
fret over the impossible task before him. It was simply what
he had to do.

"Given six months, I'd have them fit," he said.

Urmaeor sighed. "You're thinking like a fool. You have
days to prepare them, not all winter."

"If you're expecting Thyrazene help, Light Bringer's arrival will melt it."

"Just speed up their training."

Shadrael frowned. He knew just how fast a legion could
move when required. The Eleventh was now stationed
northwest of Ulinia. It could be here in a matter of days. As
could the Tenth and Second.

Shadrael's gaze swept across the muddled chaos before him. "Halt!" he shouted. "Line up!"

The men straggled to comply, most of them failing to come to attention. Many were chatting among themselves, slack and openly defiant; others were gazing around, trying to impress their comrades by puffing out their chests and looking fierce. The rest just stood, dumb and passive, no doubt wondering how long until their next meal came.

"The empire is starting to teeter. He's losing ground, and we are gaining it. We have," Urmaeor said with intense satisfaction, "the upper hand over him. And he will come straight into our trap here, as surely as though we control his mind."

Shadrael thought the priest might as well be holding a honeycomb under a hornet's nest. He held his tongue, but Urmaeor smiled.

"Do you think so?" the priest asked, clearly having discerned that thought in Shadrael's mind. "I want him angry, rash, and ill prepared. I want him moving toward us quickly. Think of him lured out here"—Urmaeor gestured at the desolate landscape of lava stone, barren ridges, and scattered boulders—"so isolated, so . . . vulnerable. The positioning is perfect for our purpose."

"Even if he brings idiots for generals," Shadrael replied, "the sheer numbers will defeat us."

"Is this the confident victor of numerous battles?" Urmaeor asked sharply. "Have you lost your nerve along with your magic, Commander?"

Once, Shadrael would have killed him for that. Now he sent Urmaeor a stony look and said, "Any good leader mistrusts such uneven odds. These men will die in the first charge. What else are you providing me?"

"Wait and see."

Urmaeor turned away, but Shadrael blocked his path.

"If I'm to plan an effective strategy, I must have information."

Anger contorted Urmaeor's face. "Who said you are

planning the strategy? Do you think you can return to us, after refusing to obey my orders before, and be trusted implicitly? You have lost your soul and your magic. You are slowly going mad. You are a rogue *donare* at best, and an ineffectual coward at worst. When the time comes, you'll be told what you should know. And you'll do as you're told."

His words were cruel, designed to hurt as much as the stoning. Shadrael bowed his head, focusing hard on nothing. His muscles had grown rigid. He found it hard to breathe normally.

Urmaeor laughed softly. "I'm glad to see that stiff pride of yours mastered. And if it will relieve your anxiety, your brother has pledged his army to our cause."

"Vordachai?" Shadrael's head snapped up. "He'll never support you, not after—"

"The warlord has changed his mind." Urmaeor's mouth stretched in a vulpine smile. "The ransom demand for Lady Lea was sent to New Imperia in his name, you see."

Shadrael saw immediately. Despite his efforts to protect his brother, Vordachai had been implicated in the plot after all. Shadrael's mouth compressed. It was all he could do to ignore the feelings that threatened to engulf him.

"Did you really think to keep him out of this conflict?" Urmaeor asked scornfully. "When his whole aim is to pull Ulinia from the empire?"

Reckless, impulsive Vordachai, Shadrael thought in exasperation. Too passionate to be prudent, he had never been clever enough to think his way completely through any situation. The priests had manipulated him as skillfully as they were now luring the emperor into their trap.

"The warlord is busy summoning his barons and levying their armies," Urmaeor went on. "The entire Ulinian force will be joining us in a matter of days."

Which meant, Shadrael thought, a force equal to one Imperial legion. Not enough men. "Who," he asked, "are you putting in command, Vordachai or me?"

"That," Urmaeor said coldly, "remains to be seen. Now get these men ready."

Stepping off the boulder, Shadrael walked down the ragged line, his thoughts carefully marshaled beneath a mental list of assessments and tasks to be done. Urmaeor, he realized, might be obsessed and zealous, but he was no fool. With a force of five legions, Light Bringer was obviously intending to crush Ulinia into submission. He would enslave the people, execute the warlord and barons, and burn the Vindicants to ashes with whatever magic lay at his disposal. For Urmaeor to calmly dismiss this threat meant that he and Lord Barthel were devising a trap with all the evil and shadow magic at their disposal.

Even so . . . Defeat of Light Bringer . . . who had broken the world and destroyed both Beloth and Mael? What did the Vindicants have planned?

Shadrael frowned. Dangerous to wonder. Pointless to speculate.

Abruptly he picked out the five men he'd observed executing the drill maneuver correctly. Among those five, now to be his centruins, was Fomo.

Wearing good armor and new boots, Fomo looked well armed with daggers, a sharply honed sword, throwing stars that Shadrael recognized as his own, and a maul thrust through his belt. He came smartly to attention, sucking in his cheeks so that his tattoo shifted in a lewd way. His small, vicious eyes stared straight ahead in the correct army manner, aiming somewhere past Shadrael's left shoulder. He was wary and tense, with good cause, Shadrael thought, having deserted his commander just before arrest.

As faithful as a prostitute, Shadrael thought. *As loyal as a flea to a dog.* He wondered what else Fomo had spent his money on, money gained from selling Lea's necklace.

"We meet again, Centruin Fomo," Shadrael said tonelessly.

Fomo held army discipline, refusing to move or react.

Shadrael turned to address the whole assembly. "These

men I've selected will be your centruins," he said, projecting his voice so that it could be heard by all. He used the
standard spiel given to all new recruits. "If you don't know
what a centruin is, you'll learn fast. Your centruin will train
you, see you're housed and fed, and punish you when you
commit infractions. You will obey your centruin's orders as
you obey mine. Without question. Without hesitation. If
you get yourself in trouble, take your problem to your centruin. You are being paid to serve this army. You are now
sworn to its service. Your loyalty will be absolute. That
means my orders are your law. Disobey, and you will be
punished. Desert, and you will be hunted down and killed.
You are now a cohort. You will train as a cohort, and you
will learn to fight—*together*—as a cohort, relying on each
other in training and battle, for your survival."

He paused, surveying the men. Most were listening to
him. A few, at the far end of the line, were not. He took
note of who they were, lodging their faces in his memory.

"When the additional warriors ride in"—he watched the
men's attention perk up—"you will remember that you are
a cohort. You will keep to yourselves. You will wear your
insignia of Cohort One at all times. You will obey the chain
of command that your centruins will teach you."

Turning, he pointed at one of his new officers, a tall,
gangly man with a gnarled face and the scars of old army
service. "You there, pick out a company of men. We're
short a full complement of five hundred, but make your
choices. You"—he pointed at the next centruin—"will
have second pick, and so on. On my dismissal, fall out your
men, and set them to drilling."

A groan rose from the line. The centruins, however,
watched Shadrael without moving. He had given them rank
and authority. For now at least they might be willing and
eager to show what they could accomplish. He felt certain
that at least half of the five had never been more than common foot soldiers, but if nothing else they could march cor-

rectly. He needed their experience, however scanty. As for
Fomo, easily the most intelligent and experienced among
them, Shadrael had deliberately given him the last choice
of men. Fomo would get the worst of a sorry lot, and he'd
be the first to whip them into fighting shape. If the other
centruins possessed any sense, they would observe and
learn from him.

Shadrael lifted his chin. "That is all."

He strode away, ignoring the howl of complaints and
the barked commands of the centruins as they started
choosing and sorting.

"**N**o, Excellency! I beg you to reconsider."

Buckled into full armor and wearing his crown of spun
gold and emeralds, Caelan left Chancellor Brellit and his
advisers without another word, refusing to listen to more
protests.

He strode through the palace into the women's pavilion
and went up the alabaster steps leading to the empress's
private apartments. He was determined to tell Elandra the
latest news, including his decision to leave his court today,
before anyone else did.

Within her rooms, so luxurious and serene, he stepped
past the bowing eunuch who ran her household and saw her
waiting for him. She wore flowing garments of azure and
cream. Her auburn hair was pulled back from the smooth
oval of her face, and a small diadem of yellow diamonds
glittered on her brow. In her slender hands was his sword,
draped with a cloth of Mahirin silk that shimmered many
colors in the light. Her clear eyes looked stern and peculiar,
as though she were fighting back tears.

Halting in his tracks, Caelan frowned. "You know?"

A smile almost curved her lips, but failed. Her eyes never
left his. "My informants brought me the news this morning.
She is found, praise Gault."

"Located, but not freed," he said grimly, his emotions trying to escape the tight control he held over them. "The Vindicants have her."

Elandra blinked in surprise. "Vindicants! But I was told Warlord Vordachai of Ulinia demands her ransom."

"Officially, yes. But I have a better spy than yours, beloved."

Pink tinged her cheeks. She lifted her chin high with an expression of resignation that her eyes belied. "Then you will not send your generals in your stead. You are going."

Her statement asked him no question. He gave her no answer save a fleeting smile. Tears suddenly sparkled in her eyes, but she blinked them back as she came forward.

"Your sword has been blessed," she said formally. "It is ready for your hand. My prayers for your success and safe return lie upon it."

He lifted the weapon from her grasp, letting the cloth slide off the blade and across the back of his hands. As it did so, he felt the tingle of its magical properties upon his skin. He felt stronger and more capable than before. His mind was clear, filled with all he intended to do. He had never loved Elandra more than at that moment of parting.

"The court believes I am riding out today to inspect a new company of archers just arrived from Cumbria." He hesitated, concerned about telling Elandra details that would only worry her more. "I shall travel to Ulinia as swiftly as possible."

Elandra nodded, her eyes searching his face as though she meant to memorize every angle and line of it. "By Choven means?"

"You must take care," he warned her, dodging her question. "I fear to leave you and Jarel unguarded here with plots so rife—"

"Let your mind be easy about us," she interrupted, pressing her scented fingertips to his lips. He kissed her hand, making her smile. "Keep safe and come home swiftly," she whispered. "That is all I ask."

"Keep safe," he echoed back to her, and kissed her hard before pushing himself away. "I must go."

She murmured something, but he was already striding out, his protector falling into step at his heels as he left her.

Keep her safe, Caelan prayed to Gault. *Let her come to no harm while I am gone.*

Chapter 18

$\mathcal{T}$ he night they were to come for her, Lea could not rest or choke down any food. Although the jailer had given her several blankets, she huddled on her cot in the orange flicker of torchlight and shivered, unable to get warm.

She had never been more afraid.

Although burned, Lord Barthel had survived, and Lea had been left alone. For days she'd done her best to disrupt the Vindicants, singing when they chanted their evil prayers, smiling at the jailer every day so that now he smiled back if they were alone and provided her with decent food and plenty of clean blankets. She called with all her might to the air spirits so that the clouds gathering daily over the camp parted every afternoon and let the sun shine down. Most of the priests fled from sight whenever she was escorted through the camp; none of them would meet her gaze. When her terrible sessions with Lord Barthel resumed, she had to be carried—weak and swooning—back to her cell. Only then did they emerge to hiss curses at her.

She suspected they were planning a battle against her brother. Bits of overheard conversations informed her that

Shadrael had come, but never had she seen him. She was
not sure she wished to. How could she bear to see his cold,
shadow-sworn eyes look at her with indifference? Twice
she'd thought she heard his voice shouting out orders in the
distance, and it had felt as though stakes pierced her heart.

Late this afternoon, she'd heard a spell being woven,
something so dark and dreadful it made her turn icy cold
just to hear it. She could not be sure, but she suspected it
was a blood curse, which meant they had decided to feed
Lord Barthel her blood. Tonight she would die, unless she
used her tiny *gli*-emerald to destroy him first.

To kill . . . to deliberately strike with the intention of
taking life . . . it horrified her. Such a violation of all her
principles, planning an attack in cold blood, and yet what
else could she do? She would not let him make evil use of
her. She dared not give him a greater weapon against Caelan than he already had.

With his black cloak swirling at his heels, Shadrael
strode through the gloomy passageways until he came
face-to-face with Urmaeor.

"I must speak to you," he said to the priest. "At once."

Urmaeor's haggard face looked gaunt and tired in the
fitful torchlight. He was carrying a bowl of blood that
smoked and stank. "I am too busy."

"Is that blood?" Shadrael asked, stepping closer despite
Urmaeor's cautious recoil. The acolytes behind Urmaeor
closed ranks, but Shadrael ignored them. "I smell blood potion," he said. "I heard the blood curse being chanted. I
need—" He broke off, swallowing hard. "I must have something."

"Later," Urmaeor said without compassion. "This is *tal
vei hadri*, most sacred."

"And potent," Shadrael said, staring at the bowl. "Let
me drink of it."

"Are you mad? Such is forbidden to you!"

"Who will know?" Shadrael gestured at the gawking acolytes. "Cloud their minds and let me drink. I perish from craving."

"This is for Lord Barthel," Urmaeor said curtly.

"All of it?"

"All. And it's not finished."

A chill ran up Shadrael's spine. "The girl."

"Yes! Now let me pass."

But Shadrael didn't budge. "The chief priest doesn't need her blood for full transformation. He can—"

"Yes," Urmaeor said as Shadrael broke off in surprise. "You used to be more clever, Shadrael. I thought you would have guessed before now what we're doing."

"I'll lead no force of the dead," Shadrael said sharply.

"You will."

"No."

Urmaeor glared at Shadrael, who didn't back down. "You will follow the orders you are given and obey Lord Barthel without question. How dare you interfere?"

"The girl's magic is Choven based. You cannot mix Choven and Vindicant magic," Shadrael said, trying to make him understand. "You will get the high priest killed."

"Your concern is touching, but I know how to cast this spell. Lord Barthel will rise to lead us, and the army of dead will destroy the usurper."

Shadrael made no effort to mask genuine horror. "And who will command the dead on the battlefield? I—I cannot control such a force," he admitted reluctantly. "Not as I am now."

"All you will do is distract the advance legion with your little cohort. Vordachai's men will harry the soldiers from the flank. Once the usurper is pushed into our trap, Lord Barthel will unleash the dead. The scent of fresh blood will draw them into the fray."

"You risk too much," Shadrael insisted.

"There was a time when you laughed at risk," Urmaeor said with scorn. "What a coward you've become."

"If the dead are not controlled with care they will turn on any living mortal, enemy or ally. I understand that my cohort is bait, but what of Vordachai and his barons? What of their men? They could all be slaughtered if Lord Barthel is not careful."

"Don't presume to tell my master what he should and should not do," Urmaeor said angrily. "You are no praetinor now; your sole responsibility is to lead your men where we direct."

Seeing implacable light burning in the priest's gaze, Shadrael silenced his protests. He realized that nothing would change Urmaeor's mind. All his protests had accomplished was to arouse fresh suspicion against himself.

Desperately Shadrael clutched at the sacred bowl. He heard the contents slosh as Urmaeor wrenched it away from him.

"You fool! Have a care!"

"Must drink," Shadrael murmured, licking his mouth. He let his gaze wander, revealing the hunger that itched and crawled inside him. "Feel weak without—"

"Get back," Urmaeor said without pity. "I offered you a blood potion days ago, and you would not drink it."

"Need it now," Shadrael mumbled.

Urmaeor spoke sharply, and a burst of flame shot up from the ground at Shadrael's feet, driving him back.

Shadrael could hear murmurs in his mind, voices hissing of the danger he was in. He closed them away.

Urmaeor walked through the flames, which did not touch him, and the acolytes nervously followed. Glancing back, the priest said, "Never interfere with me again, Commander."

"But I—I thirst."

"If you crave nourishment, partake of the filthy brew you brought with you."

"Gone."

"Then kill for the blood you need," Urmaeor said, and strode on his way, his assistants at his heels.

Left in the gloomy passageway, Shadrael lingered a moment, battling his feelings. He was certain that Urmaeor's confidence was misplaced. The plan was too risky even had they several powerful *donares* present to govern the dead. Barthel was rushing too fast, taking too many chances.

Sighing, Shadrael shoved the problem away. The blood curse was swirling around in his tired mind, confusing him and awaking hungers he'd thought safely suppressed. Farther in the tunnels a lurker howled, and he wanted to howl with it.

Well, he had given Urmaeor sound advice based on experience. If the Vindicants chose to ignore it, let them reap the consequences.

Feel nothing, Shadrael told himself. *Think nothing. You have nowhere else to go but here. Accept it.*

Swallowing a curse, Thirbe pressed his face against the stone wall in an alcove off the passageway, shutting his eyes and holding his breath as Lord Shadrael trudged past.

The man walked so close that Thirbe almost felt the brush of his cloak; then the commander was gone, swallowed up in the darkness, his footsteps growing faint.

All Thirbe heard for a moment was the drumming rhythm of his heart before he let out his breath soundlessly. Sweat was beading up beneath his leather helmet. He dared make no move for several moments, fearing that someone else might come by at the wrong time.

A hand curled around his forearm, clutching it suddenly, and Thirbe nearly jumped from his skin. His dagger was in his fist before he realized it was only Hultul beside him. Swallowing his heart from his throat, Thirbe lowered his weapon with a shaking hand.

"Gods," Thirbe whispered. "I nearly sent you to Paradise."

"A thousand curses on your filthy person if you do,"

Hultul said. "You take too many chances. We should not be in here. If Lord Shadrael had sensed our presence, he would have cut your miserable threads of life. And mine."

"He's not paying much attention today," Thirbe replied, pulling the stopper from his water skin and helping himself to a sip of tepid water.

Hultul refused the water. "There is a limit to one's luck, and then the gods make fools of us."

Shrugging off such pessimism, Thirbe dug the opal from his pocket. It had lost its iridescent sheen and lay lifeless and pale on his palm. He could barely see it in the gloom, and the sight of it made his guts clutch in a painful knot.

"She's running out of time," he whispered.

"Your plan will not work," Hultul said. "None of your plans work. Because Lord Shadrael knows you—and me—by sight, we cannot join his army as you wished. Now we have ventured deep into this filthy place of blasphemy where demons can eat our hearts, and you no longer have your guide to find her. We must leave before we are found. I do not want to feed the Vindicants *my* blood. Do you?"

"Can't just let them kill her either."

"There is no more help I can give you," Hultul said. "I must return to the warlord, and warn him of what they intend."

"Never reach him in time," Thirbe said fiercely. "His only chance—and the emperor's, too—is for us to thwart these devils."

Hultul lifted his hands, jostling Thirbe's shoulder in the gloom. "May the gods watch over us and guard our unworthy hearts. You ask the impossible."

"I tell you we've got to try!"

"There's nothing we can do."

"I have served you as you forced me," Hultul whispered. "Now I must serve my beloved master. Let me go."

Thirbe gripped his wrist to hold him back. "Wait," he muttered, and pressed the *harnush* into Hultul's hand.

Hultul gasped audibly. "You return this to me?" Without waiting for an answer he slipped the thong over his head and kissed the amulet. "O Gault, I give praise for this kindness which has risen in the unworthy heart of a barbarian—"

"Get going," Thirbe said gruffly, wanting no thanks. "I got a princess to rescue. And don't get caught."

"Farewell," Hultul said.

Thirbe grunted and turned away, only to feel something hard crash into the back of his head. For a moment the gloom of the passage brightened to a white light, and then he knew nothing at all.

𝕿𝖍𝖊 strike of a tinderbox rasped, and a pinprick of flame shot into life, driving back a fraction of the darkness filling Shadrael's quarters. He shut the heavy door grimly behind him and stuck his candle in its holder. The room was cold and draped with dusty cobwebs that reappeared no matter how many times he knocked them down. He could hear the night wind whistling through cracks in the building, and he shivered beneath his cloak.

He felt weary to his bones, yet too restless to sit down. The spells and magic being cast tonight crawled about, putting him on edge. It was time to act, he told himself. The game he played was growing too dangerous, and Lea obviously had little time left.

Without warning, the door creaked open behind him. He turned, and saw Urmaeor standing there. Fearing discovery, grimly Shadrael reached for his sword, but the priest was not there to accuse or attack him. Indeed, he seemed strangely exhausted, and his robes were torn. An angry scratch had risen in a red welt down the side of his face, and little pustules were forming there as though his skin had been blistered. His dark hair was mussed, and his eyes almost crazed.

"Come with me!" he said without preamble. "At once!"

Silently Shadrael obeyed, following the priest through a

maze of passages to the altar room. It was in worse disarray than usual, with boxes overturned and spilling their contents. Torches smoked and blazed in wall sconces. A handful of shaken priests were trying to chant, but Lea's voice was shouting louder.

"We are united by harmony and the three laws!" she said. "We are balanced on the fulcrum of tranquility and—"

Someone clamped a rag over her mouth, muffling the rest. Tied on her back atop the altar, with her wrists and ankles bound with ropes, she struggled and writhed. Some of the ropes were frayed and parting and others were smoking as though on fire. The priest holding the cloth over her mouth suddenly screamed, stumbling back, and flung the blazing cloth away.

Urmaeor rushed forward. "Hold her, you fools! Shadrael, control her *now*."

A rumble shook the chamber. The Vindicants looked up with alarm.

"She's calling the element spirits," Shadrael said quietly.

Urmaeor shot him a wild glare. "Impossible! I have made certain she can't—"

"Have you searched her for *gli*-emeralds?" Shadrael asked.

"Yes, of course. She has none."

"Clearly she does."

"Then remove them. Now!"

With Urmaeor glaring at him, Shadrael approached the altar where Lea was struggling like something gone wild. Her golden hair was tangled and dirty. Her blue eyes stared past him as though she no longer knew him. She was panting hard and fast, like a hare caught in a trap.

"Do something," Urmaeor growled in his ear. "Do something!"

Drawing off his glove, Shadrael gripped her wrist and held it fast. Her struggles stopped abruptly. She blinked, her eyes regaining focus as she stared up at him.

"You," she whispered.

The sight of her dirty, tear-streaked face nearly unmanned him. He watched sadness filling her eyes, sadness
and intense disappointment, and barely checked his feelings. The danger around them had never been greater.

"Is it by your hand I'm to die?" she whispered.

He shifted his gaze away from hers and said nothing.
Although his grip on her wrist never slackened, it was a
strain to resist the *sevaisin* that tried to form between them.

Gasping, Lea uttered a cry and averted her face.

"Excellent. Excellent," Urmaeor murmured over Shadrael's shoulder. "Keep her quiet, whatever you do. Master,
she is ready!"

The squeak of a straining axle filled the sudden quiet.
There came the sound of metal wheels grating upon stone
floor. Priests slowly pushed a flat wooden cart through the
doorway of Lord Barthel's inner chamber. The chief priest,
grotesquely obese, reclined on it while the men labored to
move him. His delicate hands fluttered and gestured eagerly. His fleshy face was actually pink with excitement.
Had it not been for his inhuman eyes, red rimmed and ooz-
ing pus, he would have looked almost healthy.

Shadrael sensed something brushing his senses. Involuntarily he glanced down and met Lea's gaze. She was
pleading silently with him, and it took all his strength to
shift his gaze away. Not even the slightest change of expression crossed his impassive face. From the corner of his
eye he saw her bite her trembling lower lip and shut her
eyes.

She drew a breath, but Shadrael swiftly spoke a word
that silenced her attempt to summon an element spirit. He
felt pain stab through his chest at even this small use of
magic and struggled to ignore it. The *gli*-power within her
was draining his strength rapidly, but he dared not release
her. *Be quiet,* he thought. *Be quiet.*

Beside him, Urmaeor finished mixing something in the
blood bowl and stared at him in approval. "So my cripple

has kept a small amount in reserve," he murmured. "Excellent. I still have a soul for you, Shadrael. I haven't forgotten my promise, no matter what you think."

Shadrael's free fist clenched at his side before he could control himself. Oh, that was a sly piece of trickery, he thought. As silken a promise as the touch of haggai flesh, and none of it true. He clenched his jaw so hard a muscle twitched.

Urmaeor's smile faded. "Have you no thanks? Are you not pleased?"

"Hurry!" Lord Barthel's shrill voice commanded before Shadrael could answer. "Hurry! I am cold."

"Master, this must not be rushed," Urmaeor said patiently. He added a pinch of something that blazed briefly inside the bowl before dying down. The fumes smoking up from the potion made Shadrael feel light-headed, yet he dared not avert his face.

"There!" Urmaeor said in satisfaction. Lifting the bowl before the crudely drawn image of Beloth, he sang loudly:

> *Eternal Chaos, hear our cry!*
> *Send down your howling whirlwinds from on high.*
> *Spin forth your dark despair!*
> *Let Death and Lamentation fill the air*
> *Till Sorrow's bitter cup doth overflow!*
> *Let wraith and ghoul and shyrieas low*
> *Sink human hearts to deepest woe!*
> *Till day is night and night is day*
> *And shadows rise to have their way!*

His words echoed in the chamber, now silent save for the popping hiss of the torches and Lord Barthel's labored breathing. The oppressive presence of shadow filled the room. Lea's face had grown as pale as death. Shadrael could barely feel the flutter of her pulse against his palm. His head felt as though it were on fire, for the voices were stirring in the back of his skull. As the last vestige of his healing *severance* faded, madness reached anew for him. He felt his concentration slipping, wondered what he was trying to do, and grimly struggled to hang on.

Urmaeor placed the smoking bowl of dark red liquid near Lea's throat. "Lift her," he said to Shadrael. He glanced at one of the other priests. "You, cut her *now*."

With reflexes trained for battle, Shadrael slashed Lea's frayed ropes and yanked her away from the priest's ceremonial knife. Clutching her against him as Urmaeor shouted and nearly dropped the bowl, Shadrael shouted the word of command, but failed to open the Hidden Ways.

Urmaeor's angry voice rang out. The Vindicants rushed at Shadrael, but he shielded Lea behind him and defended himself with his sword. Two men fell, bleeding heavily, and the rest retreated.

"You'll regret this stupidity," Urmaeor said. He called out a spell that shot fiery red trails of fire through the air, but Lea raised her hand in front of Shadrael, and a glow of light shielded them both.

Urmaeor went stumbling back, howling in pain, and Shadrael pounced on Lord Barthel, who was waving his arms ineffectually and screaming the beginnings of a spell.

The edge of Shadrael's blade at his throat silenced him. All the Vindicants froze, and there was only the sound of Lord Barthel's wheezing breath. Urmaeor scrambled to his feet, his eyes murderous, but Shadrael stared him down.

"Don't," he said in warning.

"Desist!" Urmaeor said. "Do you realize what you're doing? You cannot save her."

Deliberately Shadrael looked at Lea, seeing joy and relief shining brightly in her eyes. He frowned. "We've got to run," he said softly to her. "Take the right passage at the fork and hurry. I'll catch up."

She clutched him. "No! They will trick you if you stay."

Shaking his head, he pressed his sword a bit harder against Lord Barthel's fat throat, and the chief priest yelped. Urmaeor raised his hands, but Shadrael gave him such a look of menace that the priest did not strike.

"Shadrael, my friend," he said instead, his voice soothing, reassuring. "You are confused. It's shadow you serve, not this witch of light. Lord Barthel is the receptacle of Beloth's legacy. We implore you to resist her wiles and harm not our master."

"Hurry!" Shadrael murmured to Lea. "Don't argue. You're the only one that can stop the war and save Light Bringer from the trap. Warn him, Lea. Go!"

As he spoke, he drew her necklace of *gli*-emeralds from his pocket. They were blazing with green fire. With a shriek Lord Barthel cowered away from the light they cast, and even Urmaeor shielded his eyes.

Shadrael crammed the jewels into Lea's hand. "In Gault's name, go! Don't make this in vain."

She shot him a look he did not understand and hurried into the passageway. Her emeralds lit her path, and when Urmaeor made a move to pursue her, Shadrael nicked Lord Barthel's throat.

The chief priest yelled, babbling curses that were no more dangerous than tiny sparkles of light showering down on everyone.

Shadrael summoned the last dregs of magic he possessed, determined this time not to fail, and opened the Hidden Ways in front of Lea.

A rumble shook the chamber, sending priests scrambling in all directions, and he heard her cry out briefly. A gush of fetid air like an opened grave flowed into Shadrael's face, even as he raised his fist and pulled a veil of darkness over the priests.

Then he plunged his sword deep into the mountainous body of the chief priest, and fled. Screaming, Barthel shuddered and convulsed. Black blood bubbled from his mouth,

staining the tiny tentacles thrashing at his lips. Then a dark
mist hissed forth from his body. Where it touched Shadrael, he felt as though his skin had been frozen. Shuddering, he seized one of the torches and plunged it into the
mist.

There was a scream, and ashes rained down.

Shouts and confusion spread through the Vindicants.
Shadrael fought his way through them, driving them back
from him, while Urmaeor rushed to Barthel's side.

Ahead, Shadrael could see Lea waiting for him, just inside the Hidden Ways, her emeralds blazing green light in
her hands.

"Come!" she called. "Hurry!"

Her stubborn disobedience angered him. He ran for the
passage, feeling something give way inside his chest. A
fiery burst of pain told him it was over. Even so, with her
voice calling to him, he kept running, struggling to make it.
For a moment, he almost believed he could . . .

And then Urmaeor's deep voice rose over everyone's.
His curse struck Shadrael down from behind, knocking
him off his feet with such impact he skidded on his shoulder. He couldn't speak, couldn't command his body except
to fling out his hand toward Lea.

Realizing in a sort of haze that she was standing on the
very threshold he'd opened, keeping it from closing, he tried
to urge her to go on. He was furious that she was throwing
away the one chance he'd sacrificed everything for.

She darted to him, gripping his hand and dragging him
bodily through the opening. Half-conscious, disoriented,
nearly blind with pain, he felt something bumping him
from beneath the surface of the ground and did not understand until the earth spirit flung him off and he went tumbling into the dank refuge of *between*.

Lea knelt beside him, gripping his arms. "Quickly.
What is the command that will close the passage?"

He murmured it, and through a haze saw her hold up the

glowing emeralds and shout the command as though she'd been born to the use of shadow magic.

There came a fearful explosion of light and magic. It seemed to pick him up and fling him down. And then there was only darkness.

Chapter 19

Crouched beside an unconscious Shadrael, Lea tried to shake him awake. It was very dark here, save for the eerie green glow of her emeralds. Fastening them around her throat, she redoubled her efforts to rouse Shadrael.

A rumbling sound sent her to her feet. She stared, her fists clenched, her heart thudding wildly, unable to tell if the opening was going to reform and admit the Vindicants.

She heard the faint sound of voices and scratching, as though claws tore at rock. Swallowing hard, she sank down in a heap at Shadrael's side, not daring to make a sound.

They were searching for her, she knew. The mysterious passages of *between* were infinite, yet Lea feared the priests could sense her presence and find her. At the moment they seemed very close. The spell barrier created by Shadrael in his last moments of consciousness was much too thin.

Then she saw a cloud, like black fog, pouring into the passageway. It flowed over her head, and along the ground. Afraid, Lea squeezed Shadrael's hand, her heart racing as fast as her thoughts, while magic seethed and searched around her. Not until she realized that the black fingers of shadow were curling back from the light emitted by her emeralds did she understand why discovery had not come immediately.

Eventually the voices went away. The shadow flowed into the darkness and vanished, and in relief Lea buried her face in her hands.

But only for a moment. She dared not waste their temporary respite.

"Shadrael," she whispered urgently, shaking his shoulder. "Please wake up. Shadrael!"

He stirred, moaning. Anxiously Lea pressed her fingers to his lips to silence him. After a moment his eyes dragged open. He stared at her awhile before his brows knotted.

"Told you to run while you could," he murmured. His voice was very weak. "Warn the—"

"Hush," she whispered. "I think they've gone away for the moment. Open the barrier and let us return to the physical world."

His nose was bleeding, and more blood trickled from the corner of his mouth. Lea anxiously searched for a wound, but did not find one.

"Where are you hurt?" she asked. "Can you sit up? Can you—"

"Listen," he broke in, his voice a mere thread.

Lea heard the muted sound of voices coming back. Fear stabbed through her. "They're still searching. We can't stay here."

"The barrier is too weak," he murmured. "I'll . . . hold them. Now go. Get to your brother."

"How?" she cried.

"There are markers to guide you—"

"I don't care," she said impatiently. "I'm not leaving you."

He frowned. "Must. My blood will confuse the demons. They can't track you as well if I stay behind."

Lea heard the scratching sound again. The air seemed

suddenly hot and oppressive, making it hard to breathe. The black shadow came back, tendrils of it flowing here and there on a blind hunt for them.

Shrinking away from it, Lea took Shadrael's arm and urged him up, hushing him desperately when he would have protested.

He leaned on her, his weight staggering her, his feet clumsy and slow.

Freeing her hand to grip the largest central emerald in her necklace, Lea aimed its light into the passage ahead. Patiently, urgently, she kept coaxing Shadrael along.

Time lost all meaning. They crept forward, eventually leaving the shadows behind. Now and then the light of her emeralds reflected in the eyes of creatures that watched them from the darkness, but nothing attacked them. Although the power in her necklace had restored much of Lea's strength, she grew very tired. Yet as long as Shadrael, stumbling and obviously in pain, could keep going, she refused to rest.

And then the passage ended. She stopped, not comprehending at first that she'd reached a dead end. Putting out her hand, she touched neither dirt nor rock, yet a barrier closed their path. She lifted her *gli*-emeralds higher, hoping to see something, but even the light shining from her necklace was growing dim.

Alarmed, she asked, "What's happening?"

"He's found our Way," Shadrael said hoarsely, dragging in an audible breath. "He's trapped us."

"Can you open the barrier and let us out?"

Shadrael closed his eyes and extended his hand, only to tremble and sink to his knees with a groan. Lea went down with him, trying to break his fall. The sound of his ragged breathing frightened her.

He lifted his gaze to hers briefly. "Sorry," he whispered. "Tried . . ."

"Tell me the command. I shall open it as I—"

"No," he gasped out. "Not the same."

"But—"

Moaning, he sank onto his side, his face drawn and pale, and closed his eyes.

She shook him once, then harder. "Shadrael. Shadrael!"

The only sounds she heard were the eager scrabble of claws over rock and snuffling breaths.

Whirling around, Lea saw innumerable red eyes, small and evil, glowing at her.

𝕬 wheeled litter, its curtains closed, rolled along the sleeping streets of New Imperia. An escort of armed men went with it, quiet and watchful, alert for danger. Like many chariots and litters of the patrici abroad at night, its coat of arms had been covered to discourage thieves. On the opposite side of the city, several villas were alight with parties, but here in the temple quarter all lay quiet and dark.

The litter halted at the steps of the Penestrican temple, and the armed men swiftly dismounted. One of them glanced all around before scratching at the leather curtain.

"If you are ready to descend, Majesty," he murmured.

Elandra, wearing a cloak and hood of magically woven Mahiran cloth to disguise her appearance, climbed down with her protector's assistance. When her attendant, also disguised, would have followed her, Elandra bade the woman remain behind. She climbed the broad stone steps with only her Guards in her wake.

A Penestrican sister, robed in black, her head and arms bare, waited at the entrance beneath the portico. She was holding a fat white candle in her hand, its light casting but dim illumination on this moonless night. Although she bowed her head respectfully to Elandra, she glared sternly at the men.

"No male may pass this threshold," she said.

They bridled at that, although they knew the strict canon of the sisterhood. Elandra's protector, uneasy with the whole business, pulled forward a slender, elderly man.

Elandra smiled at the sister. "May I and my eunuch Rumasin enter?"

Frowning, the priestess moved aside. "The Magria has granted permission for this exception. Enter, and welcome."

Still wearing the faint public smile she'd perfected, Elandra respectfully touched the octagonal-shaped *bridjeti*, emblem of protection to women, and walked through the open door of the temple. Rumasin followed her silently, touching nothing, his head slightly bowed as was correct.

The vestibule inside was lit by more candles, casting a soft golden haze against the shadows of the oval room. Floor tiles depicted a vivid mosaic of entwined serpents, and more serpents—symbol of the sisterhood—had been carved in relief on the stone lintels and wall moldings.

Their escort put down her candle, and said, "Your cloaks are not necessary here."

Glancing over her shoulder, Elandra saw a shimmering blue haze of magic barring the doorway leading outside, where the Imperial Guards waited. She gave a nod, and Rumasin took her outer garments, folding them and his own neatly over one arm before the escort could take them.

The sister stared at him. "As you prefer. Come."

The temple itself was newly completed, an edifice that was rather a triumph for the sisterhood so long persecuted under Kostimon's reign. Elandra was not herself a devotee of the Penestrican order, but they were invaluable allies that she took care to cultivate and respect.

Tonight, she had many favors to ask.

It was very hot within the actual temple. Elandra had worn her lightest summer gown, but within moments she found herself uncomfortably warm. The sand pit was deep and enormous, filling almost the entire sanctuary. At the far end, narrow stone steps rose to the Chair of Visions, its pale marble already stained with blood.

Averting her gaze, Elandra followed her guide through a passageway and into the service area of the temple. Although she could hear voices coming from somewhere and sounds of activity, she crossed paths with no one. They went down steps into what felt like a dungeon. Narrow cells, one after the other, empty of contents save for the most utilitarian bed and single folded blanket, each door standing open at precisely the same angle . . . quarters for the sisters.

Elandra remembered the terrible days before her marriage to Kostimon and her elevation to the highest lady in the land, when she'd lived in such a cell, temporarily blind and very afraid, tested in numerous ways. For all their wisdom, for all the good they accomplished, the Penestricans were harsh, sometimes merciless, and cruel. She shivered.

"Your cloak, Majesty?" Rumasin murmured.

Quickly she shook her head.

Their guide halted at the end of the dreary passage and gave Elandra an impassive look. "The Magria has asked me to say that this meeting will do neither of you good. It is her suggestion that you do not proceed."

Rumasin stiffened, but Elandra checked him with a gesture. "I acknowledge the Magria's concern, but I wish to see my sister. Please allow me to do so."

As the priestess unlocked the door, Rumasin bowed to Elandra. "Majesty, is this safe? Are you protected sufficiently? The last time—"

"She has no powers of her own," the Penestrican said sharply. "All the tricks given to her by the Maelites have been removed."

Something in the way she spoke made Elandra frown. "I am ready."

The priestess swept her hand over the door, removing the spell lock. "There is no danger," she said. "The spell keeps her calm, nothing more."

As she spoke she pushed open the stout door, her ring of keys rattling at her belt. "Bixia," she said, speaking loudly and deliberately, "your guest is here. Sit up and remember your manners."

Elandra entered the cell. It was brightly lit by candles high above them out of reach. Bixia, stark naked and fatter than before, her face smeared with dried food stains, her eyes dull, sat on her bed. Her blond hair, once so thick and bright, clung lank and uncombed to her skull.

For an instant Elandra was outraged at her condition, but then she noticed the robe lying torn on the floor and the food dishes smashed on the wall, and she calmed down. When they were growing up, her half sister's tantrums were legendary. It seemed the sisterhood had not yet taught Bixia to control her temper.

Elandra looked at the priestess. "May we be alone?"

"I'm afraid not."

Displeased, Elandra stepped closer to the bed. "Bixia? I've come to see you, to talk to you about what lies between us. Do you know me?"

Bixia stretched without any modesty and began sucking on the brittle ends of her hair. When Elandra reached out to pull the hair from her mouth, Bixia snapped at her like a dog, small white teeth just missing their mark.

Startled, Elandra jerked back and shot a glare at the priestess. "You said she's not dangerous."

"There is no danger of magic attacking you," the Penestrican replied.

Bixia laughed.

Annoyed, Elandra regained her composure and turned her attention back to her half sister. "Bixia—"

"Go away!" Bixia's face contorted with sudden temper. "I hate you! I hate you! You put me here! You gave me to them! I was supposed to be empress, not you! Never you! Bastard! Bastard! *Bastard!*"

Her screaming grew shrill as more vituperation and curses spilled from her mouth. Elandra retreated from the cell, and the priestess shut the door firmly. Locking it, she murmured a soft incantation that sent prickles through Elandra's skin, and gradually the insults stopped. Bixia began to giggle instead.

The sound of that insane mirth was more horrifying to Elandra than the profanity. "Has she gone mad?"

The priestess nodded. "I will take you to the Magria now."

"**What**," Elandra asked when she was ushered into the Magria's presence, greeted courteously, and served refreshment she felt too shaken to consume, "can be done for her?"

"Very little." A young woman, coldly beautiful with blue eyes and a long curtain of straight blond hair falling down her back, Anas seated herself opposite to Elandra and gathered from a basket a tiny serpent as slender as her finger. Holding the reptile in one hand, she stroked its head while she regarded the empress in her cool way. "She was always unstable. Our work with her is unlikely to help her condition."

Elandra frowned. She suspected the Magria was keeping something from her. "The emperor said you intend to punish her."

Anas lowered her hand and the little snake slithered up her sleeve and vanished. "She still believes it is her destiny to be empress. The fact that she is here with us rather than in the palace is a considerable torment to her."

"I think there's more to it than that."

"The Maelites have controlled her since childhood," Anas said with a shrug. "Our removal of that control has rendered her simple. She remembers her hatred of you, but little else. Now that you've come, against my recommendation, you find yourself filled with pity for her. You wish to do her some kindness. What good will it achieve, Majesty? We feed her and house her. We keep her safe. If we release her, the Maelites will acquire her once more."

"Surely they would not now use her to harm me—or my child," Elandra said. "That approach has failed."

"You remain vulnerable as long as you pity her."

"What else should I feel?" Elandra retorted. "Should I despise her? Desire her death? She's my sister."

"The blood tie means nothing to her. She's been conditioned to hate you, and she will always hate you. In that sense, she's as a dog trained to attack."

"But—"

"You wish there to be some bond, some vestige of affection between you. Desire for family is strong within you, but let it center on the family you and the emperor have created." Anas gestured. "Especially the new life you carry now."

Elandra drew a sharp breath of surprise. "I was not yet sure."

"Be sure, Majesty. You will bear another child." Anas almost smiled, and for a moment she seemed softer, and feminine. "Take joy in that, and let Bixia go."

Elandra wanted to go on protesting, pleading for the Magria to find some way to restore Bixia into a person who could at least be content somewhere. "Will you keep trying?" she asked.

"Of course." The smile on Anas's face faded. "We are not finished with Bixia. As for your other request tonight, I must refuse it."

"I haven't asked it yet."

"But you want news of Lady Lea, do you not?"

"Yes, oh yes! Can you cast another vision? Caelan said that before you could not see where she was, but at least—"

"When you requested this meeting, I knew you would want it done," the Magria said, sounding a little weary. She pulled the snake from her hair and let it wrap itself around her wrist. Her gaze remained on the reptile, and her uncharacteristic hesitation made Elandra lean forward.

"You've discovered something," she said sharply. "What is it? Magria, good or bad, what is it?"

"Nothing." Anas raised her blue eyes to Elandra's startled ones. "Nothing," she repeated. "Three times did I try."

Elandra frowned, feeling a chill sliding down her spine. "Please. I don't understand."

"There is nothing to tell, nothing to see. I cannot find her at all. There is only darkness. The darkness of shadow."

Within the Hidden Ways, the demons rushed at Lea in a snarling pack, only to flinch away from the green light shining around her. She held her necklace with both hands, trying to stay calm and center her *quai*, knowing that if she panicked she would likely be torn to pieces.

With all her strength she called to the higher spirits of the Choven, the *chi'miquai*, for help. There came a slight tremor in the ground as earth spirits came to her. Dust and bits of rock rained down on her from above; then the barrier blocking her path opened and she saw a cavern ahead of her.

It was lit by some means she could not discern, a tranquil pale illumination that reassured her. When she'd been a child, the earth spirits had guided her into such a cavern concealed among the ice caves and shown her marvelous wonders. In her adolescence, she had discovered sacred forest groves as well, and had been taught that the *chi'miquai* also had places in lakes and the sea. Unlike the element spirits, the *chi'miquai* were all-encompassing, everywhere and nowhere, seen and not seen. They often took the form of a Choven and would walk for a time in the world. That was one reason why all the People were so courteous to each other. One never knew when a *chi'miquain* would be inhabiting one of the People.

Although it looked just a few steps away, Lea knew the cavern of sanctuary was probably far from here, in another level of *between* than where Shadrael had brought them. Distance and time were not measured the same in the world of spirits as elsewhere. It did not matter. Here was their means of escape. Her fear fell away, and her *quai* steadied.

A figure appeared in the opening, shimmering and ethereal, hued in many striations of color like a rainbow. Hissing and whimpering, the demons retreated from Lea into the shadows.

The fragrance of flowers reached Lea's nostrils, and she sensed only warmth and kindness ahead. It drew her as a bee to a flower. She had missed the special dwellings of the *chi'miquai*, where she'd been so happy as a little girl. How she'd yearned to return to them.

Containing her feelings, she made the gesture of courtesy. "Thank you for hearing my plea."

"You are always welcome among us," the spirit said into her mind. It beckoned to her. *"Come and dwell with us again."*

It was the invitation she'd been waiting for. Lea sprang to her feet gladly and bent down, patting the cold soil to direct an earth spirit to bring Shadrael.

"No," the *chi'miquain* said. *"He cannot enter our sanctuary. He has killed one of the People, those special to us. He has walked willingly among shadow and darkness. This is his place. Not among us."*

A pang went through her, and she was filled with confusion. "He came back for me," she said. "He saved my life."

"He cannot save you here. Come away, for you do not belong among the darkness."

Hissing and snarling came from the demons. Lea looked worriedly in their direction. "I can't leave him behind. Not after what he's done for me."

"He knows his purpose. He is to feed the darkness that comes."

"No!" Lea cried in distress. "There must be some way to save him."

"He cannot enter our sanctuary. We invite you to live among us, as you did before. It is our way to walk among the People. And so did we let you return to walk among your kind. But now you must choose. Your stones have told you that the time of transformation is on you. If you are to

join us completely and dwell forever in quaiteth *among us, then you must come now."*

Tears filled her eyes. The element spirits had saved her life when she was eight. They had taken her to the *chi'mi-quai,* and she'd been so happy and content there. True harmony, true peace, tranquility . . . all balanced perfectly. It was an idyllic existence, a safe one. It had not prepared her for the shocks of life among the Imperial Court. When her *gli*-emeralds began to alter shape, signaling her time of transformation, she had been elated and relieved, sorry to leave Caelan, Elandra, and little Jarel, but desperate to return to a life of true harmony. When she set out on her journey to Trau, she'd intended to escape into the wilderness and accept her completion, transforming into *pi'chiquai* and ascending to the first level of becoming fully *chi'mi-quai.* She'd never expected to be abducted by Shadrael, or to fall in love with him. She'd grown and changed on this journey, but it had taken her away from *pi'chiquai,* not toward it.

Sorrow rose in her heart. "Can I not have sanctuary with you for a short time? As before?"

"Not in your time of transformation. Few of your kind are worthy to dwell among us. We welcome you. Come."

"I can't go with you if it means leaving him to perish."

"He has chosen his path of sorrow and lack. His name is woe, and there is only emptiness inside him. Decide, for I will not hold back much longer the darkness that comes."

Torn, Lea fingered her necklace. "Will my *gli*-emeralds protect him if I leave them behind?"

"No. They are yours alone. They will serve no other."

Lea shook her head, unable to believe this was the only choice available to her. That she should finally reach all that she'd ever wanted, but at such a price. What harmony, what tranquility could she find if it meant abandoning the man she loved?

"Lea," Shadrael whispered.

Startled, she saw that he was awake, his eyes dark and

liquid in the gloom. She knelt beside him, taking his hand.
A shiver passed through him.

"Lea . . ."

"Yes?"

"Get out of here. I can't see what you're talking to.
Can't see the path, but take it."

Her fingers tightened involuntarily on his. "Shadrael—"

"I'm dying. You still have a chance. Take it."

She heard his words, as aloof and proud as ever. But his
eyes held fear, and the emotion trembling in his hand was
vulnerability. Gently she stroked his brow. "Hush. We can
find another way out, for both of us."

"No. You must go. I belong . . . here. I'm finished."

"I don't believe that."

His fingers squeezed hers weakly. "Thank you," he whispered, his voice fading. "Thank you for being . . . kind."

His eyes closed, and Lea found herself weeping. She
did not want it to end like this for Shadrael, for him to sink
into damnation, believing himself without a soul. She
knew better, knew that his soul remained—damaged, broken, so coated in darkness he could not find it—knew that
given time, he might be able to mend it once more. But to
abandon him, to leave him here to die alone in the darkness, believing himself lost . . . she could not do something
so cruel.

"The moment closes," the spirit said to her mind. *"Come
now."*

Dashing her tears away with the back of her hand, pearls
scattering in all directions, she turned to face the shimmering form. "I can't do this!" she cried out. "I love him. I cannot leave him."

A rumble shook the ground. *"Then there will be no
completion. So does your future change. As you foresaw."*
Abruptly the *chi'miquain* vanished, and the opening of escape closed.

As soon as it was gone, the demons sprang at her. She

cried out, kicking them away, throwing pearls at them, shining the light of her necklace on as many as she could. The filthy, deformed creatures snarled and twisted in retreat, snapping at each other in their flight.

Again there was a moment of quiet, but she noticed some of them trying to slink around behind her. She knew they would rush her and Shadrael again and again. And eventually her strength and vigilance would falter, and the demons would prevail. Even worse, in the distance, she could hear footsteps, far away as yet, but coming.

Calm clarity came to Lea. Since she and Shadrael were to die together, she thought, there was only one thing left for her to do.

Bending down to Shadrael, she took his callused hand in hers, holding tightly when he flinched. Deliberately she opened *sevaisin* between them, gasping as his pain flowed into her. Putting her lips to his, she sent her breath into him, sharing her strength and vitality, joining her light to his shadow, absorbing all that was bleak and broken inside him to give him freely what Lord Barthel had tried to rob from her. She did not know if this gift could reach the vestige of what had once been his soul, or even help it, but all she had, she gave.

The green light illuminating the passage faded as her *gli*-emeralds went dark and lifeless. Gasping and dizzy, Lea felt a terrible, creeping sensation of shadow spreading through her. Around her were only the darkness and the cold. She was so terribly tired. She shuddered, frightened at being cut off from the *gli* power of her emeralds, which she'd depended on nearly all her life. She was frightened at losing her *quai*, frightened at dying like this.

Heed not the terror of shadow, she told herself. *Put away the fear you have received from Shadrael and believe instead in the glory of light.*

Weakly she rested her head on Shadrael's chest, waiting for what was to come.

And in the dark silence, as the demons snuffled closer, hissing and growling, closing in on Lea and Shadrael from all sides, she thought she heard Shadrael whisper her name.

Then there was nothing.

Chapter 20

The inhabitants of Kanidalon were awakened at dawn by the town watchmen sounding the alarm. People rushed from their abodes or leaned out windows, only to point and marvel. Ever since the arrival of the Second Legion two days ago and the Tenth the day before that, the town had been humming with fear and apprehension, unsure of what might befall it next. Rumors were rife, saying that the warlord had proclaimed Ulinia to be in open revolt, that the emperor was coming to lay waste to the province, that its people would be rounded up and sold into slavery. The arrival of two legions in addition to the Ninth already stationed here only seemed to confirm such speculations. As for Lord Vordachai, he was said to be barricaded high in the Jawnuth Mountains in his citadel, refusing to come down from its safety to plead for his people.

Now more invaders seemed to be coming. Trumpets sounded from the city walls as the pale gray sky of early morning filled with ominous shapes.

Dragons.

* * *

Roused from his bunk by his aide's rough shaking, Commander Pendek rolled onto his feet with a sour grunt and found himself moving to pull on clothing and pick up his weapons before he was fully awake. The blare of trumpets and the running tramp of feet told him the whole camp was roused.

Blinking, he knuckled sleep from his eyes and glared at his aide, half-seen in the early light. "Is it attack?"

"I don't know, sir," the aide said briskly. "Alarm has sounded. Dragons are flying in."

Scowling, Pendek tossed down his sword. "Is *that* all? You know better than to panic over a courier."

"We've counted a hundred of them, sir."

"Are they attacking?"

"They're flying in the Imperial formation."

Astonishment rooted Pendek in place before he rushed to his window and flung it open. It seemed at first to be a dream. The sky glowing pale above the horizon, the moon sinking, a veil of thin cloud glowing in hues of red and gold from the rising sun. And against this backdrop, the dragons, their enormous wings silhouetted against the sky, were approaching in a single V, perfectly aligned, instead of their usual flying clusters.

Excitement rushed through Pendek. Then fear. He felt the sensation of balancing on a teetering surface, with nothing to grab. It could be a trick, a vile trick of the wily Viermar's. Perhaps the old scoundrel had joined the revolt and was bringing his dragon lords to an alliance with Lord Vordachai. Perhaps raiders meant to attack the town. Kanidalon would stand little chance against fire raining from the sky. Or were the dragons flying in as escort for the emperor's chariot? And if so, how far distant was His Imperial Majesty? And why hadn't couriers ridden from the checkpoints to warn of His Excellency's approach?

Pendek felt dizzy from so much rapid speculation.

Meeting the emperor would be the crowning achievement of his career, his very life.

It could also prove disastrous. He must take care that no one blamed him for Vordachai's revolt.

Outside his window, a decivate still struggling to buckle on his armor paused to throw Pendek a salute. "Compliments of the watch officer, sir!" he shouted. "The emperor is coming."

"Which road? Get the men ready to provide an escort into the town."

The officer gaped at him. "From the sky, sir. Have you any messages for your cohort leaders?"

Pendek mumbled something and withdrew his head, his thoughts swirling with thoughts of how to present his report. This was all like a dream. It seemed impossible. And yet . . . he suddenly roared for his bafboy, a wizened man who'd served him for years.

"Sir?"

"Get out my best armor, my new cloak. I must shave! And set my office in order. Great Gault, the emperor!"

Caelan Light Bringer had sworn years ago never to trust or befriend a Thyrazene. Since the horrible day when dragon raiders had burned his boyhood home E'nonhold and killed or sold into slavery almost everyone he held dear, he'd harbored a cold knot of resentment that had hardened with every day he spent chained to a galley oar, with every night he ached from surviving another fight in the gladiator games. Since he'd taken the throne, his dealings with the Viermar, supreme chieftain of all the dragon lords, had been cool at best, and his curtailment of much of their smuggling revenue had set them against him in return.

However, with Lea's safety at stake and the need to move swiftly paramount, Caelan had put aside his animosity and gone to the Viermar for help. He'd done so in secret, telling no one—not his advisers, not even Elandra—what he planned. It had been a gamble, for with Thyraze threatening revolt, he was placing himself in their hands.

But the Viermar, after much shrewd haggling for concessions, had seemed delighted with the honor conferred on him. No emperor had ever ridden a dragon. Kostimon had permitted them, in the eight hundredth year of his reign, to fly above his chariot in escort once. Never again.

This was a great day for the dragon lords, and they had shouted acclaim for Caelan as he swallowed both trepidation and unpleasant memories to climb atop one of the huge, scaly beasts.

Now, having flown through the night and nearly frozen in the cold air, his numbed hands gripping the harness as the powerful wings beat with smooth strokes, Caelan had found a measure of exhilaration in flying so high above the ground, in covering distance so quickly. Had he not been worried about Lea, he might almost have enjoyed himself.

As it was, he had no inclination to marvel at the mountains and desert in this province that had caused him trouble since the beginning of his reign. Most of the land seemed to be barren dirt or sheer precipice. Moments ago, he'd flown over a mountain peak, the clouds curling about his shoulders, and come down through a heart-stopping gorge into a land that seemed to grow almost nothing. There were few fields, rare pastures. He wondered what the people lived on and how they fed themselves. Yet no amount of poverty excused what they'd done to his most beloved sister.

The notorious market town of Kanidalon sprawled below him. He saw the rambling clusters of mud buildings nestled at the base of more mountains. To the south stretched the army outpost, and annexed to it were campaign tents pitched in orderly rows. He assessed them quickly with a nod to himself. Three legions at hand already, with cavalry and another two legions on their way. Lord Vordachai, he thought grimly, was about to learn a hard lesson about the price of treason.

Behind him, the rider whistled shrilly in the code the

dragon riders used among themselves. The formation tightened as they came down over the town, where people were running in all directions like insects. The dragon beneath Caelan was slowing, shifting its wings and grunting as it suddenly lowered its horned head and angled downward.

Caelan, aware that he could go sailing right off over the beast's neck if he did not take care, tightened his grip on the harness and swallowed the sudden dryness in his mouth. A prior landing to let the dragons rest had not been so steep.

Below, he could hear trumpets and saw the soldiers hastening to assembly.

He reminded himself that he'd wanted the element of surprise. He wanted to move on Vordachai and crush the flames of revolt before they could blaze into other provinces. Above all, he wanted Lea out of here and safely home. His sister was a delicate, unusual creature, a delight to everyone of course, but also fragile in certain ways, her spirit unable to cope with violence and unkindness. That anyone had dared abuse her, that anyone had dared frighten her or cause her one moment's misery sent fresh rage surging through him.

This stunt, this vast risk, was worth it, he thought grimly, if it meant freeing her from the terror and distress she must be going through.

The rider tapped his shoulder, and Caelan dared release one hand from its death grip on the harness to point at the parade ground outside the post. He had no intention of entering Kanidalon's walls until the province and its unruly warlord were subdued.

The rider whistled again in a series of shrill sounds. Moments later, the dragons flying behind Caelan's peeled away, bugling a sound that had once figured in his nightmares. Now he flew down alone, while the rest of his escort circled and wheeled in the sky.

Rising sunlight gilded him, glinting off his golden breastplate and armor, shining on his crown. He rode a bronze-hued dragon, the largest of their kind. It landed with amazing lightness, hardly jarring him at all. The dragon raised its

horned head and bugled, then folded its wings and knelt for
Caelan to dismount.

Officers were hurrying forth to greet him. Caelan took a
moment to draw his breath and give thanks he had landed
safely. He hoped his numbed feet would support him when
he climbed off.

"My thanks to you, rider," he said to the man at his back.

"You have granted us great honor," the Thyrazene
replied. "My dragon and I thank you." His restless beast
snorted a belch or two of fire, sending the officers scurrying
back in some alarm. The rider swiftly curbed his brute, and
the dragon lowered its horned head with a rumble that shook
its entire frame. "It's safe to get down now, Excellency."

Caelan jumped stiffly to the ground and strode forth to
meet the goggle-eyed officers as though he made this sort
of entrance every day. His gray eyes, so pale and intimidat-
ing, swept across their faces. Ignoring their salutes and
eager smiles, he kept his own expression grim as his gaze
focused on the legion commander wearing the emblem of
the Ninth.

"Commander Pendek," he said without preamble.

His disregard of the courtesies they so obviously
wanted to give him gave them pause. Pendek, a tall fellow
with the shoulders of an ox and Chanvezi eyes, looked both
apprehensive and awestruck. His spanking breastplate and
cloak were clearly new, showing a marked contrast to the
battle-scarred, although well-polished, gear of the other legion commanders.

A clerk, Caelan thought. Risen to his present rank by
possible favoritism and family influence, but certainly not
a field officer. Caelan wondered who had posted this man
to Ulinia in the first place.

Stepping forward, Pendek saluted officiously. "Excellency, it is my pleasure to welcome you to the—"

"Thank you," Caelan said, cutting off his speech. "See
that these dragons and men are given rations and anything
else they need." His gaze swept to the other two command-

ers, and he accorded them nothing more than a slight nod before turning back to Pendek. "Where is your office?"

"Allow me to show you, Excellency."

Hurriedly Pendek fell into step with Caelan, awkwardly positioning himself to one side so as not to interfere with Caelan's protector, now on the ground and coming up grimly to take his position at the emperor's heels. The other commanders followed, along with their aides, as centruins bawled orders and the long line of soldiers saluted and shouted acclaim for the emperor.

Behind him, the dragon riders whooped and shrieked, making their beasts rear up and flap formidable wings, bugling as loudly as the trumpets.

A trifle disconcerted by the ruckus, Caelan kept going.

"You can see that we have made improvements to the post's original design," Pendek said, chattering and pointing as they crossed the base to his modest little office. "When I came there were no—"

A decivate opened the door smartly just ahead of Caelan, who strode inside, taking in the modest space with a single glance. Someone had had enough wit to get a fire going, and the room was warm.

Stripping off his gloves, Caelan stretched his cold hands gratefully to the fire for a moment before swinging around to face the others.

"We have a rebellion to crush," he said quietly. "Let us get down to business."

Thirbe wasn't sure which was worse—being trussed on a donkey like chattel under delivery to its new owner, or having a skull that throbbed and threatened to split in twain while riding trussed on a donkey like chattel. He was thirsty. He was angry. He was insulted. Most of all, he was embarrassed.

Caught like a flat-footed noddy too gut-swabbed to know better than to turn his back on a devious sprat like Hultul. He must be getting old.

Aye, old and a fool who had failed the sweet lady entrusted to his charge. The frustration of having been so close to her, close enough to almost put his hand on her and get her out of those foul blood drinkers' clutches, was enough to choke him.

Thanks to Hultul, as devious a swinegullet as a Vindicant, Lea remained behind—still a prisoner of the foulest, most vile scoundrels imaginable. It was like a sick kind of joke, only Thirbe couldn't laugh. Nothing he said made any impression on Hultul, and he heartily wished the Ulinian had simply killed him rather than keep him alive.

Glancing over his shoulder, Hultul broke off the little song he was singing and asked, "Ready for your turn with the water skin, my friend? There will be nothing else to break your fast today, for we must reach Muhadim by nightfall."

Barely lifting his pounding head, Thirbe went on glaring between his donkey's long shaggy ears at the precise place in Hultul's spine where he wanted to ram a dagger. "Keep your damned water," he growled. "I hope you end up swinging from a gibbet, with crows pecking out your eyes."

"And you, my friend!" Hultul called back merrily. "May you end up chained to a rock with ten thousand vultures stripping the flesh from your bones while worms swim in your diseased bowels and four virgins whom you will never bed cry out their joy at your demise."

Thirbe blinked. It wasn't enough that he'd been knocked cold, abducted, tied up without a saddle on a donkey with a backbone like a comb, but now he couldn't even deliver an insult without being bested. Biting back a reply, Thirbe sulked instead.

"It is no good refusing to accept what is," Hultul said to him. "I was your prisoner, and now you are mine."

"We were working together, you scab of a leper," Thirbe said.

"Only because you forced me into that terrible place. You were not good to me, my friend. Yet I have saved your miserable life before you got us both killed."

"I let you go," Thirbe said furiously. "I gave you back your amulet."

Hultul gave him a mocking salute by touching fingers to lips and forehead. "And I thank you for your generosity. But you should not have taken it in the beginning. Some things are not done with honor, my friend."

"I'm not your damned friend."

"No," Hultul agreed cheerfully. "You would like to kill me now. If ever I give you the slightest chance . . . *zzzsst!* You would cut my throat."

"Filthy traitor! I was this close to rescuing Lady Lea, and now—" Thirbe broke off, his jaw muscles knotting so hard they ached. He'd said enough earlier. It did no good to repeat his protests.

"But my most beloved and esteemed lord would not wish you to rescue the lady," Hultul called back. "He would wish me to warn him of the evil that awaits him from those he considers friends. Perhaps it was not wise of him to trust the shadow priests, but they are clever and full of tricks. I think perhaps they deceived my beloved master before and now it is important that he learn what they truly are."

"Fine," Thirbe said. "Warn him. But let me help her while there's still a chance."

"I do not think the chance remains," Hultul said, the mocking gaiety fading from his voice. "There was much commotion in the priests' camp last night. Much trouble, and I think it was good that we left when we did, before they caught us and fed us to the dead."

The thought of Lea possibly sacrificed in some savage rite sent cold chills through Thirbe. *Stay alive, Lea. Stay alive,* he thought desperately, wondering what had happened last night after he was knocked unconscious. If he asked, Hultul would only tease him and refuse to give him straight answers. It was no good assuring himself that the Vindicants wouldn't hurt her. They cared nothing about her ransom. As vile and twisted as they were, they knew no honor. And if they . . .

Hastily he shut down his thoughts, knowing he was tormenting himself to no good effect. As for this fool, just one slip was all it would take, and Thirbe would gladly send him to the gods for judgment.

"No longer do you talk to me," Hultul said. "No longer do you ask questions. Are you tormented by worry for the maiden, my friend? Perhaps she is a maiden no longer. Or perhaps they have drunk all her blood."

"Shut up," Thirbe spat out. "You can mock any other woman in the world, but not her. If you had any decency in that black heart of yours, you would not joke about her plight."

"A rich, pretty princess . . . why should I care? Or perhaps she is not even pretty. Perhaps just rich. But spoiled she must be. Ordering you here and there, like her lapdog. Are you not, somewhere in your heart, relieved to be rid of her?"

"Listen, *jinja*-face, I've listened to all the insults against her I'm going to."

"No, you have not, my friend. My esteemed lord's enemies are my enemies. The sisters of enemies are my enemies. And when we are called to war, we give no mercy, no quarter. It is our way."

"Your way is puke," Thirbe said. "You've never been out of this dust pile you're so proud of. You can't imagine the rest of the empire or its wonders."

"Wonders built on Ulinian backs. Paid for with gold squeezed from Ulinian blood. We have nothing, dog. *Nothing!* And always the emperor takes from us, takes and takes, until we are dried and withered to the bone. And he wants even that."

"It's his right, damn your eyes. The emperor's wish is my law, and yours."

"No! I serve my esteemed Lord Vordachai. I obey the customs of my land, and the laws of my *aziarahd mahal*."

"Sure. You're so obedient that you could have captured

Shadrael, but you didn't. You should be dragging him home by the hair instead of me."

"Capture Lord Shadrael?" Hultul asked in astonishment. "And why should I do an unkindness to the brother of my esteemed and beloved lord?"

Thirbe scowled. "I knew you were lying to Pendek about bringing him in for arrest."

"Not then, no. Then I would have obeyed my esteemed lord. Now it is different."

"Gut-snapped nonsense," Thirbe grumbled, refusing to follow the man's illogic.

"Ah, you do not understand the force of passion."

"What?"

"The force of passion. It is the defense of vendetta, of honor. We call it," Hultul said reverently, *"halya a daulma nyaem.* When it is upon a man, you respect it, even if it means he kills. My most beloved and esteemed master possesses much of this quality. His temper is what you would call high."

"Possess a fair amount of it myself," Thirbe muttered.

"And so when my warlord ordered the arrest of his brother, he was in *halya a daulma nyaem,* and I obeyed his wishes. Now it will not be so. Sometimes you must understand what it is that your lord really wants, instead of only what he says. You must know whether he gives orders from anger or from judgment."

"Nice excuse for anarchy."

"Yes? I do not know this word, anarchy. But I know the heart of my master, and I do not hunt Lord Shadrael without new orders. The wish of your heart, that I help you to capture Lord Shadrael and do him harm, I do not obey. That is surely clear, even for a stinking foreign dog of an Imperial Protector such as you."

"Go piss on yourself."

Ahead of them something shimmered in the desert, like a mirage. Hultul threw up his hand, yanking his donkey to a halt. Swiftly he gestured, touching his fingers to his forehead and each eye. "Great One on High," he said solemnly, "preserve us from what comes."

"What is it?" Thirbe said.

Hultul kept staring, his posture alert and rigid, his hand now on his sword hilt.

Thirbe did not ask again. Instead, he watched, too. The air felt strange and unsettled. The morning sun was barely up, but already it was glaring into Thirbe's eyes, reflecting off the barren ground and making it hard to see. He refused to let Hultul's obvious alarm infect him, although he was well aware that strange kinds of danger could be found in the desert. He longed desperately for a weapon.

"Gods, you itty-witted knave," he whispered after a tense moment. "If there's trouble, at least untie me."

Hultul didn't seem to hear him. "There!" He pointed. "Behold!"

Straining his eyes, Thirbe looked through the glare at the shimmering haze. For a moment he thought he felt a shift in the very fabric of the world, as though someone was opening the Hidden Ways. Then he heard a small goat bell tinkling, and saw four individuals swathed in sand-colored robes and head wraps. They emerged from the glare and dust, approaching Thirbe and Hultul warily as they drove a small flock of bony goats before them with long staves.

Thirbe let out his breath with a grunt. "Faure's hell," he said in disgust. "Behold the great Ulinian warrior, scared of a pack of goats and some serfs."

"They are *nameids*, not serfs," Hultul corrected him. "And it is evil luck to insult them."

"Well, then—"

"Quiet. Something is very wrong. I think . . ." Letting his voice trail off, he kept watching.

By now the *nameids* had reached them and stopped. The goats stayed bunched up, bleating softly, their yellow eyes giving Thirbe a queer feeling. Or perhaps it was their owners, these nomadic people he'd heard about but never seen before.

They were very tall and stick thin, their skin extremely dark and their eyes pale and somehow . . .

Hastily he averted his gaze, knowing a mind spell when he encountered it. The *nameids* did not speak when Hultul greeted them politely. He offered them his water skin, but they ignored the gesture and instead pointed where again the mirage was shimmering.

"*Paru. Paru,*" they murmured.

"What are they saying?"

Hultul glanced briefly at Thirbe and drew his sword. "Danger."

At that moment a tremor went through the ground, startling the donkeys into braying. The goats scattered in all directions, and Thirbe caught an unmistakable whiff of rot and decay that nearly stopped his heart. For one wild moment he thought the Vindicants had come after them, but as a black maw opened, it was a lone man who stepped out. A man who staggered two steps and sank to his knees as the opening closed behind him. He was carrying a woman, either unconscious or dead. Her long tangle of blond hair dragged in the dirt as she tumbled limply to the ground.

Thirbe felt a stab of fear so deep it felt mortal. "Lea," he whispered. "Great Gault, *no!*"

Hultul, meanwhile, was staring as though he could not believe his eyes. "Lord Shadrael?" he said.

Chapter 21

Half-blinded by the sunlight, bleeding from scratches across his face, his arm trembling from the weight of Lea's unconscious form as he shook the last demon off his sword blade, Shadrael staggered out of the Hidden Ways into the world. His heart was bursting inside his chest. He could not think, except to get her out of the darkness.

One more step . . . he found his knees buckling under him. With a groan, he sank down and released the spell holding the Hidden Ways open. Pain clawed through him, and he found himself shaking in the aftermath of having used shadow magic. It felt foreign to him now, foreign and *wrong*.

What has she done to me? he wondered.

"M'lord!" came a distant shout. "Lord Shadrael!"

Instinct made him turn toward whoever was coming. "Shut up, you fool," he said, but it was too late.

A pale gray raven with a band of white at its throat came flying from the darkness just before the Hidden Ways closed completely. Cawing harshly, the bird circled over him, and landed on the ground close by.

Panting for breath, his face wet with sweat and tears, Shadrael braced his free hand on the ground even as he strove for enough strength to kill that bird. He should be masking his point of exit with another spell, and quickly, but he couldn't remember the word to say. His fingers fumbled for his dagger, failed to draw it, and closed on a rock instead. He threw it weakly at the raven, and missed. Flapping its wings, the bird flew, only to circle overhead, still cawing.

They will come, Shadrael thought desperately.

The man who had called out ran up to him. "M'lord, are you hurt?"

Shadrael squinted up at a dark face half-hidden beneath a head wrap. He slashed awkwardly with his sword, and the man jumped back barely in time. "Get away," Shadrael snarled.

"M'lord, forgive me. Let me give you water."

"Get away!"

"Hultul!" shouted another voice unfamiliar to him. "Damn you! Untie me!"

Confused, disoriented, Shadrael could barely hold his eyes open in the glare of sunlight reflecting off the desert. He knew there was danger, knew he had to keep moving, yet he seemed to be caught in an invisible web, unable to move, unable to take action.

"Quiet," he said hoarsely, but the men were arguing and did not listen.

"Release me!" the old man kept shouting. "Let me go to her. Release me, you damned spawn of a demon!"

Ignoring his prisoner, the one called Hultul crouched beside Shadrael and touched his shoulder. Shadrael flinched as though he'd been burned. He was shaking so hard he could barely hold himself upright, yet he fumbled to take Lea's icy hand and hold it in his.

"Please," he mumbled. "Please . . ."

And then he felt the heaviness in the air and that shift of reality as the Hidden Ways opened. Despair filled him. To have come this close to escape, only to fail . . .

He drove himself to his feet, standing over Lea's crumpled body like a man demented, swinging his sword and snarling curses at an enemy not yet before him. Hultul stumbled out of reach, holding out both hands in appeasement.

"Shadrael," a deep voice said behind him.

Shadrael froze with his sword in midswing. He *knew* that voice, and knew that he had failed in this, the most important task of his life. He wanted to cry aloud in despair. Instead, he pulled himself erect, still holding his sword in both hands.

"Look at me," the voice commanded.

Do not. Do not, warned a voice inside his mind.

"Shadrael, look at me."

Unwillingly Shadrael lifted his blurry gaze. His eyes were streaming from the intense light. All he could see was a dark shape coming toward him, cowled and hooded, all of shadow. Other figures followed the first. They spread out to surround him, Lea, and the two men. The menace that hung over them was unmistakable.

"No!" Shadrael whispered.

The leader's hand closed on his, and prickles of magic shot through Shadrael. Shadow magic.

Revulsion gripped him. Gasping, he dropped his sword and wrenched free, feeling as though he might vomit. And as he bent over, wracked with misery, he saw his shadow at his feet, cast by the sunlight. Astonished, his mind tumbling with confusion and disbelief, he stared at it.

Could it be true? he wondered. Was his soul restored to him? It must be true, and if so, then Lea had done more than give him enough strength to open the Hidden Ways. She had done much, much more.

"Lea," he whispered. Overwhelmed, he dropped to his knees beside her. Inside, his wits were reeling. Had he been hit on the skull with a maul and left a simpleton, he could not have been more stunned.

Urmaeor struck him aside with magic, sending him

tumbling helplessly into the dust. "Get away from her," the priest said coldly.

Burning with resentment, Shadrael struggled to his hands and knees. By then, two priests had rolled Lea onto a blanket and lifted her.

"Let her go," Shadrael said hoarsely. "What more can she do, now that your chief priest is dead?"

"Thanks to you," Urmaeor said, and struck him with magic again.

This time, Shadrael was knocked nearly unconscious. A kick brought him around, and he groaned as he forced open his eyes.

"She belongs to us until we are finished with her," Urmaeor said. "As do you. Now get on your feet."

Invisible bonds had closed on Shadrael, making it impossible to struggle. He felt helpless, caught in a queer lassitude as he dully obeyed Urmaeor's order. As the priests carried Lea away in the blanket and he followed Urmaeor like a whipped dog, Shadrael raged inside.

He had vowed to save her, but instead she had brought him back from the brink of destruction; she had made him whole.

Now, as the Vindicants carried her into the Hidden Ways, Shadrael could not bear to see her looking as pale and still as death while she was returned to the darkness. All the hope inside him, so briefly born, sputtered and died to mere embers.

"Follow," Urmaeor commanded him, and Shadrael could do nothing but obey.

Later, back in the Vindicant camp, he found himself locked in a cell with Hultul and the old man with the flat nose and caustic temper who apparently had been Lea's protector. Thirbe claimed they had met in a Kanidalon tavern, but Shadrael did not remember. He shook his head, refusing to answer Thirbe's questions, and kept a wary eye on Hultul as well. There were no friends here, and until he regained his strength and got used to the restoration of his soul he dared not relax his guard. The fact that the Vindicants had not already killed him made him worry that they planned a far worse fate for him.

"What ails you, m'lord?" Hultul asked him. "Twice have I asked you a question, yet you do not seem to hear me. What is wrong?"

"Leave him be," Thirbe spoke up before Shadrael could answer. His keen eyes seemed to cut through Shadrael, seeing too much. "Shakes and snakes, ain't it?"

The protector's friendly tone, containing just the right amount of sympathy and understanding, did not fool Shadrael. He perceived a deep vein of anger running through the protector, hidden behind that perfunctory smile and offer of false comradeship. Cautiously Shadrael gave Thirbe no answer.

"M'lord," Hultul said, removing his head wrap and sitting respectfully at Shadrael's feet. "I ask your forgiveness for what happened between us before. I was acting on my most esteemed and beloved lord's orders. And I know that you felt obliged to kill my men to save yourself. May we call a truce between us while we are prisoners of these vile men and work together to escape this place?"

Shadrael's gaze narrowed. "Perhaps."

Hultul grinned briefly and edged closer. "Thank you, m'lord. Now, this foreign dog before you has the intelligence of a donkey and the temper of a scorpion, but together he and I have explored this place, and there is—"

"Quiet!" Thirbe said in warning.

There came the sound of approaching footsteps.

Hultul scrambled away from Shadrael just before the lock was opened and the jailer appeared in the doorway.

"You," he said to Shadrael. "Come out."

Warily Shadrael got to his feet. As he stepped over the threshold, several Vindicants pounced and bound his wrists with spiked shackles that cut cruelly into his flesh. They shoved him roughly along a passage that led outdoors, crossed the camp, and skirted the mercenaries camped in makeshift tents. The men seemed oddly quiet. Among them stood Fomo, his scarred face showing no expression at all until he saw Shadrael's shadow on the ground. He gaped, his eyes nearly bulging from his skull before he grimaced and spat eloquently.

Inside the caves, Shadrael was taken through several passages until he reached the round chamber containing Beloth's altar. Half-expecting to see Lea stretched across it in sacrifice as she'd been last night, Shadrael instead found the stone bare. Only two torches were burning now, casting uneven light on the bloodstained altar. The stains were dark—old, not fresh, he was relieved to see.

The cart used to shift Lord Barthel's obese body remained near the doorway into the chief priest's private chamber, yet of Barthel's corpse there was no sign.

Wondering if they meant to execute him here, Shadrael grew tense. Unable to test his cruel bonds, he shifted his gaze about, seeking escape.

Urmaeor appeared from the gloom, standing across from him on the other side of the altar. The priest's eyes blazed at Shadrael almost without recognition.

The escort shoved Shadrael to his knees.

"Leave us," Urmaeor commanded, and the others backed away.

Shadrael climbed onto his feet, refusing to remain in a position of respect. "Where is Lady Lea?" he asked.

"Locked away."

Concern too intense to be controlled spread through Shadrael. "Is someone caring for her? Is she being kept warm? Has she regained consciousness?"

"She is not conscious. She lies very ill, thanks to you."

"Will she—"

"Enough! You've caused us all a great deal of unnecessary trouble, and you have stolen the best of her essence." Urmaeor glared at him a moment. "Congratulations, Shadrael.

I did not realize you were adept enough to tempt the very breath of life from her."

"It was—"

"I withheld the soul I'd promised you because it was the only way to control you. Now you've achieved restoration another way. How clever. You look positively sleek from feeding on the girl. As for your concern for her, stop pretending. If it's for her benefit, she can't hear you. If it's for mine, I don't appreciate the mockery."

"It's one thing to use your cruelty on me," Shadrael said. "Quite another to harm her as you've done."

"The harm came from you," Urmaeor said angrily, then restrained himself. "But why fret? You have what you want. Are you so greedy that you would take still more from her? Will you leave nothing for—"

"For whom?" Shadrael broke in, angered by what Urmaeor was saying. "Yourself?"

The priest schooled his features into a phony smile. "How perceptive of you. As you can see, I have begun to experience the less pleasant effects of withdrawal."

"Really? I thought it was from too much contact with Lea."

Hatred twisted Urmaeor's features for a moment before he smoothed his expression. "She has not been cooperative."

"Imagine that," Shadrael said. "Abduct the girl from her friends and family, lock her up in this icy ruin in the middle of nowhere, torture her, and try to drain the very life from her body to salvage a rotting shambles of a man. Why should she resist?"

"My patience with you grows extremely thin, Commander. Do not try me further."

"Aren't you grateful for what I've done for you?" Shadrael replied. "Thanks to me, you're now chief priest."

Hissing, Urmaeor raised his fist, and Shadrael braced himself, but the priest did not strike. Slowly, he lowered his hand and glared at Shadrael for a moment before he spoke.

"Despite your treachery, Lord Barthel is not quite destroyed." As he spoke, Urmaeor extended his staff so that Shadrael could see a pale green mist swirling within the crystal orb affixed to one end. "I have preserved his soul, as you see. And in due course another host will be found to hold it."

A chill ran through Shadrael. He thought of those weeks ago when Urmaeor had offered him a soul, and he could not help but wonder what horrible thing might have taken possession of him had the bargain been kept.

"But Beloth's legacy is lost," Shadrael said.

"No."

"I saw it leave Barthel's body."

"You're mistaken! I have preserved it. I have preserved everything."

"Why bother?" Shadrael asked, keeping his tone light. "I thought you had ambitions to be chief priest."

Something flashed across Urmaeor's gaunt face too quickly for Shadrael to read. "Do you think you can tempt me?" Urmaeor asked quietly, strain in his voice. "Do you think you will entice me to finish what you failed to do?"

"Why not?" Shadrael asked with a shrug. "It's what you've always wanted."

"I am not ready."

"Are you sure?"

"Be silent!" Urmaeor cried. "One more word, and I shall destroy you where you stand."

Shadrael said nothing, and after a moment Urmaeor seemed to regain some of his customary calm.

"Clever," he said flatly. "Very clever, seeking to goad my temper. You are working much mischief against us, Commander, and if I had the leisure I would personally see you boiled alive and the broth from your bones served to the demons hiding in the Hidden Ways. As it is, I still have a use for you."

"What is it?"

"Exactly what I wanted before."

Shadrael frowned. "That's lunacy. Without Barthel, you can't raise an army of the dead."

"Can't I?"

"You've admitted you're not ready to lead. Without Barthel—"

"Believe what you wish," Urmaeor said, undercurrents running through his voice. "I shall not waste time persuading you otherwise. If you think you will again trick us, or take actions to betray us, put aside such intentions. You are wholly in my power. And you will act as I direct you."

"You've never controlled me," Shadrael said defiantly.

"In the past that was true. Now you're a spent force, and I know where you are vulnerable."

Shadrael raised his chin.

"You have betrayed your devotion to the girl. You are bound emotionally to her. You perhaps even love her."

Shadrael felt his guts twist.

"Oh yes," Urmaeor said silkily. "Why else risk so much to come among us as slyly as a shape-shifter, pretending to be an ally? Why hide your thoughts so adeptly from me? Why attempt murder against Lord Barthel? All that effort to rescue one little witch." He cocked his head to one side, pretending to study Shadrael. "And now you feel so pathetically grateful to her, do you not? She has given you renewed life, as would Lord Barthel, had you waited."

The lie made Shadrael scowl.

"I confess I underestimated your charm to her," Urmaeor continued, "but then I do not have a feminine mind. Was it easy to convince her to sacrifice herself for you?"

"That isn't—"

Abruptly Shadrael stopped his involuntary defense. He wasn't going to give Urmaeor more to twist against him.

"Protecting her?" Urmaeor asked. "Such a touching, if stupid, gesture. We will make sure the girl learns a lesson she'll never forget."

"If you harm her, I'll—"

"I'm not interested in your threats," the priest said.

"Now heed me closely. Our quarry is on the move, coming to the Valley of Fires from Kanidalon. By morning he will be inside our trap."

Surprised, Shadrael stared at the priest, wondering if the information was true. Light Bringer must have ridden like the wind from New Imperia, or else he had used the Hidden Ways himself.

"Yes," Urmaeor said with a snap, apparently having discerned Shadrael's thoughts. "He rode the wind. But now he comes to us as only a mortal, determined to rescue his sister at any cost. Therein lies his undoing. And once he puts himself into our trap, you will close it."

Shadrael let his gaze narrow. "Has Vordachai ridden in?"

"The warlord camps close by. He and his barons scheme and lay their plans, but you, Commander, will take charge of all our forces. Our human forces."

"Vordachai won't accept me as commander."

"He will. From the beginning he has sought your help. He will be relieved to see you take charge."

"We've quarreled. He won't trust me now."

"Leave that to me," Urmaeor said with assurance.

"Vordachai is a law unto himself. You can't control him, or his barons," Shadrael said. "You're getting weaker every day, not stronger. Lea's influence has upset your entire—"

"The girl's presence is a hindrance no longer. Sacrificing herself for you seems to have drained her abilities to a dangerous point. Now she is too weak to matter. Even those baubles she wears—so devoted of you to return them to her—have lost their power." Urmaeor smiled. "How well things work to the larger purpose. You have lost your magic. And she can no longer interfere with our spells."

"Take care, Urmaeor," Shadrael said sharply. "If she dies, the emperor will—"

"Another threat? How tiresome. I thought you intended to deal with me so thoroughly there would be nothing left for the usurper to trample."

"Repeated threats bear heeding," Shadrael said.

Urmaeor shrugged, sliding his hand along his staff. "I don't care what Light Bringer does or intends. We shall destroy him."

"At least let the girl go."

"Why should I?"

"You've said you're through with her. Why—"

"To torment you, Shadrael," Urmaeor said. "That should be obvious."

"You've hurt her enough."

"No one has hurt her, but you."

"Then lead the army yourself," Shadrael said. "I won't do it."

"Oh, but you will. You are a key player in our ruse. You are experienced with shadow and can keep the men from panicking when the dead appear."

"Work your filthy magic alone, Urmaeor. You'll not get my help."

Urmaeor spread his fingers, and a small dark mist formed over the altar between them. The center of the little cloud cleared, showing Shadrael a vision of Lea lying pale and far too still on a crudely made bed.

"The girl," Urmaeor said softly, "grows dangerously weak. We can revive her, or we can let her die. That depends on you, and whether you will cooperate."

Anger filled Shadrael. Instinctively he reached for the priest's threads of life, but his shadow magic was gone. For a moment he raged with frustration, until Urmaeor's quiet laughter distracted him.

"Pathetic," the priest said. "For years you have played such a tragedy figure of angst and misery, pretending to wallow in despair while you yearned for a soul. And now that your wish has been granted, you long to once more be an evil *donare* murdering at will. There is simply no pleasing you."

Bitter shame spread through Shadrael. He dropped his gaze with nothing to say.

"I believe I liked you better, Commander, when you were utterly ruthless and quite despicable. Now you are dull indeed."

"I murdered your chief priest," Shadrael reminded him. "No matter how many little crystals you collect, you'll never revive him. Take care I don't run a blade through you."

"Oh, you will not try," Urmaeor said, and gripped his threads of life, making Shadrael gasp in pain. "It tempts me to see if I can capture the girl's soul as I have Lord Barthel's. Or I can simply discard it. She would make an interesting host for his essence, would she not?"

He released Shadrael, who staggered, fighting to stay upright. The priest's threat against Lea horrified him.

"Her fate depends entirely on how well you spring to-morrow's trap on Light Bringer. Now do I have your complete attention?"

"Yes."

"Convince him he faces a real army. Pull him into the fray and—"

"His legion commanders will direct the battle," Shadrael broke in. "You don't expect him to charge out there, swinging a sword himself, do you?"

"Of course. This emperor is young, and his blood runs hot."

"That's not the way a battle is fought. His officers won't let him risk himself."

"Then draw him into danger! Light Bringer *must* take the field," Urmaeor said.

"I would have to be winning," Shadrael said. "Only then would he risk danger by riding among the men to rally them."

"Then that is what you must do."

Shadrael did not understand how Urmaeor believed this pathetic plan had any chance of success, but he kept silent.

"When Light Bringer is on the field," Urmaeor continued, "I shall unleash the army of dead."

"Unleashing them is one thing," Shadrael said, thinking

of his brother's men. "Controlling them is another. Who will do that? You?"

"Leave that part of the business to me."

"Once the battle starts I can let the uneven numbers sway the outcome. I can let the Imperial soldiers overrun mine, and the battle will be over before you can unleash the dead. Why not give me a real incentive to carry out your plan?"

"Such as what?"

"Let the girl go, and I'll lead your forces to victory."

Chuckling, Urmaeor smoothed his saffron robes. "You bargain as though you actually have leverage. The girl will remain here, firmly within our control."

"Then I won't ride forth on the morrow," Shadrael said.

"Oh, you will ride and you will command, exactly as I've ordered," Urmaeor said flatly.

"Put me in the saddle, but I won't fight," Shadrael said. "Unless the girl is safe, I'll do nothing."

Again Urmaeor grabbed his threads of life.

The agony was almost unbearable, but Shadrael managed to gasp out, "Kill me, and you will have only Vordachai to lead the dead. Will he?"

"I can make you dance as my puppet." Urmaeor released him, and Shadrael sank to his knees with a groan. "I can force you to drive a sword through your own vitals should I wish."

Shadrael climbed slowly to his feet. "Yes, you can enspell me," he agreed. "But your magic is weaker than it used to be. While you govern me thus, can you also control the dead? Are you that powerful without shadow gods to help you?"

Urmaeor's eyes glittered with anger. "Very well," he said reluctantly. "I'll release the girl."

"Now?"

"She's unconscious."

"Revive her. Give her to her protector and send them out of here."

"Later."

"Now."

Urmaeor smiled, tight-lipped. "So she can ride straight to Light Bringer and warn him? When the battle ends, I'll let her go."

"Release her before it starts."

"If I release the girl before the battle, Light Bringer will have no reason to fight."

Shadrael had to laugh at the priest's naiveté. "He's here to crush rebellion. He'll fight. And if we are not the victors, our lives will be forfeit to summary execution for treason. We all have reason to fight."

"Then your quibbling over my army of the dead makes no sense."

"I want to win," Shadrael said, "not die. I do not want to be cornered by your fiends, or see my brother torn to pieces by creatures you can't control. *That* is my objection. Nothing more."

Urmaeor picked up a ceremonial knife off the altar and thrust it and a small bronze bowl at Shadrael. "There is one way to protect yourself and Vordachai. A blood oath."

Shadrael hesitated, trying not to betray his distaste. "I am no longer shadow sworn."

"Then swear anew! I will have your blood oath, Commander. Or you can go into battle unprotected, and the girl will never leave our camp."

Involuntarily Shadrael flexed his wrists, and felt the spikes dig brutally into his flesh. *Shackles of shadow,* he thought. As cruel to his spirit as to his body. Urmaeor was not content to let Lea's valiant sacrifice cleanse one tiny corner of Shadrael from all that tainted him. Why must he demand that Shadrael discard what Lea had done for him, to retreat into the smothering depths of shadow?

Because he is evil and petty, came the answer in Shadrael's thoughts. *Because he must hate anyone who escapes shadow's cruel talons, as he never can.*

What else could he do? Shadrael asked himself. If Lea was to have a chance of freedom . . . if Vordachai was to be given the slenderest hope of survival . . . there was no other choice to make. Shadrael drew a deep breath, steeling himself. "Agreed, *if* the girl is released at dawn."

Urmaeor leaned across the altar toward him. "Make the cut, and she will be."

Shadrael's fingers closed around the small knife. It was dirty and dull, the bronze blade too soft to kill with, even if he threw himself across the altar and aimed for the priest's heart.

"Quickly!" Urmaeor said intensely. "Or I shall know the truth behind your hesitation."

For you, Lea, Shadrael thought. *For you, my brother.* And swiftly he slashed his wrist.

Chapter 22

At dawn, Shadrael, his face implacable, his dark eyes as cold as stone, strode out into the wintry morning and mounted his horse.

The cohort of mercenaries stood silent behind their five centruins. By contrast, from over a nearby ridge came the sound of Ulinian cheers as now and then Vordachai's unmistakable bellow echoed on the air.

Ignoring the noise, Shadrael said nothing to the men before him. They looked hollow eyed and less than ready to fight. He hardly blamed them, for if they got even an inkling of the fate intended for them, they would bolt at the first opportunity.

Fingering the bandage wrapped around his left wrist, he waited in grim silence until he saw a horse come into sight, picking its way across the Vindicant camp. Thirbe held the reins, and Lea—bundled in a blanket—rode in front of the protector's saddle.

Just the sight of her sent a mixture of emotions churning in Shadrael's chest. After returning to his cell, he'd lain awake all night, worrying over the situation while Thirbe

and Hultul slept or pretended to sleep. He'd expected the
Vindicants to punish him for what he'd done against Lord
Barthel, and so far there'd been little retaliation, other than
forcing him to renew his oath to shadow. Punishment
would come. Of that, Shadrael had no doubt.

As for the blood oath itself, he felt sick about it and
ashamed. This morning he carried a repulsive little talisman to be given to Vordachai when the time came.
Shadrael did not trust Urmaeor to have put protection on
him and his brother at all. It might well be the reverse, and
the dead creatures might come for them before they attacked the emperor.

Impossible to know . . . impossible to prepare a defense
for. Wearily Shadrael told himself that he'd done all he
could. As for Lea's release, he feared a trick. The priests
were devious. This might not be Lea at all, but simply a
phantasm to fool him.

Frowning with suspicion, Shadrael pushed his horse
through the activity to approach her.

Lea was awake, her blue eyes dark and enormous in a
pale face. He wanted her to speak, if only to prove she was
real flesh and blood.

"Lady Lea," Shadrael said formally, saluting her.

She gave him a slight nod, but that was all. As she stared
at him, disappointment seemed to fill her eyes.

Aware that this was probably the last time he would ever
see her, he frowned, swept by a sense of unbearable loss.
He knew he could not forgive himself if he did not tell her
something of what he felt. And yet how could he, when
they had no privacy at all?

"I wish to thank you for all you've done," he began.

She simply stared at him, looking hurt, while he wanted to
curse himself for sounding so stiff, unpleasant, and ungrate-
ful. Small wonder she was gazing at him like a wounded doe.

Impulsively, he leaned over and gripped her hand, hanging on when she would have drawn away.

Thirbe glared at him, bristling like a guard dog, but

Shadrael ignored the man just as he tried to ignore Urmaeor
standing a short distance away, watching them closely.

"Lea, thank you," Shadrael said quietly, urgently. "You
have given me a gift beyond imagining. I owe you everything."

"Yet you're going to squander your life," she whispered,
her blue eyes peering right to the very heart of him.
"You're going to throw it all away."

He looked down, unable to lie to her. "The sword will
always be in my hand. I've regained my soul, thanks to
you, but I can't change what I am."

"And still you do not understand." Tears filled her eyes.
"Free yourself, and come with me, please."

Although he longed to sweep her into his arms and hold
her tightly, he forced himself to release her hand and sit
back in his saddle. He loved her so much he ached. "My
place is here."

"Not willingly!" she said in distress. "Shadrael, I know
he has coerced you. If it is for my sake, if it is to make
them let me go, then I—"

He leaned over and kissed her, possessing her sweet
mouth until it yielded to his. When he drew back, yearning
to gallop away with her, he saw pearly tears rolling down
her cheeks. He took one, tucking it into his glove for luck,
and regretted all they might have had together if only . . .

"I'm sorry, Lea," he said. "I can't ask you to wish me
victory, for soon I will be fighting against your brother. I
can only say, Gault bless you for all you have done. Go
now, and keep safe."

"If you continue," she said sorrowfully, "if you go to
fight, then terrible tragedy awaits you."

An involuntary chill ran through him. Was this prophecy
she spoke? he wondered. He shook off his doubts impatiently. All war held tragedy. "Your sympathies must side
with your brother," he said stiffly. "I understand."

"No, you understand *nothing*—"

Urmaeor, however, was suddenly standing at his stirrup.

"Your touching farewells have been spoken. Lady Lea, you are free to go. Do not keep our commander from his assigned tasks. As for you, Protector, remember you have given us your pledge to take her to Kanidalon and nowhere else."

As he spoke, he stroked the neck of Thirbe's horse. The animal shifted with a nervous whinny, and Thirbe—looking preoccupied—curbed the horse harshly.

Urmaeor gestured. "Begone, Lea E'non!"

Her gaze shot to Shadrael as though she would speak, but he was already reining his horse away. As he did so, he gave Thirbe a curt nod. The protector spurred his horse to a trot, heading in a direction opposite to the battlefield.

Urmaeor chirruped to the raven on his shoulder, and the bird flew after Thirbe and Lea.

Shadrael frowned uneasily. His instincts continued to tell him something was wrong. This was all too easy. Urmaeor was being too agreeable. Shadrael stared very hard at the priest's back, and after a moment Urmaeor sent him a stony glance.

"My minion will inform me if he tries to circle around and warn the emperor," Urmaeor said. "But I think the spell I've cast on his horse will see him straight to Kanidalon."

Shadrael nodded, forcing his emotions down to a cold, unhappy place. The symbol painted on his wrist in blood—a reminder of his reluctant, renewed oath to Beloth and Faure—seemed to burn his skin as much as his conscience, yet it had been worthwhile to see Lea go free. Urmaeor had won his little game for the time being. *Let him be satisfied,* Shadrael thought.

"Satisfied? Never," Urmaeor murmured. "It begins, Commander. If you want to survive this day, you and your brother both, then you will do exactly as I have ordered."

A Ulinian horn sounded from over the ridge to the west, and more cheers rose in the distance from Vordachai's camp. Shadrael's horse tossed its head, prancing eagerly.

"Go," the priest said, touching Shadrael's boot and

sending a frisson of magic through him. "Hurry, or the warlord will not wait for you."

Shadrael turned his gaze toward his men. They were no army, he thought in contempt, yet even so he felt the old habits stirring inside him, causing him to straighten in the saddle and face them with the cool assurance of a born leader.

"Men," he said, projecting his voice so that it rang out in the cold dawn air. "Today we face Imperial legions, the toughest opponents in the world. But they fight under the banner of a nameless man, a former slave, undeserving of the throne he holds. *We* fight to bring down the usurper! We fight to break the injustice of Imperial law! We fight for ourselves! Let every one of you face your foes as though a demon rides your shoulder."

A halfhearted cheer rose from them. He studied them from beneath knotted brows.

"There will be glory awaiting you."

They hooted in derision.

"And plunder."

They cheered.

"The more kills you tally, the more weapons and armor you'll bring home. We'll melt down the usurper's crown and strike new coins for every one of you."

Lusty cheers. Eagerly they laughed, brandishing their weapons.

Shadrael drew his sword and held it aloft. "For Beloth and shadow!" he cried.

And they echoed his war cry: "For Beloth and shadow!"

Without glancing back at Urmaeor and the other Vindicants, Shadrael led forth his rabble to die.

Clad in plate armor polished to a dazzling sheen, Vordachai was riding his horse in restless circles and brandishing his sword in a waste of energy that made Shadrael frown.

As soon as Shadrael arrived, however, the warlord bellowed a welcome.

"Well met, brother!" he shouted gladly. His eyes were shining, and his bearded face burned red with excitement. "I thought this day would never come, eh?"

"The last time we met," Shadrael said, keeping a wary eye on the warlord's sharp sword, "you were out for my blood."

"Old quarrels." Shrugging, Vordachai dismissed the matter. "Do you think I can hold a grudge today? The usurper is within our grasp at last!"

Glancing swiftly around, Shadrael drew his brother out of earshot of the nervous barons and any possible Vindicant spies. Fomo was close by, but not looking in their direction. Shadrael watched the former centruin for a moment through narrowed eyes, but Fomo strode away, shouting at some of the men, and Shadrael turned to his excited brother.

Under the pounding of the war drums, he said urgently, "Vordachai, this is a trap."

"Of course it is. I have scant use for Vindicants at the best of times, but if they've conjured a nasty surprise for the usurper, so much the better."

"No, hear me! The Vindicants don't care if your men are massacred with the Imperial troops. If we withdraw now, we stand a chance of escaping."

Vordachai's expression froze. "Withdraw?" he roared so loudly several men glanced their way. "I, Vordachai tu Natalloh, Beloved Lord and Master of the Mountains and the Sand, *withdraw*? Tuck my tail between my legs like a worm-afflicted dog and slink away? Are you mad? I've cut out men's tongue for less—"

"Vordachai—"

"*No!* Impossible! I'll listen to no more of this!"

"You have to listen," Shadrael said. "Damn you, stop yelling and heed me, or you and Light Bringer will *both* die today."

"If the usurper falls, then I am blessed of all men," Vordachai announced. "I'd gladly forfeit my life if this wish is granted to me."

Shadrael swiftly spat on the ground to deflect such bad luck. "Don't talk like that," he said. "Do you want to see your barons and the whole Ulinian army massacred as well?"

"If necessary." Vordachai lifted his bearded chin. "We will have died to set Ulinia free. No matter what you think, you whining pustule, we will have covered ourselves with honor."

"There's no honor in walking blindly into a trap just to satisfy a clutch of exiled priests too frightened to step into the sunlight. They are the cowards. Why aren't they here, to fight beside us?"

Vordachai was staring at something. Realizing his brother wasn't listening, Shadrael scowled at him. "What's the use of talking to you? I'm trying to help you, you fool."

But the warlord pointed at the ground, where the rising sun was throwing a long shadow out behind Shadrael. "What's happened to you?" he cried in amazement.

"What do you think?"

"You're different. You're casting a . . . *Look!*" Joy filled Vordachai's face. He gripped Shadrael by both arms and shook him until his teeth rattled. "Can it be possible? Is Gault this merciful? Have you regained your soul?"

Wincing, Shadrael twisted free and pulled out the talisman. "At least carry this for protection."

Vordachai ignored it. "Tell me straight. Are you human again?"

"Why should it matter to you?"

"Why not tell me?" Vordachai stared at him in open wonder, scrutinizing him so closely that an embarrassed Shadrael looked away. "Are you not rejoicing in Gault's mercy? Are you not pleased by this?"

Tangled emotions, too knotted to explain, crowded Shadrael's throat. He felt his eyes going moist, and fought to keep himself from becoming unmanned. "Yes," he muttered.

His gaze went unwillingly to the bandage on his wrist. "I rejoice," he said, wishing he could confess the truth to his brother. "But what matters now is that we forget this battle and—"

"And what? Let him go? I can see that your wits must be tumbled, but this is no time to lose your head and start preaching encompassing love like a Reformant monk. Think of it! Fighting the usurper, Light Bringer himself! When will we ever again have this chance?"

"He'll never take the field," Shadrael said.

"It will be glorious." Vordachai was obviously not listening. "Our names will be sung into legend. On this day we'll free Ulinia from the yoke of oppression."

Shadrael gripped his arm. "You cannot win this battle, Vordachai."

"Does that matter?" Vordachai's brown eyes met his. "I will have fought him. I will have stood up and defied this tyrant. Besides"—Vordachai spread his arms wide—"he has named me a traitor and an outlaw. He has put a price on my head as though I am a common road bandit. A former slave condemns *me*! The insult is too great. I can never forgive it."

"Vordachai—"

"No! This is my chance to be great, and I must seize it. Think of it, brother," he added, laughing in sheer excitement. "The emperor himself, forced to come to my corner of the desert just to swat me down. What can be more glorious?"

"Winning."

Vordachai gave him a swift grimace of agreement. "Well, yes, that much I will grant you, sour face. A victory would be joy beyond all expectation. A delight, a boon from the gods. But even so, I shall be content just to fight him."

"But—"

"I will have rattled his power a little. I will have pinched the bully's nose and made him squeak, even if for only one day. Gods, Shadrael, is it not marvelous? This battle is the sublime moment of my life. How can I turn away now?

And you . . . I don't understand you at all. I thought you would be itching to get your hands on a sword and meet the man that's treated you so shabbily."

Shadrael felt his old resentment stir.

"Yes," Vordachai said, watching him. "The man who wronged you. Light Bringer!" he whispered, curling his fists. "Here, for the taking, as we've always dreamed."

Shadrael blinked. "In what nightmare? You talk as though you have him cornered."

"It can be done. It can be tried. Ulinia could rise again. Think of the glory!"

"I'm thinking your wits have left you," Shadrael said in a blighting voice. "Five legions against your army . . . you'll lose half or more of your men in the first charge."

"He doesn't have five. By all accounts, he came early to Kanidalon, ahead of his forces. As for the Ninth Legion . . ." Vordachai twiddled his fingers airily. "Polished breast-plates and no substance. Their commander is a fool. No match for us."

Shadrael caught his brother's arm urgently. "The Ninth can fight, and you're forgetting the Second and Tenth. They're seasoned enough to cut us to pieces. As for the Vindicants—"

"May the pox shrivel their parts and drive them mad."

"You and your army are the bait, and they will let you be destroyed."

"So be it."

"No! If they raise the dead to fight—"

"Can they do that?" Vordachai asked, wide-eyed.

"I think so. And once their foul army is unleashed, Urmaeor won't be able to control it. The creatures will attack everyone on the field. Everyone! Do you understand why I want you to retreat now, while it's still possible to escape?"

"But I can't back down, not before the emperor," Vordachai said, blinking. "He would think I fear him."

"Write him a letter of explanation. But don't give your men to the Vindicant slaughter."

Vordachai frowned, beginning to look doubtful. "If you're sure—"

The sounding of trumpets cut him off. Vordachai stood in his stirrups. "They're coming onto the field."

Shadrael gripped his arm. "Back off now while—"

"Not when they're entering the field!" Vordachai shook him off. "Now stop talking like a toothless old woman and tell me squarely—do you stand with me or do you intend to retire like a coward?"

Shadrael glared at him, but it was obvious that Vordachai wasn't going to listen to sense. It was like trying to stand against a mighty sandstorm and blow it onto a new course with his puny breath. He sighed. "I stand with you."

Vordachai beamed. "That's the spirit!"

"But in Gault's name, take this!" Again, Shadrael proffered the talisman.

Vordachai eyed it with distaste. "Why do you give me such a filthy thing?"

"To protect you from what's coming."

Vordachai's brows knotted. He stared at Shadrael. "Wear blasphemous shadow protection when my men, my barons, have none? What do you take me for?"

Heat crept up Shadrael's throat into his face, and his cheeks burned. "Damn you! I've broken my conscience to obtain this, and by the gods you're going to wear it."

Vordachai grabbed it from his hand and threw it under the trampling hooves of horses. "And here I thought we could fight shoulder to shoulder, like brothers should. If turning human has made you a coward, then I'm ashamed to know you. Ashamed, Shadrael."

Before Shadrael could answer, Vordachai wheeled his big warhorse and rode away. "Sound the horns!" he yelled at the top of his lungs, waving his sword.

As the trumpets sounded, and the men cheered, Vordachai glared at Shadrael. "Better collect your rabble and creep away, little brother."

"I said I'd stand with you."

Vordachai didn't look pleased. "Don't expect my gratitude. I'd rather see you dead than without your nerve."

"Vordachai—"

"I had meant to ask you what sort of commanders we're
facing, but you've wasted the time with your mewling. We'll
charge straight through, and mind you keep those ruffians
you brought to one side and out of the way of my men. And
keep well away from me today. I want no part of you."

"Wait—"

But his brother was spurring his horse, making it rear.
"With me, men!" he roared over the noise. "To victory!"

Everyone cheered except Shadrael. He sat there, fuming
in his saddle, not knowing whether to curse his idiot of a
brother or beg his forgiveness.

"M'lord." It was Fomo at his stirrup, his ruined rasp of a
voice barely heard in the din of shouts and war cries. The former centruin held up the battered talisman that Vordachai had
thrown away. "The warlord dropped this."

"Keep it," Shadrael snarled, and joined the stream of
warriors galloping to battle.

Wrapped in silence, Lea rode inside the shelter of
Thirbe's arms as the morning sun rose higher in the sky.

They'd reached the foothills to the south and were climbing away from the old lava fields in the Valley of Fires when
Lea suddenly frowned and leaned forward.

"I've been so foolish," she said aloud.

"What's that, m'lady?"

"We must turn back and help them."

Thirbe grunted. "Ain't likely."

"Commander Shadrael means to fight Caelan," she said.
"We have to stop them both."

"Can't be stopped now," Thirbe said. "The fight's well
joined by this time. There's not a thing you can do."

"But—"

"No," he said firmly. "I've got my orders, and you're

going to where it's safe. You've been through enough, and I ain't seeing you jeopardized again."

"And who gave you those orders? Commander Shadrael or the Vindicant?"

Thirbe cleared his throat gruffly. "Sworn to safeguard your life, ain't I?"

"No, Thirbe," she insisted. "It's not that simple. Shadrael worked some bargain with the Vindicants to get me freed, didn't he?"

"As to that, I couldn't say."

"Can't? Or won't?"

Thirbe didn't answer. She leaned forward and gripped the reins, stopping the horse.

"Now, m'lady—"

"Don't argue," she said.

Shrugging off her blanket, she reached for the *gli*-emeralds fastened around her throat. Balancing them in her hand, she breathed over them, and their lifeless, dull appearance suddenly sparkled into a glow of power. She ran her fingers over the jewels, feeling their *gli*-energy flow to her. Their power did not feel quite as strong as before, but that was because she knew shadow now. She had felt it coil through her spirit and forever leave its stain. And now she knew she must go back and face whatever evil lay in wait for both Shadrael and Caelan.

"You can tell me not to argue, but that don't mean I'm following any itty-witted orders," Thirbe was saying with spirit. "You ain't about to go to no battlefield, not with Vindicants and monsters—"

"What monsters?" she asked sharply.

When he didn't answer, she twisted around to look at him. "What monsters?" she asked again.

"Don't know. Don't know anything, except I'm taking you to Kanidalon."

Abruptly she slid off the horse, stumbling as her feet hit the ground.

Thirbe reined up fast. "Now, don't give me trouble, m'lady. You're going to Kanidalon, and that's all there is to it."

"No!" she said stubbornly, watching for the pale raven. In a moment she saw it, gray wings almost the same color as the early morning sky.

"Gave my pledge to take you there."

"You gave your pledge to an evil man sworn to shadow," Lea replied, watching the bird fly closer. "But I did not."

"Now, that's no way to be," Thirbe said. He reached down to offer her his hand. "Climb back on the horse, and let's get well away from this blasted—"

"Thirbe," Lea said, half-closing her eyes as she touched her necklace and summoned an air spirit. "That priest has put a spell on you. Don't you feel it?"

"No."

"I was foolish enough to let myself be distracted," she said, calling the air spirit again. "Too worried about Shadrael to pay attention to what Urmaeor was doing. This isn't the direction to Kanidalon. Why did we come this way, Thirbe? Why?"

The protector didn't answer. With the raven flying straight at Lea, she had no time to wonder why.

The air spirit came, ruffling her hair affectionately before it surged up and knocked the raven tumbling from the sky.

The bird landed on the ground hard enough to bounce. It lay there, its wings crumpled and beak open. Momentary compassion touched Lea, until she saw its small form shrivel and blacken into a misshapen lump as dark as the chunks of lava stone lying scattered about.

"Beware. Beware," the air spirit whispered in Lea's mind. It slid around her, blowing her hair and whipping through her clothing.

Hearing a sound behind her, she turned and saw Thirbe changing shape, his familiar features blurring into the nightmarish countenance of a creature with bulging eyes and an elongated snout. Saliva dripped from the shape-shifter's jaws. It sprang off the horse, charging at her with the lurching, stumbling gait of a lurker.

And as it came, it laughed.

Chapter 23

Panting hard, Shadrael drew rein under the over-hang of a huge rock, and gave himself and his horse a breather. His arm and shoulder were trembling with fatigue, and sweat was pouring down his face from beneath his helmet. His fingers had gripped his sword hilt so hard they were starting to cramp.

The battlefield was a melee of confusion, with riders and foot soldiers fighting in all directions. Vordachai's initial charge had met the advance of the Second Legion with a brutal clash that had seen an enormous amount of bloodshed on both sides. Meanwhile, the Tenth had bided its time, letting the Ulinians tire themselves before surrounding them and cutting off retreat.

That's when Shadrael had led his poorly trained cohort into the fray. The element of surprise had carried his men long enough to give them heart, so that they fought harder than they'd known they could. But then the surprised soldiers regrouped, turning away from beleaguering Vordachai's men in order to deal with this new threat. Shadrael's men had been cut down systematically by ruthless Imperial forces that

fought—not for glory or loot—but to win. It ended as the
slaughter he expected. Cohort One, he'd called them, and
they'd died around him while he did his job and kept them
from fleeing until he had none left to lead. But they'd given
Vordachai a chance to break his warriors free of the corner
they'd been in. And while Vordachai regrouped, his bellow
carrying over the din of screams and clashing weapons,
Shadrael had fought his way clear, and paused here to re-
assess the situation.

Across the battlefield, he could see other officers doing
the same thing. The sun hung high overhead, casting shadows from the spikes at Shadrael's shoulders. He pulled off
his blood-spattered gauntlet and wiped perspiration from
his face before grimly unwrapping the bandage from his
wrist.

Sweat and grime had worked their way across the symbol painted there, smearing it. Shadrael rubbed it off with
his palm, unswearing himself to Beloth in a tired mutter,
and pledging his soul and conscience instead to Gault. The
uneasiness did not leave him, but at least he felt free of the
degradation Urmaeor had put him through.

He pulled open the cut on his wrist, and let a few drops
of fresh blood fall on the ground before tying it up with a
fresh cloth pulled from his saddlebag. He drank thirstily
from a water skin and pulled his gauntlets back on.

He was surprised the Ulinians had lasted this long. The
battlefield was cramped and tight, bordered by low ridges to
the east and a series of arroyos to the west—time-consuming
to travel through. The north was blocked by a canyon too
deep to cross. The south lay fairly flat, opening to desert
devoid of water holes or much life. Shadrael had chosen
this location because such a small battlefield was ideally
suited to the Ulinian's advantage since the Imperial foot
soldiers could not maneuver well. Yet the numbers of
Ulinians were clearly dwindling, and there seemed to be an
endless supply of legion cohorts—fresh and rested—coming
over the ridge to join the fight.

By the numbers of dead and wounded sprawled on the ground, this battle had clearly become a tiresome slog, grim and entrenched, with little movement. Outnumbered and flagging, the Ulinians could not last much longer. Shadrael knew all too well that this kind of fight always went to the general with the greatest number of men.

"You fool," he said under his breath, watching Vordachai galloping past a line of retreating warriors to send them back into the fray. "Fall back while you still can."

From his vantage point, Shadrael could see the Imperial Banner waving proudly in the wind above the emperor's standards. High atop one of the ridges bordering this field, the emperor sat astride a white steed, his crown and breastplate shining in the sunlight. His men could see him watching and feel cheered. His enemies could see him watching and feel despair.

Shadrael's emotions churned. For a moment he felt anew his black anger at what Caelan Light Bringer had done to him, but tempering that old resentment was his gratitude to Lea. Now Shadrael realized the only thing he truly hated was his brother's stupidity in provoking a fight he was doomed to lose.

The valor of the Ulinians impressed Shadrael's heart. They were fighting for the worst reasons—for land they loved, for honor, for freedom. As a professional, Shadrael had been trained to fight without emotion, to feel nothing but determination to win.

Now he knew that he must stand by his brother, for Ulinia, no matter how hopeless, or never forgive himself.

A roar of shouting caught his attention. He saw the standards of the Ninth lifted high as at least three cohorts poured onto the field to surround the Ulinians. Vordachai and his men could not flee even if their courage deserted them.

"Fight," he whispered, knowing they could not surrender in the circumstances. "Fight, you poor devils."

Unable to watch the massacre to come, Shadrael drew

his sword and kicked his horse toward the battle, determined to die with his brother.

Crying out, Lea stumbled to one side and barely managed to avoid the shape-shifter's leap.

"Earth spirits!" she called.

The ground shook beneath her feet. The wind blew harder as more air spirits joined the first, slinging sand into the creature's face and driving it back momentarily.

It howled and clawed at its hideous face, emitting a foul stink.

Choking, Lea squinted against the lash of wind and sand. "Earth spirits, help me!" she cried.

Again the ground trembled beneath her feet, and numerous furrows appeared, converging on her and the beast. There came a tremendous crack of sound as the ground split open under the shape-shifter. It screamed and toppled, clawing desperately at the edge to keep from falling completely in. The ground closed, crushing it, but the gush of fluids splattering from its death throes created serpents and black lizards and queer, misshapen things that scuttled on their bellies toward Lea.

She retreated, desperately looking behind her, and scooped up a handful of stones to pelt the creatures and drive them back.

More furrows appeared in the ground, and a fissure opened almost at Lea's feet, between her and the demonic reptiles.

At the same time, a whirlwind sprang up, twisting and flinging sand. A voice said in Lea's mind, *"Enter my heart."*

She obeyed, shielding her face with her hands as she leaped into the center of the whirlwind. A loud roaring noise nearly deafened her, but inside the swirling cloud of dust and whipping sand, the center was calm. Lea felt as though she were floating. Stray wind currents tossed her from time to time, and then the whirlwind died down to a

mere whisper and was gone, leaving the ground scoured of
sand down to hard-baked dirt.

She saw no serpents or lizards, no demons. Just a scattering of tiny bones blown apart and scrubbed clean.

Lea found herself panting and shaking in the quiet aftermath. She crouched a moment, for her legs did not seem to
want to hold her. *Thirbe,* she thought, trying to rebuild her
shaken *quai* as she pushed back her tangled hair and
brushed sand from her face, *what have they done with you?*

Fearing for him among the evil Vindicants, she estab-
lished her inner harmony as best she could. A sense of rising urgency made her turn her gaze back toward the Valley
of Fires. She blamed herself for having been weak enough
to let Urmaeor cloud her mind and trick her.

But now she knew clearly that she must go to the battlefield. Caelan needed her. Shadrael needed her. Both of the
men she loved must be kept from fighting each other directly, for she did not intend to let either of them fulfill the
evil purposes of the Vindicants.

Knocking a soldier aside with his sword, Shadrael
heard Vordachai's voice shouting over the noise and saw
his brother surrounded by five soldiers. Hemming in the
warlord with tall shields, they were hacking at him from all
sides.

Horseless, and with only one warrior at his back, Vordachai stood roaring curses and fending off attack with a
sword in one hand and a maul in the other. A soldier feinted,
drawing his attention, while another struck him from behind, making him stagger.

Swearing, Shadrael spurred his horse and rode right into
the back of the nearest soldier, knocking the man down and
trampling over him while his sword took off the head of a
second one. By then, his charging horse had carried him
through the circle. He took down a third man, improving
the odds for Vordachai, who yelled with renewed fervor

and found the strength to fell his fourth opponent. The remaining soldier picked up his shield and fled.

"Shadrael?" Vordachai shouted, panting so hard he wheezed. "That you?"

"Who else?" Shadrael replied.

Still panting, so red faced he looked as though he might burst in apoplexy, Vordachai peered up at Shadrael. His beard was soaked with sweat, and a trickle of blood was running down his face. His weapons were smeared with gore, and there was a fearsome dent in his breastplate. Even so, his dark eyes were dancing with the joy of battle.

"Well fought, brother!" he gasped out, lifting his sword in brief salute. "Gods, what work this is."

Shadrael fended off a man in a fierce skirmish that cost his foe an arm. As the soldier staggered away, spurting blood and screaming, Shadrael turned back to Vordachai.

"Where's your horse?" he asked.

"Killed under me." Vordachai wiped sweat from his eyes with the back of his hand. "These brutes are tireless. They never stop coming."

Shadrael bit back the obvious comment and pointed. "The Ninth has joined the fight."

"May Gault blight them," Vordachai said, sucking in air. "My men are cut off. Surrounded, I think."

"Yes."

"Yours?"

"All dead."

A pair of soldiers ran toward them, yelling the war cries of the Tenth. Shadrael spurred his horse forward, blocking them from Vordachai. He made the animal rear, its forefeet striking at one soldier while he swung at the second. The man staggered backward with a cry, clapping his hand to his bleeding face. As the horse came down on all four feet, Shadrael met the first soldier's grab for him with a quick short blow that gashed the man's arm. Blood spurted, and Shadrael gave him a second, fatal blow in the neck.

Wheeling his horse around, he saw Vordachai in trouble once again. The warlord was exhausted, staggering on his feet, and barely able to lift his weapons. His opponent knocked him down and knelt on him, raising his short sword to drive in a fatal thrust.

Shadrael's blade cut off the man's head, sending it spinning through the air, helmet and all.

"Vordachai, quickly!" he shouted, reaching down his free hand. "Up behind me!"

Thrashing about like a beetle flipped on its back, Vordachai managed to roll over and climb to his feet while Shadrael fought off more attacks. Finally, panting too hard to speak, Vordachai scrambled up clumsily behind Shadrael's saddle.

Shadrael's horse shied under the extra weight, but he sent the animal in the direction Vordachai was pointing. Riding across the field, fighting off every attempt to bring them down, Shadrael heard his brother laughing aloud and marveled at Vordachai's ebullient spirits even in defeat.

Ulinians cheered them as they rode by, and Vordachai waved as though he had victory instead. Heartened by the sight of him, his warriors fought on with enough courage to make even Shadrael proud of them.

Shadrael dodged a pair of soldiers determined to pull him from the saddle, and spurred his way through the line, breaking free and fetching up beneath a vantage point of jutting black rock where the surviving Ulinian barons were crouched, surveying the progress of the battle and arguing among themselves.

As Vordachai greeted them and plunged into the discussion, Shadrael kept a frowning eye on the battle. More and more Ulinians were being cut down while their leaders chattered, apparently unable to agree on how to proceed. It angered Shadrael to see such weak leadership and lack of preparation displayed before the men. These warriors—exhausted and outnumbered, obviously close to throwing down their weapons in surrender—deserved better.

"Vordachai," he said impatiently, overhearing some fantastic scheme, "in the name of the gods, have done—"

Trumpets sounded, causing him to break off. He turned that way, seeing the emperor riding toward the battlefield on his white horse. Drums were beating, and standard bearers and flag bearers proceeded Light Bringer.

Gasps of astonishment came from the Ulinian barons, while Shadrael and Vordachai exchanged looks of outrage.

"Who has told him the battle has ended?" Vordachai shouted. "How dare he ride forth to claim this field?"

"He insults us!" Shadrael said furiously. "Damn him!"

"Arrogant puppy!" Vordachai said. "Get me a mount!" he roared. "I'll teach this upstart some manners."

Men scurried to bring him a horse. Vordachai climbed into the saddle and drew his sword. "Ulinians, to me!" he cried.

The barons cheered him, spurring their mounts forward.

But by then Shadrael had realized that the emperor's entry onto the field meant something far worse than a premature claim of victory. He could feel a growing heaviness in the air, a shifting sense of something about to happen.

"Vordachai," he said urgently, breaking in on what his brother was saying to the barons. "Call your men to retreat. I'll help break them through the line . . . there." He pointed. "Lead them into the canyons as fast as you can."

Everyone stared at him as though he'd suddenly turned blue and begun to speak in Madrun.

Vordachai scowled. "Not this again. Damn you, Shadrael, what mean you by this treachery? Dishonor myself by fleeing the field just as that leprous dog takes it? Never!"

"The army of the dead is coming," Shadrael said urgently. "The emperor has entered the trap, and now the priests will close it."

Disbelief filled Vordachai's face, only to be replaced by the dawning light of glee. "At last!" he said in relief. "I was beginning to think there might not be any of us left before they brought their aid."

"You don't want to be here—"

"Shut up! I won't listen to you a moment longer. Men, to me!" Vordachai shouted, and galloped forward.

At that moment the world seemed to shift. The air grew unnaturally still, and Shadrael felt shadows forming, forcing open the Hidden Ways. Horrified, he whirled his alarmed horse around just as the opening gaped wide. The all-too-familiar stench of evil rolled out, as sour and rotten as the grave, and he heard a peculiar clattering sound that he recognized from his past and had hoped he would never hear again.

Years before, when he was just a young cohort leader and Kostimon still sat on his ruby throne, Shadrael had been forced to fight with the dead. As a *donare*, he'd shared the duties of controlling the vile creatures with their shambling gait and dead stares. Mindless, they had moved here and yon as directed, attacking anything in their path and tearing it to pieces. Shadrael had heard the clacking of bones in his dreams for months afterward, exactly as he heard it now.

The hair rose on the back of his neck, and it was as though his past nightmares had sprung to life. From the Hidden Ways poured an army of walking skeletons, their bony feet clattering on the hard ground, their eyeless skulls questing blindly as they emerged into the open air.

A howl that came from no human throat rose from within the shadow realm, and it made Shadrael's blood run cold.

Beside him, Vordachai sat rigid in his saddle, his eyes protruding from their sockets. "What in Gault's name—"

"The army of the dead," Shadrael said grimly. "As promised by Urmaeor. Hear me now if you value your life! These are *not* your allies."

Around him fell silence, as more and more men stopped fighting and turned to face what was coming. Brawny soldiers with gore-smeared swords suddenly gripped their amulets. The Ulinians fell back, ashen with shock.

A horse and rider came galloping up, reining before Shadrael with a flourishing salute. It was Fomo, his stringy hair tied back from his eyes, the stink of fresh blood potion hanging on his breath. Grinning at Shadrael, he positioned his horse in front of Vordachai.

"Compliments of Lord Urmaeor," he said, his hoarse, rasping voice straining to make itself heard over the clatter of moving bones. "Your army is delivered, as promised."

Still staring at the skeletons, Vordachai seemed incapable of answering.

"That'll do," Shadrael said in dismissal.

Resentment flashed across Fomo's tattooed face. "Best you set about sending 'em that way, m'lord," he said, pointing toward the emperor.

A scream pierced the air, a man's death cry. Shadrael saw that the first of the walking skeletons had reached an Imperial soldier. The soldier backed away from the skeleton, which had swung out of the column to attack. Stumbling back, the soldier had slashed frantically with his sword, but the skeleton sprang at him and bore him to the ground, tearing him apart in a grisly death.

And even more were coming, an infinite number pouring from the Hidden Ways.

Too many, Shadrael thought in growing alarm. He turned to Vordachai. "Now do you see?" he said urgently. "Vordachai, recall your men now."

"Too late for that," Fomo rasped. He pointed, and Shadrael saw that the skeletons were splitting, half of them heading southward as though to block the only real exit from the battlefield. "Now," Fomo said eagerly, "we show the upstart's light lovers what death's all about."

More screams rose as men began to fight and die. Others ran, but the skeletons chased them like hounds, bringing them down.

"Vordachai!" Shadrael said, gripping his brother's shoulder.

The warlord breathed out something, his horrified gaze still locked on the sight before him. "How can Beloth still be with us?" he asked. "What are these unholy things?"

"They're your army, as requested," Fomo said, maneuvering up beside his horse.

Vordachai struck him with the back of his hand, nearly knocking him from his saddle. "And they're killing my men, as many of my men as the enemy," the warlord said furiously. "Get back to those damned priests and have them call off this spell. I won't be a part of it. I won't!"

"Not even to see Light Bringer die?" Fomo asked slyly.

"That'll do, Centruin!" Shadrael barked. "You have your orders. Go!"

Glowering, Fomo galloped away. Some of the skeletons turned as though to pursue him, but movement from the men on foot caught their attention and they marched onward.

Like the giant white ants of the desert, Shadrael thought. Ravenous, mindless brutes that consumed the flesh of any living thing in their path.

He turned to his brother, but Vordachai was already issuing orders. "Sound the retreat," he said. "Hurry!"

"Careful," Shadrael warned him. "The men must not run, or the dead will chase them."

"Gods," Vordachai muttered, still staring. "I never thought—I didn't believe you. Can you control them, as that knave said?"

"Not anymore."

Turning pale, Vordachai looked at him then. "You mean you've done so in the past?"

"Only once," Shadrael said grimly. "I wasn't proud of that day."

Vordachai swallowed visibly. "How are they killed? I mean—stopped?"

"With magic."

"A pox on that!" Vordachai swore. "The shadows are supposed to be gone. What evil has brought this back upon us?"

"Our only hope now is Light Bringer," Shadrael replied, glancing in the direction of the emperor. Although halfway across the battlefield, the emperor's progress had stopped, and soldiers were running now to position themselves between the skeletons and His Imperial Majesty. "He destroyed Beloth. Surely he can burn this evil away as well."

"I won't surrender to *him*," Vordachai said in renewed fury. "Not for all the bones in this world or the next!"

"Then hack them to bits," Shadrael replied grimly, swinging his horse around and drawing his sword. "For they are upon us."

Chapter 24

Catching the horse, Lea galloped back into the Valley of Fires with an air spirit guiding her through the folded maze of canyons until at last, shortly past midday, she topped a ridge and came to the battlefield.

She heard the screams first, then saw a scene of terrible carnage. Men were running in all directions, pausing only to desperately fend off the creatures swarming them. Hacking, chopping, smashing . . . Lea had never seen so much blood, nor could anything have prepared her for the dreadful slaughter taking place. The field was full of *na-quai*, and all benign spirits of the elements seemed to have fled.

Even her little guide, the gentle air spirit that had coiled around her neck during the ride back to this valley, now vanished. All Lea found before her were death and fear and evil. It was as though shadow had returned to darken the world, and it frightened her.

Many of the Imperial soldiers had drawn themselves into a tight column, holding their shields across each other in a defensive wall as they retreated slowly and steadily in

good order. Others had been caught on the field and now
fought for their lives against the terrible creatures seeking
to kill them. Screams of the dying filled the air. Officers
were riding frightened horses back and forth, shouting and
trying to keep the men in better order. As for the Ulinians,
Lea saw no flag flying, and far too many of the trampled
corpses wore Ulinian mail and clothing.

She saw Caelan on the opposite side of the field, well
away from the carnage, astride an enormous white horse
that pranced and pawed. Her brother, wearing his crown
and a breastplate of hammered gold, seemed to be yelling
orders, but he was not fighting.

She saw a few Ulinians bunched tightly around a
bearded man in armor that reflected the sunlight in bursts
of silver, but Shadrael did not seem to be with them.

From her vantage point, she saw an opening to the Hidden Ways, where even more of the skeleton creatures were
spilling forth, running toward their living prey with a
deadly kind of intensity. And just inside the opening, she
glimpsed a tall priest in robes of saffron.

Lea's heart quailed a moment before it beat with fresh
determination. If Urmaeor had wrought this horror, she
told herself, he must be stopped.

"M'lady!" a voice called out.

Startled, she looked around, and saw a bedraggled man
stumbling toward her. His cloak hung in tatters, and his
breastplate was dented and streaked with grime and blood.
A drawn sword was in his hand, and his eyes looked wild.

Lea instinctively tightened the reins, making her horse
back up. "Thirbe?" she called uncertainly.

Gasping for breath, he stumbled to a halt a short distance
from her, holding up his hand as though for mercy.
"M'lady, what are you doing here? It's not safe for you. Not
safe for anyone."

Lea frowned. He looked like Thirbe. He sounded like
Thirbe. But she'd been fooled once today. She could not risk

being deceived a second time. Digging into her pocket, she removed the tiny *gli*-emerald that had served her so well.

"Come to me," she said breathlessly, aware of what she was risking. "Come very close. Now."

Still panting, he obeyed her, putting out a hand to grasp the reins as her horse tried to swing away from him. Then he was at her stirrup, close enough to pull her from the saddle and kill her if he chose.

"Hold out your hand," she said. "I want you to take this."

He frowned. "M'lady, this is no time for—"

"Do as I say."

Still frowning, he turned up his grubby palm, and she placed the *gli*-emerald on it. He peered at the stone, looking bewildered. "What am I to do with it?"

"Oh, Thirbe!" she said gladly, reaching down to grip his callused hand. "How relieved I am to see you."

"Wish I could say the same," he muttered, squeezing her fingers to belie his gruff tone. "You shouldn't be here, not in this bloodbath. Are you well? The last time I saw you, you looked mighty poorly. How came you to escape?"

"I can't tell you now. Climb up behind me. We must put a stop to this terrible evil."

"You leave the fighting to the emperor," Thirbe said in alarm. He climbed onto her horse with alacrity and would have reached around her to take the reins if she hadn't stopped him. "M'lady, let me—"

"No," Lea said firmly. "I must find Shadrael."

"M'lady, don't be daft. That blackguard could be anywhere. Run off or dead by now. You haven't a hope of finding him until this is over."

An agonized scream rent the air. Lea flinched, tears filling her eyes, but she blinked them away. She could not bear what she was seeing, yet she had no intention of retreating to safety. Again she gazed across the battlefield, searching for Shadrael. "He cannot withstand this," she said to Thirbe. "He will forget what has come so new to him. He will try to fight in the old ways he knew before, and—there!" She pointed. "I see him!"

A rider in a black cloak was galloping at an angle between the retreating Ulinians and the advancing skeletons. Lea could see that Imperial troops—instead of assisting the Ulinians—were closing in from the rear, cutting off their flight from the dead. The warlord and his men were trapped, unable to escape certain destruction. And Lea found herself outraged at her brother's army for taking such unfair advantage of the Ulinians. All the men should be united against the army of the dead, she thought. And yet they were not. It shamed her that her brother had not called a halt to such actions.

As for Shadrael, he was galloping away, angling closer to the skeletons than he should.

"Running, by Gault," Thirbe said in contempt. "The surly knave—"

"No!" Lea protested, leaning forward. "He's trying to draw them after him. Oh, he risks too much. Too much!"

She saw Shadrael spur his frightened horse forward when it would have turned. The animal slung its head and shied, bucking with him. And during that pause the skeletons rushed at him, moving faster than Lea thought possible. Shadrael reined in his terrified horse, keeping it from bolting.

"He *is* leading them away," Lea said in excitement, her heart in her mouth. She saw one of the creatures leap at his back and gasped aloud as Shadrael shook it off. "I understand where he's going. Do you see, Thirbe? Do you?"

"Leading 'em back to the Hidden Ways," Thirbe said, sounding astonished. "Damned cool of him."

Lea saw Urmaeor move, turning about and lifting his arms. "No!" she cried out, kicking her horse forward. "He's closing the Hidden Ways. He can't. He mustn't!"

"M'lady, what are you doing?"

Lea bent low over her horse's whipping mane, urging it faster. "We must stop this!" she shouted.

Thirbe's protest was lost in the wind. Lea kicked her horse even faster, skimming along the top of the ridge bordering the battlefield until broken terrain forced her to angle her mount down the slope into the actual field.

Her protector was still yelling at her back, reaching forward in an effort to grab the reins from her. Lea fended him off as with all her might she called for the earth spirits to come to her aid again.

A pair of bloodied men sprang up as though from nowhere, yelling at her, and trying to stop her horse. Lea yanked the reins and sent her horse dodging them. The horse stumbled, and Lea was nearly thrown over its head, but she clung tightly and escaped the ambush, galloping on with her heart thudding in her throat.

Skeletons came at her, bony fingers grabbing at her skirts and arms. Lea screamed, and Thirbe's sword smashed one of the arms in twain, sending splinters of bone flying. Ahead, Lea saw Urmaeor standing within the safety of the shadow realm, watching without expression. The wide opening to the Hidden Ways was closing, nearly shut now. Desperate to stop him, Lea reached for her necklace and pulled one of the *gli*-emeralds from its setting.

Light flashed as the stone came free. With all her might, she threw the jewel into the opening. Her aim was true, and there was an explosion of brilliant greenish white light that seared deep into the Hidden Ways. Nearly blinded, Lea shielded her eyes while Thirbe swore and pulled her close against him as though to keep her safe.

The Hidden Ways closed, and the air stank of sulfur and heat.

Through watering eyes, she glimpsed Urmaeor thrown to his hands and knees as though ejected from the shadow world. He scrambled nimbly to his feet and fled, holding up his robes in order to run. In moments he had vanished from sight among some boulders.

"Like a rat, bolting into its hole," Thirbe said angrily.

"Not his hole," Lea said. "He hasn't escaped yet."

Intending to go after him, she gathered her reins. Thirbe, however, was tapping her shoulder.

"M'lady, look!"

The skeletons suddenly milled about aimlessly, stumbling into each other, attacking each other. Others collapsed on the ground or stood still, bony arms waving. Howling so bestial and wild it could not be human filled the air. The creatures pursuing Shadrael, however, did not pause. They were gaining on him, Lea saw now.

She cried out a warning, but he did not seem to hear her. And as he approached, still heading for the opening that no longer existed, Lea saw him realize it. He reined up his horse involuntarily. The animal slowed and stumbled, its flanks heaving, and the skeletons caught up with him.

Standing in his stirrups, Shadrael fought off attack from all sides, but they were swarming him now.

"Earth spirits!" she cried, and they came, rumbling through the ground in rapid furrows. "There!" she shouted, pointing.

A tremor shook the ground as a chasm opened, sending many of the skeletons plunging into it. Shadrael's horse reared dangerously close to the edge, and for a heart-stopping moment Lea feared he would topple from the saddle and be lost.

But he clung to his mount and sent it forward away from danger.

"M'lady, to the west!" Thirbe shouted.

Lea looked and saw that the remainder of the skeletons had regrouped. They were now heading toward the Imperial forces. "Caelan!" she whispered.

She saw soldiers fighting off the attack. Now Caelan was entering the fray, fighting with his men, putting himself in danger. Wheeling her horse around, Lea galloped in that direction with Thirbe yelling at her to stop.

"Earth spirits!" she called again.

But no fresh furrows appeared in the ground. Glancing over her shoulder, Lea saw the spirits following her, but too slowly. She frowned, uncertain what held them back, and looked ahead in time to see a skeleton leap at Caelan, nearly dragging him from the saddle.

"No!" she screamed. "Caelan!"

But her brother straightened, his sword slashing hard. Relief filled her, but only for a moment. He was attacked from behind. This time his horse reared up, and he was pulled off, vanishing from Lea's sight as though the ground itself had swallowed him.

"Caelan!" she screamed in horror. And then the skeletons were all around her, too.

$\mathfrak{S}$hadrael's horse was starting to pull away from the skeletons pursuing him when the animal stumbled and went down. Shadrael heard the unmistakable sound of a fetlock snapping as he was tossed through the air. He hit the ground hard, rolling over from the impetus, and found himself fending off a human foe before he hardly had his wits about him.

Driving his dagger in the man's ribs, he forced himself to his feet. His head was ringing, and he could not seem to orient himself, but instinctively he kept moving. By now the skeletons had caught up with him. Shadrael pulled his axe from his belt. Using it in one hand and his sword in the other, he started knocking the skeletons back.

Behind him, his horse was kicking and thrashing, unable to gain its feet, and moaning in pain. Shadrael saw more skeletons closing fast, but he ran to the horse and killed it out of mercy, not wanting the shadow creatures to attack it. Even so, they swarmed the animal as though attracted to its blood.

Ahead of him came a flash of yellow, and his wits pulled together. He remembered seeing Urmaeor running for cover. He'd been chasing the devil when his horse went down. The only way to truly stop the skeletons was to kill the priest controlling them.

"Gladly," he muttered.

With a wary eye on the skeletons still clustered around

his dead horse, Shadrael ran after the priest on feet that felt too clumsy and slow. But as he gradually gained on his quarry, he saw that it wasn't Urmaeor after all. Several priests were scurrying among a scattering of boulders, like mice in search of cover.

Grunting with effort, Shadrael heard the horrible clatter of bones as pursuit resumed behind him. His outstretched fingers closed on the robes of the priest, and he yanked hard, pulling the priest off his feet. Shadrael was on him in an instant, striking hard.

His axe hit something unseen that was not flesh or bone, but rigid like an invisible shield. Shadrael's blow, however, broke through and the axe bit deep into the man's body.

The priest's scream rent the air, and black shadow flowed forth from the wound instead of blood, becoming ashes that blew apart in the wind.

Forcing himself onto his feet, Shadrael left the man for the skeletons to pull apart. He caught another priest and killed him the same way. Behind him, the skeletons began to fall, more of them crumbling to dust. A ragged cheer in the distance went up from human throats.

Shadrael paused only to wipe sweat from his brow with a weary hand. He had to find Urmaeor if this bloodbath was to stop.

Halfway up the ridge, he found a narrow track of sorts that twisted through the rocks. Pulling himself past larger and larger boulders, he suddenly caught up with Urmaeor. The priest was clinging to his staff as though it were precious. He was guarded by two cringing mercenaries and a mutilated lurker.

The lurker shrieked at the sight of Shadrael and fled, lurching awkwardly as it vanished. Urmaeor spoke sharply to the mercenaries to keep them from fleeing also. They stared grimly at Shadrael, their hands white-knuckled on their weapons, and when their gaze shifted to look at what was coming behind him, Shadrael attacked.

One man fought him, only to die as Shadrael struck him down. The remaining mercenary ran.

And then it was Urmaeor and Shadrael alone. The priest lifted his hand and Shadrael felt something push past him. When he glanced over his shoulder he saw the skeletons held back by some invisible barrier.

"How long can you hold them off?" Shadrael asked, gulping in deep breaths while he had the chance.

"You will not prevail," Urmaeor snarled at Shadrael, his deep voice raw with strain. And he grabbed at Shadrael's threads of life.

In agony, Shadrael felt the ground heave and tremble beneath his boots, and he was released. Urmaeor swayed, nearly losing his balance, and Shadrael sprang at him.

He knocked Urmaeor sprawling and pinned him fast, smashing one hand across the priest's mouth before magic could be uttered. Even so, he felt Urmaeor's power pulsing against his palm, burning him until he had to grit his teeth to keep from releasing the man.

They were too close for him to use his sword. Dropping the weapon, Shadrael drew his dagger while Urmaeor's eyes widened and he struggled harder. There came a tremendous cracking sound, and the ground heaved again just as Shadrael struck.

He missed, losing his hold on Urmaeor, and tumbled off as the priest scrambled for freedom. Shadrael tackled him and pinned him again, but Urmaeor was spitting out curses that flamed in the air. Some of them struck Shadrael, and they hurt like darts piercing his skin. He could not seem to get his dagger close enough although he strained to break through Urmaeor's resistance.

And then a fissure opened in the ground, coming toward them as the earthquake shook boulders loose and sent them tumbling dangerously in all directions. Flung about on the heaving ground, Shadrael lost his hold on the priest and scrambled away from the fissure. It ran beneath Urmaeor, who flailed wildly and fell into it. His cries abruptly cut off as the ground closed, crushing him.

The tremors continued, while Shadrael dodged a boulder in time to avoid being knocked flat. He stumbled over Urmaeor's staff and saw the green mist swirling inside its crystal prison. Picking up the staff, Shadrael swung it with both hands and brought it crashing down upon a stone.

The crystal broke, and the mist that was Lord Barthel's essence spilled out into the sunlight and fresh air. It turned into black ashes that the wind blew away.

The earthquake stopped abruptly. There was complete silence for a moment as though the world struggled to catch its breath; then Shadrael heard the sound of voices calling out. Men began to cheer and whoop.

He climbed to his feet, wearily gathering his weapons, and saw that the fighting had stopped. Across the field, the skeletons were all crumbling to dust. Someone raised Vordachai's banner, its tattered ends catching the breeze only for a moment before Imperial soldiers closed in, pulling it down.

Shadrael saw the surviving Ulinians throwing down their arms. His heart squeezed in anguish for a moment; then he collected himself and ran in that direction.

Pulled off her horse with Thirbe separated from her, Lea kicked and struggled against her captor, only to be crushed against a breastplate with enough force to nearly squeeze the breath from her lungs.

"Be still, little one!" her brother said in her ear. "When did you learn to fight like a hellcat?"

"Caelan?"

"Who else?"

Disbelieving, she twisted around to gaze up into her brother's face. His silver eyes smiled a little quizzically into her blue ones, searching as though he had questions of her. A tremendous rush of joy swept through Lea. "Oh, Caelan!" she cried, and flung her arms around him.

Chapter 25

Long before Shadrael could stumble wearily across the field to rejoin his brother's force, he was captured and made to surrender his weapons. Eventually, however, he was pushed into the midst of the Ulinians—perhaps less than two hundred men by the looks of things. Vordachai, hale and safe, was roaring his displeasure at the top of his lungs.

"I'll surrender to the emperor and no one else, you damned, verminous pox mark! I'm the warlord of this province, and—"

"You're a filthy traitor and a prisoner of war," a grimy centruin said, unimpressed. He was tall, with the height and size of a Traulander. He wore the insignia of the Tenth Legion. "Strip that armor and look sharp about it. Strip!"

Faced by a man who could yell louder than he, Vordachai unbuckled his armor and let it fall in a loud clatter to the ground. He kicked it, muttering in his beard. "And it comes to this, eh?" he said to Shadrael. "Begone, brother! No need for you to stand with us now."

Shadrael gave him a rueful smile. "When you go before the emperor, some contrition might gain you mercy."

"My head will be on a spike in his quarters by nightfall," Vordachai grumbled. "And don't give me more advice! I'm no diplomat and never was. No, and no court posy either to mince about and flatter His Imperial Damned Majesty."

"Keep quiet!" the centruin barked.

Shadrael grimaced at Vordachai in fresh exasperation. "Do you want your tongue cut out for insulting him? Have a care!"

"A condemned man taking care," Vordachai said with a snort. "I'll be dragged before him and he'll sneer at me and I'll break my sword and fling it in his face. Then some brute will run me through." Vordachai rubbed his face with both hands and sighed. "Damn."

"Ask for his mercy," Shadrael suggested. "Tell him why his taxes are choking you. Ask for another chance."

"Beg, you mean."

Shadrael raised his brows. "Better a beggar with your head on your shoulders than the alternative. Show some sense now, at least."

"You," the centruin said to Shadrael. "Strip that armor and be quick about it."

Shadrael had just unbuckled his breastplate and felt the cool kiss of air through his sweat-soaked undertunic when he felt a hand tap his shoulder from behind. He turned around and saw Fomo, wild eyed and grinning nervously, right behind him.

Shadrael took an involuntary step away from the man.

Fomo's gaze darted in all directions. He held up the talisman Shadrael had tried to give Vordachai earlier that day. "Worked sweet, didn't it? Never thought I'd make it, did you?"

"Fomo—"

"Still here," Fomo went on, unheeding. "And now look at you, going to get off free as air, because of that witch making eyes at you. Leaving the rest of us to be executed."

"We'll all go to the executioner's axe," Shadrael said quietly. Beside him, Vordachai's hand gripped his shoulder as though offering comfort. Shadrael glanced at his brother and gave him a quick, rueful smile.

But Fomo wouldn't go away, not even when they were pushed into a line and marched forward. He stuck close to Shadrael.

"Not you," he whispered to Shadrael, his gaze darting in all directions. "No execution for you. Got your soul back," he said raggedly, hugging himself as though he were cold. "Ain't sworn to shadow now. Ain't going to die like the rest of us. Got that witch to speak up for you, but you won't speak for us. Too good for us now. Too—"

"Shut up, Fomo," Shadrael said.

In front of him, Vordachai turned around. "Who *is* this piece of lice and why does he plague you?"

Before Shadrael could answer, Fomo screamed in rage and pulled a knife from his undertunic. He grabbed Shadrael, trying to pull him onto the blade. Shadrael twisted his torso and missed being impaled, but Fomo was already striking again.

Only the blow fell short because Vordachai punched him hard in the chest. "You filthy whoreson!" he shouted, and punched Fomo again.

Staggering back, Fomo doubled over, coughing harshly. But he hadn't dropped the knife, and he sprang at Shadrael a third time. Shadrael had seen him pull that trick before and was ready, but Vordachai stepped between them.

Shadrael heard his brother grunt and saw Fomo back away with a scowl. Vordachai sagged, and Shadrael caught him, trying to support him as his brother sank down with Fomo's dagger in his chest. Too late, their guards restrained Fomo, who was swearing at Shadrael like a man demented.

Ignoring him as he was bound and hustled away, Shadrael knelt beside Vordachai. He watched blood bubbling up around the blade and heard the wet, sucking rattle in Vordachai's lungs. The knife had been driven deep, clear to the hilt. Grief welled up inside Shadrael, burning his throat and eyes.

After surviving today's harrowing battle with no more
than a few bruises and scratches, for Vordachai to be struck
down like this, so senselessly, so stupidly . . . frustration
swelled inside Shadrael until he could barely hold back his
rage.

"Vordachai," he said in a little moan. "Ah, gods, *no!*"

His brother's eyes sought his. He smiled a little, tried to
speak, and slumped over.

Shadrael lifted him up, tipping his chin. "Vordachai?"

But his brother was dead, sightless eyes staring at the
wintry blue sky.

The other Ulinian prisoners gathered around, heedless
of the soldiers that tried to move them along. Everyone
looked shocked. The two surviving barons hurried up and
stared at their fallen lord. And Shadrael bowed his head,
unable to release his grasp on his brother although nothing
remained to hang on to.

"He saved your life, my lord," someone said.

"That madman would have killed you," another agreed.

The Traulander centruin strode up to them, looking exasperated. "Back in line! One dead prisoner means one
less—" He broke off, looking surprised. "The warlord?"

The wounded baron, cradling a bloody arm, spoke to
him in a murmur while the other baron suddenly knelt before Shadrael. "My fealty to you, Warlord Shadrael. May
your governance be long and prosperous over us."

Having quelled the impatient centruin, the wounded
baron now knelt with assistance. "My fealty to you, Warlord Shadrael," he said hoarsely, his eyes dark with shock.
"My sword, my lands, my honor are yours to command."

The remaining Ulinians also knelt, one by one to swear
their fealty, while their guards stood silent, allowing it.

Numb and silent, Shadrael barely listened to what they
were saying. His thoughts were on his brother, burly,
hot-tempered, impulsive Vordachai, who had bullied and
teased him throughout boyhood, resented him and felt jeal-
ous of him by turns through their adulthood. Vordachai had

always turned to him for advice in a pinch, yet seldom followed any of it. And now his foolish, impulsive elder brother had saved his life.

For what? Shadrael wondered bitterly. *For what?*

Eventually the centruins moved the prisoners on. Shadrael was pulled away from his brother's cooling corpse. A cloak was laid over Vordachai, and his official seal on a small silver chain was unfastened from his throat and handed to Shadrael, who took it without a glance. Still holding it as his wrists were bound, Shadrael was herded with his fellow prisoners to await the emperor's decision.

The afternoon waned and grew cold. Shivering, Shadrael was surprised when two decivates came, saluted, and escorted him to the emperor.

It was his first time to see Caelan Light Bringer face-to-face. Shadrael knelt, his expression grim and set, and regarded the man who had so long been his enemy.

Seated on a camp stool draped with fur, wearing his crown and a face as stony as Shadrael's own, the emperor was a bigger man than Shadrael had expected. Caelan Light Bringer was a man head and shoulders taller than most, with a brawny chest and muscles any man would envy. His blond hair hung loose to his shoulders, and his silver eyes were hard to meet.

No mercy softened his face, and Shadrael could well believe this was the man who had hounded so many capable officers from the army during the Reforms. He had the look of one who had walked through fire and worse. He clearly knew shadow, knew evil, knew the devious hearts of men, yet there was nothing idle, dissipated, or corrupt about him. In that sense, Shadrael found him nothing like Emperor Kostimon at all.

Forcing himself to return that steady silver gaze, Shadrael frowned at this emperor whom he'd hated since the day of Kostimon's death. He suddenly found that he had no more hatred left. Vindicants and their monsters had been the enemy, the only enemy.

The silence between them grew long, but Shadrael did not fidget or seek to break the quiet. This, he knew, was the end of him.

"So," the emperor said at last. "You are the new war-lord, I hear. And the man so long a thorn in my side, the man who would not pay his taxes, who would not bow his stubborn neck to my authority, the man who dared steal Her Imperial Highness from family and friends—jeopardizing her life—lies dead."

"I abducted her, Excellency," Shadrael said gruffly.

"But on his orders," the emperor said.

Shadrael met those silver eyes and could not lie. It was time, he reminded himself, to stop protecting Vordachai from his folly. "Yes, Excellency. He gave the order."

"And so I am robbed from dealing justice to this miscre-ant, this traitor who dared rebel against my authority."

Shadrael's mouth closed to a thin line. "We served him gladly."

"You are his successor?"

"Yes, Excellency." Shadrael frowned in an effort to con-trol his emotions . . . and his voice. "His younger brother."

"Praetinor Shadrael tu Natalloh."

Shadrael looked up. He could not speak.

"Dishonorably discharged, I'm told."

"Yes."

"Yet once a hero and a legion commander. A man given a triumph through the streets of Imperia. I remember hear-ing about it. For a legend of the empire, Lord Shadrael, you have not behaved respectably. Have you more sense than your hotheaded brother?"

The conversation began to puzzle Shadrael. He frowned. "I used to think so, Excellency."

But the emperor grunted and leaned back. He did not seem pleased by Shadrael's answers.

There came a commotion from somewhere in the crowd

surrounding them. The Imperial entourage parted to let Lea walk through. Her unbound hair hung in a shining veil around her shoulders. Her eyes were as intense a blue as the sky. She wore a gown of cream and fawn and gloves a bit too large for her dainty hands. Her necklace sparkled at her throat.

Amazed, Shadrael could only stare at her. "How did you—"

Abruptly collecting himself, he broke off the rest of his question, knowing he had no right to speak unbidden in the emperor's presence. Lea stood at his side with her hand resting on his shoulder. His heart thudded wildly at her proximity, her touch. He did not know how she came to be here, but she was alive and well. He felt dizzy with relief.

With a happy smile, Lea turned to face her frowning brother. "And now you have met him," she said. "This man of whom I have spoken. Shadrael tu Natalloh."

The emperor's gaze went to her smiling face and softened fractionally, but when he looked again at Shadrael he grew stern. "You have accepted your new role?" he asked. "You mean to take Vordachai's place?"

"I have accepted fealty," Shadrael replied cautiously.

Lea's grip tightened on his shoulder. "I'm sorry," she whispered. "I know how much you loved your brother."

Shadrael frowned fiercely, his grief as yet too raw to express. "He was a dolt," he muttered, and barely kept his voice from breaking.

"If you take his place," the emperor continued, "then do you also accept the present charges laid against the warlord of Ulinia?"

"They are my responsibility," Shadrael replied. He thought of how once he would have shrugged off everything, believing he didn't care about Ulinia or its people. And now . . . he wished with sudden intensity that Light Bringer would stop toying with him and just pronounce his sentence.

"You accept the charge of treason?"

"I abducted Lady Lea," Shadrael said. "My guilt is equal to my brother's. Greater."

"No," Lea breathed. "Do not say it that way. As though you are . . . Caelan, don't accept what he tells you."

"He is telling me the truth, Lea," the emperor said. "Would you prefer he begged for mercy and lied to me?"

"But I have explained everything to you," she said impatiently, stamping her small foot. "Why need this be dragged out? Why do you not pardon him, as I have asked?"

"Lea!" Shadrael said involuntarily.

The corners of the emperor's mouth tugged although he did not smile. He glanced at his sister. "Are you sure about him?"

"Yes," she said clearly, her voice containing no hesitation.

The emperor's frown deepened. "This is a man so sworn to shadow that he could not accept reform. This is a man reputed to have no soul. Blood and death are on his hands. How can you bear his proximity? What has happened to you, little one?"

"All that I have told you," she replied serenely. "Test him if you wish. He will not fail."

Alarmed, Shadrael rose to his feet, and the emperor's protector stepped forward with a half-drawn sword.

"Free his hands," the emperor ordered.

Shadrael's bonds were cut. He flexed his wrists, keeping a wary eye on the emperor's protector. Thirbe, he noticed, was also standing close by, squinting fiercely with a hand on his sword hilt.

Lea unfastened her necklace and held it out to Shadrael. "Will you hold this, please?"

He hesitated, glancing at the emperor, who gave him a nod. A priest in the robes of a Reformant pushed forward to stand nearby. Shadrael held out his hand, and Lea draped the necklace across his palm.

For the first time since he'd met her, the *gli*-emeralds did not sting his skin. He felt nothing at all, and marveled a little.

Smiling, Lea picked up her necklace. The Reformant bent over Shadrael's hand, examining it closely.

"He is not burned, not affected," the man said. "He is no longer of shadow."

A murmur ran through the onlookers, and even the emperor seemed startled. "Are you sure?"

"Quite certain, Excellency." The priest turned his gaze back to Shadrael. "Will you accept the public swearing of your soul to the devotion of Gault?"

Uncertain of what might happen, Shadrael glanced at Lea and saw nothing but absolute confidence in her expression. He returned his gaze to the priest. "I will."

The priest touched his shoulders. "Then kneel, Lord Shadrael, and repeat these words of cleansing and renewal."

When the rite was finished, Shadrael rose to his feet, feeling rather amazed by the simplicity of it. He felt no different; certainly there had been no alteration inside him as when he'd first discovered the return of his soul. But neither did he feel sickened and filled with self-disgust as he had after every Vindicant ritual he'd ever participated in.

The emperor waved everyone back. "I would speak to this man alone."

In some consternation, the assembly of men, guards, and officers retreated. When Light Bringer shook his head at Lea, she smiled, squeezed Shadrael's hand briefly, and joined the others out of earshot.

"Lea has told me all that happened," the emperor said quietly, keeping his voice to a low murmur. "I am not inclined to forgive you or grant you a full pardon as she desires."

Surprised that apparently the emperor had even considered it, Shadrael blinked. "I did not expect you to consider mercy. I am grateful for the chance to swear my soul before my execution."

"You abducted my sister like a brute," the emperor said.

"For a time I thought you had corrupted her. For that alone, I could kill you."

Shadrael said nothing.

"You also saved her life. And possibly mine."

Frowning, Shadrael remained silent.

"You do not plead very hard for your life."

"I know my guilt," Shadrael replied. "I have been a bitter man for far too long. I have done evil acts. Whatever changes Lady Lea has wrought in me, I remain *donare*. Damaged, yes. Unable to perform magic as before. But still stained in some way by shadow."

"As are we all," the emperor said. He tilted his head. "I, too, am *donare*."

Startled, Shadrael blinked. The emperor gave him a slight nod, saying, "Even Lea is not exactly what she was before."

Guilt burned through Shadrael. "My fault."

"You condemn yourself faster than I can," the emperor said with a snort. "Are you as much a nuisance and troublemaker as your brother? Do you share his political views?"

Shadrael, amazed by this small opening, tried hard to take advantage of it. Thinking rapidly, he replied, "Ulinia is poor. In no condition to be independent."

"The taxes I have levied are harsh," the emperor said. "Since coming here, I now understand Ulinia's level of poverty as I did not before. But that doesn't mean I condone treason or rebellion. Neither is a solution to the problems here."

"If you execute me and the barons," Shadrael said, "you can mold the next warlord into whatever you please."

"Who is your heir?"

"My five-year-old nephew."

"Warlord Vordachai's son?"

"Our sister's son. Vordachai sired no children."

"A child cannot rule this province. I would have to annex it into a protectorate." Light Bringer shook his head. "No solution there."

Shadrael held his tongue.

"Lea has spoken to me most earnestly on your behalf," the emperor said with a scowl. "It seems she's in love with you. Do you deny it? Do you not return her feelings?"

"I deny nothing," Shadrael said in surprise. "My feelings are strong, but I cannot attain to her hand. I—"

"Are you bound to another?"

"No, and never will be. She is all I—" Shadrael halted, not daring to continue.

"I find her choice a poor one," the emperor said. "And you do nothing to convince me. You will not plead for yourself. She would offer you my empire and throne if she could. Yet I find you sullen and proud, too prickly to accept the opportunities thrown to you."

Shadrael shot the emperor a suspicious look. "I have reason to be cautious with a sword at my neck."

"Cautious? Or too surly to assure me of how much you will cherish her forever?"

"Of course I cherish her," Shadrael said hotly. "I—"

"Everyone does," the emperor said. "She has that effect on people, especially men."

Shadrael flushed. "Then I can convince you of nothing, Excellency."

The emperor laughed. "A clever remark, even if a sour one. Lea is not a melancholy creature. I don't understand what she sees in you . . . beyond the obvious attributes."

Shadrael found his face growing hot. "Are you saying I have a chance to win her hand, Excellency? Am I to be pardoned for all that's happened?"

"My sister is impulsive, merry, but wise. Her judgment is astute. I would not dream of questioning her decisions on anything important. And her happiness is one of the most important things in my life."

Shadrael felt his heart beating faster. He barely dared breathe. Could Lea have this much influence over Light Bringer? he wondered. It was rumored that she did, but until now he would not have believed it.

"Lea says you are to be trusted. She insists that, despite your reprehensible actions, it was the Vindicants behind the plot rather than you. And she's explained your motivations."

"My motivations were hatred of you, Excellency," Shadrael said stiffly, determined to be honest. "And a desire to strike at you for my discharge."

The emperor grunted, but did not rise to this bait. "Your record in the army, before your discharge, proves you to have been an excellent and loyal officer. Lea also insists that you will serve me as an exemplary warlord. Is she correct?"

"I—What is asked of me in exchange for so much mercy?"

The emperor frowned. "My conditions are these: that you squelch this propensity for uprisings, that you make this province loyal so that I don't have to station a legion here to keep order, that you stop the corruption robbing customs of most of its profit, that you eradicate all Vindicants from within your borders, that you find ways to improve the economy of this blighted land instead of exhausting it further, and that you alert me at once if shadow returns in any form. Is that agreeable to you?"

Astonished, Shadrael blinked. "Is that all?"

"I think you'll find it sufficient to keep you busy."

"You don't ask much of me, not after—"

"Lea does not wish to return to New Imperia with me. What have you to say about this? Have you asked her to remain with you?"

Shadrael found himself hot faced and clammy by turns. His heart was racing. "I—I've been in no position to—"

"Have you claimed her? Touched her?"

Shadrael met the emperor's stern eye, feeling the man's temper barely held in check. He swallowed hard. "Through *sevaisin* only, Excellency."

"Then she is not dishonored?"

"No!"

The emperor stared at him as though he could see every thought, every intention, every emotion inside Shadrael.

"You are much I dislike, but at least you don't lie. Do you want my sister in marriage?"

"I—" Shadrael lost his breath and had to start again. "Yes, Excellency. But—"

"I do not approve of the match," the emperor said, casting a look over at Lea, who smiled at them both. "You're hardly better than a brigand, despite your lineage. You aren't worthy to hold one of her slippers. And exiling her to this barren wasteland appalls me. Letting her marry you is nothing but an endorsement of the barbarian acts you've committed. But she loves you, and she's asked me to permit you two to marry."

Shadrael felt awash in confusion. He couldn't believe Lea had told her brother so much in such a short time. And he felt miffed that not only was she making the offer, but that he hadn't been permitted to speak to her first. He was used to being in charge, and longed to court her, but everything was moving so fast he felt as though he were dreaming.

"Feeling as though you've been caught in a snare and are hanging upside down from a tree?" the emperor asked.

"Yes, Excellency."

"Get used to it, for that is life with Lea. Have you a question?"

Shadrael hesitated, then drew a quick breath before he could lose his nerve. "I should like to court her. I—this is sudden—and I love her as though she is my heart, but this is not the Ulinian way of seeking a maiden's hand."

"With Lea nothing is ever ordinary," the emperor replied. "It says little for your ability to govern if you fail to understand how this business needs patching. If I force Lea to return to court, she will always be talked about. If she stays here, it will be much the same. Either way, her reputation is ruined."

"Scandal?" Shadrael frowned, ready to defend Lea against anyone. "Do you care more about her reputation than her happiness?"

"If I did, sir, your head would already be off your shoulders."

Shadrael flushed, his chin lifting.

They glared at each other a moment before the emperor said, "Lea dislikes life at my court. She will be unhappy enough there to try escaping again. Gault knows what kind of trouble she could land in next."

"But she—"

"Don't you think she knew what would befall her on her journey?" the emperor asked him. "She sees the future. Sometimes she makes the future."

Startled, Shadrael looked up. "Are you saying she—"

"You'll find out soon enough." Light Bringer gestured. "I don't want to crush this province, or enslave its people," he said wearily. "Let us come to terms. By all accounts, you've inherited an empty treasury. What bride price can you pay?"

Embarrassed, Shadrael cursed his brother's notorious problems with money and scrambled for some clever reply. "The gardens of Bezhalmbra will be hers to enjoy. They are like nothing in the world, Excellency."

"Insufficient," the emperor said coldly. "Flowers will not feed or clothe her."

"She is no ordinary maiden, Excellency, as we both know. She cares nothing for trinkets and fripperies."

"I think you'll discover that she likes pretty clothes more than you can imagine . . . or afford."

Shadrael smiled involuntarily. "And who weaves prettier cloth than Ulinians? Would you have me offer jewels and wealth to a lady who can pick up precious stones from the ground? I cannot compete with the riches of your court. All I can offer is my love, my devotion, and my steadfast heart. And the freedom to walk among the spirits that serve her whenever she wishes."

The emperor was nodding. "And twenty percent of your income for ten years."

"Five."

"Done!" Suddenly the emperor smiled at him, and

Shadrael saw that he possessed charm similar to Lea's.
"Let her do as she pleases. Make her happy. Never be un-
kind to her . . . again. Have I your word on this, Praetinor?"

Shadrael stiffened. "As a Ulinian first, I give my word.
As a praetinor, I doubly pledge it."

The emperor beckoned to the others to rejoin them.
"Kneel before me, Lord Shadrael."

Shadrael knelt in the dust, hardly able to believe he was
about to swear fealty to a man he'd always considered his
enemy.

Lea came running to him, her face radiant with joy. "He
accepts you," she whispered. "He likes you. I'm so glad!"

Eying the emperor warily, Shadrael wasn't so sure, but
on demand he gave his oath. He felt very strange, as though
he didn't know himself.

"Rise, Warlord Shadrael of Ulinia," the emperor announced for all to hear. "Your transgressions are pardoned.
But let this day be a lesson to you, your barons, and all of
Ulinia. Let the tragic loss of your army be a reminder of
the emperor's wrath. Let your pardon be an example of the
emperor's mercy."

Shadrael bowed low, his face rather hot.

"Serve us well," Light Bringer continued. "With Lea
to guide you, prosperity will soon touch this province.
Lord Shadrael and Lady Lea are now betrothed, with my
blessing."

A gasp ran through the onlookers. Everyone looked
stunned.

Laughing aloud, Lea ran first to the emperor and
hugged him with the abandon of a child, then came skipping to Shadrael's side. With her at his arm, he felt complete. Her radiant happiness made him smile. Gazing down
into her blue eyes, he felt himself lost in their depths . . .
and her magic.

He pulled her close, desirous of claiming his betrothal
kiss, but she was already wriggling free of his embrace,
bending down to pick something off the ground.

Baffled, very aware of people staring, he watched her a moment. "What are you doing?"

Lea paused in her gathering to show him a handful of small, glittering jewels that reflected the sunlight. "These are emeralds," she said happily, "for my wedding crown."

Acknowledgments

The Pearls and *The Crown* came about because Christi Schemm and Liz Kiser read *Reign of Shadows* and subsequently urged me to write "more about Lea." My editor, Ginjer Buchanan, kindly gave the project a green light.

I'm grateful to Kent Graham and Vicky Woodward—each possessing brothers, as I do not—for their invaluable feedback regarding the relationship between Shadrael and Vordachai.

Most especially, I want to thank Karen Mahaffey for believing in Shadrael all along and providing language assistance in a pinch. Dee Nash and Curtiss Ann Matlock—writing buddies with busy careers and deadlines of their own—found time to share plenty of encouragement.

Even my Scottish terriers, Dash and Dundee, "helped" by snoozing wedged behind the wheels of my desk chair and making it difficult for me to wander away from the keyboard.

THE ULTIMATE IN FANTASY!

From magical tales of distant worlds to stories of those with abilities beyond the ordinary, Ace and Roc have everything you need to stretch your imagination to its limits.

Marion Zimmer Bradley/Diana L. Paxson

Guy Gavriel Kay

Dennis L. McKiernan

Patricia A. McKillip

Robin McKinley

Sharon Shinn

Katherine Kurtz

Barb and J. C. Hendee

Eliza

T. A

Bria

Rob

penguin.com

M12G1107